VALLEY FORGE

* * *

ALSO BY NEWT GINGRICH
AND WILLIAM R. FORSTCHEN

Gettysburg

Grant Comes East

Never Call Retreat

Pearl Harbor

Days of Infamy

To Try Men's Souls

VALLEY FORGE

* * *

GEORGE WASHINGTON
AND THE
CRUCIBLE *of* VICTORY

* * *

NEWT GINGRICH,
WILLIAM R. FORSTCHEN
AND
ALBERT S. HANSER,
CONTRIBUTING EDITOR

* * *

THOMAS DUNNE BOOKS
ST. MARTIN'S PRESS ≈ NEW YORK

THOMAS DUNNE BOOKS.
An imprint of St. Martin's Press.

VALLEY FORGE. Copyright © 2010 by Newt Gingrich and William R. Forstchen. All rights reserved. Printed in the United States of America. For information, address St. Martin's Press, 175 Fifth Avenue, New York, N.Y. 10010.

www.thomasdunnebooks.com
www.stmartins.com

ISBN 978-0-312-59107-6

First Edition: November 2010

10 9 8 7 6 5 4 3 2 1

There is only one dedication that is fitting for this work: for George Washington and those who endured the winter at Valley Forge. May the sacrifices they made forever be a guide and inspiration to us, the inheritors of their dreams.

ACKNOWLEDGMENTS

✳ ✳ ✳

Across the years of our collaboration and now writing this, our seventh book together, we are always profoundly touched by the help and advice so many are willing to offer. Trying to thank all would now require a chapter in and of itself, and it is difficult to even remotely attempt a listing of all, so if a name is missed, we hope you do not take offense.

First and foremost, a thank-you is due to our readers. With the launching of each new book all of us are on the road, doing interviews and going to signings. It reaches deep into our hearts when those of you reading this now take the time to show up to an event. The fact that so many hunger for stories about our shared experience as Americans is heartening and a constant reinforcement that love and pride for our country is still very much alive. There are hundreds of stories of friends we have met along the way and we wish we could share all those stories.

This series on the birth of our new Republic, the insurmountable odds we faced, and our legendary hero George Washington started with a suggestion from our editor Pete Wolverton. His wish to move forward on the project, his support and understanding when, as with any book, we hit some "speed bumps" along the way, and his suggestions were always appreciated, along with those of our publisher Tom Dunne, and the staff who work at St. Martin's Press.

Our work is fiction, following in what we hope is the grand old tradition of such authors as Kenneth Roberts, Howard Fast, and others. Guidance was definitely found in Pulitzer Prize—winning works by David Fischer, David McCullough, and Joseph Ellis. As three historians with Ph.D's, we believe that historical fiction can often serve as inspiration for readers to turn to the "real" story. We highly recommend that when finished with these pages you consider turning to theirs. A special thanks as well to Paul Lockhart, who just prior to our starting this work released the seminal study of Baron von Steuben, *The Drillmaster of Valley Forge*. Paul and William Forstchen were graduate students together under the tutelage of the noted historian Gunther Rothenberg and it was a pleasure to reconnect after twenty years.

The launch of the first volume in this series, *To Try Men's Souls*, was supported by the dedicated team at Mount Vernon. The home of George Washington is managed by a private foundation and one of the best examples today of how ordinary citizens can take upon themselves the preservation of a national treasure. Our thanks go to director James Rees, historian Mary Thompson, a most extraordinary docent, Sue Keller, and board member Gay Gaines.

Now in our second volume of this series, we are grateful to the Valley Forge Archives & Library, especially their amazing Archivist Dona McDermott for her assistance on much valuable research.

In the creation of a book, there are so many behind the scenes who work hard to ensure that all things come together. On Newt's team, our thanks go to Randy Evans, Joe DeSantis, Stefan Passantino, Vince Haley, Liz Wood, Chris Paul, Rick Tyler, Sonya Harrison, Alicia Melvin, Bess Kelly, and that genius of organizational skills Michelle Selesky. Of course as always a special thanks must go to our agent Kathy Lubbers.

From William Forstchen's side of the fence, the support of his school, Montreat College, must be recognized for dealing at times with the eccentricities of a professor under a publishing deadline! The very special Dianne St. Clair was always ready with advice, cups of hot tea, and red pencil. Bill Butterworth IV (W.E.B. Jr.), trusted editor with *Boys' Life* for more than twenty years and lifelong friend, was always there with advice and encouragement as well.

Perhaps there should be some sort of conference for the families of authors. It would most certainly be an interesting session! The patience of our wives Callista Gingrich and Krys Hanser is legendary. As for Bill, the patience and support from Dianne and his daughter Meghan are invaluable. "Just give me fifteen minutes and I'll be ready to go," more often than not means hours of waiting until a chapter is done. Thank you for your understanding!

We hope that this story, as already said, triggers a deeper interest in the subject of our Revolution. Our greatest inspiration of all simply came from the accounts of those who did indeed forge a nation, bringing thirteen very different colonies into a single force that could defy an empire, endure eight long years of suffering for a higher ideal when all others thought it a forlorn hope, and in the end stayed true to those ideals as they created the constitutional republic we have today.

We owe all to them, that their vision of America as a constitutional republic where the government as the servant of "we the people" shall continue on into the twenty-first century and that our children's children will take pride in a nation that will forever be the hope and inspiration of the world.

INTRODUCTION

*Why George Washington, Valley Forge, and the Making
of the American Army Matter to Americans Today*

✳ ✳ ✳

At a time when many Americans despair over their country's future, worry about their political leaders, and find themselves looking to the Founding Fathers for guidance, there is a lot to learn from the difficult challenges that faced Americans in the fall of 1777.

The ordeal of Valley Forge in the winter of 1777—1778 and the emergence of an American Army trained to stand up to veteran British professionals was in many ways the crucible in which American freedom and the American tradition of self-government were forged.

The leadership of George Washington was so central to this process that it is hard to imagine how America could have either won the war or created a free country without him.

The challenges Washington faced should make present-day Americans ashamed of any complaints we have about the difficulties of self-government and the problems of big government, big deficits, high taxes, and arrogant politicians.

Washington and his colleagues were taking on the most powerful empire in the world.

They had substantial opposition from those colonists who remained loyal to the British king and helped the British military. For more Americans remained loyal to the Crown than Americans today realize.

In many ways American politicians in revolutionary times were as big a challenge as were the British. The Continental Congress routinely failed to meet its obligations. Politicians were eager to meddle, interfere, and demand, but they seldom took the time to learn about reality and seldom provided needed help to Washington and his army.

Much of the historic importance of Washington comes from his determined commitment to the rule of law and to the principle that the army must be subordinated to civilian authority. No matter how incompetent, meddling, or infuriating the members of the Continental Congress were, Washington insisted on treating them courteously and respectfully and obeying their instructions, even if at times he deeply disagreed with them.

The principle of civilian control remains to this day one of the greatest bulwarks of the American system of self-government.

Washington did not just have political meddling on the civilian side. What came to be called the Conway Cabal was a serious effort to undermine Washington and replace him with General Horatio Gates.

While we look back and see Washington as the father of his country and the man upon whom our traditions rest, it was not nearly so clear in the winter of 1777—1778. Even though Washington had managed Boston well (maneuvering to force the British to withdraw), he had then suffered defeat after defeat, from Brooklyn across Manhattan and White Plains to the Palisades and down through New Jersey.

In *To Try Men's Souls*, we captured the story of the desperate, bold attack designed to turn the war around on Christmas Day 1776. General Washington's courage in deciding to gamble everything was one of the most important building blocks of America.

Without Washington's courage in crossing the river at night and marching nine miles in a blinding snowstorm, the American Revolution might well have collapsed at the end of 1776.

Without the courage of the men who served in the army, Washington's courage would have been to no avail. By himself, George Washington could not have created a free country. As a leader with thousands of dedicated followers, he had a chance.

Over the last year, audience after audience has responded emotionally to the story of a small group of dedicated patriots changing the course of history by their devotion, their dedication, and their endurance.

When audiences learn that fewer than one out of every thousand Americans was with Washington during that desperate time, they are amazed. Even more they learn that one-third of the 2,500 men who crossed the Delaware at night on an icy river during a blinding snowstorm had no shoes, they are astounded.

When they learn that these men left a trail of blood on the icy, stony road to Trenton, they have tears in their eyes.

For all of our complaints and all of our problems, THIS is the cost of freedom, and THIS is the courage, determination, and persistence that made America a free country.

Washington's great victory at Trenton was followed by another great victory at Princeton two weeks later. Then he drove the British from most of New Jersey back toward New York City and their naval base.

After that exciting winter campaign, most Americans believed they were on the edge of winning the revolution. Freedom seemed to be at their fingertips. Yet the greatest empire in the world was far from done with its efforts to reconquer the Americans. After all, the British Empire had put down rebellions in Ireland and Scotland, and peasant uprisings in rural England. Such policing was just a necessary part of running an empire.

Throughout 1777 Washington found himself on the defensive, and when the British used their command of the sea to move the army from New York City to Philadelphia, he found that his undertrained army was incapable of staying in the field against British and German professional soldiers. At Brandywine and Germantown the Americans came tantalizingly close to winning and then fell apart. The sheer discipline and routine competence of British and German professionals outlasted the enthusiasm and energy of the American amateurs. At Paoli an American unit was surprised at night, and (at least in the American view) many of its men were massacred by British troops using bayonets.

While Washington was fighting a frustrating series of losing battles, the one glorious bright spot was in the north, where General Gates was winning. Gates was born in England and had served in the British Army, but he had lived in America for a long time. He saw himself as a professional soldier and had contempt for Washington, whom he saw as an incompetent amateur in over his head.

Washington sent forces to help Gates contain General John Burgoyne at Saratoga in the fall of 1777 and then force his surrender. This was an extraordinary moment of optimism. An entire British Army surrendered. It proved to be the *key* event in convincing the French to enter into an alliance with the Americans. Every American was impressed with this great victory, and it contrasted vividly with Washington's failure to win in New Jersey and Pennsylvania.

Washington loyalists knew that General Washington had generously sent some of his best troops to help Gates. They also knew that at the *key* moment in the campaign, Benedict Arnold had provided leadership when Gates faltered. Finally, they knew that Washington had kept the vast bulk of the British Army facing him instead of marching north to rescue Burgoyne.

Nonetheless, to much of the American public, it was Gates who had succeeded and Washington who had disappointed. Gates had supporters both in the Continental Congress and in some elements of the army.

Washington's genius as a leader and as a politician is at the heart of the survival of the American system of self-government in the winter of 1777—1778. Faced with a terrible lack of supplies (the Congress, as it so often has, talked a lot and achieved virtually nothing despite its promises), a treacherous plot inside the army, and overt questioning of his authority in the Congress, Washington calmly and steadily focused on first the survival and then the rebuilding of his army.

There is no episode of American history more poignant, more painful, and more difficult than Valley Forge in that terrible winter. Thousands of the twelve thousand men who entered camp died. The lack of shelter, lack of food, malnourishment, and collapsing morale all plagued the army and threatened to dissolve it, leaving the revolution lost and the British victorious.

Not least of the keys to the survival of the army were the five hundred women who helped with cooking, cleaning, sewing, nursing, and a host of other noncombat duties. Washington thought so highly of them that he gave them half pay and a 50 percent pension. They were the unsung in the survival of the American Revolution and are a key part of our history. Martha Washington spent February to June 1778 at Valley Forge with her husband, and, in providing leadership alongside him, she was far from unique among wives.

The agony of the American forces seeking simply to survive contrasted painfully with the situation of the British eighteen miles away in Philadelphia. Having occupied the largest city in North America (where the Declaration of Independence had been written and proclaimed), the British Army spent the winter in comfort.

In contrast to the desperate conditions at Valley Forge——muddy streets, drafty log cabins, and limited food——the British Army officers and men lived in fine houses in a comfortable city with plenty of food and drink. The difference between the conditions experienced by the two forces was so great that it is little wonder the British high command fully expected the American Army to simply disintegrate through desertion.

Washington, in fact, was worried that the British would prove to be correct and that the American Army would collapse. He himself warned that "unless some great and capital change suddenly takes place this Army must inevitably . . . starve, dissolve, or disperse in order to obtain subsistence in the best manner they can."

The real problem was not desertion, although some did desert. The real problem was the legitimate refusal of units to reenlist. Men who had served their time felt that they had every legal right to go home with honor. As much as he needed them, Washington agreed they could legally exercise the right not to reenlist without its reflecting poorly on their character.

Once again, Washington's insistence on the rule of law and following the rules, even when it was to his disadvantage, was a key part of the moral leadership on which the American system of freedom came to be built.

Those men who did stay were deeply committed to the cause and were determined to learn how to defeat the British. The arrogance of the British in living well and holding parties and dances in Philadelphia did not demoralize these Americans as much as it infuriated them. A deep determination to learn how to win began to take hold in that painful winter.

Just as the role of women at Valley Forge is often understated, so, too, is the role of people from other nations in the survival and ultimate success of the American Revolution is often understated or simply ignored.

At a time when we are trying to think through our immigration predicament, it is useful to remember that, without foreign help and foreigners themselves coming to Washington's assistance, we might never have won the war with Great Britain.

In many ways these foreign volunteers were the freedom fighters of their generation. They saw the Americans fighting what they believed was a universal fight for freedom from tyranny and monarchy. In our earlier *To Try Men's Souls* we note the importance of Englishman Tom Paine, whose pamphlets were vital in winning the intellectual argument for freedom and in sustaining the morale of the revolutionaries during dark periods of defeat and deprivation.

Among military figures, the Marquis de Lafayette and Baron Friedrich von Steuben were the two most prominent European supporters, but there were dozens more who came to America to fight for freedom, like the Polish revolutionary hero Casimir Pulaski.

Lafayette mattered because he validated the American cause for the French Court. While Benjamin Franklin and John Adams were busy trying to convince the French that they should support the revolution, they had an uphill struggle. The French monarchy was burdened with debt and had been defeated by Britain too frequently to enter into a war lightly. Lafayette's eyewitness accounts in letters to Paris played a major role in convincing the French government that Washington and his cause could win.

Lafayette was also important to Washington as the son he never had. Washington was deeply fond of the young man and was sustained emotionally by his enthusiasm and his commitment and courage. Lafayette was a significant factor in convincing the Continental Congress that Washington was indeed, as the scholar James Thomas Flexner has called him, "the indispensable man."

Lafayette's importance is signified by his portrait in the U.S. House of Representatives, hung in the chamber in 1824. A decade later, George Washington joined him on the wall on the other side of the speaker's chair. To this day they are the only two people thus honored.

As we deal with immigration issues, it is helpful for our congressmen to look to the wall and realize just how vital foreigners have been in the making of America.

Baron von Steuben played an equally important role in creating the American Army. Washington knew that he needed a disciplined, trained, full-time army if he was to stand toe-to-toe with the British professional forces. He had spent years in the wilderness during the French and Indian War and understood guerrilla warfare as well as anyone in his generation. He also knew that the militia around Boston had played a decisive role in driving the British into abandoning that city.

However, the simple reality was that the center of power in America rested on a coastal plain from New York to Virginia. Only when an American army could defeat a British army in an open battle on that plain would it be possible to win independence.

Washington understood that modern warfare required very steady infantry, disciplined volley fire, and strong artillery support. That combination required training and more training.

While Washington understood the need, he lacked the principles for training and the ability to train. That is where von Steuben became invaluable. There is a remarkable subtlety in what von Steuben did. He did not try to transfer rigid European systems designed for conscript armies. He intuitively understood that Americans had to learn faster and had to understand and participate instead of being coerced. The result was an approach that was learnable and which combined intense training with realistic goals.

By Monmouth, Washington's army had survived the crucible of Valley Forge and emerged with a level of training that enabled them for once to fight the British Army in the open and win.

The French entry into the war forced the British government in London to reinforce their troops in the sugar colonies in the Caribbean (which were far more profitable and, to the British, more important than the American mainland). That transfer of troops from Philadelphia to the West Indies forced the British Army to abandon Philadelphia and retreat to New York.

During their retreat, the unthinkable happened. They collided with a disciplined and determined American Army. At Monmouth, the survivors of the long Valley Forge winter got their revenge against the troops who had enjoyed Philadelphia comforts throughout the winter. The result was a decisive British defeat and a huge increase in American morale and in Washington's personal prestige.

Washington is at the heart of America's success and of our definition of ourselves as a country of freedom under the rule of law. By virtue of his honor, dignity, and integrity, Washington attracted an extraordinary group of men around him, including Nathanael Greene, Anthony Wayne, Alexander Hamilton, and, of course, the allies already mentioned.

Through defeat, despair, deprivation, political intrigue, endless frustrations, and a host of problems we can barely imagine in our modern, comfortable world, Washington behaved as the leader of freedom's cause. His being——not his intellect, not his speechmaking, not his personality——but, rather, his very being as a force of disciplined righteous patriotism made success possible.

There was no doubt in Washington's mind what the struggle was all about. It was about freedom under the rule of law.

Washington's favorite play was Joseph Addison's *Cato*. It is the story of a man who loves freedom so much that he sacrifices his son and himself rather than bend to Caesar's will. Washington never tired of the play. It was also clear that he saw himself in that tradition. He would rather have died than given in to British tyranny.

It is our hope that this story of freedom emerging from difficult times will inspire our generation to do our duty to protect the rule of law and reassert the classic provisions of American liberty.

Nothing we face is as difficult as Valley Forge. We have no excuse for not serving our country and dedicating ourselves to the cause of freedom. That is the real message of this book.

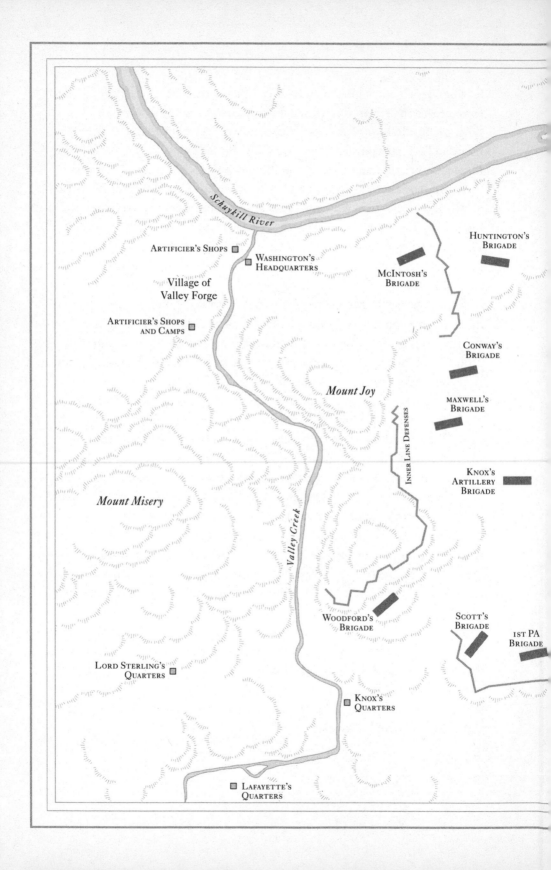

Schuylkill River

Artificier's Shops

Washington's
Headquarters

Village of
Valley Forge

Artificier's Shops
and Camps

Huntington's
Brigade

McIntosh's
Brigade

Conway's
Brigade

Mount Joy

Maxwell's
Brigade

Inner Line Defenses

Mount Misery

Valley Creek

Knox's
Artillery
Brigade

Woodford's
Brigade

Scott's
Brigade

1st PA
Brigade

Lord Sterling's
Quarters

Knox's
Quarters

Lafayette's
Quarters

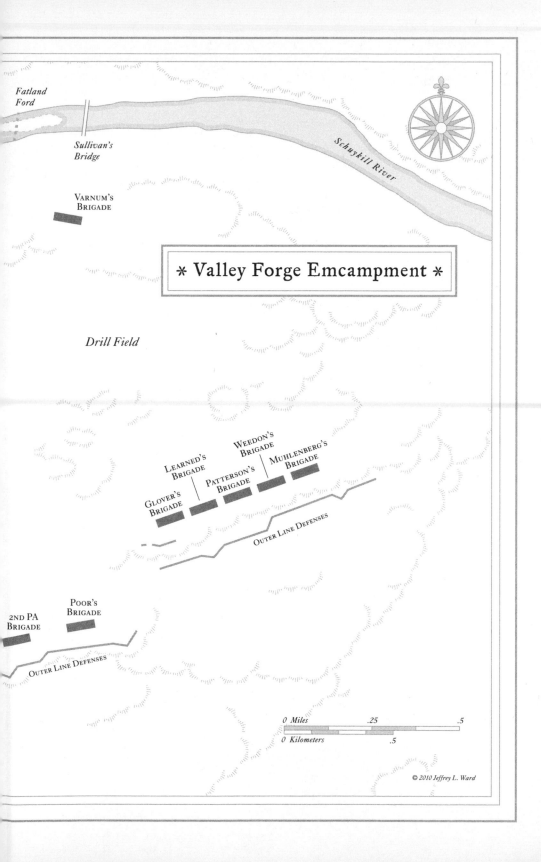

Fatland
Ford

Sullivan's
Bridge

Schuykill River

VARNUM'S
BRIGADE

✳ Valley Forge Emcampment ✳

Drill Field

WEEDON'S
BRIGADE

LEARNED'S
BRIGADE

MUHLENBERG'S
BRIGADE

GLOVER'S
BRIGADE

PATTERSON'S
BRIGADE

OUTER LINE DEFENSES

POOR'S
BRIGADE

2ND PA
BRIGADE

OUTER LINE DEFENSES

0 Miles   .25   .5

0 Kilometers   .5

© 2010 Jeffrey L. Ward

PROLOGUE

✳ ✳ ✳

Near Paoli, PA
10:00 PM, September 20, 1777
Battle of Paoli

"Fix bayonets!"

The order was whispered hoarsely. Lieutenant Allen van Dorn, a Loyalist from Trenton, in the rebellious colony of New Jersey, was in a column of more than a thousand British light infantry, arrayed in a formation of company front by column. He could hear the order echoing softly behind him, followed by the cold, chilling sound of long bayonets pulled from scabbards, then locked on to the muzzles of Brown Bess muskets.

He caught a glimpse of General Charles Grey as the blanket of clouds, concealing the moon, parted for a moment. Tall, slender, and supremely fit, Grey's presence was sensed——even in the cover of darkness. His whispered words carried self-confidence and command. The battle plan was his. This fight would be his, and Allen sensed that this man reveled in the moment.

Allen, serving as one of the scouts for the attack, observed Grey from a respectful distance. With soldierly ardor, the general addressed the knot of officers surrounding him.

"I want every man checked yet again," Grey hissed sharply. "Flints are to be removed from all weapons except officers' sidearms. If any enlisted man disobeys and fires his weapon, I will personally flog him. If any of you discharge your pistols before the attack is well joined, by God I will not only flog you, I will see you broken to the ranks and sent back to England in disgrace.

"Do we understand each other?"

There was a muffled chorus of assents.

"Rejoin your commands and await the order to advance. Once this column begins to move, guide on the unit in front of you. Keep the formation tight. Do not lose contact with the line in front of you. Once the attack is launched, fan your men out as we discussed earlier and then in with the bayonet and finish the bastards. No one is to escape. No one!

"Rejoin your men."

The officers scattered and dispersed into the blackness. The clattering of a sword sheath broke the unnerving stillness.

"Who was that?" Grey snarled.

There was a momentary pause.

"Captain Neilson, sir, he has fallen."

"You are relieved of command, sir. Stay to the rear. I will deal with you tomorrow."

There was no reply.

"Officers, drop your sword sheaths," Grey added.

The order had been given earlier, but some were reluctant to comply; their scabbards inlaid with gold were worth a pretty penny. Neilson would pay far more in terms of shame.

Grey turned to face the men gathered around Allen.

"You men know your orders."

Each man quickly whispered his orders, to deploy to the left of the flank, to the right, to move ahead and secure the several farmsteads in their path of advance. Finally, it was Allen's turn.

"I am to stay with the prisoner, sir, to insure he does not try to escape."

"And if he gives false directions?"

Allen hesitated.

"I will kill him myself," came a whispered reply. It was muttered by a captain who had recently joined their ranks. John André was beloved and esteemed as a soldier, a poet, a duelist, and above all else, a gentleman with courage. As part of a prisoner exchange, he was recently assigned to act as a liaison for Grey during the attack.

"I will see to it, sir," Allen interjected.

He looked over at the prisoner, a civilian blacksmith who had come to their camp earlier in the day to report that a division of rebel troops, under the command of Anthony Wayne, was encamped near Paoli Tavern. That was already known, but the blacksmith carried the additional information that the men were demoralized after the drubbing they had received at the Battle of Brandywine, fought nine days ago. He reported that many were grumbling about deserting, cursing Washington and Wayne. Drunkenness was rampant and his own personal grievance was that they had looted his barn, insulted his wife, and threatened to loot and burn his forge. He added that they were keeping poor watch; the men were drinking gin and corn liquor even while on picket duty. That was enough to spur Grey to action.

The blacksmith, however, never expected the next turn of events. He had been "volunteered" to lead this midnight attack column, and had openly wept when ordered to do so, crying that he was only a civilian, had done his duty to the Crown, and should be let go.

The burly man was trembling, stifling back sobs as the soldiers around him prepared to go forward.

Allen went to his side.

"You heard the general," he whispered.

"Why? I did my duty."

"Listen to me," Allen whispered. "There is no escaping it now. You are in this to the end. Once the fighting starts I will let you go, but if you try to bolt, my orders are to run you through."

He hesitated, looking over his shoulder at Captain André.

"And if I don't, he will."

"You're not one of them," the blacksmith whispered.

"What do you mean?"

"You sound like you're from Jersey."

Allen did not reply for a moment. The man had a good ear for accents and guessed right.

"Yes. Trenton."

"Why are you with them?"

"I could ask why are you with us," Allen snapped.

"I was only doing my duty. I am not a soldier, though."

"Well, I am."

"If my neighbors see me with you tonight, they'll burn me out."

"Not if we win," Allen replied coldly, knowing it to be true.

With Brandywine and the utter rout of the rebel army, political feelings in the countryside around Philadelphia were in upheaval. More than a few of the populace were already Loyalists, and in the days before the fight, as some of the undisciplined rabble serving with Washington took to foraging for food, feelings had shifted even more. After the victory, many were now hanging the Union Jack in front of their homes.

For Allen, it was a source of intense inner confusion. He had joined the

Loyalist cause a year ago, after his brothers Jonathan and James had run off to join the rebels, when the war was being fought near New York. James had deserted and was now back home running the family tannery and store. Jonathan, though, poor Jonathan had stayed with the rebels and died the evening after the battle for Trenton.

Taken prisoner along with the Hessians, Allen had been allowed by the rebels to help carry his brother back to their encampment . . . and held him as he died from exhaustion and pneumonia. By his side was their childhood friend, Peter Wellsley.

The following day, Peter took Allen to General Washington and appealed for his release in exchange for the sacrifice of his brother.

Allen was now one of the very few serving the Crown who had met Washington, talked with him, and taken a measure of the man. Though he could never embrace Washington's cause, he nevertheless respected the man for his personal integrity. Washington readily granted Wellsley's appeal, saying that it was a fair exchange to a family who had lost a son who had served with valor.

Washington tried to press him for some details of British positions, which Allen respectfully refused to answer. The general immediately desisted, though he offered the opportunity to join their cause, which Allen refused as well. The general had then made him swear that he would reveal nothing of what he had seen or heard while within their ranks and let him go.

A week later, when the rebels returned to Trenton, Allen left his family behind, rejoined the ranks, and reported to General Grey. Grey asked the same questions Washington had, and again he refused to answer, saying he had given his oath. Rather than enrage the supposedly hot-blooded Grey, the general clapped him on the shoulder, saying he carried the proper honor of an Englishman and assigned him to his staff as a liaison to Loyalists.

So now he stood, keeping careful watch on a terrified blacksmith who was in way over his head with this war. He had, without doubt, slipped through the lines to try and curry favor, assuming that in another day his village would be occupied. . . . He had never bargained for this.

"For your own sake," Allen whispered, "you better guide us correctly. Are you sure you can do that?"

"I grew up here, I know every field and woodlot like the back of my hand," the man whispered in reply, voice trembling.

"For God's sake, don't try to play false or run."

He nodded back to the regular British officer who was huddled with Grey.

"That man hates colonials and will run you through like a dog if you try to take off."

The terrified blacksmith did not reply. André stepped away from Grey to join the two.

"Forward, and you better lead us straight in," André announced.

"He will," Allen offered.

The three set off and seconds later Allen could hear the whispered command for the column to follow.

No matter how hard they tried, a thousand men stepping off into an attack could not be totally silent. There was a clatter as someone apparently tripped or dropped his musket, muted curses, and the sound of boots scuffing across the stubble of the recently mowed hay field.

Light infantry formed most of the column, supported by a second column behind them, the famed and rightly feared Scottish Black Watch.

Crossing the open field, the blacksmith led them down into a hollow. Fording a shallow stream a dozen feet wide and only several inches deep, the column slowed for a moment as the advance churned the ground into a morass, slowing the rear of the attacking force. They moved by the oblique to the right, angling across the next field, and then experienced several moments of confusion as the attacking force made its way through a farmer's woodlot, which the blacksmith stated would conceal their advance.

Allen looked back over his shoulder several times. Light from the rising moon occasionally broke through the thick veil of scudding clouds, revealing the men as they advanced. He could only hope that the pickets were indeed drunk or foolish enough to have campfires. Gazing into a fire for just a few seconds would blind a man's night vision for several minutes afterward.

The blacksmith muttered to himself, repeating the Lord's Prayer over and over again.

"Be quiet there," André finally snarled, "or you won't need to pray, you will be able to explain it to God personally."

Emerging out of the woodlot, Allen could see a glow on the horizon, easily recognized by any soldier as the campfires of an opposing line.

"Where are their pickets?" It was General Grey, who arrived to join them.

"The what?" the blacksmith gasped.

"Their scouts, the guards!" Allen hissed.

"Over there, I think. I saw them posted on the road."

He waved vaguely to their right.

"Just keep moving, but, by God, if this is a trap, you will be the first to die," Grey snapped, and turned back.

"Skirmishers and dragoons forward, deploy fifty yards ahead," Grey whispered, pointing toward the glowing fires, and seconds later a swarm of light infantry sprinted forward in advance of the main column.

They were now halfway across the open field. The clouds parted again, illuminating a low rise ahead. It was the perfect location for forward pickets to be in position. Grey caught glimpses of the dozen or so mounted dragoons, crouched low in their saddles, cresting the rise.

And then the darkness was cut by the flash of a musket——a snap of light followed a second later by two more, and the crack of rifle fire echoed across the field.

"In on them, my lads!" Grey roared. "In and after them!"

"If this is a trap . . . ," André repeated, glaring at the blacksmith who stood stock-still and terrified.

The column behind them broke into an exhilarating run. Allen turned back and saw the glint of leveled bayonets and a wall of men charging toward them.

"Come on," Allen cried. He dared to lay a hand on a superior officer, and push him forward.

André hesitated for only an instant, his sword poised as if to stab the blacksmith, but then turned to join the charge.

"You, for God's sake, lie down!" Allen cried, shoving the blacksmith forward. "Just lie down and claim later . . ."

He didn't have time to explain further or to offer advice for this poor soul, who, if found out, would likely find himself at the end of a rope if the rebels won, and at the end of a rope as well if he had played false to the Crown.

The man collapsed, almost as if shot, and lay on the ground quivering. Allen felt a measure of pity as he left the man behind, racing to keep ahead of the wall of bayonets. Reaching the low crest, he saw the bodies of the unfortunate advance pickets; their campfire, dug into the ground in an attempt at concealment, was still glowing hot. Several of the light infantry skirmishers were bayoneting the bodies, one still alive and shrieking for mercy.

The column reached the top of the hill and began to spread out as ordered. From this position, the men had an unobstructed view of the enemy encampment directly ahead, along the edge of the woods. The Americans sprang to their feet in confusion, clearly silhouetted by the flames of their campfires. As if with one voice, the advancing column let loose with wild shouts of battle lust. The sharp battle cries of the Black Watch were terrifying, even to Allen.

The charge swept straight into the rebel camp and the slaughter began.

"My God, what is that?"

General Anthony Wayne turned in his saddle. Three shots had come from his right. Throughout the night and the day before, rumors had inundated him that an enemy column was nearby. Repeatedly he had tried to push scouts and mounted vedettes forward, only to have them driven back in by the damned British light infantry.

It had been a bitter week since the disaster at Brandywine, as various parts of the army attempted to hold the approaches to Philadelphia. His own position was to hold the advanced position on the road through Paoli and await "developments." Caution had caused him to pull back two miles during the day.

He had not slept in two days, constantly riding out to check the picket lines. He was looking for an opening he could push into——take some prisoners and gain intelligence. His men were exhausted from the battle and the frustrating days of retreat, maneuver, and then falling back yet again.

Most of his command was encamped forward of the Paoli Tavern, his headquarters, while even now he moved with a small column along the flank, responding to rumors of an impending attack from that direction.

The shots sounded more like rifle fire than the heavier, duller boom of musketry.

He looked imploringly at his staff, repeating the question.

"What is that?"

No one spoke.

And then more shots sliced the black night, and, only seconds later, a nerve-rending cheer, more like a shrieking——the distinctive cry of the Black Watch resounded.

"Merciful God!" was all he could gasp, as he savagely reined his horse about and raced back toward his main encampment.

"Oh God! God!" Allen gasped, trying to back up, jerking his sword back and out of the guts of the man he had just impaled.

He was a veteran of half a dozen skirmishes and two major battles, but until this moment he had never really known if he had killed a man. This time the evidence was before him, so close that he could hear the convulsive screams of his victim, and the vomited blood, splashed into Allen's face.

He had stormed into the rebel camp at the front of the charge, trying to keep pace with André. And then this man, this man he was killing, came bolting out of a wigwam and all but thrust himself straight onto Allen's sword in his blind panic.

The man's eyes shone in the moonlight, wide, terrified, his open mouth a black hole contorted by his screams.

With one hand he clutched Allen's jacket, with the other he feebly waved a knife about; with one slash he opened a wound on Allen's left arm. While still clutching the hilt of his sword with his right hand, Allen used his left to grasp the arm that was holding the blade. It was like trying to restrain a child, there was no strength in his enemy now, just a terrifying gasping as he started to sag, but the blade was still lodged in the man's stomach, and, try as he could, he could not extract it.

He was screaming as well, cursing, crying, oblivious to all that was around him until he saw André striding toward him, pistol raised and cocked.

The dying rebel saw him as well, and now tried to push back from Allen, whimpering, his cries like that of a girl, which filled Allen with even more horror, wondered if his victim was a woman caught up in this madness.

André pressed the pistol to the man's brow and pulled the trigger. The explosion was deafening; the ball tore off the top of the skull. The body collapsed, and André put his foot on the man's chest and, grabbing hold of Allen's right wrist, pulled back hard.

The blade slipped out with a grating noise of steel against bone.

"Never thrust upwards into the chest!" André shouted. "The blade usually gets stuck."

Allen stood there dumbstruck, looking down at the mutilated body.

"Come on!" André shouted, grabbing Allen by the shoulder, "keep moving or it will be you that gets it."

He had seen many a man die in this last year but this was the first time that he had looked into the eyes of someone he was killing, the first time blood had been coughed into his face. A sudden wave of nausea flooded his body as he choked back the taste of vomit in his throat.

"Come on!" André screamed, urging him along.

A wigwam shelter set into the woods was ablaze. Men were inside, screaming in anguish, while at the entry half a dozen light infantrymen stood with bayonets poised, shouting for them to come out. One man burst out and the light infantry fell upon him, stabbing and stabbing again. Another came out to the same terror.

Two more tried to fight their way out and were slaughtered in turn.

"For God's sake," Allen screamed. "Prisoners."

His cry was ignored as the light infantry stood ready, taunting the men who were burning inside to come out.

"Stop them!" Allen cried. He started to run over, but André grabbed him.

"You can't stop it!" André shouted. "Their blood is up! You can't stop it."

Allen, dumbfounded, looked around as dozens of wigwams burned, and at nearly every one, men were fighting with terrible desperation to escape.

All was mad confusion, light infantry, dragoons, a solid line of the Black Watch swarming into the encampment, while hundreds of rebels ran in every direction. Here and there fragments of companies and regiments tried to rally, one group even managing to fire off a ragged volley before being swarmed under.

With Grey's order forbidding musket flints, the attackers could not form into volley lines but instead absolutely had to press forward. The injunction had been meant to ensure that no weapon was accidentally discharged, thus spoiling the surprise, but Allen could see that now it was unleashing a murderous frenzy. They had to close with their enemies in order to drive them, and in so doing, a murderous melee of men on one side was driven into a killing frenzy and, on the other, caught by surprise and so terrified that some did not even offer resistance. In their attempts to surrender, they were clubbed down and bayoneted like sheep being slaughtered.

The attack swept past him and into the woods. Scores of men were on the ground; most were dead, some twisting and writhing, others curled up, yet others were trying to crawl away.

Two light infantrymen came up to a man on the ground who held his hands up, begging for mercy. Laughing, they raised their muskets high and pinned him to the ground. Allen stood as if frozen, unable to respond. Still laughing, as if drunk with some mad hysteria, they approached their next victim, who looked to be not much more than a boy.

Allen sprang forward.

"No! Prisoner!"

The light infantrymen, joined now by several of their comrades, paused and then one turned on him.

"You sound provincial! You're one of them!"

He raised his musket as if to run Allen through.

"Stand in place or you're a dead man!"

It was André, at Allen's side. Though his pistol was empty he cocked it, aiming it at the light infantryman.

"This officer is one of us. By God, lower that musket or I'll blow your damn head off."

The infantryman did as ordered.

"Name and regiment."

He snapped out the question with such authority that the man replied, so drilled was he to respond without hesitation.

"Fredericks, sir, Second Light Infantry."

"I will see you come morning, Fredericks, now move along."

The man actually came to attention and saluted.

"Begging your pardon sir. It's dark, he sounded like a rebel. Thought he had snatched an officer's jacket, sir."

He looked at Allen.

"Begging your pardon, sir."

"Damn you, start taking prisoners," Allen replied, trying to control the trembling in his voice.

The man saluted and ran off, followed by his comrades, and Allen could see that as they disappeared into the dark, they looked back . . . and the order would not be obeyed.

"Stay close to me and keep your mouth shut," André snapped, "otherwise our own men will run you through."

"We must stop it," Allen cried. "They're surrendering."

André sighed.

"It can't be stopped now. It can't be. In the dark, like this, all men are savages."

He spat the words out as if filled with an infinite weariness.

The battle, if it could be called that, had swept into the woods. From within several of the burning wigwams Allen could hear screams, the death cries of men who preferred the agony of dying by fire to facing the terror of the bayonets. One of the wigwams exploded with a flash, bowling over several men of the Black Watch who had been standing outside, boxes of ammunition within having lit off.

Some semblance of battle briefly flared on the left, as if fresh enemy troops were coming in or had rallied.

Allen caught a glimpse of General Grey, now mounted, riding in that direction, and woodenly followed André. Even before they arrived at the flank, resistance had collapsed.

Bugle calls began to sound, some of them signals for regiments to rally and reform, others the ubiquitous foxhunting calls which everyone knew so galled the rebels.

Grey dismounted to confer with the commander of the Black Watch. The battle was already winding down.

"Start pulling your command together, sir. They still outnumber us, even though we have them on the run!"

The Scotsman laughed.

"They're runnin' clear to the Ohio."

"Keep control of your men!" Grey replied.

The colonel saluted and ran off, followed by his staff.

The general looked over his shoulder and grinned at André.

"Hell of a foxhunt it is now, André. Keep driving them!" Grey shouted as he remounted.

Allen stepped forward as if to interrupt and Grey looked down at him.

"You got one, I see," Grey announced, pointing to Allen's blade. The crimson blood appeared as black oil in the moonlight. "Good lad!"

"Sir——"

André's hand was on Allen's shoulder, pulling him back.

Grey spurred his mount and was off.

Allen turned on André and shrugged his hand off.

"It would have served no purpose, Lieutenant," André said. "He sees you now as one of us. You got your man."

"One of you?" Allen replied with astonishment.

He looked back toward the forest and the burning wigwams. The blood frenzy was abating and he could see a column of prisoners, most of them wounded, staggering out of the woods, prodded along by guards with bayonets lowered. One of the men staggered and fell, and in an instant, two guards were on him, bayoneting him.

André again grasped Allen by the shoulder.

"With your damn accent you can't stop it. Let the fury leave them. By morning more than one will be on his knees to God asking for forgiveness."

"And the other side?" Allen asked coldly, nodding westward. "What will be their prayer?"

By the early light of dawn, Anthony Wayne pressed along the road leading west. Staggering behind him was the wreckage of his command. Except for the cries of some of the wounded carried on stretchers or helped along by comrades, nearly all were silent, heads lowered, numbed, dejected.

Their general, however, boiled with silent rage.

He had lost a battle, which was shame enough. He had also endured a massacre and he would have his vengeance, he swore to God———if it meant his life, he would have vengeance. Gone forever was any thought that this was a conflict of gentlemen. In his heart it was war as savage as any fought on the frontier, and he would fight it thus until the end.

CHAPTER ONE

* * *

A cold and blustery wind blew out of the northeast, carrying with it the promise of yet more snow. Undaunted by the wintry blast, Zebulon Miller faced the rising storm from the doorway of his spacious barn. The pitiful mooing inside was an abrupt reminder of the abandoned predawn milking. As the ominous darkness gave way to a pale dawn light, a startling revelation was now confronting him: The war was once again coming to his farm, his land, and this time it had caught him by surprise.

His wife, Elsa, ran from the house and clung nervously to his side. A sudden gust of wind caught her cap, revealing auburn tresses that whipped wildly about her face.

"We can still try to hide them," she pleaded breathlessly.

He shook his head. "Too late," was all he could say bitterly. His voice trembled with the seething rage that was beginning to erupt within him.

Over the past four months, Zebulon had unfortunately come to know the paraphernalia and uniforms of this war: the threadbare rags of the so-called Continental Line, the ridiculous foppery of the militias that would turn out boldly enough but then turn and run at the mere rumor of an approaching enemy. What he saw now was a striking contrast, for the men advancing in open lines across his neighbor's fields were professional soldiers of the king.

They were British light infantry, their hat feathers dyed red in mocking defiance of pledges made by the Pennsylvania Line to show them no quarter in battle after the bitter memories of what was now called the Paoli Massacre.

[13]

The red feathers were a taunt, a statement that boasted, "Here we are, we defeated you at Paoli, and there's not a damn thing you can do to stop us."

Deployed into open skirmish lines, the light infantry advanced toward Miller's farm. A mounted troop of dragoons in the center of the formation held the road leading up from Middle Ferry Road and the village of Darby. The synchronized movements of the formations resembled the choreography of a dance; they were leapfrogging forward at the run, flanking a hundred yards to either side of the road. Half were moving, half remained still, with weapons raised to provide covering fire for those who in turn would then leap forward another couple of hundred yards. Taking advantage of every bit of cover, they crouched behind trees and ducked into ditches. After hurdling the split rail fence that divided Zebulon's fields from his neighbor, Snyder, half the men dropped down on one knee with their muskets at the ready, the other half sprinted toward his home.

There might have been a time when British infantry would foolishly march up a road, and straight into an ambush, as some militia boasted, but he doubted it. Perhaps at Concord and Lexington, in 1775, when the British thought they were just sweeping up rabble, there might have been a certain complacency. But now, after nearly two years of grueling war, they were well trained and exceptionally efficient. The events of the last four months, from Brandywine to Germantown, were proof that no militia could ever stand against them. Zebulon Miller knew he was watching the best-trained infantry in the world. He stepped out from the entry of his barn. Resolved to make the best of it, he tried to force a welcoming smile. He could at least claim to look like a Loyalist, now that his troublesome son had run off to join the rebels.

A light infantryman ran swiftly toward Zebulon and Elsa. The soldier fought to catch his breath as he raised his musket to his shoulder and steadied his aim at the farmer. His eyes darted to size up Zebulon, then looked past him to the barn, and focused again on the farmer and his wife.

"Show your hands there!"

Zebulon did as ordered. In the last four months, he had faced a loaded musket more than once. He recalled a frightening incident when he caught some foolish militiamen trying to loot his chicken coop. His blunderbuss won the standoff, and the men ran like hell at the sight of the gaping muzzle of his weapon.

With his hands held high, he took a daring step forward.

"I am loyal to the king," he announced.

The soldier didn't move or reply, glaring at him coldly, his musket still poised. Several comrades forced their way into the farmer's home; the sounds of breaking glass were mixed with jeers and raucous laughter as they took great delight in ransacking the home for plunder.

"No need for that!" Elsa cried, stepping out from behind Zebulon to defend the sanctuary of their home.

"Damn you, woman, don't move!" the soldier snapped.

Zebulon lowered a hand to pull her in by his side.

Zebulon studied the countenance of the soldier before him. The pale light of dawn that broke through the turbulent skies revealed a young, ruddy, weather-beaten face; the lack of expression in his eyes disclosed a stoic detachment.

"I have some cider in the barn. My good wife would be glad to heat it for you and your comrades. Would you care for some?" he offered.

The barrel of cider left out in the open would be lost anyhow; he hoped they would not find the other barrels concealed in a pit dug under the floorboards of the barn.

The soldier didn't waver. A comrade came out of the house, held up his musket on the porch, and waved back to the support line covering their advance. The second line got up from their ready position and dashed forward in turn. As the other two in the house came out, one stuffed a slab of bacon, which would have been Zebulon's breakfast over the next few days, into his haversack. Elsa began to object, but Zebulon squeezed her shoulder to warn her not to move.

Seconds later, the support line burst forward, barely glancing at the couple as they raced through the farmyard, past the barn, and out into the orchard to the west.

Two infantrymen dashed into the barn and came out seconds later with jubilant expressions.

"Plenty in there," one exclaimed, and they raced to join the rest of their detachment, already moving through the orchard.

Zebulon's heart sank with those words.

He owned twenty acres of woodlot to the north. In the center there was a deep hollow cut formed by a creek that meandered down to the Schuylkill. With considerable effort, he had dug into the bank and covered its approach with deadfall. With each appearance of armed men, he had been able to conceal his prize team of draft horses, his breeding bull, two of the milk cows, and the last of his sows, old Beatrice. Elsa had declared that Beatrice would never be slaughtered; the old grotesque thing had become like a pet to her.

Up until this moment, he had managed to keep enough hidden to see them through the winter and into the planting and breeding time of spring.

But this time, war came without warning.

He turned anxiously to look back into his barn. Before this damn war started he was planning to add on to the barn, built by his grandfather, who had cleared the land fifty years ago. Two years ago he owned thirty head of dairy cows, creating a thriving business of selling the milk in the city. Each year rich litters of pigs were slaughtered in the autumn, smoked or salted down, barreled and sold to the ships that docked in the busiest port of North America. His orchard yielded hundreds of bushels of apples to be pressed into cider and sold in the city as well.

He had prospered until the coming of this damn war. After Brandywine, he lost the herd of dairy cows, along with most of the harvest. It was a war in which he saw no part for himself. The cries about taxation and liberty? What taxes had he ever paid, other than what the local commissioners extorted for his rich farmland? As a young man, the call of adventure enticed him to serve with the militia, along with a promise of simple garrison duty without any prospect of fighting. He had never ventured farther than the east bank of the Susquehanna for the tedious duty of garrisoning a fort, and then returned home satisfied that he had done his service to his king.

The young soldier who confronted him slowly lowered his musket.

"Why are you still here?" Elsa snapped angrily. "Your thieves of men have left, and they've stolen our breakfast!"

"Orders," he responded sharply.

"Whose orders?"

"The officers will inform you."

"Support line! Forward at the double!"

The young soldier looked toward Middle Ferry Road. A sergeant, with his short musket raised, was pointing westward.

"Stay here and don't move," the soldier commanded. As if pulled along by some vast machine, of which he was but one cog, he took a deep breath, exhaled, and sped off, running past the barn and into the orchard.

Zebulon and Elsa stood aghast as the soldier retreated.

"Can we still hide something?" she whispered.

"Too late," he replied despondently. Down on Middle Ferry Road, a company of heavy infantry was advancing at the double; a sergeant urged them forward with obscene cries. Behind them was a company of mounted troops, uniforms blue and green. Zebulon gazed at them coldly. These were the mounted Hessian riflemen, the dreaded Jaegers.

A long, sinuous column of dozens of wagons followed. Mounted troops covered their flanks. Several of them turned off the road into his neighbor Snyder's farmyard.

The lead wagon in the column reached the pathway to his farm and turned in, followed by two more.

"Three wagons in here," announced the leading officer, as he dismounted and stretched, tossing the bridle of his horse to a waiting private. He studiously ignored Zebulon and Elsa for the moment; his gaze swept the farm with the air of a buyer contemplating an offer of purchase, or an overseer inspecting his property.

He finally turned back to Zebulon.

"Lieutenant Peterson of the Commissary Department of His Majesty's Army," he announced languidly, as if already bored with the proceedings.

Behind him, the wagon drivers dismounted; several soldiers in the back of each wagon jumped down to join them.

Zebulon knew that it was not customary to shake hands with king's officers, but he offered the friendly gesture anyhow. Peterson limply accepted his grasp, but only for a second, and then stepped back.

"The Commissary Department is requisitioning supplies for the army," he announced.

Zebulon tried to keep his smile.

"Lieutenant, let's get out of the cold. We were about to have breakfast, that is, until your men stole it. Perhaps Elsa can still find something to prepare."

He tried to force a friendly wink: perhaps something to drink as well.

"No time for that now."

He turned his back on Zebulon, a gesture that the farmer saw and was meant to see as an insult.

"Corporal Henson, move lively there, move lively!"

A soldier who was headed toward the house stiffened to attention, saluted, and turned back to the others, barking orders.

"Sir. We are loyal to the king here."

"Of course, that's what you all say."

"Sir, we are loyal," Elsa interjected.

Peterson barely nodded, looking past her.

"Jones, what's in that barn?"

A soldier appeared at the open doorway and stood stiffly to attention.

"Sir. A rich haul, sir. Two fat cows, two horses, big 'uns they are. Plenty of hay and feed too, sir."

"Move lively there."

"Sir, what are your intentions?" Zebulon asked, trying to force some authority into his voice.

The lieutenant glowered at him with cold eyes.

"How many live here?"

"Sir?"

"You heard me, how many live here?" he retorted.

"Just the two of us," Elsa replied anxiously.

"No children, hired hands, or slaves?"

"No children," Elsa whispered. "We had two girls; they died of the smallpox six years ago. No, no children . . ."

Her voice trailed off. She made no mention of her son, trying to artfully dodge the question.

"No sons with the damn rebels?"

"She is a godly woman and answered truthfully, sir," Zebulon shot back. "We have no children."

"Don't take that tone with me. I am doing my duty as a soldier of the king." A hint of menace now filled his voice.

"As I told you, we are loyal to the Crown."

"If that is so, why do you still have that livestock? This area is crawling with rebel raiders. Why the livestock? Did you pay them off?"

"I hid them, sir. I had thirty head at midsummer; this is all that is left."

"And would you have hidden them if you had known we were coming?"

He didn't reply. Did the man take him for an utter fool?

The lieutenant pointed toward the east; a plume of smoke was rising with the wind. It looked to be the Mueller farm, down near the river.

"He got off lightly; he'll live, by orders of General Howe. I would have shot the bastard for striking one of my men. But his house is being razed."

Neither replied.

"Slaves or hired hands?"

"They ran off."

"Joined the rebels?"

"I didn't ask them about their personal business when they left."

A loud bellowing interrupted them. Zebulon looked back to find a soldier trying to lead the bull out of the barn. As if sensing his fate, the bull was fighting back. More soldiers joined in, prodding its butt end with their bayonets to force him along.

"He's all that's left of our breeding stock," Zebulon protested. "The bull, the two cows, and our horses, we will need them for spring plowing."

"They are being requisitioned for the army. I'll give you a receipt, and you'll be paid in hard cash."

"We can't eat money," Elsa replied sharply.

"Still better than what you can do with that damn Continental money the rebels would have given you instead. There's only one use for that paper," he said with a salacious grin.

"You are no gentleman, sir," Zebulon fumed. "How dare you speak to my wife in such a manner?"

A heavy rumbling shook the ground as horse-drawn wagons approached. After a break in the line, several officers, resplendent in scarlet and white, led a company of mounted troops across his field and toward his house.

"Is that General Howe?"

The lieutenant looked over his shoulder and then back at him.

"None of your damn business."

He reached into his cloak, pulled out a note pad, and jotted down a tally.

Elsa watched in horror as the soldiers seized their livestock. The soldiers' vociferous laughter and cheering filled the air as if to make it a celebratory event. The draft horses, Caesar and Pompey, the cows, and the bull were tied to the wagons. Some carried the chickens; a few twitched spasmodically but were already dead. A soldier filled his hat with fresh eggs, dropping several on the hard ground; others lugged baskets of dried apples and turnips. A pig squealed in terror as their breeding sow, Beatrice, was dragged out of the barn. The lieutenant scanned the men as they loaded the goods. He quickly finished his notes, signed his name, and tore the sheet of foolscap from the pad and extended it to Zebulon.

"Report to Philadelphia, swear your oath of allegiance to the Crown, and you'll be paid fairly."

Zebulon took the receipt with unconcealed rage. The lieutenant had noted but one horse and a cow; there was no mention of the bull.

A shrill cry of agony interrupted the farmer; he looked on with repulsion as a soldier stabbed a bayonet into Beatrice. She thrashed about wildly, trying to pull herself free of the blade; another soldier cheered and joined in, stabbing the animal again and again until she collapsed, convulsing weakly, in a welter of her own blood.

"No!" Elsa cried. "She was only a pet. A pet!"

She moved as if to strike the offending soldiers and Zebulon grabbed her by the shoulders and pulled her back.

Out on the road a knot of scrupulously dressed officers rode past, barely sparing a glance at the confrontation in the farmyard. He could instantly tell by their finery that they were men of rank, far superior to the lout who handed him a document of blatant lies about what was being taken and now smiled as his men finished off Beatrice.

"Damn you, sir!" Zebulon cried. "This is an outrage, I wish to protest!"

He stepped away from the lieutenant and moved toward the open gate of his farm.

"Sir, you there! You!" he shouted, pointing toward the officers.

"Shut up and don't you move a damn inch," the lieutenant hissed.

"You can go to hell," Zebulon snarled, breaking free from his wife's grasp and shoving his way past the lieutenant and starting for the road. Surely these gentlemen would stop this outrageous abuse.

"Zebulon!"

The blow from behind knocked him to the ground. The world was suddenly red-rimmed, distant, as if about to fade away forever.

Groaning audibly, he rolled on to his side and looked up at the lieutenant, who was clutching the barrel of the pistol, the handle smeared with blood from the blow.

"Lieutenant!"

The man stiffened, looked past Zebulon, and came to attention.

"No excessive force with the civilians, if you please."

At this command, the lieutenant stood rigid and saluted.

Elsa scurried to Zebulon's side; as she flung herself on the ground, she took him into her arms, and tried to stanch the flow of blood from his scalp, which had been split open by the blow.

"Madam," the lieutenant hissed, "control that husband of yours or, by Jove, I will come back here later and blow his goddamned rebel brains out."

She gazed up at him, unable to reply.

"Damn, they are coming on fast!"

Colonel Daniel Morgan slipped his large frame down behind the tree. He returned the telescope he had been using to its owner, Major John Clark. Clark, commander of his detachment of spies and scouts, had been assigned by General Washington to shadow the British in Philadelphia.

Clark focused the telescope back on the road and continued counting. He absently reached for his notepad as he watched, and made hatch marks as he counted the wagons, companies of infantry, and the mounted Jaegers and dragoons.

There was a tense moment as the first wave of light infantry rode past, but they did not penetrate into the woods where Morgan, Clark, and their men were concealed. Foolish mistake, but then again, the men were at least two hundred and fifty yards from the road, nearly three times the range of a musket shot.

Morgan smiled. The enemy had no idea that his riflemen were lurking.

Keeping diligent watch, he stretched his long legs out on the cold ground. He reached for his long rifle beside him; it was his most prized earthly possession, and the same rifle he had carried since the last war, the one against the French and Indians. Crafted by Adam Haymaker to his specific demands, it had cost him twenty-five pounds sterling. And that was over twenty years ago, when such a sum could buy a man one hundred acres of prime land in the Shenandoah Valley.

The barrel was almost four feet in length; its black walnut stock measured precisely to fit just under his chin. If he had dared to cut a notch in it for every man he had dropped with this rifle——French, Indian, British, and Hessian——such a sacrilege would have destroyed the beauty and symmetry of the weapon's lines. Besides, such a vanity was considered exceedingly foolish by anyone from the frontier. If he was ever captured alive by the less than friendly Indians of that region, such a tally would insure even greater lengths of creativity with their tortures.

"Damn it. That can't be him." Clark spat.

"Who?"

"General Howe!"

"Where?" Morgan cried. He sat up and squinted against the cold easterly wind.

"On the road there, just before that farm down below."

Morgan watched for several seconds. It would be a long reach at three hundred yards to the road with this wind, but damn it all!

He slipped the rifle up, cupping his hand around the lock, flicking the flash pan open to check the powder.

"Dan. You aren't?" Major Clark asked.

"I'm going to try a shot at the son of a bitch."

"Dan, we're here to scout, not start a fight."

Morgan said nothing as he blew the powder out of the pan, drew up his horn, and opened it to pour in some fresh priming.

He knew Clark was right. The man was General Washington's master of spies for this region, tasked with infiltrating agents into Philadelphia to ascertain what the lobsterbacks were up to. Clark was here to spy, not to start a fight. Morgan and his men were ordered to provide cover and support, and then raid on their own, but not to upset or interfere with Clark's efforts. It was at least a brigade down there, and he had only fifty men with him at this spot. But still, if that was Howe . . .

Clark was obviously a bit unnerved this morning because he had failed to gain warning of this move and was trying to reassert himself by determining an accurate count of strength and the line of march. He had already muttered that Washington needed to be told of it at once, that perhaps this was a chance to cut off part of their army out in the open, perhaps another Christmas coup like last year at Trenton, to restore the collapsing spirit of the revolution.

They had watched as the lead scouts crossed at the first light of dawn from the cold morning mists rising off the river.

Company after company emerged out of the fog. Most were light infantry; several units were the dangerous mounted Hessian riflemen, and then the column of wagons. They counted over two hundred on the far side of the river, lined up and waiting to cross.

The intent was twofold and obvious. The first, to sweep along the west bank of the Schuylkill River, strip the countryside of all supplies to feed the ten thousand British troops garrisoning Philadelphia, and, in so doing, deny those supplies to the patriot cause.

Dan could easily see the second intent as well. It was a taunt, a challenge. At this very moment, only twenty miles to the north, General Washington and his army were struggling to establish a winter campsite at Valley Forge. Howe was offering a dare. If he himself was moving this column, the challenge was an even greater affront. The commanding British general, leaving the comfort of his headquarters and the beds of his mistresses for a few days in open challenge and defiance, would be a chance too good to miss.

The target momentarily disappeared from view behind the house. His rifle primed, Dan Morgan waited.

Morgan sighed as he contemplated the spectacle nearly three hundred yards away. It was a far cry from what he had witnessed several months ago, up north in the forests of New York and the field at Saratoga. Back then, it was his men in the open sweeping the countryside with victory.

With the first rally cry for volunteers in 1775, he served with his comrade of the last war, George Washington, bringing with him a hundred riflemen recruited from the Virginia frontier. Sent north to join one of the great heroes of this war, Benedict Arnold, he then fought at Quebec in '75, taking command when Arnold was wounded and captured. The campaign turned into a debacle and he, too, was taken prisoner. Exchanged along with Arnold for a couple of British officers, he returned south, raised a regiment in Virginia, returned to the war, and then went north to join in the climactic struggle to hold back the northern invasion by General John Burgoyne.

How he had lusted for that assignment; he was filled with a fervent though ungodly prayer to once——just once——have Burgoyne within 250 yards of his muzzle.

Years ago, as a boy of eighteen, he ran off to join the army of General Braddock as a teamster. There he first met Washington, a young officer in command of militia, and the two became fast friends. It was there, as well, that he ran afoul of Gentleman Johnny Burgoyne, a young, foppish officer who should have stopped a bullet when the army was all but annihilated on the Monongahela.

After one of Burgoyne's comrades slashed at him with his sword over some alleged rude remark, he gave the man the thrashing he deserved for insulting a free man. In retaliation Burgoyne ordered him to be bound to a wagon wheel to suffer four hundred and ninty-nine lashes.

As he contemplated it now, Dan rubbed the back of his neck. What were intended as scars of humiliation had become a source of pride. He had openly stripped to the waist before the men of his command more than once to show his wounds. He swore before them that he would not rest until every lash was repaid in full. His men followed him with an eager determination to fulfill that oath.

Four hundred and ninety-nine lashes were tantamount to a death sentence. He later learned that Washington had tried to intervene with an appeal but was rebuffed, and had been warned that it was time colonials learned the meaning of discipline. He was told that those gathered to watch saw the bones of his ribs and spine, the flesh hung in bloody strips . . . all in the name of proper discipline. His indomitable spirit and the fact that he had survived the ordeal made him a legend of survival and defiance against the increasingly hated officers from England.

When he joined the northern army with his sharpshooters, they had set to work with a passion. A wonderful moment indeed when he spotted an officer more than two hundred yards off, and put a bullet through the man's head with an offhand shot.

The British, under a flag of truce, sent a representative to protest the deliberate shooting of officers, as if it were against the rules of war, stating that it would only create unruliness and a collapse of discipline on both sides. The British officer exclaimed that it was not at all proper, and was genuinely upset and utterly confused that his protest was met with mocking disdain.

Morgan was supremely delighted to send a personal response back to the "Gentleman," asking him if he remembered a young teamster who received four hundred and ninety nine lashes and was now eagerly waiting to see him anywhere within two hundred yards of the front lines.

It was later said that Gentleman Johnny never again ventured anywhere near the forward trenches during the final siege at Saratoga.

He almost regretted sending that taunt. He ruefully thought that he might otherwise have been able to get his vengeance after all.

With the victory at Saratoga, created in large part by his old comrade Benedict Arnold, he assumed the war was nearly over. His men were ordered to rejoin Washington; their triumphal march down the Hudson Valley, into New Jersey, and across Pennsylvania turned somber when they received word of the disasters afflicting Washington and his command. Howe had finally stirred from New York City. Rather than go north to link up with the beleaguered Burgoyne, as everyone assumed he would, he took ship with nearly his entire force, leaving only a small garrison to hold New York City. Sailing south as far as Chesapeake Bay, then north, he disembarked near Wilmington, then maneuvered to seize Philadelphia, the capital of the newly proclaimed United States. To the British way of thinking, when an enemy capital fell, the war was decidedly over. Disaster had befallen Washington at the Battle of Brandywine, and repeatedly throughout the autumn.

Congress abandoned Philadelphia and fled to Lancaster. Frightened that the British would launch a surprise attack and capture them, they finally ran to the far bank of the Susquehanna at York, while Washington's army staggered northward to what was supposed to be their retreat position at Valley Forge. Some had described it as a march into oblivion.

Now Morgan had been tasked by Washington to bring his men down the river to support Major Clark with his spying efforts; to harass, observe, and provide warning if the enemy should bestir themselves from the comfort of their winter quarters.

As he waited for his target to reappear, he glanced over his shoulder. Thirty or so yards back, half a dozen of his men were concealed in a cave dug into the side of a creek bed. Someone had most likely dug it out as a hiding place for what was left of his livestock.

He whistled softly. As if on cue, a bare head popped up; it was old Moses Wheeler. He was a disturbing sight for many. Twenty years ago, Moses had been taken prisoner by the Shawnee and made a source of entertainment. They had scalped him while he was still alive, along with the usual practice of slowly roasting his feet. He endured it without a whimper, taunting his "hosts" to try their best, that surely they could do better. Impressed by his stoic fortitude, the torture was stopped and he was offered adoption into the tribe. Considering the alternative, he readily agreed and later said he actually came to like his new family, but with the return of spring the next year he decided to end the adoption and get out.

Moses could not tolerate a hat. Even in the dead of winter, he claimed it caused his skull to ache. Now that it was free of any covering, the sight of his mangled, hairless crown made many living east of the mountains decide that venturing westward was something they would no longer consider.

Moses crawled up out of the creek bed and hobbled forward. His toes had been burned off, so he had learned to walk again with a strange bearlike shuffle. He crawled the last few feet to Dan's side and settled in.

As Moses moved in beside him, the cavalcade reappeared, riding slowly along the road, out in the open between the house and barn.

"Can you see that son of a bitch on the road?"

Moses squinted and then smiled, spitting as he offered a chew of tobacco to Dan. He gladly accepted the thick, solid cake, took a bite, and handed it back.

"Think one of 'em's Howe."

In spite of his infirmities, Moses had the best eyes of any man in his detachment. Vanity forbade Dan to admit that he feared his own eyes were beginning to fail a bit.

"What do you think, Moses?"

Moses studied them for a moment using Clark's telescope. The cavalcade had stopped. Moses lowered the telescope, looked east for a few seconds, into the eye of the wind, then back to the men on the road.

"I reckon it is. And if it ain't, it sure as hell is some high ranker. Figure it to be near on to three hundred yards, Dan. But dammit this wind's gonna make it a tricky shot."

"It's not Burgoyne, but the commanding general is worth the try," Dan announced.

"Colonel Morgan!" Major Clark hissed. "Damn it all, sir. Do you see how many light infantry they have down there! And those mounted riflemen. For God's sake, don't. We're supposed to scout and report!"

"You write your reports, while I do me some shooting," Morgan replied with a grin. "And maybe, just maybe, you can report that Howe has gone to hell and I sent him there."

He slipped his rifle up over a fallen log, found the point of balance, and squinted down the four-foot length of the barrel.

"God help us," Clark sighed. He snapped his notebook shut and slipped it into his haversack.

"You boys get ready for some fun. Dan's gonna shoot himself a general," Moses cackled. The other riflemen strained to look up from their hiding place. They were already placing wagers on the shot, betting their wads of Continental money.

Dan sighted in on the officer in the center of the group, took a deep breath, and exhaled half of it. His finger lightly touched the trigger, and his gaze shifted to the tufts of grass in the pasture before him. He watched as they bent over with the wind, judging the distance and time the ball would be in flight, and shifted his aim a dozen feet to the left of his target, elevating the muzzle to half again the height of the man.

A surge of wind eddied around him, moaning through the forest; the tree-tops swayed. Muttering a curse, he withdrew his finger, exhaled, and could hear Clark sigh with relief.

"Thank God . . ."

The horsemen moved again along the road that dropped down behind the orchard. Morgan raised his rifle again, judged the wind, the movement of the target, and the bullet's destination. *Just a few seconds*, he prayed, *hold this wind back, just a few seconds . . .*

The prayer went unanswered as another gust swept across the fields and through the trees. The target disappeared from view behind the barn, the road farther on turning south was concealed as well by the orchard.

The shot was lost.

"You lucky bastard," he whispered. "You don't know how close it was."

Clark exhaled with a grunt.

"Let's just settle back and watch them for a while, Colonel. It's swarming with light infantry and Jaegers down there. They'll be on us like flies to manure if they know we are here."

Morgan nodded, his attention focused back on the farmyard.

And then he saw it. The farmer stepped away from the officer and headed toward the road. The officer came up behind him, pistol drawn, and hit the man across the back of the head, causing him to drop to his feet.

"You see that!" Morgan exclaimed. "You see what that bastard did to that farmer?"

Morgan snapped his rifle back up, not even bothering to rest it on a log, and sighted in. The range to the farmyard was about two hundred and twenty, maybe two hundred and forty yards, the wind from the left was dropping off . . .

"Colonel Morgan, please, . . ." Clark exclaimed.

Morgan squeezed the trigger.

The familiar recoil slapped his shoulder; it felt much like a caress to Dan. The muzzle of his rifle leapt up slightly as the .45-caliber ball cracked out and arced upward. The greased patch that had encased the ball fluttered to the ground a dozen yards out into the pasture. A puff of smoke swirled up around him, whipped away by the wind, but not before more than a dozen watchful skirmishers in red uniforms and the blue and green of the Jaegers had spotted it.

The report of his rifle thundered across the field and echoed around Zebulon Miller's farmyard as the bullet shattered Lieutenant Peterson's right arm——the arm that had been holding the pistol. The impact of the ball shattered the bone from just below the shoulder to halfway down to the elbow.

"Dear God, that's done it for certain," Clark cried.

"You shot a little too far to the right, Dan," Moses announced laconically. "Not your best, but still rather fair, I'd say."

"Damn wind," Dan muttered, as he pulled his rifle back and hurriedly started to reload.

"They're on us!" Clark shouted.

Dan looked up and saw where Clark was pointing.

From out of the orchard to the west of the farm, several horsemen were already emerging, urging their mounts to a full gallop. Behind them, skirmishers and the light infantry were turning and coming on fast. To the east of the farm, he could see other mounted troopers approaching as well. In the farmyard, every lobsterback was scattering. The man he had just shot was on the ground, writhing with pain.

One more imaginary notch for this rifle, he thought with grim satisfaction. Last time you'll ever hit a civilian, you bastard.

Moses raised his rifle to shoot.

"Don't give 'em more smoke!" Clark cried, as he turned to run back into the woodlot.

Moses laughed and fired anyway. Dan saw a horse go down, its rider tumbling to the ground.

"You shot the horse, not the man!" Morgan shouted. He fell in behind Clark and reloaded as he ran.

Moses shuffled beside him, sliding down into the creek bed, and then they were up onto the other side. The six men with him already up, two of them behind trees, rifles lowered, aiming, waiting.

Clark cursed the lack of military discipline of all riflemen as he continued to run with Dan.

A scattering of shots erupted behind them. Musket balls whizzed through the trees, one smacking a branch above Dan. He turned and looked back. The Jaegers were on the edge of the woodlot he had rested in but a minute ago. Several of them were dismounting; one had just fired while still mounted.

The two men bringing up the rear fired in reply, and the mounted Jaeger leaned forward, clutching his stomach.

Two more of his men covered the retreat of their comrades, who were now running full out. None of the Jaegers dared to venture into the woodlot, but from the corner of his eye he saw a troop of mounted dragoons galloping hard across a field of winter wheat, trying to flank the north end of the woods and cut off their retreat.

Their own horses were at the far end of the woods; four of his men waited with the mounts.

It was a hard run on the cold, frozen ground. Old Moses cursed as he shambled along on the stumps of his feet, but he still kept the pace.

More shots could be heard. Glimpses of red uniforms flitted in the woods behind them. A line of light infantry moved fast, dodging from tree to tree; some were already across the creek, where they lay flat on the far side to take advantage of the natural trench.

One of their horses screamed, kicked up its hind legs, and collapsed onto its side. Dan realized it was Moses's horse. He muttered a curse under his breath. "Double with me, Moses!" he cried.

As he reached for his mount, he flung himself into the saddle. Moses needed no urging to grab hold of Dan's waist and pull himself up as Dan spurred on.

Clark was in the lead, racing at a full gallop fifty yards ahead into an open pasture. Dan did not blame him in the least. Clark knew the names of every spy and counterspy working in Philadelphia. Although the Brits did not condone the Shawnee way of torture, if he were to be captured they would still try to persuade him to talk before he finally danced at the end of a rope.

Perhaps Major Clark had been right after all. Perhaps that shot was not worth it. The response by their light infantry and mounted troopers was indeed getting faster and more effective.

The British dragoons to their right were momentarily stymied by a high, well-made split rail fence; they were forced to ride parallel to their quarry for a hundred and fifty yards until at last they came to a gate. The troopers were filled with rage as one finally dismounted to lever the gate open.

The delay gave Morgan and his men just enough time to pull ahead of their pursuers; they galloped down a long slope, leaping a low stone wall bordering a shallow frozen creek half a dozen paces wide, crossed a field of corn stubble, and took cover in a wooded ridge. His reserves were waiting dutifully. Fifty of his riflemen had anxiously watched the pursuit and cheered him on as he came in. One of the riders shouted that "Ole Dan" had gotten himself another officer.

The line of British light infantry skirmishers emerged from the abandoned wood, sprinted halfway to the ridge, stopped at the low stone wall, and got behind it. A dozen mounted Jaegers galloped in to join them and dismounted while Dan's men opened up at a long two hundred yards. Dan realized these men were not fools. He had hoped to lure them on to his reserves, but they were well trained and would have nothing to do with being caught in an open field, armed with smoothbore muskets, while their opponents in the woods were armed with rifles.

Civilians who still dismissed the British as wooden soldiers——who said they were nothing more than targets waiting to be shot——had never faced them in a real fight, especially the light infantry and the mounted German riflemen.

Some of his men opened up anyhow, but given the wind and cover the enemy had taken, it was more for sport and harassment. Their pursuers were not so imprudent as to press forward against concealed riflemen.

Moses slipped off Dan's horse and cursed soundly that the ride had all but gelded him. Dan leapt down, ordered his men to keep a sharp eye, and walked over to Clark, who was glaring at him coldly.

"Did that accomplish anything?"

Morgan grinned.

"One less officer, I'd say."

Clark shook his head as a smile creased his face.

Dan beamed with great satisfaction. Part of the game of legend, he thought to himself. Four hundred and ninety-nine lashes. The message back again to Burgoyne. By tonight his men will joke how he had put another British officer where he belonged. Indeed, it was part of the game of legend, leadership, and command.

Clark walked to a hollow where several shelters cut of pine branches were well concealed. A clean fire of seasoned hickory rails was crackling in front of the shelters. One of Clark's men, a former slave Clark now employed as a regular spy, sat by the fire. Seeing Clark approach, he scooped a tin cup of coffee from the kettle over the fire and handed it to him. Morgan followed directly behind him, and the black man gestured with a second cup, which Morgan accepted with a nod. "David, when did you get back?" Clark asked. He sipped his coffee and patted the towering black man on the shoulder.

"Just after you left here, sir. I found out about this raid and was trying to get word to you, but you were already out watching them, so I thought it best to wait," David replied, his voice as rich and cultured as any British officer's.

Dan was a bit startled by the man's tone. He could have sworn he was hearing some upper-class Englishman, fresh off the boat.

So this was David. Clark had spoken of him the night before. The use of this man was obvious. He could easily move between the lines and was able to mimic the dialect of a runaway Jamaican slave who wanted to find shelter inside the British lines from his master. Or he could be a servant of a proper English gentleman carrying a secret love letter to a mistress now so sadly caught behind rebel lines. Since the British seizure of Philadelphia, this man had run the lines half a dozen times, returning from each trip with invaluable information to be forwarded to General Washington.

David gave a quick report of what he had observed and the intelligence he had gained, now evidenced on the road below. A full brigade, with Howe rumored to be personally leading it, had crossed the river and was attempting to lure Washington out for a fight. The price of all foodstuffs in the city had dropped now that the Continental forts that had blocked the lower Delaware had at last fallen and supply transports were coming in daily. Though the city was now well supplied by transports, this raid was a spoiler, meant to sweep the countryside around Philadelphia clean of any provisions the Continental Army might still try to seize. The report was a picture of the British well secured and comfortable in the richest city in North America, ready to live out the winter in luxury, with the lowest British private eating as well as a general on the American side. Weekly balls were already in vogue. Officers were finding merchants more than happy to rent out living quarters for real guineas stamped with the image of the king. More than a few of their daughters were willing to be seen clinging to a redcoat's arm, the less proper willing to share rather more. Most of the populace seemed content with their conquerors—— more and more, they were calling them their liberators. Rumors from spies for the British were that the rebel army was disintegrating, that not a single head of cattle or barrel of flour was found when the Americans marched into Valley Forge three days ago.

Dan listened quietly, pondering all that was said. Three months ago, he believed it was all over. After Saratoga, victory for the Revolution had seemed inevitable. An entire British Army had surrendered. But now, all of this? The excitement of the hunt and chase of only minutes ago evaporated and was replaced with exhaustion and hunger. He had placed the strictest injunction against looting and foraging, an order personally given to him by Washington, and thus his men had ridden past many rich farmsteads, leaving them untouched even as they felt the pangs of hunger. It was becoming increasingly difficult to prevent his men from going back to steal. However, General Washington's orders had been strict. The populace would be kept on the patriots' side by forbearance and hunger. Now, the British were the ones who were plucking the land clean.

Clark sighed and thanked David, drew his notebook out, and started to write.

"Can one of your men take this report back to General Washington?" he asked, looking over at Dan.

Dan nodded. With this cold ground, Old Moses wasn't much good for running. He could take a horse and get off his feet for a few days.

Clark finished his report and, as an act of courtesy, handed it to Dan, who scanned it. He was ashamed to admit he could barely read or write, but he could figure out some of it. Clark gave what he thought was an accurate account, not claiming that Howe was with the column but suspecting he might be, and closed by urging that, if a flying column was rapidly dispatched to this place, the general could cut off a goodly portion of the British Army and achieve a telling victory.

Dan quickly folded the message and called for Moses, who took Dan's horse and rode north to report to Washington.

Clark squatted down by the fire alongside David, staring morosely at the flames.

"A year ago today, I was with General Washington," Clark finally said. "Today's the twenty-second of December, isn't it?"

"I think so," Dan replied.

"A year ago today, December twenty-second, the general asked me to send a few men into Trenton to take a look around. David was one of them. A good act he played with that runaway slave routine of his. And he came back with an accurate count of how many men were with that Hessian Colonel Rall."

"I knew then what the general was thinking. A year ago exactly," Clark sighed.

He held his hands up to warm them as a gust of wind screamed all around them.

"And now look where we are. This damn war will go on forever. We're worse off now than we were a year ago. You heard what David said, and I believe every word of it. At least when we retreated across the Delaware a year ago, there was food waiting and Philadelphia was still ours. Damn it all. After Trenton, Princeton, and our driving them clear back to New York, I thought I'd be home by now with my family and friends, rather than out here freezing . . ."

A muffled pop interrupted him. Dan looked up with a start as a bullet smacked into the tree he was leaning against, sending bits of bark raining down all over him.

Another pop, and then a scattered volley was heard.

"They're on our left!"

One of his men ran in from the east and pointed back over his shoulder; a second later he collapsed in a crumpled heap, his blood and bits of brain and skull exploding in a vaporlike mist in the air even as he fell.

A line of British light infantry, intermingled with Jaegers, came down off the crest of the ridge to their left and rear.

Dan raised his rifle and snapped off a quick shot, not sure if he had gotten his man but hoping, at the very least, that he had made him duck. He whistled and gestured for his men to run for it.

Clark and David were running hard along his side.

Caught by surprise! My men caught by surprise!

He looked back up the slope. Moses had dodged out of the trap and rode hard to the west to get around them, carrying the dispatch for Washington.

It was time to run, and Colonel Dan Morgan was not at all ashamed to lead the way. This was not Saratoga, and he had a gut-wrenching sense that the shoe was now indeed on the other foot here in Pennsylvania, and that this winter had only just started.

Zebulon Miller, still weak at the knees, stood silent as the men loaded their lieutenant into the back of the wagon. The man struggled to stifle his anguished screams as the wagon jolted off back to Philadelphia, where most likely the knife of a surgeon would amputate his arm.

The sergeant in command of the looting party, his attention now relieved of ministering to his wounded officer, resumed his task, and barked at his men to hurry and strip the barn clean. From within the barn Zebulon could hear enthusiastic cries of delight as someone, prying up floorboards, uncovered the barrels of hard cider and the two ten-gallon barrels of corn whiskey.

Before the barrels were loaded into the wagons, men were already filling their canteens, and one of the corn liquor barrels was partially drained.

He saw by their angry glances and muttered comments what was to come, and he fought to choke back tears when the thought struck him that perhaps God, in His infinite wisdom, had taken his two daughters away before this war had descended upon this land. For they would have been sixteen and eighteen now . . .

Over the distant ridge by the Mueller farm he could see puffs of smoke and the echo of gunfire.

"Our lads are giving the bastards hell," one of the men cried. The sergeant nodded in acknowledgment.

"That's the last of it, Sergeant."

Zebulon saw a soldier come out of the barn, holding a couple of geese up high, their necks already broken. Elsa stifled back a sob. One of the geese was indeed a pet. On summer days it used to follow their two girls around, honking loudly until attended to, hand-fed, and petted.

"Burn it," the sergeant announced.

The men needed no urging. Inwardly Zebulon searched for a biblical reference as to how men were driven mad by the lusts of war, but the verse would not come to him or comfort him when, within minutes, flames leapt heavenward, consuming the barn.

The sergeant looked at him closely, drawing in his breath, heavy with the scent of corn liquor.

"That woodlot yonder. The one the shot came from?"

Zebulon did not reply.

"You own it?"

He was silent. A second later, the sergeant slapped him hard on the side of the head with the butt of his musket. Zebulon collapsed, knocked out by the blow.

"Do you own it, damn you?"

"Yes, it's ours," Elsa cried. "Now in the name of Christ please leave us alone."

"Your farm was harboring rebel traitors. And I lost my lieutenant. He was a fair bastard, he was, and let us have our fun at times. God knows what kind of officer we'll be stuck with next, thanks to you. Most likely some preachy type who will tell us you Yankees are just like us and we got to be respectful of you."

He looked back at his men.

"Burn the house."

The sergeant led his detachment away. As their home collapsed in flames, their neighbor Snyder and his wife came to help Elsa carry her husband back to the Snyders' house, where they would be sheltered, at least for the moment, from the storm.

CHAPTER TWO

* * *

Valley Forge, Pennslyvania
Twenty-two Miles Northwest of Philadelphia
Noon, December 22, 1777

Heavy flakes of wet snow danced on the wind, intermingled with bursts of sleet and freezing rain as General George Washington, his hat pulled low against the chilled blast, rode slowly along the crest of the ridge where he had planned his defensive positions.

Not a single spadeful of earth had been turned for the defensive line he had been promised would be constructed before his army arrived here. The slope was bare, open, and could easily be taken by assault. To hear a curse escape his lips was indeed rare, but for several long minutes he gave vent to oaths of rage and frustration.

Weeks ago he planned for this place to be his fallback position if he could not drive the British out of Philadelphia. Twenty miles from the center of the city, it was close enough to keep watch, but far enough away that he would not be caught by surprise if they should sally forth.

To the east and north, the Schuylkill River turned in a broad arc, providing flanking cover, and then twisted back down to the southwest to serve as an anchor point for his right flank as well. The ridge in front of the river was dominated by two heights, Mount Joy and Mount Misery, where he had laid out plans for sturdy redoubts. At the moment, he felt the latter was most aptly named.

The site was chiefly wooded with secondary growth, the old forest cut back long ago to provide fuel for the nearby iron forge for which the ridge and valley below were named. The trees of the reemerging forest were well sized for easy felling and conversion into logs for huts and to serve as firewood.

He had conveyed these plans to Congress weeks ago. He had been promised by the Congressional Committee for the Conduct of the War that militia would be roused to build the defensive lines and construct enough shelters to house his men, and that rations would be in place to feed them for the winter.

Nothing, absolutely nothing had been done!

Rage gave way to dejected silence as he rode across the empty plain. No fortifications, no shelters, and thousands of shivering men squatting, sitting, lying on the bare ground, crouched around sputtering fires. Only a few even rose to their feet as he rode past, so lost were they in their frozen misery.

Rations had run out two days ago as they marched to this place. For the first time in this war, they had truly run out. In the past there had been some flour to be passed out to be fashioned into johnnycakes——nothing more than dough rolled out on a flat rock or frying pan——to be eaten half cooked, with perhaps several ounces of salt pork, usually spoiled. For the last two days, there had been nothing at all for any of them. As he surveyed the men, he felt a pang of guilt over the one-pound slab of bacon "acquired" somehow by his servant, Billy Lee, and shared with the men of his staff, along with a mixture of coffee and parched barley to wash it down.

There were no tools for making their shelters as the storm increased its fury. At the break of dawn that morning, when word reached the ranks that rations had not yet arrived, hundreds of them crowed like birds, a signal in their ranks of their intent to fly away. And morning muster reports showed that indeed more than three hundred had walked off during the night.

Washington contemplated the sheer failure of the promises made to him by Congress. Congress, of course, was utterly indifferent to its inability to deliver, and now blamed him for this debacle. It was a harsh denouement after a year of bitter disappointments.

After the string of blazing victories this time a year ago, the great surprise at Trenton with eight hundred Hessians captured, followed a week later by a second battle at Trenton, then the rout of the British column at Princeton, he had driven the enemy clear back to the banks of the Hudson, and finally made winter camp twenty-five miles to the west of New York City at Morristown.

At that time, spirits were high, although rations were short and the winter brutal. The victories and the dozens of successful skirmishes that drove the British garrison out of New Jersey, combined with the stunning words of Thomas Paine in his *The Crisis,* sparked new life into their cause. After laying in their spring planting, thousands rallied to join the ranks. New recruits came in believing that this would be the year that independence would be secured, and the last of the British and their Hessian hirelings would be driven from America's shores.

The news from the north had been heartening as well. He had little regard and virtually no trust for General Gates, who had all but betrayed him by refusing to cooperate in the opening moves of the Trenton campaign. Nonetheless, he had to concede that Gates had gone on to stall Burgyone in the wilderness of upstate New York. Gates's persistence had forced the surrender of over seven thousand men in October: the worst defeat handed to the British Army in the last century.

And yet, concurrent with the glorious news from the north, Washington's own forces had been defeated at Brandywine, maneuvered out of Philadelphia. His riposte at Germantown had come within a hairsbreadth of victory but then disintegrated into yet another humiliating defeat. Other battles and skirmishes failed as well, including the humiliating and ghastly defeat suffered by Anthony Wayne at Paoli.

Of course he must shoulder the blame for battles lost, but he sensed that something was most definitely afoot. Gates was lodged with Congress, appointed to head up the oversight committee, and he sensed that more than a few saw him as the new commander in chief, a position Gates obviously had sought since the start of the war.

He could not denigrate Gates's victory at Saratoga; in fact, he loudly applauded it, eager to extend his congratulation. But it was one thing to win a fight in the northern forests, against an enemy with overextended supply lines hundreds of miles long. It was an entirely different war here on the coastal plains. He could not give the rich lands and cities of the coast over to the enemy without making some effort of resistance, especially when the capital of their new nation was in the wager. He had to stand and fight, but he could never succeed with rabbles of militia, or men who signed for only six months and then went home.

America, if it was to survive, needed a trained professional army for this war, an army that could stand and face the dreaded volley fire of the best-trained army in the world. Increasingly, his light forces of riflemen were more than overmatched as the enemy formed their own light infantry companies into fast-moving strike forces supported by mounted riflemen.

But no one in Congress seemed to listen. Valley Forge was the barren fruit of his appeals, and he could not help but wonder if this was the final setup for a failure.

At this moment he did not care a whit for what Congress might do to him.

But these men, merciful God, he cried inwardly, the suffering of those who sullenly gazed at him as he rode by was nearly more than he could bear. Brave men, who had fought by his side, risking all, were now dying from hunger, for want of a pair of shoes, for lack of even the rudest shelter to shield them from winter's storms.

Across the last year and half, since declaring independence, Congress had been hard at work forming numerous committees. No one was sure how many there were; the last estimate approached nearly two hundred. Some members of Congress served on twenty or more such committees.

There were committees for recruiting, printing declarations, and handling recommendations for promotion. Increasingly, especially in the last few months, that usually meant that the ones promoted were not those recommended by him but rather by Gates, men who hung on Congress's coattails, accompanying their general to meet with Congress after the triumph at Saratoga.

There were committees to decide on their own pay raises, committees for the design of the money they printed to give themselves pay raises; they even had a committee to oversee the creation of more committees and, in a move of downright madness, a committee to oversee the supplying of the armies.

The supply committee was actually two committees. One made appeals to the various state committees, which in turn referenced the requests to yet other committees. The other was tasked with gathering supplies directly for Washington's army. That committee passed a resolution that granted him the power to seize supplies from "those disaffected with our gallant cause" but in the next breath admonished him not to antagonize the local populace and to win over the "disaffected." The Continental Committee would appeal to the various state committees for those supplies that would be forthcoming when and where needed.

Months ago, a delegation of patriotic citizens, horrified by the sight of their boys marching barefoot and ragged to what would be the Battle of Brandywine, had approached Congress, pledging to fund the building of a tannery in a safe location to manufacture shoes for all the armies in the field——but the government would have to provide the hides. The last Washington heard, that resolution was mixed in with all the other paperwork Congress had dragged with it to Lancaster and from there to York. The location where the tannery was to be built was still just an empty field.

A month ago, with the onset of autumn, he had issued a direct appeal to

Congress that his men were in rags; not one in twenty possessed a proper winter cloak, and nearly half of them were barefoot.

The reply was a haughty one: A request had been sent to France for eight thousand uniforms, properly tailored and of sufficient weight for winter wear. The note should be in Paris by the end of the year, he was told, with uniform delivery expected by March; Benjamin Franklin would guide the request through the various French committees, get the uniforms loaded, and then run them safely through the British blockade. Meanwhile, he was told to look to local patriots for relief. Their task and obligation to him was therefore done, and the concern was now his, with the clear implication that they had fulfilled their duty to him, and that if his men were not properly clad it would be his fault.

And now this final blow, the army's arrival at Valley Forge two days ago.

During the bitter march north, he had repeatedly promised his men that upon arrival they could set to making proper winter quarters. He had sketched 10 × 14 foot log cabins, ten men to a cabin, arrayed in neat, orderly streets, with regimental cookhouses and hospitals for the sick.

When he arrived with the vanguard of the column, his heart felt a despair he had never yet experienced in this, the third year of the war.

He was greeted by a barren, tree-studded plain. His choice of this low ridge had been made first with tactical requirements in mind. As an agricultural area, Valley Forge was a poor piece of land. At best, the cleared land could be used as pasture. Further west, or up toward Reading, the land was far richer, but it did not fulfill his desire to be close enough to Philadelphia in order to be able to strike swiftly if an opportunity presented itself. This was something he was already planning; the notes for the attack were locked safely in his secured footlocker. The plan was obviously based upon the success at Trenton almost exactly a year ago to this day.

What greeted him at Valley Forge was worse than Long Island, worse than the desperate days before Trenton, when at least he had a plan and a target to strike back at, but also a secured base on the west bank of the Delaware beyond British reach and with some trickle of supplies coming in.

Congress assured him that the proper committee from the Pennsylvania delegation had been informed of his intent to make his winter camp at Valley Forge, which, for reasons of security, had to be kept secret. This committee would rouse the local militia to bring in supplies, heads of beef, barrels of flour, and tools for cutting and shaping trees into the hundreds of cabins that had to be built quickly. They would have proper fortifications along with the shelters. In the retreat after Germantown, his army had lost a fair part of their baggage train and, with it, the siege equipment of heavy picks, shovels, axes, ropes for dragging, and wheelbarrows——what Caesar and the Romans had called the "impedimenta" of the army, the baggage that slowed an army down but was needed for their survival.

What greeted him at Valley Forge was nothing. Absolutely nothing.

He stopped, unable to bear the sight. Listless, starving men hunkered down in the open around smoky fires, many of them too weak and sick to build shelters, even if proper tools could be found. They gazed at him sullenly; some showed their respect by standing and coming to attention, but many could not move.

When he turned his mount to ride back, a cry rose up.

"Meat, meat. We have no meat!"

He could hear officers and sergeants yelling for the malcontents to fall silent, but the cry cut into his heart.

Merciful God, what am I to do? Go back and lie? Go back and promise that by this time tomorrow herds of cattle and sheep and droves of hogs would be driven in? If only he could give them all just a single pound of meat for one meal. He needed at least twenty head of cattle a day, or three times as many hogs or sheep, and that meant not a single ounce wasted; everything——from innards and brains to boiled-out bone marrow——would have to be consumed. To give each of them but a pound of bread, he needed six tons of flour a day, and the bakehouses and cords of dried firewood to bake the loaves.

He needed tons of corn, dried fruit, vinegar for the surgeons to clean the hospitals yet to be built, stout ale and broth to feed the sick, at least thirty pounds or more of good fodder per horse, at least fifty wagonloads a day for fodder, though he wondered if a single horse would still be alive in another few days. There were reports that artillery crews were killing off the weakest animals to eat them. Along the Guelph Road leading to this place, he had seen the frozen and butchered carcasses of more than one animal that had collapsed and within minutes had its flesh stripped clean from the bones by hungry troops. Even the bones had been scooped up to be boiled.

It was worse than the nightmare retreat across New Jersey. The small cadre of men who had endured the campaign a year ago, and stayed on with the army, was now enduring another season of misery. Two winters in a row was asking too much of any man.

And what am I asking of myself, he wondered, as he rode back toward his headquarters tent.

"Meat, General! For God's sake, where's our food?"

One of the men lay on his back and held his feet up in the air for him to see. His feet were black, swollen, and cracked; it was obvious that in a few more days the surgeon would take both of them off.

"Is this my reward for standing with you since Long Island?" the man cried. His voice broke into sobs of anguish.

Washington lowered his head so they would not see his own tears, and he rode back to the command tent, pitched in an open grove of chestnuts. Even nuts from the trees had already been scavenged by his hungry troops.

As the storm increased its intensity, sleet slashed down on the melancholy landscape. The tree limbs glistened and the tent groaned under the weight of the ice. It would certainly not survive this storm; he made a mental note to send guards out to approach the nearby farmers with a request to rent their homes as headquarters.

He had become quite firm on that issue. For Americans, this was a war for the hearts of a people who were indeed wavering after two and a half years of bitter fighting. To loot, to forage, and to take without asking only created yet more enemies to fight. It brought to mind the rejoinder of Henry V just before he hanged an old comrade for looting: that at times the gentler of souls gained the greater victory with the people who must endure the passing of armies.

He came to a halt in front of his tent. A headquarters guard immediately took the bridle of his horse.

"Thank you, Peter," he whispered.

The young soldier forced a smile. He was one of the men who had joined the headquarters guards before Trenton and then stayed on rather than return to his Jersey militia unit.

Major Tench Tilghman, his aide-de-camp, waited by the open tent flap.

"Did the ride help at all, sir?" he asked.

"No, it did not," he replied wearily.

Tench offered his general a tin cup of tepid coffee mixed with roasted barley. Washington refused; the guilt of having indulged in a meager meal of slightly rancid but tolerable bacon and coffee with his staff this morning still gnawed at him.

"Have you thought of a reply, sir?" Tench inquired, as he sat across the conference table and motioned to the stack of correspondence. Atop it were the three letters, the cause of his explosive rage an hour ago. He had ordered the ever-present Billy Lee and the rest of his staff to stay behind as he stormed out and mounted to ride. They had waited nervously for his return.

The tent began to leak through a burst seam; a steady trickle dropped onto the table, splattered the papers, and caused the ink to smear and run.

"Will all of you, except Tench, please excuse me," he sighed.

His staff and the waiting generals obliged and filed out into the storm. Billy Lee closed the flap of the tent behind him. He overheard General Greene ask profanely where in the hell they should go now.

He promptly turned his attention back to Tench.

"Tell Sergeant Harris to go back down the Guelph Road toward the forge. The first house he reaches, I believe the name of the owner is Potts, tell him to ask respectfully if we might move in there for now. We will pay a fair price."

He hesitated.

"That is, in Dutch silver, not Continentals."

"Yes, sir."

Washington picked up the three papers that had come in over the last day. It never ceased to amaze him just how much correspondence arrived. There were the letters from parents begging for news of the fate of a son last heard of during the Battle of Long Island. There were letters of complaint——a representative of Congress stated that soldiers had stolen five pigs and a cow, that he was shocked to hear of such behavior by troops under Washington's command, and now threatened an investigation. Washington picked up the first of the three letters that had set off a long-simmering rage. The first bore a formal title: "A Letter of Remonstration."

It was an official note from Congress declaring that the patriots of New Jersey were suffering under the yoke of British and Hessian depredation. He was hereby ordered to send the appropriate number of troops needed to drive the interlopers out of that state, reassert control, and capture the governor appointed by the Crown.

Incredible. Over twelve thousand of his men were huddled on these hills of Valley Forge, not one hut was yet built to shelter them, he possessed at most a hundred axes to fell the trees, there had been no food for two days . . . and he was to detach sufficient numbers to reoccupy New Jersey in a winter campaign? And while he was at it, capture the son of Ben Franklin, who had stayed loyal to the Crown?

He clenched the letter with his gloved hands and with frustrated disgust tossed it to one side.

"Sir, do you have a reply?" Tench asked. He made the gesture of trying to find a dry spot on the table to spread out a sheet of paper and produced a small ink pot from inside his jacket where he kept it ready during cold weather so that it would not freeze.

Tench, along with Billy Lee, was among the few he allowed to see his emotions of the moment. He was, after all, a gentleman and, as such, bore the responsibilities and displayed the expected behavior of a gentleman. He did not subscribe to the extravagant and overdramatized diffidence of the English aristocracy and their officer class, but instead always strived to portray the quiet, resolute gravitas of a leader of a free people, attempting to shape a republic.

And thus, in spite of the boiling rage, he forced a smile.

"Nothing we can write down yet, Tench. Let it wait for now."

Tench returned the smile.

He scanned the next letter. It was yet another letter of remonstration. This one was from a committee of state representatives of Pennsylvania, proclaiming that there were no Tory loyalists left in the region surrounding Philadelphia, that all were patriots who supported the cause of freedom, and that, therefore, he, General Washington, was hereby ordered to cease this unwise retreat to the north, turn around, and defend the patriotic citizens of the region to the west and south of Philadelphia. In addition, it was expected, before the year was out, that Philadelphia and those within the city who cried out for liberty would be free of the brutal occupation and, in so doing, restore trust in the name of General Washington.

The last line stung deeply. *Unless I wager this army in a desperate bid, Congress itself is now openly saying it has lost its trust in me.*

Deep in the pile of papers was a note that only Tench knew about. A note from "a friend" within Congress. Gates, the hero of Saratoga, was even now being feted in York, where food was plentiful, of course, and already he was being held up as the appropriate replacement for the incompetent Washington, who had lost Philadelphia and with it, the hope of French acknowledgment and support.

He knew the rumors to be true. A year ago he had placed great trust in his friend Doctor Benjamin Rush, but, since the fall of Philadelphia, and the reported looting of Rush's home, even his private correspondence had grown somewhat icy. Rush was asking if there was any hope whatsoever of retaking the city by a coup de main such as the one that had brought success at Trenton this time a year ago.

If even Rush was now doubting me, when would the axe fall? If ordered to do so, of course, he would resign and return to Mount Vernon. In some ways he even longed for that release. But he knew as well, without any sense of self-inflation, that his forced resignation would doom this Revolution.

Gates was a strutting political fool. If anyone had gained the victory at Saratoga, it was his own friend Benedict Arnold. But Arnold was down with yet another crippling wound; this time he had nearly lost his leg, and he would not be fit for field command until spring. Arnold would not be the right choice anyhow. He remained a New Englander of volatile temperament who still needed grooming before being given an independent command. Washington's personal choice would be Nathanael Greene, but he was, unfortunately, another New Englander like Arnold. He had learned to set aside his prejudices against these hard-shelled Yankees——they had proven their worth often enough in battle——but there was a firm realization that the leader of this war had to come from the middle states in order to hold the thirteen independent together.

Gates tried to claim he was a son of Virginia. In reality he had been born and bred in England and had served as an officer with the British army for nearly two decades, leaving for America only when his ambitions for higher command were thwarted because he lacked the proper influence and the money needed to purchase command of a regiment.

And now Gates was maneuvering for the highest command of all, the entire army. Every general beneath him had come close to mutiny during the Saratoga campaign——in fact, Arnold had been under arrest when the climactic battle started, for calling Gates, in front of the troops, a damnable fool who would serve them all better by going over to the other side. Arnold had broken free from confinement, rushed to the front line, and was nearly killed rallying the soldiers who were beginning to flee, and then himself led them to victory.

Gates, ever the consummate politician, through dispatches and by personally appearing before Congress, garnered the laurels of victory for himself while at the same time denouncing every other general. He had even taken the nearly unbelievable step of seeking a political appointment, head of a congressional committee, the Board of War, while still serving in the field, technically under Washington's direct command. As head of that board, he bypassed his supposed superior officer, routing all of his correspondence and self-aggrandizing reports directly to Congress. At the civilian level, Washington now technically answered to the board, even while its head served in the field and was supposed to answer to him. The arrangement was so absurd that even the British were laughing at it, as yet another sign of the irrationality of this rebel experiment, which was obviously descending into an arguing mob whose self-serving and factional maneuverings would inevitably lead to self-destruction.

If Gates gained ultimate command, Washington knew with utter certainty that the Revolution would be lost.

He sighed and tossed the second letter to one side.

"Same as the first, Tench," he announced. "I'll send some reply in a day or two."

What reply? That I take umbrage with the statement that Congress feels I need to restore my honorable name?

It was the third letter on the pile that he had to face next, and that truly produced an explosion of rage. It was a letter from the Commissary Department of Congress, informing him that supplies, or lack of supplies, at Valley Forge was now his responsibility.

"My responsibility," he hissed through clenched teeth, picking up the note and looking at it again.

If, by some miracle, using some strange device conceived of and built by Doctor Franklin, he could fly to York in an instant, he would pick up the authors of this infamous tatter of failed promises and lies, wing them here, deposit them in front of his troops, and let them endure the taunts he had just heard, the agonies he had just witnessed.

If only the Congress could spend a week in the field with his men. If only they could come out of their warm rooms, pleasant banquets, and evenings of good drink in front of a fire and learn what the War of Independence was really like. But then they wouldn't be the same politicians who now infested this Congress.

He had communicated his intention to retreat to this place weeks ago and here build winter quarters. There was, as well, more than a hint of advice on his part that rather than adjourn themselves to the far bank of the Susquehanna, the Congress should reconstitute here, with the army, and share their lot with them. Or at least choose Reading instead. The British were openly mocking the flight to York as an act of wanton self-preservation and cowardice, and asserting that by spring a few companies of dragoons would cause them to spring in terror to the far banks of the Mississippi or perhaps even seek refuge in the Spanish lands of the far Pacific coast.

And now this? He thought of the man holding up his frostbitten, dead feet. Chances were good he would not survive the amputations.

"Is this my reward for standing with you since Long Island, sir?"

If but Congress would convene here. Would any of them offer to take that man and put him in his bed tonight, and would any stand his watch, having first taken off his shoes and humbly offering them, as if any shoes at all could now fit those swollen, disfigured members.

He knew what some whispered. It was the same whisper down through the long millennia of history. The same whisper that had beguiled Sulla, Caesar, Cromwell, and so many others. It was the whisper that if at this moment he rode back out, called his men together, and announced they would march on York, arrest Congress, and seize the food they most likely had well hidden away, nearly all would follow him.

He let the thought dwell for a moment. Whether, he were in control of this fight and by placing officers such as Greene, Wayne, and Arnold in the right commands, finding the supplies needed, he could drive the enemy out of Philadelphia and into the sea next spring.

He sighed, sitting back, rubbing his eyes.

He knew, only too well . . . it was the voice of Satan.

It was the voice that had betrayed every revolution throughout history. The voice whispering to a general so falsely used by the politicians he must take orders from, until at last came a day, for some out of their own desires, perhaps for others out of sympathy and loyalty to the men who followed them, that they should strike down the very government they were sworn to obey, with the wild, mad dream that once things were set aright, the "proper authorities" could be restored.

It was the whispered voice of Satan, of betrayal, of a history to come that would then be stained by coup, countercoup, revolution, and yet another revolution, a dream for a future nation that, in the end, would be a land as blood-soaked and tyrannical as Europe and the realms of the Eastern potentates.

He held the letter between thumb and forefinger, and then, with a defiant gesture, tossed it to the frozen ground.

"No reply at all to that one, Tench," he said, his voice husky with emotion.

"Yes, sir."

"We can no longer count on Congress for our supplies. I will therefore use the authorization given to me. I still have several hundred Dutch dollars in my possession, some English guineas as well. Pass the word to the other officers of some worth that I expect them to make the appropriate contributions as well."

He hesitated, Tench smiling. Tench, he knew, was a wealthy man, but of a family that this war had torn apart. His father was a king's official appointee;

all his male siblings and relatives were either serving the Crown forces or wearing the uniform of Loyalist regiments.

"I still have three pounds sterling, sir, and a brooch containing a portrait of my mother mounted in gold that is worth several pounds more." Tench fell silent for a moment. "Put that in with the rest, sir."

Washington, his throat constricted with emotion, was afraid to reply.

"Parties to be formed of reliable, trustworthy men who for good measure should be devout Christians as well and not given to thievery. They are to fan out, seeking to purchase supplies for this army, along with all tools necessary for the construction of shelters. I will authorize that if such tools cannot be purchased they are to be borrowed, with receipts given, to be returned once our encampment and proper fortifications have been built."

"Very good, sir."

He settled back on the stool. The thin stream of ice water dripping down through the tent from outside was increasing now to a steady cascade. If they had not been in so desperate a situation, there would have been almost a strange, comic quality to the moment. He wondered how General Howe would react if caught in similar circumstances. Undoubtedly a dozen men of various ranks would be expressing their dismay, holding up their cloaks over Howe's head, thinking themselves to thus be immortalized the way Sir Walter Raleigh had been with the gesture of a cloak laid beneath the feet of a queen.

"Sir."

It was Billy Lee, half opening the tent flap and peering in.

"What is it, Billy?"

"Dispatch rider reporting in from Major Clark and Colonel Morgan."

"Show him in."

Tench stood up to open the flap wide. Washington, at this moment strangely cognizant of his role, remained in his seat, as if under this cascade of ice water he was simply carrying on the routine of a commander in chief. Willing himself to endure the discomfort rather than avoid it. Feeling it as one more proof of the virtuous burden of freedom.

The man came in, walking in a strange, shuffling gait that somehow triggered a memory. Washington stood up, his stool falling backwards. "Old Moses?" he exclaimed.

The man gazed up at him with genuine delight, a toothless smile cracking his face, even offering what he thought was a salute, a quick knuckling of his forehead with his left hand while he produced the dispatch with his right.

Breaking custom, Washington grasped the man's hand.

Moses was old, at least by the reckoning of the frontier, twenty years ago. As a young man, the general had shared more than one campfire with this unusual frontiersman out along the Ohio, never tiring of hearing his story, which with time became more embellished, of his capture, torture, and scalping by the Shawnee. He had had no idea that this old man, who surely must be an ancient of sixty-five years or more of age, was actually serving with the army.

"General, you got anything to drink? It is colder than the devil's tail out there."

He smiled and shook his head. "Nothing but some half coffee, half chickory."

"Damn, I should have stayed with Dan, he could always find a jug or two, properly, of course, begging your pardon, sir."

"Maybe one of my men can find you something I'm not aware of," he offered, nodding to Billy Lee to find a drink for his guest.

Taking the crumpled dispatch, he opened it up. He read slowly at first, but then hurriedly sweeping to the end. He handed it over to Tench, who read it as well. His aide broke into a grin.

"A full brigade?" Washington asked, looking back at Moses.

"Yup, sir, seen them myself, and you know I got the sharpest eyes of any man alive, and be damned to my age."

"I believe you. Now tell me their composition. What units?"

And Moses rattled off the details just as Clark's letter had reported, a mixed command primarily of light infantry, dragoons, several companies of heavy infantry, perhaps a battalion, more than two hundred wagons——and the most tempting of all . . . no artillery sighted, and the belief that Howe himself might be with them.

He looked over at Tench.

"Find Generals Greene and Wayne immediately."

Tench leapt from his chair and ran out to fetch the generals.

"Moses, thank you. I'll have a reply written to Colonel Morgan for you to take back. Billy Lee will bring you something warm to drink."

"Thank ya, General."

Moses looked at him appraisingly.

"And you, barely out from behind your mother's skirts when I first laid eyes on you, begging your pardon, sir. Knew then you would be an important man some day, God bless ya. Never dreamed it would be this important, though. You're the future we fight for."

Embarrassed by this outpouring, and glad that Tench and Billy Lee had not witnessed it, he shook Moses's hand again and guided him out of the tent.

The two generals came in, each reading the note in turn, but his enthusiasm was not reflected by the gazes they exchanged when they finally passed the note back to him.

"What is it, gentlemen?" he asked.

"Sir," Wayne asked. "Are you proposing that this army march now, today?"

"I doubt if we could today. Let us see how this raid of Howe's develops. They might be back across the Schuylkill by nightfall. But if they stay on this side, I would propose we march at midnight, just as we did last year before Trenton. The left wing of the advance to seize the Middle Ford and block retreat. The main body to then fall upon this brigade and defeat it in detail."

Neither spoke in reply.

"Gentlemen?"

Greene nervously cleared his throat.

"Sir, you rode out there an hour ago. You saw the men."

"Yes, I saw them."

"And you heard them."

He did not reply.

"Sir, this army is finished. It is played out."

Washington bristled at the blunt words.

"Sir," Greene quickly replied, "I do not mean played out forever. It is still an army loyal to you. But as an offensive force?"

"They did it last year at Trenton."

"Sir, at least they had half a meal in their stomachs, and a march of but nine miles. It is more than twenty to Darby. This storm is still rising. Most of the men have not eaten even a single morsel in more than two days. If you try a forced night march, you will lose the entire army before dawn."

"Lose them? What do you mean lose them?"

Greene hesitated but, ever the blunt-spoken Quaker turned warrior, he would not shy away now.

"Half will collapse and freeze to death. The other half will desert and head for home, looting as they go, and the Revolution will be lost."

Washington could not reply.

"That is what Howe is all but begging you to do by this raid. We know he has spies among us. They know our situation as well as we do. He is goading us and we must not rise to the taunt."

The general shifted his gaze to Anthony Wayne. If ever there was an officer in this army thirsting for vengeance it was he. Two months ago, at Paoli, a surprise attack at night had caught him totally unprepared. The attackers were a column of light infantry led by General Grey. Rumors had exploded after the battle that it had in fact been a massacre, though a court of inquiry had found no evidence of actual butchering of prisoners. The terrible injuries of the dead and wounded had been caused when Grey ordered his attacking column to remove the flints from their muskets and go in with bayonet alone in order to avoid the accidental discharge of a weapon and thus give warning to their intended victims.

It had been a swift action at bayonet point, barely a shot fired in return as Wayne's men panicked and fled, many of them found stabbed in the back.

Grey had even sent a note through the lines denying the reports of the American newspapers of savage butchering of fallen wounded pleading for their lives, pointing out that over a hundred wounded had been taken in and were now being well treated in Philadelphia, which was more than could be said for their comrades who had fled and were now starving in the country-side.

It had been such a nightmare for Wayne that he had demanded a formal court-martial and there had faced down the whisper campaign that he had been drunk and derelict that night.

"I must concur with the judgment of General Greene," he finally replied. "This army is no longer fit to move another mile in attack or retreat. And if we do not find food by tomorrow morning, by tomorrow night we will have no army at all."

Washington snatched the dispatch back from Tench and gazed at it with anger. It was a reproach; yes, actually a deliberate taunt by Howe, who knew as well as he did just how desperate he truly was. It was defiance, a parading of British strength before a starving rabble in arms.

Washington turned away from the two, went back to the table, pulled the camp stool back up, and sat down with a sigh. No one spoke.

How could he tell them now of the even grander plan he had already mapped out and tucked in the locked box of secret papers that he would not share even with Tench?

Starting three days ago, just before arriving here, he had sat up late and mapped out a bold plan modeled after Trenton. More than anyone, he knew that the new country needed another such victory as Trenton if this army was to be held together by the first of the following year. Many of the reports he had requested from Major Clark had been for the purpose of developing this plan. Which men were to be quartered where, would officers live separately from their troops and if so where, how many ships were to be tied off along the wharves and what cargo would they carry.

As at Trenton, the new attack would be launched on Christmas night. Safe and secure in Philadelphia, he knew without doubt that almost every enemy officer would be up late at dances, or in the taverns. The reports from Major Clark and his spies indicated plans were already being openly discussed and anticipated in the city for a night of revelry. Though the Quakers and Presbyterians of the city did not hold much with celebrating Christmas, the English gentry and German officers did, and they were feeling safe in what had been the former capital of the rebels. It would be a time to celebrate.

His plan was for the army to break camp late in the afternoon. Flying columns of the few mounted men left with his command, reinforced by Morgan's riflemen, would precede the advance, securing every Tory household ahead of the line of march. By the time the army reached the upper fords of the Schuylkill, night would have fallen and the parties within the city would be in full fling.

His men were to ford the river at three different points and then advance at the double. Once into the city it would surely be chaotic, but the chaos would favor his side with the drunken British officers and enlisted men and commanders separated from their units.

Specially designated units of raiders were to move along the wharves, torching every ship moored at the docks. A conflagration would be started that would sweep the length of the waterfront and adjoining warehouses, consuming millions of rations and hundreds of thousands of pounds' worth of military supplies.

Once into the city, he would establish headquarters where Congress had once convened. If all went perfectly to plan, by dawn he would there accept the surrender of General Howe. He was pragmatic enough to know, however, that no action ever went according to plan once combat was joined. If he sensed he could not hold the city, he would order a withdrawal . . . and grim though it must be, the city would be set to the torch as they pulled out.

A grim and terrible act, but in so doing it would force the British to withdraw as best they could after the loss of so much shipping. Their only other escape route would be to march back across Jersey to New York, and in that event he would harass and attack them every inch of the way. It would send a message straight to the king and to all of Europe as well that this Revolution was far from over. That we are willing, if need be, to destroy even our own capital as an act of final defiance, to then draw back and be ready to pounce yet again and again until the last of our foes left our shores forever.

A city could be rebuilt. Freedom? Freedom, as Thomas Paine had written, was so celestial an object that it could never be purchased cheaply. The destruction of Philadelphia would stand as a statement to the world of just how determined Americans were to see this through to final victory.

That had been his plan for this Christmas night. And now two of his most trusted generals were telling him that even a response to a raid by a single brigade, without artillery and hindered by the need to guard hundreds of wagons, could not be mounted.

"Surely something," he finally said, looking back at Greene and Wayne.

The two looked one to the other and finally Wayne spoke up.

"May I suggest this, sir? A call for volunteers. Fifty men from each brigade of the army. That will be close on to a thousand men. No artillery. If not enough volunteer, let officers chose the men they think best and most fit for the task. Those men, joining in with Morgan's riflemen, would be a sufficient strike force to hit a strung-out column on the road and send them reeling."

"But not enough to capture the supplies they have taken intact and bring them back," Tench interjected.

Wayne sighed and shook his head.

"Cattle, sheep, and swine on foot, yes, we might be able to drive them here. But the rest? We'll then be the hunted with that many wagons, especially if the weather turns and the roads thaw into mud. Their light infantry will then have us by the throat.

"At best we can spoil their fun and take some of the food for ourselves."

"And Howe?" Washington asked.

"He'll be too well guarded and they will make sure he gets out. He is simply using himself as bait, sir, to try and lure our entire army out. That would be the most intemperate of moves this day. I can mount a flying column to be ready at dawn, sir, but I beg you, leave the rest of the army here. Find food for these men, find tools for them to build huts so they can survive through this winter.

"General, this army is here, at Valley Forge, for the winter. To ask anything more of them will be the death of most of them and probably the death of our independence."

Washington took it in, thoughts turning back to his elaborate plan for the seizing of Philadelphia on Christmas night . . . and at that moment, cold ice water dripping down through the burst seams of his tent, he finally realized the reality he must face.

There would be no attack this Christmas night . . . though a gesture would be made by Wayne tomorrow. The Continental Army was finished as an offensive force for this winter. There would be no second Trenton, and at that moment he wondered: If, before the winter was out, Howe decided to bestir himself, could he even mount a defense?

Valley Forge must be a place of survival to keep some nucleus of his army intact and, from that nucleus, to rebuild with hopes for a spring to come, if they should live that long.

"Do as you suggested, General Wayne," he whispered. "Do as you suggested. Report to me before you leave at dawn."

Wayne saluted, Greene as well, and the two left. Through the thin canvas wall of the tent he could hear their whispers in spite of the rising storm, which now was buffeting the tent, Greene thanking Wayne for convincing the general not to commit double suicide, for himself and for the American cause.

Tench stood silent as if awaiting orders.

"Some time alone, Tench," he said softly.

His aide nodded and withdrew.

Alone, he stared around at his command tent, water pouring in now from half a dozen leaks, men outside cursing and then laboring as one of the tent lines uprooted, fighting to drive it back in place into the frozen ground.

He was hungry, but then again he knew his hunger was not that which the common infantry of the line were suffering out in the open in this storm. At least there had been a bit of bacon and coffee at dawn, and Billy Lee would surely find something later and most likely lie if he pressed too closely as to where it came from.

He had boots, though his feet were cold and wet, and a uniform that decorum demanded be well fitted and relatively clean. The general in command must set some sort of example. No one would dare to steal his horse tonight to butcher as food.

And only twenty miles away, his foes paraded through the rich countryside, looting as they went, stocking up their larders for the Christmas feasting to come.

In York, the congressmen he must, as duty demanded, answer to, sent him letters, chastising letters about drunken soldiers stealing a pig, demanding he send his army hither and yon on mad, insane orders, and then openly accuse him that the debacle they had created here at Valley Forge was now his fault. Soon he would, without doubt, face their inquiries, with Gates, as head of the Board of War, standing behind them, ready to seize command.

There was nothing he could possibly do now at this moment other than what his inner spirit told him to do.

Lowering his head, he clasped his hands tight and silently began to pray.

CHAPTER THREE

* * *

Valley Forge
December 22, 1777
Early Morning

"God, this is cold," Sergeant Harris exclaimed, as the frigid wind cut into his face, causing him to turn aside and put his back to the icy blast.

"Come on, Peter," Harris gasped to the private he had chosen as company for this task. Peter, with a hopeful ulterior motive in mind, had fallen behind.

The boy caught up.

Peter Wellsley was barefoot, his swollen feet fortunately still red, not turning black, a sure guarantee of a lifetime as a cripple. Typical of the lad, he was silent. Oftentimes, days would go by when he barely said a word. He was a good soldier but had not made a single friend in the rest of the unit. It was without doubt because he was not a Virginian, as were the rest of the company, but from New Jersey.

"I think it's just around the bend here," Harris announced, turning back into the wind and freezing rain, pushing on. The boy was supposed to look like some sort of official escort, but that was a farce. True, they were both wearing the famed buff and blue uniforms of the Third Virginia, the guard company for the commander of the Continental Army of America, or at least what was left of those uniforms. Shoes and boots had worn out long ago. The buff trousers were threadbare, thighs, knees, and backsides black from countless days of service in the field. The joke now was that no one dared to wash his uniform, since it was only the ground-in dirt and muck that was holding it together. At least with this company material was provided to patch up the tears, rents, and burst seams——it certainly would not do for a headquarters unit to have men standing on parade with knees, elbows, and in more than a few cases bare backsides sticking out. Jackets were nearly black and brown as well. The few buttons still in place, at least, were polished with a paste mixture of charcoal from the morning's fire pit. The white cross-hatchings for their cartridge box slings and haversacks were all but invisible. On occasion, attempts had been made to whiten them, but that was a futile effort of late, for no whitening paste was available.

Two ragged scarecrows off on a quest to find quarters for their general, Harris thought with a wry smile as they turned the corner of the road. Before them was a neat, small stone farmhouse. It was of two stories, the farm, yard, and barn were well tended, and smoke was curling from the chimneys that flanked the east and west sides of the house.

"Now look sharp you and remember what the general said——be respectful."

"And what if they say no?" Peter asked.

"Leave that to me," Harris muttered as he approached the door. Peter stopped several feet behind him, grounding his musket and standing at ease so as to not look threatening.

Harris knocked on the door and but a few seconds later it cracked open, the resident within having obviously seen their approach.

"What do you want?"

The door was opened only a few inches. A tall, bony woman of middle age nervously peeked out from the opening.

"Ma'am, by request of his Excellency General George Washington, may I speak to a Mr. Potts?"

"If you're looking for food there's none here. The British took most of it, and then some scoundrel with your army took the rest and left me with a worthless piece of paper."

"Ma'am, I am not here seeking food," Harris replied patiently. "May I come in and talk with you?"

She glared at him defiantly and started to close the door without replying. He leaned against it, trying not to appear as if he was forcing his way in, but not relenting, either.

"Ma'am, as an act of Christian charity, we are two soldiers out here in the cold. May we please come in and talk with you for a moment?"

She didn't reply, but did not open the door, either.

"You have my solemn oath as a God-fearing man that I am here with an official request from General Washington. Please just hear us out, and if you then wish, we will be on our way."

"Tell me what you want."

He sighed, the cold wind whipping around him and his companion.

"The general wishes to rent your house as a headquarters."

"Go on and tell another." He couldn't help but smile at her response even as she refused entry.

"May I be struck down if it is a lie," he replied, trying to smile in reply, his teeth near to chattering with the cold. "Please may we come in, or frankly I think I will be struck down, from this cold."

She finally conceded, and opened the door to let him in. She was tall, nearly six feet, angular, with more the build of a gangly boy than a middle-aged woman. She had a long, pinched face with a hawklike nose, graying hair tucked into a mobcap, and a heavy shawl wrapped around her shoulders. Harris motioned for Peter to follow, as with her hand on the door she seemed ready to close it on him.

"Come now, ma'am, would you leave a boy out in the cold?"

She hesitated, then opened it back up.

"In and be quick about it, and wipe your feet first." She shooed them in as if they were wayward boys back from a romp and would now face punishment.

As they wiped their bare or canvas wrapped feet, she looked down at them, shook her head, and sighed. Peter's feet were bare and Harris's wrapped in canvas.

She slammed the door shut once they were inside, and without comment went into the kitchen off to the left, the two following.

The warmth of the room, the smell of something cooking in a kettle over the open fire, struck Harris like a wall. His head swam and for a few seconds he feared he would faint.

The room was saturated with warmth. Strange, almost confining, to feel four walls around him and a solid roof. And the smells! Bread was baking. A stew that smelled like potato, perhaps, with some pork mixed in, simmered over the fire. His stomach convulsively constricted. He looked back at Peter, who was actually leaning against the doorway into the kitchen for support, gazing wide-eyed, as if he had been raised to the gates of a paradise thought to be lost forever.

She turned in front of the fireplace with arms folded, fixing the two with a cold, sarcastic gaze.

"Well, on with it, state your business, and then be off with you. I don't have time to waste on a lot of foolishness."

Harris had to swallow hard. Strangely, he actually felt nauseated from the smell of food. As she gazed at them, she wrinkled her nose.

"Merciful God, the two of you stink like a manure pit in August. Now out with it and be on your way, and if it's food you're begging for . . ."

She sighed, looking past Harris to young Peter Wellsley.

"How old are you, boy?"

"Eighteen, ma'am," he whispered.

"Eighteen," and she shook her head, sighing. "Oh, damn it. Sit down. One bowl apiece and not a drop more, then out of here. Got barely enough for myself and now you starving boys are swarming all over the countryside. Whoever thought of this war should be shot."

There was no need for urging as the two leaned their muskets against the wall and sat down on a narrow bench before the kitchen table. Muttering to herself, the woman opened a cabinet, took down two wooden bowls, and stirred the soup simmering over the fire with a wooden ladle. She measured out just one ladleful for Harris and set it before him. She poured one ladleful for Peter, and looked back at Harris.

Muttering under her breath, cursing soldiers, generals, armies, and boys playing at war, she added half a ladle more to Peter's bowl and set it before him.

He looked up at her, still wide-eyed. He wore the expression of one overcome with awe and gratitude who might shame himself with tears, but he just sat there silent, staring at her.

"Grace," she announced, but did not bow her head. Instead, she looked up as if about to deliver a lecture to the Almighty.

"God . . . end this war, send a plague on those who started it, and return these boys home to their mothers. Amen."

She didn't offer spoons, and after hesitating for several seconds, Harris simply lifted the steaming bowl. It was a thick potato soup with several slices of pork floating in it. It was near to scalding, but he swallowed it down in several gulps and sat back. Peter sipped at it slowly and actually set it back down with a little still in the bottom. He stared at it. Harris struggled with himself not to ask if the boy was leaving the last few ounces behind. Peter shifted uncomfortably and then looked up at the woman.

"If you will excuse me, ma'am," he gasped, and without waiting for a reply he bolted for the door and back out into the storm.

"What the devil's got him?" she asked.

"He's got the bloody flux, ma'am, begging your pardon. I think the meal hit him with another bout."

She started toward the window to look out but then turned away.

"Well, I hope he made it to the necessary place," she announced. "Your army marching past here these last few days, you'd think they'd been taught to at least find some bushes to hide behind when taking care of such things. Merciful God, what a mess, right on either side of the road, it's disgusting."

"The flux, ma'am, I'm sorry. Don't give you much time to decide when it hits you."

She sighed.

"A boy like him should be home in bed."

She stiffened and looked back at Harris.

"Now state your business."

"I am looking for Mr. Potts. I was informed he owns this property."

"He isn't here."

"May I ask where I might find him?"

"Try Philadelphia. He's a Quaker. He owns the forge, but he decided to stay in the city even after the British came."

"And am I addressing Mrs. Potts?"

"I should say not!" For the first time she allowed the trace of a smile. "I was married to his brother, that is, until smallpox took him off. Quakers they are, and maybe my temperament wasn't suited to him and them. Then I married Mr. Hewes.

"I am Deborah Hewes. My husband, Colonel Hewes, is off with the state militia. God knows where, though. Haven't got a single letter from him in months. Months, I tell you. Darn fools, I'm willing to bet he is sitting safe and snug in some billet out there in Pittsburgh or wherever instead of being here, where he belongs. When the British came in September and burned the forge, he certainly wasn't here to defend it. The hired hands ran off, so I'm the only one left. Now, does that satisfy your questioning?"

She looked at Harris as if he was to blame for the straits she was in. He quickly nodded in agreement, then shook his head with sympathy.

"And if my husband happens to be lurking with your army, tell him he better come home now. We got cleaned out once when the British raided and made off with my milk cow, and now another army's at my doorstep. So if you see him, tell him his wife is looking for him, and, by God, I'll come up to the camp looking for him if need be, and drag him back by the scruff of his neck. And don't think I won't do it!"

Harris tried not to smile. He could well imagine the reception Mr. Hewes would receive upon his return. It would not be a pleasant one.

"No, ma'am. I mean, yes, ma'am, I believe you would, indeed."

"What does your general want?"

"His Excellency the General humbly requests the privilege of renting your house as his headquarters for the duration of our army's stay in this place."

He recited the words slowly, exactly as Major Tilghman had conveyed them.

She stood with arms folded.

"How long and how much?"

"Ma'am, I can't say as to how long."

"A week, a month, perhaps till Judgment Day? Which, with the way things are looking, I pray comes sooner rather than later."

"I would say the winter, ma'am."

"Four months, then. Now, how much?"

Tilghman had been specific on this delicate point. Owners of the scattering of houses in the region were being approached the same as Mrs. Hewes to house the other generals. Word would spread in a flash as to what the going rate would be once the general had settled on a place to stay, so he had to negotiate carefully.

"The general suggested a hundred a month."

"A hundred of what?"

"Why, Continentals, of course."

She threw back her head and laughed.

"For what? I don't need kindling for the fire. Maybe that poor boy of yours out there could use it for what he's suffering from."

Harris tried to smile. It was a common joke with the troops, even though they had only been paid twice in the last six months with the paper currency, at ten dollars a month. Ten dollars could actually buy a man a dozen eggs or a couple of loaves of bread if he was lucky enough to find someone selling such luxuries. A dozen eggs for a month of marching, freezing, sickness, and defeats.

"Sorry, no Continentals, and before you say a word back, Sergeant, I am a patriot, not a Tory, so don't insult me."

He fell back to the next step.

"Would you consider a Pennsylvania promissory note? Your husband is a colonel with the militia, so surely it will be honored."

"How much?"

He hesitated.

"Ten dollars a month, Pennsylvania promissory?"

"Don't insult me."

He extended his hands in a gesture of futility. Only as an extreme last resort was he to reveal that if need be, hard currency, Dutch dollars would be offered, dipping into the last few dollars, guineas, and silver crowns left in the general's reserve.

She turned and looked back at the fire, using her ladle to stir the soup. The door opened and Peter slipped back in, pale-faced, shivering from the cold and the attack he had just suffered through.

She looked over at him.

"You all right, boy?"

"Yes, ma'am. Thank you."

"You get to the necessary?"

His features reddened and he shook his head.

"No shame, boy, when you got the flux, you got the flux. Now sit down."

She fussed around in one of the kitchen cabinets, pulled out a jar and another wooden bowl. Spooning some of the contents of the jar into the bowl, she then put another half ladle of soup into the bowl, stirred it, and set it down in front of Peter.

"Now drink that down slow, it will bind you up."

Harris looked over at Peter and saw that the boy had tears in his eyes as he looked up at her. He felt a lump in his own throat. Six months ago, before the British came up the Chesapeake and the campaign in defense of Philadelphia started, they were all hailed as heroes. But after the unrelenting defeats, Congress fleeing helter-skelter, and the bitter retreat out of the city, doors were now bolted shut, fall harvests hidden, and the countryside sullen, silent, and uncaring. Rage had grown in the army, particularly among regiments not from Pennsylvania. The soldiers wondered why they were even bothering to defend this state, which seemed poised to shift fully to the Tory side. Yet they were restrained by the strictest orders of the general to not forage, loot, or even speak crossly to the locals.

She looked down at Peter as he slowly drank down the concoction. Then back at Harris.

"One-hundred-dollar promissory note from the state. Not a penny less."

"For how long?"

She shook her head.

"Chances are the bloody British will sweep you out of here in a fortnight. So let's just say this. One hundred for however long you stay, be it for a week or until the last trumpet sounds, and that is my final offer."

Harris smiled and stood up.

"It is agreed. One of the general's staff will be down with a written agreement and payment within the day. And I thank you."

Harris looked over at Peter.

"Come on, son."

"No," and she glared at Harris. "The boy can stay here."

"Well, ma'am . . . ," and he hesitated.

Peter, finishing the last of the soup, shook his head and stood up. "I'm going back," he said.

"Maybe you should stay and keep guard on her house," Harris offered, as Mrs. Hewes's gaze bore into him. He returned the gaze, hopeful that his ploy was working. The lad was at death's door, if they didn't get him out of the weather and some food in his belly. It was why he had brought him along, having heard the word that the old woman here had a sharp tongue, to be certain, but that perhaps she could be "worked on."

"I think the general would want that, now that this is his headquarters, at least until he moves in," Harris added. "Stand guard and make sure the place is kept safe. Consider that an order, which I am certain Major Tilghman will confirm."

Peter looked from him to Mrs. Hewes.

"Stay, Peter," Mrs. Hewes whispered, voice husky. "No shame in it. Besides I'd feel better with someone garrisoned here to keep off marauders and such."

Peter reluctantly sat back down.

"Only until the general moves in."

"Thank you, ma'am," Harris whispered, turning back at the doorway. "He's a good lad."

"Tell your general, tell all the generals, to take a damn good look at what they are doing to the boys that follow them."

"I can assure you, ma'am, General Washington knows and is in as great an anguish over it as you are."

She stood silent for a moment.

"Damn all war," she sighed.

"Yes, ma'am, damn all war," Harris replied.

Closing the door, she returned to the kitchen. Peter looking up at her, anxious and embarrassed. She stepped closer and patted him on the shoulder.

"I had three boys with my first husband. Don't know if they're in this war or not, or on which side, for that matter. Haven't seen nor heard from them in years."

She didn't say more, and then she pulled her hand back.

"Merciful God, you are crawling with lice!" She vigorously brushed her hand, knocking the offending creature to the floor and crushing it with her heel.

She stood back, hands resting on hips, glaring at him.

"Young man, you are getting a bath and don't even try to say no. I'll drag out the bathing tin and start some water boiling."

Peter reddened with embarrassment.

"Ma'am, I cannot."

"And why not? And don't tell me you hold with the foolishness that bathing in winter will be the death of a person. You are filthy, you are lousy, and you are not staying in this house until you've bathed."

"I can't accept, ma'am. I'll quarter myself in the barn."

"And freeze to death. Not while I'm here."

He struggled to hold back the tears that were clouding his eyes. She softened and stepped closer.

"I know, boy. You're ashamed, aren't you?"

He lowered his head and nodded.

She stormed out of the room and returned a minute later with a blanket.

"I've had three sons, so nothing will surprise me, young man. You strip down and I'll keep my back turned. Now go on."

She handed him the blanket and turned away. Bustling out to the storage shed, she pulled out the tin tub, dragged it back into the kitchen, clattering and rattling, set it down directly in front of the blazing kitchen fire, then went out to the well, returning half a dozen times with buckets of water that went into the large kettle over the fire.

Peter stood silent, blanket wrapped tight, shivering. She ordered him to pull a stool up by the fire and stay out of her way. The water was soon at least tepid and she started to ladle it into the tub. Going back to her larder, she returned with a small brick of soap and motioned for him to get into the tub.

"Ma'am, I must ask you to please leave."

She laughed and shook her head.

"Boys and their modesty. Guess you all forget how many times your mothers wiped you clean."

He looked at her, absolutely mortified. She set the soap down by the tub and turned to leave, picking up a fire poker. Using the poker, she prodded at the pile of clothes Peter had stripped off, which were nothing more than foot wrappings, the uniform jacket, a tattered shirt, threadbare and literally dark gray from sweat and dirt, and trousers. The tails of his uniform jacket had covered his backside, but now the trousers were revealed.

She choked back a sob. They were stained with filth and blood.

"Merciful God, when will this end?" she whispered. The jacket at least she could boil, the rest she would burn.

She spared a glance back at the boy. He was sitting in the tub——squatting, actually——shaking, his white, naked flesh marred by the red welts of bites from lice and fleas. He settled into the tub and a sigh escaped him. Using the poker, she dragged the shirt and trousers out the back door of the kitchen and threw them into the yard and then returned.

In those few minutes it looked like the boy had actually drifted off to sleep sitting in the tub in front of the fire.

The hell with his modesty, she thought. Going to the large kettle over the fire, swinging it back out, she scooped out what was now warm water. She poured it over his head and he awoke with a start as she picked up the soap and began to scrub him.

"Please no!"

"You're nothing but a boy," she said softly, "Now let me take care of you . . ."

She acted like she didn't hear his shuddering sobs of humiliation as he stopped being a soldier and retreated to simply being a boy who was scared, sick, hungry, and in need of some gentle mothering.

York, Pennsylvania
December 22, 1777

A cold rain beat against the windowpane. A gust of wind worked against the window sash, prying the window open a couple of inches, flooding the already chilled room with an icy blast.

Dr. Benjamin Rush, a former member of the Continental Congress, signer of the Declaration of Independence and now surgeon general of the army for the middle states, watched impassively as the keeper of the inn where he and most of Congress were lodged went over to the window, cursing, and slammed it back down. From experience Rush knew it would slip open with the next heavy gust, and he wondered if the thick-headed man had ever come to the conclusion that having it fixed, or repairing the broken lock to keep it in place, might be the better solution.

"Rush, are you listening to me?"

He turned and looked back at the general sitting across from him in their small booth off to one corner of the room.

"I was listening," he replied absently, and even as he spoke his attention again drifted down to the letter.

It was from his wife and had been smuggled through the lines from Philadelphia. She reported that she was well and that the occupying British had not despoiled their home, even though he was a signer, because of the influence of her father, yet another signer. Her father had turned coat, going over to the Tory side, persuading Howe that if the house and the offices of his son-in-law's medical practice were not burned, he might be persuaded to return to the royal side.

He wondered, scanning the letter, if between the lines she was indeed begging him to abandon the cause and sign the allegiance to the king.

After the carnage of Brandywine, and with Washington abandoning the capital, he had managed, as the most widely known physician in America, to gain a pass from Howe to move between the lines to help tend to the wounded on both sides, under the pledge that he would not use anything he saw to the advantage of the rebels. Although he was a signer and, as such, on the royal list of men who would be condemned to hang, Howe had accepted his parole and his word of honor not to use what he saw to advantage, and in return to use his famed skills for the benefit of injured British and Hessian soldiers.

The experience had shaken him to the core, and he realized that Howe had, without doubt, played a subtler game with him, letting him see the power England was bringing to bear and, in so doing, breaking down his resolve.

The British and Hessians typically had a well-organized medical corps. Immediately after Brandywine they had shown mercy to the hundreds of American wounded, abandoned by the retreating army, and allowed him to tend to their needs, in more than one case a British surgeon aiding him in a particularly difficult amputation. At least among physicians there was still civility in this war, and he had shared meals and traded experiences and knowledge with more than a few of them.

As surgeon general for the army in the middle states, he had felt shaken in his belief in the general who commanded that army.

Few medical supplies had been set aside for the eventuality of a major campaign, in spite of his months of pleading. No proper field hospital had been constructed outside of Philadelphia in the event that the city was lost. He was forced to rely on the charity of the British for bandages, splints, tonics, and broth, a supply that had dried up as the fighting continued around Paoli and Germantown.

The impact on the large number of wounded and prisoners had been dreadful. At this very moment, hundreds were locked up in the prison house, which stood but a few blocks from where, a year and a half ago, he had put his name to the copy of the Declaration of Independence. What a staggering collapse of fortunes in just one year. The bravado of the colonists was gradually being overwhelmed by the wealthiest and most powerful empire on earth.

The occupiers announced that, given the stubbornness of Washington in not conceding defeat after the loss of the capital, and in not disbanding his army under the good terms offered by General Howe, rations for the prisoners, sick, wounded, or able-bodied, must be provided by the city or sent through the lines. Rush had to admit it was a fair response, since the American side had offered to buy rations from the British, but only with Continental currency, while demanding hard payment in British guineas for the ration supply of the thousands of prisoners now being held after the victory at Saratoga.

Unable to do anything more, he had at last turned in his parole and departed the city to rejoin the army in its retreat. Before he'd left, one of the British surgeons had informed him that the medical staff would quarter in his house, pay fair compensation, protect his property and the wife and servant left behind . . . and then conveyed the suggestion that he should use the power of his position to persuade Washington that the struggle was finished, that the suffering of tens of thousands must be brought to an end. Even Washington himself would receive a royal pardon if he surrendered honorably.

He suspected the suggestion had come straight from General Howe.

Rush scanned the room. Congress was down to barely a quorum——at times, fewer than twenty would show for the daily meetings in the courthouse across the street in this rude frontier town of western Pennsylvania, nearly a hundred miles from the front lines of the war.

General Thomas Mifflin, former quartermaster of the army and now a member of the Board of War, sat in a booth in the opposite corner of the tavern room, head bent low, obviously plotting away with several members of Congress, joined by the recently promoted General Thomas Conway, who would leave tomorrow as newly appointed inspector general of the army.

Rush sighed and looked back at his after-dinner companion, General Horatio Gates, hero of Saratoga, who had arrived from northern New York to confer with Congress as to the current course of the war and to head up the newly created Board of War.

"Do I have your attention again, Dr. Rush?" Gates asked, his tone a bit peevish.

Rush sighed and rubbed his eyes.

"My apologies, sir. It has been a long day, and the arrival of this post from Philadelphia distracted me. I had to read it at once."

"I pray the news is good, sir," Gates replied.

Rush nodded.

"The British are respecting my property as promised to my wife by the surgeons I worked with after Brandywine."

"Brandywine," Gates sighed. "Sir, forgive me, but I must say it again. It is hard to give credence to the accounts of that disaster which unfolded while our northern armies under my command were surging forward to triumph.

"When I took Burgoyne's surrender, I believed that before the onset of winter I could retire my sword and return to the warmth of my family. If only Brandywine had been the victory our nation deserved, and should have been, rather than the debacle that army was led into. I daresay even now we would be seeing the last ships of the king fleeing with the last of their soldiers and mercenaries, and our freedom assured."

Reluctantly, Rush had to nod in agreement at this little impromptu speech, spoken with sufficient gusto that others in the room could hear. Nearly all turned, and several nodded in agreement.

"I tell you, sir," and as he spoke he motioned for the innkeeper to refill their tankards of buttered rum, "this talk of trying to create a permanent standing army as the only means of achieving victory is ruinous and smacks of Cromwell and Caesar."

"Hear, hear," replied one of the congressmen, well into his after-dinner cups and sitting by the fireplace smoking a pipe, raising his tankard in salute.

"I tell you, sir, I wish all of you had stood with me at Saratoga and had seen the way my militiamen stormed forward like heroes, driving before them the so-called professional long-serving minions of the king. I know, sir; I know their mettle because I saw it with my own eyes. Officers who know how to lead free men who but set aside the plow and their tools to serve until a battle is won can wring miracles out of them. I must, as a member of the Board of War, question the sanity of a general who demands an army of dullards, of such lowly sort that they are willing to sign away their liberty and freedom for three years, five years, in exchange for what? A chance to plunder, a chance to become like Cromwell's army and put a despot on a throne once the revolution is won and then betrayed?"

Rush sighed and extended his hand in a gesture of moderation.

"Sir, please lower your voice. Not everyone in this room is of the same sentiment at this moment."

"I speak only the truth, sir," Gates replied pompously.

Rush leaned back in the booth, examining this man.

It was near to heartbreaking, but he found he had to agree with him . . . Washington had to go.

A year ago, without hesitation, he would have given his own life for that of the Virginia general. But that was a year ago.

That was before the summer campaign, with New Jersey again lost and in Tory hands. That was before Howe appeared in the Chesapeake below Wilmington and stormed forward to victory after victory. That was before the horrors he had witnessed on the battlefield, in hospitals, and in prisons where hundreds of men now languished. He turned his gaze back to the room.

And that was before this Congress, of which he had once been a member, had fled to this frontier outpost.

While in the north, Gates had indeed, according to all dispatches, wrought a miracle by whipping a retreating American army back into shape in a few short weeks, rallied them to stand at Saratoga, cornered the arrogant Burgoyne, and taken the entire lot——more than seven thousand of their elite infantry, including entire regiments of once-haughty Hessians.

In the nearly two years since the heady days of early 1776, when the British evacuated Boston, General Washington had achieved but two victories. Glorious at the moment, to be sure, but in the grander scheme of things they remained not much more than skirmishes at Trenton and Princeton. He had lost every major engagement before and since, lost the capital, perhaps the war. When word of Saratoga reached Congress, dispatches had been sent flying by the fastest ships to the courts of Europe. Surely by now his old friend Benjamin Franklin was using that news to push France forward into recognition of this new nation and aiding it by declaring war on their old rival.

Franklin would know how to fan the ancient jealousy and hatreds of Europe and, in so doing, divert England, bring much-needed supplies through the blockade, and, with diplomatic recognition, perhaps bring the rest of Europe into the war against an overweening and arrogant England.

News of the defeat of Washington, who commanded what all Europe knew to be the main army of resistance and, along with that, the loss of the capital of their nation, had, however, flown to Europe as well. The news was delivered by the English as proof that the war was near an end, and that any nation so foolish as to ally with the rebellion would, in the spring, face the full fury and might of England, undiluted by a minor annoyance in one of her colonies.

Washington's failure, Rush reasoned, had canceled out Gates's brilliant success.

Rush leaned forward, his voice pitched so that others could hear. Though he was in agreement that Washington had failed, he believed him to be an honorable man. "This call for a Continental line, serving for the duration of the war, that Washington keeps insisting upon. I cannot believe he carries an ulterior motive. I know the man. He is a Roman of the old school."

"So was Caesar."

Rush fixed him with a cold gaze, and Gates, sensing he had pushed a bit too far with this man, retreated.

"There are those around him who would see differently," he quickly interjected, backing away from an outright accusation.

Rush nodded. He had seen the near-fanatical devotion of some around Washington. Men like Greene, Lord Stirling, and Anthony Wayne, who more than a few were calling "Mad Anthony" for his fury in battle, and especially that French boy, Lafayette, were outright slavish in adoration.

It would be an unsettling mix. A permanent army, made up of those who saw their general as the country's only hope, and who openly detested Congress. The French boy, for one, had been secretly writing letters denouncing Congress for the supposed failure to provide supplies.

Suppose Washington should fall on the field of battle. There was no denying that he was brave in action to the point of utter recklessness. It was known as well that he was prone to fevers and other complaints. It was hard to imagine him harboring dreams of Caesar, but without doubt, others around him did. Cromwell had not started off with plans for the Protectorate; he was just another general in the field against the tyranny of a king. But in the end? Washington's followers were more than eager to push him forward.

The danger of a revolution, as nearly all who were educated knew, was that ultimately, in nearly every case, it had been betrayed, usually by a triumphant general in the field.

He thought of his old friend Thomas Paine. His first chapter of *The American Crisis* had set the nation ablaze with renewed calls for resistance and lent fire to the soul of the army that night before Trenton. But now? A year later? Last word was that Paine had taken refuge somewhere in the countryside, his writings of the last year a mere dribble, perhaps, sadly, drowned out by his old nemesis, drink. What little he had written were polemics calling for the revolutionary fervor of the common man and not for a war of Fabian tactics, defeat, and demoralization, and continued pleas to the independent states to create a single unified army.

"General Conway leaves for Valley Forge tomorrow, sir," Gates said, again interrupting his thoughts.

"And?"

"Would you consider going with him to see for yourself the abysmal state the army is now in?" Gates offered.

Rush shook his head.

"For what good? My recommendations were for naught."

He sighed.

"I fear, sir, by the time I arrived there, what little is left of the army will already have melted away, and my duty as a physician would then come first, even over that of a patriot. I would tell them to go home until spring and restore themselves from the deprivations of the field and battle, to heal, regain their strength, and then to plant their crops in a timely manner before returning to arms.

"Without a city to quarter the men, they will die out in those fields. Washington lost the city and now payment is upon us. No, there is nothing I can do by going there now."

The innkeeper had brought over a steaming pitcher, stirring it with a hot poker drawn from the fireplace, and refilled their tankards with hot buttered rum. He did not withdraw until Rush had fished out a shilling and handed it to him.

Rush took a sip. The mix was tolerably good. He had never been much of a drinker of hard liquor before the war, preferring instead the refinement of a good port or sherry. But out here? It was either buttered rum or the vile corn liquor brewed by the frontier settlers. The only real use of that, Rush believed, was to deaden a man's senses to some degree before putting him under the knife.

Gates, though a Methodist before the war, and behind his back called by his men "Old Granny" because of his portliness, spectacles, and tendency to lecture the troops about drink and immoral vices, did not refuse the buttered rum. At the banquet earlier this afternoon, another one given in celebration of the "hero of Saratoga," the general had insured that his rotund form would be maintained. He had consumed, with relish, the platters of venison, fresh ham, roasted ears of Indian corn, pea porridge, baked potatoes, roasted lamb, and pumpkin and apple pies spread before the gathering.

Rush did feel a twinge of guilt that he was privileged to eat and drink so freely, and he looked back over at Mifflin, whispering away with the new inspector general, Conway. He knew the reports coming in by fast courier from Valley Forge. No supplies, not one barrel of flour, not one head of cattle or swine were there, though the committee responsible stated that they had clear enough evidence that it was the failure of General Washington, who had not heeded their written warnings sent out weeks ago, which Mifflin had confirmed by his own reports and lengthy manifests. True, more than a hundred barrels of flour were reported to be lying by the banks of the Susquehanna, not twenty miles from here, left out in the open and now spoiled by rain, but that was the failure of army supply to present sufficient wagons for transport.

He looked back at Mifflin and then to Gates again. The army would need a thousand barrels of flour a month, a hundred head of cattle or five hundred swine and sheep a week until spring.

The figures were staggering.

Washington, it was obvious to him, had failed to work with Congress.

Gates, the hero of the hour, held Congress in the palm of his hand.

For Dr. Benjamin Rush, the answer was obvious, though he was dismayed that they had ever reached this point.

He stood up, hesitated for a moment, then decided to take the tankard with him, for he had, after all, paid for it. He knew that most in the room were watching him, and that Gates had come to sit in his booth with obvious intent.

"You shall have my support when the time comes, General," he whispered, and left the room, leaving those behind all abuzz that even the legendary doctor had now openly switched sides.

Valley Forge
December 22, 1777

"General."

He looked up from his desk. There was, of course, no door to knock upon, since he was still quartered in his tent, half of it all but collapsed under the weight of ice. One of his sergeants had returned by midafternoon with the report that the woman who resided in the house in question had agreed to rent it out as headquarters. To pack up all and move it before nightfall was out of the question. Besides, to hurriedly abandon this sagging tent so late on the afternoon of this day of anguish, while his men huddled around fires out in the open . . . he could not bring himself to do it.

He had to maintain an efficient running of this army, and that alone assuaged any sense of guilt over taking quarters in a solid fieldstone house while twelve thousand men shivered in the cold. He needed quarters for his staff, for the reams of paperwork that flooded in each day from Congress, from every state, from committees and more committees. And he knew as well that he needed to present some sort of show. That he was indeed an actor performing a part on the stage, and that proper form required a proper headquarters and not this sagging, collapsing marquee.

He turned to face the tent entrance.

"You may enter."

It was Colonel Tilghman, with the Marquis de Lafayette by his side, the two of them forcing smiles.

"Sir, there is a delegation from the First Pennsylvania here to see you."

"What is it?"

He tried to sound confident and calm, but if it was a demand for food, he could not bear another such delegation today.

"They wish to show you something."

Lafayette, who at nineteen seemed to actually relish the extremes of this climate, stepped into the tent.

"Sir. I can assure you, it will be for your pleasure."

Washington smiled. The young man had indeed won his confidence over the last year. Viewed with curiosity at best by many in the army, and with open disdain by some as a rich French aristocrat playing at war, the lad had nevertheless shone forth, earning the open admiration of all by his reckless display of courage at Brandywine: Racing to Washington's side when for a few moments it appeared that the general might very well be captured, he had rallied troops to the general's defense, and nearly died from the bullet wound to his leg. He still walked with a bit of a limp, and Washington could sense the young man was actually proud of that limp, a proven mark of his courage and devotion to the cause of America and of freedom.

"All right, then," Washington replied, setting aside his quill, putting on a cloak, and stepping out into the storm.

Half a dozen men of the First Pennsylvania, led by a beaming captain, were lined up and saluted as he emerged.

"Sir, we wish to show you something," the captain announced proudly, and amusingly his voice actually broke into a high-pitched squeak from nervousness.

"What is it, sir?" Washington replied calmly, not allowing himself to smile at the young man's nervousness. Besides, the weather was brutal, the storm a mix of ice and rain, though at least it was shifting more to a northerly, which would mean snow——more tolerable for those out in the open.

"Our regiment is camped yonder, sir," and he gestured to the other side of the low ridge upon which he had planned to lay out fortifications.

"Lead the way, Captain."

He did not call for his horse, rather, he silently followed the men on foot across the field. In this period of pain and suffering he wanted to be on their level, working with them and talking with them. Horseback would have created too big a gap. He already towered over them by sheer height. The ground beneath his feet was a mix of trampled hay coated with ice and mud, making the footing somewhat slippery. The six men accompanying the captain fell in on either side of Washington, Lafayette, and Tilghman, trying to march like an honor guard. One of them was wearing new boots, well made, and Washington was tempted to offer a stern inquiry as to how the man had acquired them, but thought better of it. The others were shod with a mix of battered shoes, or they were barefoot, or had the ubiquitous canvas and burlap wrappings.

They crested the low rise and he slowed at the sight of what was before him . . . a log cabin, made to his directions, 10 × 14 feet, no shingles for roofing, covered instead with several tents, complete with a wattle and mud fireplace, chimney smoking.

Nearly a hundred men were drawn up before it, formed into two ranks, coming to attention as he approached, their colonel standing before them.

The colonel saluted as the general approached, and he returned the salute.

"Sir, my regiment begs to proudly report we have completed the first cabin as per your orders."

He gazed at them in the gathering twilight. In the fields beyond, clouds of roiling smoke from hundreds of campfires were drifting over the landscape while at the flickering fires men hunched around the feeble flames, those stuck on the south side coughing from the smoke. Some stood up and looked toward where he stood, but there were no defiant cries like those that had greeted him at midday. Anthony Wayne reported at midafternoon that a dozen head of cattle had been brought in, along with twenty sheep. Maybe half a pound of meat per man if every ounce of meat, bone, and innards were used, which they surely would be.

Half a pound of meat this night, all that stood between the army still being here come next morning or melting away during the night. And now this.

"Would you care to inspect it, sir?"

"It would be my honor, sir," Washington replied formally, trying to hide the depth of emotion he was feeling.

The colonel led the way, pulling aside a tent half that served as the doorway, beckoning for him to enter.

The doorway was cut only five and a half feet high, forcing him to duck low, and once inside he could distinguish little in the darkness other than the flickering blaze at the far end, which actually cast a slight offering of warmth. Pegs to support cots had already been driven into the opposite walls, supporting either thin branches or a rough weaving of rope, bunk space for twelve men.

"I've assigned this to our sickest men; get them in out of the storm for the night, sir."

"Of course, very good of you, Colonel. So this is the first?"

"Yes, sir. We thought the boys over with the Third would beat us to it, but my lads finished it an hour ago."

"A noble accomplishment, Colonel."

His words struck him as strange. "A noble accomplishment." This single cabin a noble accomplishment? Yet in the long course of winning freedom, this simple construction might match any achievement of destruction on the field of battle. This was an effort at survival that might well allow the men, the army, and the nation to survive.

"Sir?"

He looked over at the colonel and sensed that now would come something else.

"Go on."

"Sir. It took my entire regiment two days to build this one cabin. My entire regiment."

He did not reply.

"Between us we had one axe, the blade worn down so my men said to sharpen it was futile, since it was nearly into the soft iron. Several hand axes, maybe a dozen or so light hatchets, a couple of shovels, and a pick. That's all the tools I have, sir. And each log sir, we had to drag them from the woods a quarter-mile off. And that's green wood, sir, and not enough rope to go around for the task."

He nodded. "I'll see that you have more tools tomorrow."

The colonel started to speak but then fell silent, and Washington was grateful. He could sense that the man would break down. That with a hundred proper felling axes he could house his entire regiment in two more days. Instead, it would be weeks of suffering out in this weather before the task was done.

As he turned and left the cabin, he forced a pleasant and gracious expression. Again, the actor on the stage.

"I am proud of you, men," he announced, loud enough so that all could hear. "You are an example for the entire army."

Without waiting for a reply, he turned and started back to his tent. There was a call from someone for a "huzzah" for the general; the result was feeble, at best.

Tilghman and Lafayette fell in by his side.

"Sir, it is the first of many——it is a beginning," offered Lafayette, ever the enthusiast.

Washington did not reply. One cabin for the entire army completed in two days. Nine hundred and ninety-nine more to go, along with several miles of entrenchments, two major forts, and half a dozen bastions, a bridge across the river behind them as a means of escape if this place were stormed, regimental streets to be laid out and corduroyed, a hospital for each brigade, a warehouse for supplies for each brigade . . .

He was proud of his ability to handle complex calculations in his head. As a young man he saw such as a means of training his mind. Then it prepared him to be a very good surveyor. Now it prepared him to be an effective commanding general. If tools, thousands of tools, were not found, it would be well into the next decade before this camp was complete.

And in the meantime the other calculations were before him. Six tons of fresh meat a day, six tons of flour, and all the other supplies needed to keep this army alive.

Darkness was settling on the encampment at Valley Forge, and he welcomed the end of this, the third day in this godforsaken place. Darkness at least would hide the frustration and fear he knew he could now barely conceal.

CHAPTER FOUR

✳ ✳ ✳

Valley Forge
December 24, 1777

Private Peter Wellsley shifted uncomfortably as the general approached. It was not just General Washington, but most of his staff as well——Major Tilghman, Major Hamilton, General Lafayette, and even General Greene. As they came up the walkway to the house, all eyes shifted to the lone private, now standing at attention in front of the door.

He raised his musket to the present position in salute. The general nodded, and there was a hint of a grin.

"Private, ah, Wellsman, isn't it?" Washington asked.

"Yes, sir," he replied, not daring to correct him.

"I must say you look much improved since I last saw you."

Peter reddened, not sure how to reply.

"Though I daresay that, except for the jacket, your uniform is slightly unorthodox."

Peter stammered and could not reply. The trousers he was wearing were of finest doeskin, boots of a quality almost matching that of the general. His tricorner hat even had some silver braiding on it. The trousers and hat, though, were both far too big for him; Mrs. Hewes's missing husband must have been a portly man with an extremely large forehead.

He had shaved, and his hair was tied back neatly. Under his tattered uniform jacket was a pullover of wool and beneath that a fine linen shirt, freshly boiled. As for his stomach, it was full. Whatever it was that Mrs. Hewes had dosed him with, the meals of the last day had managed to stay inside him.

As if in answer to the general's query, the door behind Peter was flung open and there stood Mrs. Hewes, in her usual pose of balled fists resting on her hips.

"So you are General Washington?"

He removed his hat and bowed slightly.

"Yes, madam, I am he, and I thank you for the use of your home."

"You should be ashamed of yourself, sir," she snapped. "You send that poor boy here to do your bidding in nothing but rags, covered in lice, and I will not even shame the lad by telling you what his bowels were like."

Washington reddened slightly, and Peter could see the variety of reactions of the entourage behind him. Lafayette stood in absolute shock, as if staring straight into the bore of a six-pounder about to be fired, while Greene could barely suppress a grin at his general's predicament.

"Was near the death of me cleaning this one lad up."

"Be certain, madam, I am most grateful, as I know he is as well. The clothing he wears, madam?"

"A gift, so don't go chastising him, which he swore you would do."

Peter, who felt caught in the middle, stared straight off into space, still at rigid attention between Mrs. Hewes behind him and the general in front of him.

"My reaction would be different if I had not heard that from you, madam. And I thank you for the concern you have shown for such a fine soldier."

Peter reddened now as well with that praise.

"If I should see him again reduced to such a state of beggary, he a fine young Christian lad who is serving our country, believe me, you will hear from me!"

"I believe you, madam," Washington said gravely.

She shifted back and forth on the balls of her feet, reaching up to pull her shawl tight over her bony shoulders to ward off the chill. It was obvious she was not finished, though.

"The house is yours, sir. I am moving in with relatives but will be by regular to check on the state of things. No tracking in mud. I prefer to think there is no consumption of hard spirits under the roof of my home, but if you and yours can't observe that, at least do not do so on the Sabbath. Nor card playing or other sorts of gambling."

He nodded gravely.

"The linens are freshly boiled. When you depart I expect the gesture to be returned."

"But of course."

She gazed past him to the others.

"Are any of you lice-infected?"

Peter, absolutely mortified, lifted his gaze to heaven, praying silently that this inquiry would cease. Lafayette stepped forward as if to offer an angry reply. Washington was struck silent, for the discussion of such things in mixed company was not at all proper. Surely a woman of Virginia would never pose such a question so directly.

Even Washington stammered and finally Tilghman cleared his throat.

"Madam, I can assure you we are not."

"Well, it better be so. This poor boy was covered with them, gentlemen. Covered, I tell you. To allow such is shocking. The British, as you know, raided here in September, and I can tell you, not one left a louse behind, even though they are a rapacious band of thieves."

No one could reply.

"Fine, then, we understand each other?"

There was a moment of silence. She sighed, again pulled her shawl tight around her shoulders, and came down off the porch. She stopped by Peter's side, gazed at him, and then, as if by impulse, she leaned over and kissed him on the check.

"If you are hungry because they can't find food for you, Peter, I'm staying just down the lane. Keep your feet dry and take that medicine I left for you for two more days——that should bind you up good and proper."

Peter looked at the general, who was gazing at him, features fixed, not sure what to do, and could see Major Tilghman standing behind the general, grinning, near to the point of laughing at his embarrassment.

"Thank you for your kindness, Mrs. Hewes," he whispered.

"God be with you, lad."

She kissed him again and choked back a sob, looking back at Washington.

"When will this damn war end, sir? When can this boy go home to his mother, where he belongs?"

"Madam, that is in the hands of Providence, but I pray it shall be soon."

She sniffed and shook her head.

"I am a God-fearing woman, General Washington. My first husband was a Quaker. Those silent meetings near drove me to distraction at times. My second husband is with the state militia, and if you see that fool, tell him I expect him home immediately and no more hiding from me. But as for God's will, sir? I am not of the Presbyterian persuasion and thus do not see our lives as preordained. I believe the Lord helps those who help themselves. It is in your hands, sir. And you damn well better seize the moment. If this boy and others like him are killed in one more battle without results, it shall rest on the heads of all of you."

She swept them with an icy gaze and none replied.

She extended her hand, offering him the key to the house, which he took, nodding his thanks.

"Good day to you, gentlemen," she announced.

She started to walk past them.

"Madam, may we offer you a ride to where you are going?" Major Tilghman asked.

"With what? I will not sit astride a horse, sir. That is unladylike. I have two good legs for walking and it is but a mile off. Good day to you."

She paused, spared a quick glance back at Peter, sighed, and, shaking her head, stepped out onto the muddy road and stalked off.

The general watched her go, and a flicker of amusement lit his features. He turned back to Peter, who was still at rigid attention.

"You seem to have found a protector, young man," he said.

"Ah, yes, sir. I mean, I'm sorry, sir. She forced the clothes on me, sir, and the bath."

"I am certain of that. I trust you behaved as a soldier should." As he spoke, he put a hand on Peter's shoulder.

"I wish I could offer the same for every man of this army on this day," he said softly. Stepping past Peter, he went up the few steps of the porch and looked back at the road and the figure of Mrs. Hewes purposefully walking on, occasionally stopping to shake the mud off her shoes.

"Women like her are the backbone of this country," he announced, gazing back at his staff as if to still any critical remarks. "Sons from a woman such as her are what we need now, more than ever. She would make a Roman or Spartan proud."

And then he forced a smile.

"But God save her poor husband when he finally shows up. I would not want to be in his shoes."

The others laughed, and the tension and embarrassment of the moment broke as Washington led the way inside. They followed him in, the last of them Lafayette, who slowed, stopped in front of Peter, and told him to stand at ease.

"Are all your countrywomen such as she?" he asked. Though his English was fairly good, it took Peter a few seconds to grasp the question.

"Yes, sir. You could say so."

Lafayette grinned and shook his head.

"Hard to imagine a peasant woman of France speaking thus to a famous general. I must say I am surprised. As to actually ask such an intimate question as to whether we are cursed with lice, it is shocking indeed."

Peter did not reply.

"What are you thinking, young man?"

Peter found that question almost amusing, since this general was barely a year older than him. He did not take any real offense. The snickers and comments around the company campfires about the Frenchie officer were most definitely stilled after Brandywine and his near-insane heroism to protect the general as they fell back in rapid retreat. The headquarters guard company that Peter had fallen into after Trenton was perhaps better informed than most units, always up on the latest gossip regarding politics, and all knew how crucial this young Frenchie had become to their cause.

Lafayette was a connection straight back to France, to their king, to their hope for foreign aid. He might talk in a dandified way about various philosophers, some Peter had even heard of, such as Voltaire, but when it boiled down to the simplest of facts, all agreed this marquis truly did believe in their cause and, equally important, would not hesitate a moment to give his life to protect their general, whom he openly worshiped like a dutiful son standing in the shadow of a noble father. A man who would do that for the general had, as one of the backwoodsmen from Virginia announced, "a backbone of hickory" and, French or not, was all right.

"Permission to speak freely, sir?" Peter asked, looking straight into Lafayette's eyes.

"But of course."

He nodded to the receding figure of Mrs. Hewes.

"God bless her, it is her right to speak thus to the general. You could say that her honesty is what we are fighting for, sir."

Lafayette took it in, saying nothing.

"And, sir, she is a patriot through and through. Her family had a share of the forge here and lost everything when the British burned it out and looted this farm. Two thousand pounds of investments burned to the ground and she bore the loss without complaint. Her sons from her first marriage are either Tories or have simply gone to sea on merchant ships flying Dutch or Swedish colors till the war is over, and then will cheer for the winning side, and she has all but disowned them. Her husband has run off with the militia. Chances are he is in some safe billet out on the frontier. And yet she stayed here, and, God bless her, sir, she nursed me back to health."

He paused, afraid that emotion would show.

"My family is in Trenton, sir, currently under British occupation yet again. My mother is far more pleasing to the eye, sir, but she is of the same independent spirit and I pray for her and my father every day."

He lowered his head, and now his emotion did surface.

"Mrs. Hewes saved my life, sir. I think another day out in the cold, the mud, the rain, and with the flux, I'd have died."

He looked back up into Lafayette's eyes.

"Sir, I would die to defend her right to speak as she just did to General Washington. God bless him sir, he took it as a man should, an American should, and I love him for it. Mrs. Hewes has been living on boiled potatoes and a barrel of salt pork that neither the British nor our people had been able to find. Her supplies were all but gone. She doesn't have a single shilling, let alone a Continental, to her name, and yet she took me in."

He hesitated, not sure he could control his voice.

"She was sharing the last meals she had with me, demanding I take it, and I will confess, sir, I was so sick, and so hungry, I could not refuse."

"I see" was all Lafayette could say in reply.

"Sir, when you write to your king, to your friends in France, tell them of her. As long as women like her believe, and send their sons forth, we cannot lose. I beg you, sir, write of that."

He could not say more. He was a private, speaking to a general whom he assumed would indeed discuss this later with Washington.

"Her freedom to speak her mind," and now he smiled, "and she most certainly loves to speak her mind, is precisely what we are fighting for."

General Washington, standing at the second-floor window of what would be his sleeping quarters, looked out the window as Mrs. Hewes continued down the road. He could not help but grin and knew, of course, that their conversation would spread through the army in the days to come.

"The house is rather small, sir, considering how many will be living here, along with visitors, but it shall do," Tilghman announced, standing in the doorway to the bedroom.

"It is sufficient. We need nothing ostentatious at this time, Major."

"The daily reports on supplies?" Tilghman announced, holding up a sheaf of papers.

Washington motioned for him to hand them over, and he scanned through the quartermaster reports filed by each brigade, adding the figures in his head as he did so. When done, he looked back at Tilghman.

"Fourteen head of cattle, eight sheep, twenty-three pigs for meat and that is it?"

"It is evident, sir, that the locals are hiding what they can. General Wayne reports on his march south to join commands with Colonel Morgan that from reliable sources the word has spread that Congress is voting an increase in payment for all foodstuffs and therefore people are waiting for that increase before revealing where food is hidden."

"Voting an increase? I have not heard of this."

"Well, sir, the locals around here have."

On top of the insanity of how supplies were to be procured, the former head of the quartermaster division, General Mifflin, whom he had once trusted and who had served well in the '76 campaigns, had instituted an iron-clad price policy enumerating the fixed prices to be paid for dozens of items, right down to a bushel of dried corn, a dozen eggs, or a one-pound loaf of bread. Payment would only be in Continental scrip. Needless to say, many in the countryside openly preferred to sell to the British, who were offering hard currency in shillings and silver half crowns and guineas if items were voluntarily brought in. It was infuriating at this moment, but he was bound by the mandates of Congress, and none of his brigade quartermasters could step outside those bounds.

"And reserves for tomorrow?"

Tilghman said nothing.

"Let me guess. Nothing."

"Something like that sir, though the afternoon foraging parties have yet to return."

"Tools?"

"Sixty more felling axes came in, along with some shovels and picks. Some men poking through the ruins of the forge found several hundred pounds of quality wrought iron along with several anvils. Blacksmiths are already at work rebuilding one of the smaller furnaces, and the report is that within a few days they can start working that iron into additional tools."

"We could use barrels of shingling nails as well for the cabins," Washington replied.

Tilghman shook his head.

"Only eight cabins up so far, sir, though with the additional tools coming in, the pace should increase. I'd suggest converting the iron to tools first rather than nails for shingles."

The general gave a nod of agreement after thinking about it. What good were the nails if there were no cabins to shingle? And only eight cabins had been completed so far——about a hundred men out of the entire army within proper quarters, with over ten thousand still out in the open. And not even sure of food for Christmas dinner tomorrow.

He looked back out the window. The clouds were lowering, though the temperature had risen above freezing. It would most likely rain tonight. Taking out his watch, he absently wound the stem as he looked at it.

Exactly one year ago, at this very moment, thirty miles away, he had left his headquarters, heading toward the Delaware to start the move across the river. One year ago. *And now I am here. What is left of my army is here. After those victories, we naïvely believed the war would indeed be over by midsummer.*

And now we are here.

He thought of his grand plan of but a week ago: that before dusk on this Christmas Eve night, his men would be leaving this encampment site, embarking on a forced march to Philadelphia to either take the city back by storm or, if need be, set it ablaze and, by that act of defiance, deny the enemy their winter quarters. The act would have reverberated through every court of Europe. Unlike in the game of kings, where a lost capital was the signal for a negotiated peace, the burning of Philadelphia would be a sign to the entire world that he and his men would never surrender. His only regret now was that he had not put the city to the torch before withdrawing.

Looking out across the open fields at his army, the utter folly of his dream of storming the former capital was there before him. Some men were moving about, listlessly working, but few with any energy. Dozens of cabins were going up, but with precious few tools. Most of the shelters were only three or four tiers high, and at nightfall men would crawl inside, tying what was left of tents together to form a roof over shelters not much more than thigh high. Regimental cooking fires were blazing, smoking heavily because of the use of green wood. The already butchered cattle, sheep, and pigs could then be carefully doled out. Maybe a pound per man this day. As for tomorrow, no one could say.

To have asked this army to march even a mile would have been the end of it. The result would have been, if not outright mutiny, then quiet desertion once night fell and, even with the most dedicated, collapse from sickness and exhaustion. No men could be asked to force-march twenty miles at night, then fight a pitched battle with only this meal and a smaller issue of about four ounces per man from the day before to sustain them.

There would be no victory this night with Philadelphia ablaze or captured, and with it the boost of morale that had allowed him to hold together at least some semblance of force when nearly all enlistments ran out six days after Trenton. No victory this time, and the vast bulk of this army could well, in seven more days, ground their arms and turn and head for their homes——duty, as they saw it, done.

The madness of expecting to field an army made up primarily of short-term enlistments was all too clear now, and the British knew it too well. Why even bother to fight, they reasoned with scornful disdain, when the Americans would just simply melt away?

His one hope now, at this moment, was the column sent off with Anthony Wayne yesterday. Five hundred men had been picked from the various brigades to lend some small support to Morgan. Given that two of his best commanders were leading them, perhaps a raid might even sweep up Howe himself, if he was indeed across the river, raiding for supplies and stripping the countryside clean. If those supplies could be captured . . . He did allow a smile with that thought. A legal technicality would take hold. If already purchased or stolen from the locals by the British, and then captured by his own men, they were legitimate spoils of war for the use of his army——return or payment not required to the original owners. Morgan had sent up a report that over two hundred wagons were on the move. Troops were scouring the countryside, and hundreds of head of cattle, swine, and sheep were being driven back to the ford at Darby. If taken in a quick coup, enough food to see his army through for a month or perhaps two months or more was waiting. And at this moment of desperation he was not above bribing the listless men making camp in the fields beyond the Hewes house. He would shower them with a week of full rations, even rations and a half, to fill their stomachs, and perhaps thus move them to sign a piece of paper to pledge another year, six months, even three months to stay with the colors and keep the Revolution alive.

Hope for survival for the next few days rested with his most aggressive commander, Anthony Wayne, even now leading five hundred men into battle alongside Colonel Morgan's riflemen and raiders.

Five Miles West of Darby, Pennsylvania
December 24, 1777

"There they are," Colonel Morgan sighed, handing his telescope over to General Wayne.

Wayne braced the instrument in the crotch of a tree and focused it. He felt like some damn primitive savage at this instant, saliva actually filling his mouth to the point he feared he might drool, stomach constricting with pangs of hunger. Half a mile away redcoats were pouring out of a large smokehouse, lugging heavy hams and long links of sausages. From the barn, barrels were being rolled out, needing three and four men to hoist them up onto the bed of a wagon, which was sagging down under the weight, while out on the road cattle were been herded along . . . back toward Philadelphia.

He shifted focus to a farm farther out, a mile or more off. Hard to see individual figures but the sense of it was the same, wagons backed up to the barn, smokehouse, root cellar. Ringing the entire operation, light infantry deployed several hundred yards out, not standing in the open but instead taking advantage of stone walls, trees, woodlots. Intermingled with them, those damn Hessian riflemen on horseback, casually moving back and forth. Wayne focused on one of them, passing just a few hundred yards away, and felt a knot in the gut. The man was chewing on a turkey leg. Satisfied with his repast, he threw most of it away, only half eaten.

"Damned son of a bitch," Morgan whispered, pocket spyglass trained him.

It was almost as if the Hessian could hear the curse. He turned, looking straight in their direction, and started to ride toward them.

"Don't move an inch," Morgan hissed.

Had the man seen them? Perhaps a glint of light off the lens of the telescope and spyglass?

He was within two hundred yards. Cursing softly, Wayne edged back, tight against the tree he was hiding behind. Looking behind him, he saw the few dozen men who had come forward with him.

"Nobody move," he whispered. "Don't shoot unless I do."

The Hessian was down to easy rifle range for Morgan and his men, who remained motionless, not yet hoisting a single weapon. At last the Hessian slowed, stopped. Someone was shouting to him. He turned and looked back.

"Ich glaube es gibt etwas im Wald da!"

One of Morgan's men whispered a translation.

A shouted command echoed back. The Hessian leaned forward in his saddle as if squinting, Wayne feeling as if the man's gaze was boring straight into him. He wondered if this was one of the bastards who had surprised him at Paoli. He struggled to keep that thought buried, for it would most certainly overrule his judgment and lead him to do something rash.

The Hessian finally turned and started to ride back at a trot.

Morgan let out a sigh of relief.

"The angel of death brushed over that one," Wayne announced. "If he'd come within range I'd of killed the bastard."

"It ain't over yet," Morgan whispered. "He could be a smart one. Seen us and knew if he gave it away, he'd have a bullet in the head. Keep an eye on him."

The wagons down by the nearest farm were pulling out, gaining the main road to head back toward Philadelphia.

He'd been watching this same drama, over and over, ever since coming up to Morgan at dawn and offering to serve under him. That had been a humiliating moment. When Morgan had seen the troops he had with him, the old colonel had exploded with rage.

"Didn't Washington get my damn message? A brigade and we could raise havoc, and you bring me this instead? A couple of hundred men barely fit to stand, let alone fight?"

Wayne, noted for his temper, felt so humiliated he could not bring himself to reply.

The order had been given directly by Washington, upon receipt of Morgan's urgent message to form a column of men. The fifty men from each brigade who either volunteered or were in the best condition to march and fight were promised abundant food once they routed the British raiders.

Wayne had set out before dawn, with the hope that by forced marching he could join Morgan by the end of the day. First light and little more than two miles from Valley Forge the truth of it all started to unfold.

Only a handful of the men were actual volunteers, nearly all of them men from his own command, spoiling for a vengeance fight against the British light infantry that had taken his brigade apart at Paoli. They were men he knew he could rely on. The rest? The other brigade commanders had found this to be a convenient way to dump off their shirkers, the men who would not help with the building of cabins and bringing in firewood, the troublemakers and those ready to desert anyhow. If they disappeared while under Wayne, their own units would not be held accountable for the loss.

Within hours, the column had melted away by more than half. A few of them at least, it was pathetically obvious, were played out, and he had found himself kept busy, even while riding, jotting out quick "This man has my permission to leave the ranks to rest" passes and signing his name. Most, though, at every bend in the road or whenever they passed through a wooded stretch, had just dodged out of the line and disappeared. He had sent the three men of his mounted staff back along the road to try to round some of them up, but they had returned empty-handed. They had returned as well with reports of angry civilians cursing them, saying that the damn stragglers were now armed bands, looting their farms.

There was a part of him that felt little pity now for those civilians. They had refused to sell, keeping their stock hidden. The army was starving to death but ten miles away. The men no longer with him, many of whom had been good soldiers, standing on the volley lines at Brandywine and Germantown, and with little or no food in their stomachs for almost five days, and after a march of twenty miles——could he really blame them anymore?

When he finally joined up with Morgan he had fewer than a hundred men fit for duty still with him. Another hundred had kept up, but were only fit for a hospital ward and clearly not for running, skirmishing, and raiding.

Wayne watched the lone Hessian riding back into the forward picket line. He glanced over at Morgan, who was down on his stomach, soaked clean through from hours of crawling through woodlots, following the narrow defiles of creek beds, keeping out of sight as they dogged the outer edge of the foraging enemy. All the men with them were soaked to the skin, the day having been one of intermittent cold rain, the ground now only congealed mud.

Not a shot had been fired; Wayne had been surprised at first by Morgan's caution at the first sight of the enemy, just several dozen strong, cleaning out a crossroad tavern, a blacksmith shop across the road, and an adjoining farm. As much as the food, Wayne craved to get at what was in that shop: axes, horseshoes, tools, and yet more tools.

"You ain't been out here for four days the way me and my boys have been, Wayne," Morgan had replied, as if lecturing a new recruit. "Run with me for a while and you'll see what I mean."

He had seen quickly enough. The British had learned a lot in two years of war. After looting the tavern and blacksmith shop, that party had moved on farther west. Then, from out of a nearby woodlot, a company of light infantry emerged in open skirmish line, a dozen mounted Hessians emerging as well from concealment in a barn not two hundred yards from where he and

Morgan had been hiding. If his small band had attacked, they would have been cut to pieces.

"They're on to us, trying to lure us in. They know we're out here," Morgan announced calmly. "And they've got horses; I lost most of mine when they surprised me a couple of days back."

As they talked Wayne watched the Hessian scout, talking with what was now obviously an officer, pointing back toward the woods.

The scout saluted and rode off, clods of mud kicking up behind his mount as he urged it to a gallop. It was a good horse with a good horseman, Wayne observed, as the man easily jumped a low fence, disappearing down into a hollow and lost from view.

"Time to get out of here," Morgan announced, "they've seen us. You watch our left as we pull back, Wayne, and I'll watch the right and center."

Morgan crawled back from the edge of the woods, Wayne following him to where their small command waited.

"Up, boys, time to start running again."

The order was greeted with muttered curses, men coming to their feet, some of them already turning north and setting off at a trot. Wayne pointed the way, those still with him following. Through a gap in the woods he saw that Morgan had indeed been right. A company of British light infantry, accompanied by a troop of mounted dragoons, was emerging out of a creek bed a quarter-mile off, moving at the run, heading north as well with the obvious intent of circling into the wooded ground they were now fleeing.

The Americans came to the edge of the woodlot, open pasture about a hundred yards wide before them. A low, rocky crest, thickly wooded, awaited them. There Morgan had kept his reserve and those too sick and exhausted to keep up.

"Across now, boys!" Wayne shouted, riding into the open.

As he rode into the open ground he suddenly heard a distant bugle call, and it made his blood boil. It was a foxhunting horn, a call for the chase. The same taunting call the British had used after they broke his regiments at Paoli, his entire command fleeing in panic from the sudden onslaught.

"Sons of bitches."

He stopped, looking back. His men were coming out of the woods, some running, more than a few barely able to walk. He did a quick head count. Some of the men would never get out of the woods in time, and he could only hope they would find good ground to hide in. The memory of Paoli burned deep, the light infantry now pursuing him the same ones that had surprised his command three months ago, nearly wiping it out. He didn't give a damn what some "neutral observers" claimed. A number of his men who begged for quarter had been bayoneted to death. He had eagerly volunteered for this expedition the moment he heard they'd be facing that light infantry. It was to be his chance for vengeance. And now he was running yet again.

Again that damn fox horn!

Their pursuers were still a couple of hundred yards off, slowing, knowing that in this game the hunters could, within seconds, be the hunted, if reserves armed with long rifles were in the next stretch of woods. They continued to move northward, though, seeking to flank their enemy.

He heard Morgan shout. The man was not slowing down. A troop of dragoons were skirting the west side of the woods in which they had been concealed, riding hard to close off retreat.

"Move it, boys, move it!" Wayne shouted, and he spurred his mount. A couple of puffs of smoke snapped from where they were heading, and for an instant Wayne felt his heart leap. Had they been cut off?

But it was Morgan's men, firing at the dragoons to keep them back, the mounted men quickly turning.

Wayne, not pushing his blown mount too hard, trotted up the slope, gained the woods, and turned.

The last of the men on foot cleared the pasture and came into the woods, many of them collapsing in exhaustion. They were played out, driven now far beyond even a remote attempt at a raid.

He had a dark image in his heart as he surveyed the scene. Something would have to change. He must convince Washington of it. This was now a no-holds-barred fight of gouging and kicking, not some gentlemen's game, no matter that the overtures of the Howe brothers called them to just come in, surrender, take the oath to the king, and go home.

Enough food was being swept out of this one valley to feed the army at Valley Forge for a month; instead it was going into the overstuffed larders of the enemy. If he was in command and the locals had not been willing to sell . . . he would have burned it all, scorched the earth for a dozen miles around Philadelphia, and then watched them starve in the city.

This was for him now a war of no quarter.

Raging with frustration, he drew his pistol, aimed it in the direction of the dragoons, and fired.

Distant laughter echoed back seconds later, followed by another call of the foxhunters.

"Ten minutes' rest here," Morgan announced, breathing hard, as he pointed north, "then we pull back another mile. They're still on to us."

No one spoke. Wayne could see that more than a few would not get up again, but instead would burrow under the leaves and hope to hide till nightfall.

Morgan looked at Wayne.

"Helluva lot of good that did," he said, and pointed at the still smoking pistol.

"At least it did something here in my soul, Colonel," and he pointed to his heart. "Damn all of them, we're not giving up. Just once, just once I want to see their backs and, by God, hear them plead for quarter."

Valley Forge
December 26, 1777

It had been a cheerless Christmas. The minds of all, Washington knew, were dwelling on the past, on what they had achieved but a year ago. As for dinner, one of his guard details had come in with an old sow, enlisted men and officers sharing alike. No amount of effort by Billy Lee and the company cook could render it more than barely chewable. The last of Mrs. Hewes's stockpile of potatoes were added in, along with some boiled ears of Indian corn the men had scavenged from a muddy field.

He had ridden around the camp, offering Christmas greetings to each of the brigades. The sense of near rebellion of three days before had stilled somewhat. The most troublesome of the soldiers, close on to a thousand, had simply deserted. Others were just too sick to complain. As for the rest, there had been something of a Christmas miracle after all. Twenty head of cattle and two wagonloads of potatoes and one of flour had come in, actually gathered up by some patriots over at Plymouth Meeting as a present to the army. He had not pressed too hard on the inquiry as to how they obtained them. The gift givers were rather closed-mouthed when General Greene inquired as to where this largesse had come from.

It was enough for two full days of rations, and at that moment, to have an extra day's rations on hand seemed indeed to be a Christmas miracle almost as profound as the one of a year before.

The weather had at least moderated, skies clear, temperature until late morning above freezing. It had been a blessing but brought with it a midday thaw. Until the roads were paved with corduroy logs, the pathways and supply roads would be calf-deep quagmires.

Washington turned back from the window, delaying the next meeting for a few more minutes, a deliberate move, making the person he was about to receive wait and thereby know, even before they started, precisely where he stood.

He turned his attention back to the letter on his desk, a copy of correspondence between General Gates and the current president of Congress, John Laurens. Laurens would not have been his first choice after John Hancock resigned, but then again most definitely not his last. The copy of the correspondence had been forwarded up by "a friend," and contained with it the gossip of what was transpiring in York.

Gates was fuming to Laurens about "leaks" of his own correspondence, and Washington smiled as he read the accusation. It was a war, an open war between the two now, one that had been simmering ever since a year before, when Gates had refused to cross the Delaware in support of the attack on Trenton, and then stayed on to politic with Congress when they so cravenly fled to Baltimore during the dark autumn of '76.

He knew Gates had his informers right here at Valley Forge, spreading rumors, and, of course, he had his own sources in York. He would indeed be a naïve fool if he had not. The duplicity of Gates was now all too apparent. The man was openly maneuvering to use the victory at Saratoga, which he had arrogated to himself, stealing most of the true glory from those who had earned it, such as Arnold and Morgan, as his stepping-stone to what he believed should rightfully have been his all along.

What was enraging, though, was the nearly open accusation from Gates to Laurens that whoever had leaked their correspondence, had, without doubt, leaked information as well to the British. Then Gates went on to make the absurd claim that he, Washington, would not be above such an act if by so doing he could somehow retain command.

That burned deeply, and he read it several times. What burned as well was that a man he had once counted as a friend, Benjamin Rush, had switched sides in this fight and now belonged to the party that felt that command of the armies had to be changed. To Washington's deep personal sadness, Rush was now supporting Gates.

He reread the letter one more time, committing it to memory, crumbled it up, and threw it in the fireplace. He trusted his staff, but in such matters he could never be so foolish as to risk the random chance of someone's finding the letter and sending it back to Laurens and Gates.

And now to the next task. One that his correspondent had warned him of.

"Major Hamilton!"

The door flew open as if the young artilleryman had been hovering on the other side. It startled him for a brief instant, and after what he had just read there was a sudden wondering. But a look at the twenty-year-old he had picked out to serve on his staff after repeated displays of gallantry, from Trenton through to Brandywine, told him yet again that this boy was loyal.

"Show the officer in and then close the door."

Hamilton stepped back from the open door.

"Colonel Conway, the general will see you now."

Washington did not let a flicker of expression change. He knew Hamilton had just opened the meeting with a deliberate insult.

The short, burly officer stepped halfway into the room, stopped, and turned his back on Washington without offering a salute or bow of acknowlededgement.

"Your name, boy?" he snapped.

"Major Hamilton."

"You are addressing Major General Conway, boy."

Hamilton stiffened but did not reply. There were a few seconds of tension, Hamilton looking straight into his eyes.

"Sir, the general awaits you," was all that Hamilton offered in reply. He gestured for Conway to turn, and, withdrawing, he closed the door.

Washington made it a point to remain seated. He was tall enough that he was near to eye level anyhow with Conway, who, red-faced, turned to face him.

"Your staff needs a lesson in manners and etiquette, sir," Conway announced sharply. It was loud enough so that those out in the small corridor could easily hear.

"Sir, when you address me," Washington replied coolly, "you will do so as a gentleman, and not shout as if we are in a tavern. Do I make myself clear?"

Conway did not reply.

"As to Major Hamilton's greeting, sir. The last we saw you with this army, your rank was that of colonel. I have not been officially informed of any change in that rank, nor presented with papers which require me or my staff to recognize and acknowledge promotion to such a rank."

He stared straight at the man, someone he had actually trusted only a few months before. Born in Ireland, Conway had fled to France as a young man, entered their army, and served twenty years with distinction. He had then become part of the flood of professional soldiers who had all but swamped

America over the last year, arriving from Europe with flowery letters of introduction and the usual endorsements of brilliance. All of them sought high
rank, commensurate, of course, with their vast professional experience, to
now serve the cause of freedom. Unlike Lafayette, who had come as a gentleman volunteer, announcing he was willing to serve if need be as a private in
the ranks, Conway had bulled his way through Congress and emerged with a
promise of a colonelcy which Washington had reluctantly agreed to, and
signed the man's commissioning papers. At Germantown he had proven himself as having some skill, but in the bitter months after that fight, he had suddenly found reason to head off with Congress as it fled to Lancaster and then
York.

Of course, Washington knew that, clinging to their coattails, Conway had
joined with Gates, Mifflin, and others. He also knew that but a few weeks past
Conway had finagled not just a promotion to the rank of major general, but a
new post created by Gates's Board of War. He was to be inspector general of
the armies.

It was a position that many had urged Washington to create, and he had
agreed. In the role, Conway was to advise the commander as to the means of
improving the condition of the soldiers; give recommendations as to promotions and, when needed, demotions; see to the general improvement of the
welfare of the troops and act on their behalf; and provide a system of training
and organization. A man holding that position, if on his side, Washington
had reasoned, could be a powerful voice for the reforms for which he had been
begging. An enemy in the position could be deadly. He would be a spy free to
move among the ranks, garner support, write whatever reports he pleased in
secret, and maneuver for the political gain of others.

For the moment, Washington could still minimize Conway's role on the
technicality that one of the powers granted to him as commander of all
armies was the power to approve or veto promotions to the rank of general,
and that the request for this man had yet to cross his desk. He sensed it was a
game, a struggle between the power Gates claimed as head of the Board of
War and his own authority as commander of the armies.

Conway was serving as Gates's stalking horse. For that matter, he might
even be stalking for himself . . . and Washington detested him as much for his
personal ambition as for his lack of loyalty.

Washington leaned back in his chair, still refusing to stand.

"Sir, I have received no official letter of confirmation from Congress as to
your promotion to the rank of major general and inspector general of the

armies. And might I add that, by the authorization given to me by Congress as commander of all armies, I have and still do retain the right and authority to approve or disapprove of any promotions granted to the forces of the Continental forces for the ranks of colonel and above."

Conway bristled, features darkening.

"Sir," Conway replied, "you undoubtedly know that with the establishment of the Board of War, of which General Gates is now director, the power to grant promotions and offices of position rests with that body as well."

"Regardless, I have seen no signed documentation affirming your promotion. While in this encampment, sir, you will be addressed as Colonel."

He seethed inside with this dueling of words. The contemptible Board of War was leading straight to an open confrontation, and this man was leading the charge. If he denied its power, created by Congress, he could be charged with mutiny. He was in a way trapped by his own position. Throughout, in spite of their utter failures, he had affirmed again and again that the army must answer to the civilian authority. If not, the Revolution would devolve into a bitter civil war, a mad scramble for power by rival generals so that even if they did gain victory over England, one tyranny in the end would simply be replaced by another. He would not play the role Cromwell had in the English Civil War and lead his army to take power. That would betray every republican principle he believed in.

Could the members of Congress not see where this was leading? If his resignation was demanded by the majority of Congress, by his own code of conduct he would comply. He had, however, the measure of Gates and those around him. They would lose the war by spring, unable to hold what was left of this army together. And even if they did win, afterward a Caesar-like scramble for power would ensue. This man was but the spearhead of that threat.

"However you address me," Conway retorted, "as inspector general I must state my shock, my absolute shock at the condition of the army that I see literally at your doorstep."

"I am fully aware of the condition of the men, sir. Believe me, I am fully aware. I have been living their lack of supplies every day."

"I have been out among them these last few days, sent here by Congress to examine the situation and then render a full report," Conway replied. "Are you aware that more than half the men are without shoes, thousands of them near naked and fully exposed to the climate?" Conway hesitated, looking at the fireplace. "Though at least it can be said that some of the officers are warm and dry."

Washington stood up, chair falling back, and leaned forward, balled fists resting on the desk. A lifetime of discipline, of keeping passions in check, was trembling at the breaking point. To strike this man would be a pleasure. It would also end his command, for it was obvious the man was deliberately baiting him.

Conway stepped back. The controlled temper and even demeanor of Washington were legendary among those who served with him, and yet there had been moments when that passion had come to the surface. A towering giant of a man, capable of holding an iron bar or double-bladed axe out rigidly without trembling, a man who could stay in the saddle for days on end, he had the physical strength to kill a man with a single blow if ever pressed far enough.

The knowledge of such physical strength was exactly one of the reasons why, when still a young man, Washington had struggled within to control his passions. Dueling was part of the way of life of more than a few from his world. He had gone a lifetime without ever engaging in what he saw as folly and little better than murder. And yet there were times when he felt so angered that it was only with supreme self-control that he managed to turn an insult aside. This was such a moment.

But his gaze, without doubt, conveyed his inner wishes, and Conway backed off.

"Of course, sir," Conway replied quickly, voice trembling slightly, "I mean no insult——a commander must have proper quarters in which to carry on the business of the army."

Washington said nothing, not offering to accept the weak attempt at apology.

"I am, though, sir," Conway added, "entitled to acknowledgment of my rank with proper observation of that rank from your brigadier generals as I go about my business."

Washington replied bluntly in a firm, controlled voice the more menacing for its lack of passion or anger. "My various brigadiers, as you call them, are men who have served with me since Trenton, some from before Long Island and some as far back as Boston. You, sir, have only arrived upon our shores these six months past and now you claim an exalted rank?"

"General Washington, you without doubt know that the office of inspector general in Europe carries with it the rank of major general and, in some of the more advanced armies, the rank of lieutenant general."

In spite of his rage at this man, Conway's arrogance was such that Washington actually fought with the desire to burst out laughing. Six months and already he sought rank second only in command to himself. And he could see in that instant that if given enough rope, this pompous popinjay would hang himself in the end. But for the moment he was dangerous, extremely dangerous.

"Of course, sir," Conway continued, "the Great Frederick, who it was my honor to meet in Prussia, and you the Great Washington here in America, understand how such things are organized and done."

This was truly too much! Washington took a deep breath. "When I receive such verification from Congress I will render appropriate judgment," he finally said.

"After completing my inspection I will return to York tomorrow."

"Perhaps, then, you may point out that the Commissary Department of Congress is still required to supply this army with rations, tools, medicine, uniforms, and other supplies as promised before I arrived here."

"At times an army in the field, when engaged in active campaigning, must see to such things itself," Conway replied haughtily. "It is the responsibility of the commander in the field——at least thus I observed at times in European campaigns fought by professionals."

He thanked God that what Conway had just said had not been uttered in front of the staff, for though he himself would not call the man out, his entire staff would be lining up with the offer of pistols at dawn.

He leaned forward again, fixing Conway with an icy gaze.

"This is not a war of king against king," he said slowly, each word measured, pitched to barely above a whisper. "It is not a war of rampaging armies, despoiling everything in their path. Every farmer stripped bare by one side will surely go to the other. Congress knows that. We won back New Jersey at the start of this year because of the depredations of the British when they occupied it. Howe realizes that now and is playing the same game, offering hard currency for supplies. Congress must somehow do the same, and you may tell them that for me."

"And the letters of remonstration?" Conway replied, shifting position. "Do you intend to respond to the one from New Jersey to now protect those who were loyal to us? Do you intend to move out of this skulking place and protect those on that side of the Schuylkill River?"

"Sir, your position is not one that requires me to discuss my strategy and plans with you," Washington replied icily.

"But as to the letters of remonstration," Washington went on. "Please convey, in whatever role it is you now operate under, that this army needs, today, ten thousand uniforms, ten thousand pairs of boots or proper winter shoes, and at least a quarter of a million rounds of ammunition for muskets and ten thousand rounds for the artillery. Oh, yes, and sufficient tools for the construction of housing, fortifications, and roads. Might I add as well a quarter of a million rations a week, along with fodder for more than a thousand horses? All such things were promised to me months ago and I am still waiting. That message alone, sir, should keep you busy enough."

"The letters of remonstration?" Conway pressed again. "You will obey them, of course."

"You have my answer."

"I see."

"Yes, I assume you do."

"So you will not march as ordered?"

"You, sir, are in no position to question my response to those orders, nor do I see any reason to have you privy to secret plans I will not even discuss with my other officers."

He offered a cold smile. "Even the Great Frederick kept his own counsel at times."

"I had hoped for better cooperation," Conway replied.

"You have received all proper respect as befitting your proper command as defined by the authority given to me by Congress. If Congress should wish to openly change that procedure, they are, of course, free to do so, and I shall comply."

He knew his last words were an open challenge, and he instantly regretted saying them. This crisis was balancing on a knife's edge. Conway's actions now made it all too clear that in short order Gates and his Board of War would push to have a change in command. Conway's visit to this army served no other purpose than for him to be an errand boy, to run back to York with a scathing report as to the abysmal condition of the army to be used as ammunition against Washington and his officers.

"Be certain, sir, I shall give a most accurate report. I shall leave in the morning."

"Then good day to you, sir."

Conway actually hesitated. He was obviously waiting for some display of protocol, an invitation to remain here for dinner and shelter for the night, but Washington would not budge.

Conway stepped back from the desk and offered a curt nod.

"Good day to you, General Washington."

"Good day to you, Colonel Conway."

The man pulled the door open and stalked out. Seconds later Washington could hear the door out of the house slamming shut.

Lafayette, Hamilton, and Tilghman, without bidding, stood in the doorway to the small office, which had until the day before been Mrs. Hewes's parlor.

He looked up at them.

"What is it?" he asked crossly.

Tilghman nervously cleared his throat.

"Any orders, sir?"

"No! No orders!"

The three withdrew.

He sat silent, staring at the fire.

He had to fight fire with fire. This move by Gates was in fact a mistake, an open warning of what he intended. Conway was too ambitious in his own right, lacking in any subtlety. The smart move would have been to ingratiate, to act as a supposed ally.

He had learned much of politics in the last two years, more than he had ever learned in his years in the Virginia House of Burgesses at Williamsburg. He would have to fight back, even as he fought a real war, one that was far easier in his mind to grasp.

"General Lafayette, Major Tilghman."

The door opened as if they had been waiting for the summons, and he motioned for them to enter and pull up chairs by his desk.

"We need to discuss a few things," he said quietly, feeling more than a little uneasy with what he was requesting.

Lafayette, of course, had his own supporters and enemies both on this shore and abroad. Tilghman, though his family had gone Loyalist, knew more than a few influential members of Congress who might still be sitting on the fence. He was also friends with John Laurens, who now served with this army, his father the current president of Congress.

He would not ask directly, but if they were aware of what Gates and his messenger Conway were planning, they would know how to act and to whom to write.

Another war was now to be fought to determine if this army and with it this Revolution were to survive.

The task of standing sentry before the entryway to headquarters was an easy and coveted position which Peter had been more than glad to take when

Tilghman, through Sergeant Harris, had offered it to him. He was, after all, one of the few men of the headquarters guard company who looked at least something like a proper soldier, and, thanks to Mrs. Hewes's dosings, he did not need to run off every thirty minutes to relieve himself.

Harris stood with him on the other side of the door, and as Lafayette and Tilghman emerged, heads together, whispering to each other, the two exchanged knowing glances, though nothing would be said between them until they were relieved of the watch.

Peter had stood directly beneath the window of the general's office and had heard more than a few words of the exchange with Conway. He was not in any way eavesdropping, to be certain, for the window was shut fast, but the voices of both at times carried. The way Conway had entered the building with such a haughty air and stormed out an hour later was evidence enough. The snatches of conversation between Lafayette and Tilghman added to the information he and Harris had garnered without any intention of listening in.

Since joining the guard company, Peter had learned to keep his mouth shut. Wherever he went, if men recognized his uniform they would try to pump him for "the latest word"; even officers would approach him at times, and Harris had drilled him hard to keep his mouth shut. A private did not last long with this company if it became evident he was spreading gossip.

But this?

What would the army say if they knew a move was afoot to overthrow the general? Some might jeer, even greet it, but most of those would be gone in five more days when enlistments were up.

But of the others, who would stay? What would they think and do as soldiers loyal to Washington?

He knew that he and his sergeant would talk long into the night about this one, for he would be damned if he would ever serve under someone who betrayed the general he had fought beside at victories at Trenton and Princeton, and even the defeats at Brandywine and Germantown. In his eyes, Washington was indeed the Revolution, and he would not see him betrayed.

CHAPTER FIVE

* * *

"Are they assembled?"

Tilghman, Hamilton, and Lafayette stood by the doorway without speaking. There were simply nods of affirmation and that told Washington all that he needed to know of what was to come. Most likely, while he had slept for a few fitful hours, his tireless aides and comrades had been hard at work trying to change the opinions of the men he was about to face . . . but to no avail.

He took a deep breath and felt a moment of self-consciousness as he looked at the small mirror next to the coatrack. He must look the part, cheeks still glowing pink from shaving. Though the blood from a razor nick had stopped, Billy Lee was beside himself with apologies for the cut, which Washington had dismissed with a smile. Poor Billy, so accomplished in so many things, had never mastered the art of barbering. His skills came into play when he had mounted and was on the chase. Not to mention that most annoying habit of trying to put himself between his master and the volley fire of a British line, or simply sitting quietly, when his master needed to speak out loud his innermost thoughts, thoughts that Billy would never share with another.

Ironic, he thought, as he looked sidelong at Billy standing in the kitchen. Billy, of course, had never learned to write. What a book he could someday write if he were able. Then again, he was the servant of a gentleman and would never violate his trust, for what would history say if Billy Lee recorded all that he knew and felt about his master, but also his general, his confidant and, yes, his friend?

Major Hamilton opened the door. Taking a deep breath in the frigid air,

Washington stepped out. It had snowed several days before, the temperature falling well below freezing. Almost a blessing, since the ground was frozen, making walking a bit easier on the men than trudging through the thick, glue-like mud encountered on the march to this place.

His mount, bridle held by the young New Jersey private, awaited him. The guard company was drawn up, colors unfolded, fluttering in the cold morning breeze out of the west. He gained the saddle, took the reins, and turned toward the open gate. The guard company fell in behind him with a ruffle and flourish of drums and fifes. They struck up "Chester," and the small procession went out the gate of Mrs. Hewes's farmstead and up the slope to the main encampment.

He rode in silence, staff behind him, followed by the color guard, escorts, and musicians. He spared a quick glance back, a pathetic procession, men and horses struggling for footing on the icy slope. Troops that he passed as he rode up the slope paused in their labors, coming to attention and saluting. At least there were no shouted taunts like those that had greeted him a week ago, for a trickle of food was finally coming in. Not enough for full rations, though he had ordered that for yesterday and today, which meant that tomorrow they would again be out of food unless Providence were kind with today's attempts to buy supplies. But in this tragic farce he was now engaged in, even two days of full rations might make the difference, and divert thoughts about tomorrow for at least some.

The troops he was about to address were arrayed in formation below the crest of the ridge——just where the defensive works, of which not one shovelful had been turned yet, would eventually be dug.

Nearly three thousand, a quarter of his entire army, awaited him, deployed in regimental columns, most of them men of the Pennsylvania Line, but some units as well from New York, Jersey, New England, and even his own Virginia.

By and large, they were good troops, veterans of Brandywine and Germantown, men who had endured much. But now their enlistments, of six months or a year, were up. If not for the military formation and the fact that they shouldered muskets, few would ever mistake them for soldiers. There was still a scattering of regulation uniforms, but most were dressed in cast-off civilian breeches or ankle-length trousers, nearly all with threadbare blankets drawn around their shoulders to ward off the cold wind. A momentary scattering of snow flurries greeted his approach as low, scudding clouds raced across the sky.

As usual, most of the men were barefoot, feet wrapped in winding cloths of canvas, burlap, or torn blankets. At least with the ground frozen solid, the foot wrappings were relatively dry.

He turned to ride parallel to the formation, passing a dozen or so feet in front of each regiment, saluting the colors of each unit as he passed, color guards looking up at him, saying nothing, officers rigid, swords drawn in salute.

And none spoke. There was no spontaneous call for a cheer for him, for the army, for the Revolution. Only silence, and that silence told him everything . . . that this was indeed a forlorn hope.

He reached the center of the formation, musicians behind him falling silent. As he had done so often in the past, he humbled himself and began his appeal.

The words were the same, an appeal that now was the time to stand firm with the ranks. The enemy was but twenty miles distant in Philadelphia, and even as they now met, by this evening spies would report all that transpired here. If a quarter of the army this day marched off, it would only embolden their foes, but if they stood firm, it would strike as hard as any victory that could be gained on the field of battle.

He spoke of the promise of food, uniforms, fresh supplies soon to come pouring in, and those words nearly stuck in his throat, for he knew that such promises bordered on untruth, for their staying would mean the need for thousands of additional rations to be found between now and tomorrow.

The very act of their leaving would in fact reduce his burden by a quarter for the total need of food and shelters yet to be built.

He implored them to think of their honor, so hard fought for and won on the battlefield, which would now melt away. He closed with another promise, which again stuck in his throat, the promise of pay if only they would sign on for but three more months . . .

And then he was done.

Silence greeted him. He swept the ranks with his gaze. Some lowered their heads, but many returned his look with cold, dispassionate eyes.

There were no spoken rejections, as he had feared there would be when riding to meet them. Just silence, and that in a way was even more terrible. He could have borne cries of protest, a release of passion that perhaps could somehow be turned around in the end with at least some stepping forward to put their names on roster rolls.

But not a word was said. Those protests had been voiced the night before,

when he had called a meeting of the commanders of these regiments to implore them to try to convince their men to stay. He had not been able to move
them, though more than a few of those now stood before him with heads lowered. Some had been in tears as they spoke of how many of their men had died
in the last month, not in battle but of starvation, disease, the flux; of men
screaming in agony as unclad feet froze and then had to be amputated.

"My God, sir," one of them had cried, voice breaking, "my own brother
came with me to this fight, and do you know what he died of? He was found
frozen to death, out on the picket line during the storm of three days ago. He
was thrown into a pit with twenty-three others that died that night, sir. We
buried him naked; the men cast lots for his blanket and rags."

There was nothing more he could do or say. The final gesture had been
made. Without another word, he turned and started back to his headquarters.
The staff, guards, and musicians fell in behind him, the instruments silent.

He heard commands echoing and spared a glance back. The regiments
were turning and began to march off . . . leaving Valley Forge behind.

Those still destined to stay, at least for now, stood along the crest to watch.
There was silence from them as well. No taunts were being uttered at the men
leaving, and he sensed, if anything, envy rather than disdain. The three thousand leaving had fulfilled their honor as they saw it. Their enlistments were
up; they were not deserting. If anything, their mood was that the country had
deserted and abandoned them, and this was the only response now left to
them. Gone was the spirit shared after Trenton and Princeton that the tide
was turning and, by hanging on just a bit longer, they would make a final push,
and the British would collapse and go home.

Lafayette came up by his side, his youthful face forcing a smile to try to
cheer him. He said nothing, looking away, fearful that the boy would see the
tears in his eyes, his control about ready to break with the shame of it all.
Shame and an ever-growing rage——he knew full well how this would be reported to Congress.

Reaching Mrs. Hewes's house, he dismounted without comment and
walked inside, his staff not sure if they should follow. The way he closed the
door behind him made it clear that, for now, he wished to be alone.

Peter Wellsley, after stabling the general's horse, went over to the campfire
near the barn door, where the company rations were being cooked. A small,
skinny suckling pig was turning on a spit, barely enough meat for everyone
this day. The men waited eagerly as slices were cut away. The ritual was played

out, with Sergeant Harris turning his back, the company cook calling out "And who shall have this?" and Harris replying by calling out a name, a fair way to distribute the food when rations were as meager as they were.

Luck was with Peter; he got the jowls, ears, and tongue, which were slapped onto his tin plate. There was even a small barrel of hard cider, mixed with some water from the well. Sitting down inside the shelter of the barn, where the company was quartered, Harris came over to join him, cursing under his breath that when he called his own name the portion had been the feet of the pig, which of course were just roasted and not even pickled.

Peter forced a smile. Harris could somehow sense by the looks of those gathered round when a less than tasty morsel was up for choosing and would then usually call his own name out.

"You think for once you bastards would all grin and rub your stomachs to let me know when something worth eating was up for grabs," Harris announced, as he picked up one of the feet and stared at it with disdain, but then chewed on it anyhow.

Peter struggled with the idea for a moment, then finally made the offer of trading one of the ears for a foot, but Harris shook his head, as Peter knew he would. After a year and a half with this army, Peter knew a good sergeant was a rare find. He would have gladly agreed to the exchange even as he knew Harris would refuse. He had figured out that Harris had, without doubt, saved his life by dragging him along on the day they went to meet Mrs. Hewes, bringing him with the hope that the old woman would take pity on him.

"The general shouldn't have issued out rations to those runaways," someone grumbled. "I heard they got fresh meat at parade this morning before they marched off."

There was a chorus of approval from the others, but Harris shook his head.

"They'd of looted the countryside clean as they marched off," the sergeant sighed. "Besides, they did their part——can't blame them for leaving. At least give 'em a meal to send them on their way."

"How many you think will run tonight?" Peter asked.

"Oh, the usual number."

"Anyone care to bet?" asked Justin Putnam, the company gambler. He could find almost anything to wager on, his latest venture being louse races, with each man nurturing a favorite on his body, plucking him off to put on a tin plate, and then betting which would be the first to scramble off.

Putnam usually won with a big fat one that he boasted he kept warm and happy under his armpit. Peter had lost his own favorite at the hands of Mrs.

Hewes, though others in the company had offered him replacements, which so far he had managed to avoid acquiring.

"What are your bets, gentlemen?" Justin asked. "How many deserters with tomorrow morning's report?"

There were snorts of derision at first.

"But before we start, my friends, what do we bet?" he asked.

The debate went on for some minutes, the company at last settling on the winner getting a double portion of tomorrow's ration.

Justin pulled out a scrap of paper and jotted down initials and bets, casually mentioning that, since he had thought of the event and was the record keeper, he was entitled to a few bites of the chosen morsel, a request greeted with derisive taunts as to what he could go eat.

Peter chose twenty-eight deserters, his bet met with gales of laughter that he was ever the optimist, Justin waiting to be the last to bet, capping the high number at 151, announcing that anything above that number and he automatically won.

Harris, still worrying over one of the pig's feet, looked up from the circle of men sitting on the barn floor, saw that an officer was coming into the barn, and called for the men to come to attention.

The officer standing in the doorway smiled, extending his hand.

"Please, do not let me disturb your meal," he announced.

It was Lafayette.

"So you think more than a hundred and fifty will leave us?" Lafayette asked.

"Well, sir," Justin replied, not at all ruffled, "it stands to reason, don't it?"

"How so?"

"Three thousand men marched off today. Enlistments for half of those left here run out before spring. Stay here and starve, or light out while you still can."

"And you, soldier? Why, then, do you stay?"

Justin, ever playing the role of the cynic, looked around at his comrades and shrugged.

"The sergeant here would hunt me down and shoot me if I ran," he said with a grin.

Harris looked over at him.

"You can leave any time you want, Justin Putnam," Harris replied, barely sparing him a glance. "Same stands for all of you sons of bitches."

He looked back up at Lafayette.

"Sorry, begging your pardon, sir."

Lafayette smiled and shook his head.

"No offense. I am still learning my English. Let us see, you called your men sons of dogs, is that it?"

A round of chuckles greeted him and Peter smiled.

There had been little if any respect for this effete-looking Frenchman when he first showed up with the army. As for the Virginians of the guard company, more than a few had fought against the French along the frontier in the last war. Besides, he was barely more than twenty, but because of some noble title, the very thing they were fighting against, he was all but automatically a general.

And yet, Lafayette had finally won over the headquarters company directly responsible for guarding the general's life——first, by insisting he sought no rank whatsoever and would fight as a private volunteer. Major Tilghman then tipped those in the headquarters off that this young man had the direct ear of the king of France, and that if anyone could help to wrangle out new uniforms, muskets, and rations, it was Lafayette. For that reason alone they should play along with the pretense.

His all but worshipful approach to Washington was, at first, in the eyes of more than a few, defined as little better than bootlicking. Over time, however, derision gave way to at least a level of respect: that this strange young man actually did indeed admire and love their general. He also appeared to revel in hardship. While other generals were quick to find dry, warm quarters, Lafayette could often be found out on the picket line in the very eye of a driving storm, ready to share a warming flask of cognac with a private, practice his English with the sentry, and then go off on some strange talk about Voltaire, Locke, and others, confusing most of his listeners, though Peter at least found he could follow some of what he said, as long as he spoke slowly.

The final doubts were laid to rest at Brandywine when the line broke. For several long and frightful minutes it appeared that Washington himself would be shot or, worse, captured, and Lafayette had personally ridden to his rescue, rallying some men and staying in the saddle even after taking the bullet in the leg, which had almost cost him that limb and his life.

So these grim men, some more than twice his age, chuckled at his attempt at mastering English, his joke about the term "son of a bitch"——after so long with the army, surely he was familiar with the term.

"Well, sir, 'tis better than saying that one has *merde* for brains," Justin replied.

Lafayette threw back his head and laughed, though only Peter and a few others got the joke, and Peter was more than a bit shocked by the temerity Justin had shown.

"So why do you stay?" Lafayette asked, smiling, but his tone now serious as he looked at Justin.

"*Merde* for brains, I guess," he replied with a shrug.

Peter blushed over such a flippant answer.

"And you, soldier? Peter Wellsley, is it?"

Peter looked up with surprise to see Lafayette smiling, directing the question now at him.

"Well, sir," and he started to come to his feet.

"No, no, I insist, please be at ease," and even as he spoke, Lafayette went down on one knee, the gesture bringing him into the edge of the group.

Peter found he couldn't respond.

"The question is with you, Jersey," Justin said with a grin. "Go on, why do you insist upon hanging about with us Virginians?"

"Americans," Peter replied quietly, looking back at Justin. "We're all the same in this outfit."

There were grunts of approval from others in the circle.

"Why do they call you Jersey?" Lafayette asked.

"He ain't from our state," Sergeant Harris interjected, "but I'll vouch for him, even if most of his neighbors are Tories."

"Then why are you not with a Jersey regiment? There are several with this army of good standing."

"I didn't like the one I was with. So I joined these madmen," Peter offered, trying to smile, his reply greeted with laughter.

"No, seriously," Lafayette said. "I am curious. You Americans seem so concerned about which colony or, now, state that you come from, when I would say you are all Americans first, and I hope I can perhaps earn the honor of being called an American, too."

"You already have, sir," Harris offered, and there were grunts of approval from the others, which caused the young Frenchman to smile and then blush.

He fumbled for a few seconds, cleared his throat, obviously deeply touched and honored by Harris's words, and then looked back at Peter questioningly.

"Well, sir. I was with a Jersey militia unit a year ago. My closest friend and I . . ." His voice trailed off for a moment and he swallowed hard with the memory of Jonathan. "My friend and I volunteered to serve as guides for the Christmas night attack on Trenton, since that is where we grew up. After the battle, I asked the general if I could stay on with this detail. He agreed and I was entered on the muster roll."

"And your friend?" Lafayette asked.

"He died from the lung sickness on the march back from Trenton," Harris quickly said, sparing Peter the embarrassment. The young man could barely speak of his friend without emotion taking hold. "He was a brave lad, as is this one. We were honored to have him join us after that fight. Peter guided the general at Princeton as well and has done right good service since."

Peter nodded his thanks to Harris, and lowered his head, unable to reply.

Lafayette studied him closely.

"So why do you stay?"

Peter looked back up at him.

"Sir, may I ask a question in reply?"

"Certainly."

"Why are you here?"

Lafayette stared at him intently, as if startled by the directness of the question, and those gathered around were silent.

"It is a fair question. I will answer fairly. It is because I believe in your cause. May I dare to say it is my cause?"

"And yet you are a nobleman. You hold high rank back in France, or so I have heard," Peter asked, voice soft but firm.

"Yes, that is true, I am of noble birth. In the old world, such is the way of things. It is easy for me, having such rank. And yet I believe in what I heard and read. What is said in your Declaration, that all men are equal? You here in America, this is some new thing. It is a Revolution that I think will take the world in a direction undreamed of but a few years ago. Victorious as I know it shall be, I will take all that I learn with me back to France and hopefully plant the seeds of freedom there."

"Would you give up your noble titles then?" Justin asked.

Lafayette looked over at him.

"I cannot deny what I am. You ask a hard question, of which I am not sure I can answer. I love my king. I believe him to be a just monarch. But I love as well my country and my people. I think in France such change will come hard, but it will come, and the title given to me allows my voice to be heard. Yes, I think I would give up my title if in so doing I could assure all men were treated the same as you fight for here. Your general, do I dare say our general, is a noble man. I think we agree upon that, do we not?"

There were nods of approval.

"I would like to see a world where men such as he can rise to the greatness they deserve regardless of birth. You and I are of near the same age, Mr. Wellsley, is it?"

"Yes," Peter replied.

"I see nobleness in you. You have not answered my question directly but I think I know your answer. You are here because you believe in this cause and if need be will give your life for it."

Peter did not reply. No one said anything. The Frenchman was speaking of things they rarely spoke of. Such questions themselves would bring the usual soldier's words that they were with the army to flee from a wife, a mistress, or perhaps both, who had discovered each other's existence and now sought vengeance. That they had escaped from jail, the bedlam asylum, anything other than the real reasons, which after the first halcyon days at the start of this war had been buried under a tidal flow of unrelenting defeats and humiliations.

"I am here because I believe as you do in your hearts," Lafayette said softly. "The same as I know our general believes, even after the humiliation we all witnessed but a few hours ago."

"Sunshine patriots," one of the men grumbled. "Damn bastards, nothing but sunshine patriots."

"They did their part," Justin interjected. "They signed on for their terms and stuck to it and left with honor intact. They fought; many of their comrades died. And what thanks did they get? You saw them. No shoes, half of them with bloody butts from the flux. At least we got this barn to sleep in, with them still out in tents. To hell with Congress, I tell you. We die and they sit out there in York stuffing their faces, surrounded by wenches as bed warmers. Win or lose, those political bastards will survive it. Most likely they will even help to shovel us into the ground as they sign pledges to return to the king."

There was a chorus of agreements.

Lafayette, still part of the circle, said nothing, his attention still on Peter.

"And you, how do you see them? The men who left today?"

"I'd like to think, come spring, they'll be back."

"If any of us are left," Justin interjected.

"That's true," Peter replied. "True enough. If any of us are left."

As he spoke, he looked straight at Lafayette.

"So what do you suggest with Congress?" Lafayette asked, looking back at Justin.

Justin smiled.

"For starters, it's a hard choice. Shooting or hanging them all as a first step, it's a hard choice." He smiled. "I'm leaning toward stringing them all up. Slow like. No drop gallows to break their necks fast. Slow like so we can watch them do the open-air jig for a while before they strangle. And by God, while they dance in midair we'll pick up the money raining from their pockets."

Several of the men laughed, others were silent.

"That's mutiny," someone sighed. "You could be hanged for that yourself, Justin Putnam."

"Then make the most of it," Justin retorted. "Hang 'em. Shoot 'em, then let the general sort it out. By God, he'd at least see we have shoes and food after we finished with them."

"He'd never agree to that," Lafayette replied heatedly. "That would be acting as your Cromwell. It is against everything he has stood for, that he has fought for."

"Such issues of political morality are all well and good," Justin replied, voice rising. "All I want is some respect. Congress was more than happy to urge us to fight two years ago, but I've seen precious few of their faces when we was at Long Island, Trenton, and Morristown. I saw neither hide nor hair of them as we bled at Brandywine when they were packing up and running away, while urging us to continue to fight."

"The Revolution is not about Congress," Sergeant Harris interjected. "It is about us."

"Well, when it comes to us, I'd start with a decent pair of boots and a full stomach, and the ten dollars a month promised me, and not in their damn scrip but in hard silver."

"So why in hell don't you just leave? I told you to go whenever you want, and that stands true for all of you," Harris snapped.

"Damn you, James Harris. If you weren't wearing them stripes I'd thrash you for that insult," Justin retorted.

"I'll take my jacket off at any time you wish, Justin Putnam. I can lick the whole lot of you but won't raise a finger if you are running away. But by the great God Jehovah, I'll not listen to mutiny."

"I'm as good a soldier as you are," Justin replied heatedly. "All I am saying is I'll fight to the end, but damn it, at least give us shoes and meat so we can fight. As it stands right now the damn British and their Hessian scum can all but bayonet us in our sleep like babes in the crib. Damn it, have we forgotten Vincent already? Did he deserve to die like that after all that he did?"

Peter lowered his head.

Vincent Upshaw had been his age. A veteran of every battle since Boston, he had been wounded at Princeton, some said because he stopped a bullet that would have hit the general. Offered a discharge because of his crippled arm, he had stayed in the ranks. He had died of the flux two weeks ago, crying and calling for his mother while Harris and his childhood friend Justin held him.

"Congress killed him as certainly as any British bullet would have," Justin cried. "Some decent food, a hospital bed, some blue mass to plug up his guts and he'd still be with us. The politicians killed him and I won't forget nor forgive that."

Justin's voice was harsh in an attempt to hide the emotion he felt for the death of someone all knew had been his closest friend.

"The British killed him. This damn war killed him," Peter interjected. "The same as any bullet."

"Says you."

"Yes, says me, and damn it I have a right to say it," Peter replied. "I lost my friend too . . ."

The two stared at each other and there was a moment of uncomfortable silence.

"Damn all wars. Damn all kings and politicians that start them," someone whispered, and there was a chorus of agreements, breaking the tension, Justin at last nodding an acknowledgment to Peter.

"You saw who was out there watching as those men marched off?" Justin said coldly.

"Who?" Peter asked.

"Wilkinson."

A mutter ran through the circle of men.

"He's all right," Peter offered. "Remember he marched with us at Trenton."

"And he's back with Gates," Justin retorted. "What happened out there, Gates and Congress will have a full report as fast as he can ride to York."

"They'd have known anyhow," Harris sighed.

"And then what?" Justin interjected, tossing his greasy empty tin plate on the barn floor in the middle of the group. "Another arrow in the quiver for the damn War Board, I tell you. They'll blame it all on the general."

As he spoke, he nodded at the barn door, open toward the headquarters house.

Peter turned away from Justin, fixing Lafayette with his gaze.

"Will they, sir?"

Lafayette said nothing, as if unable to reply.

"And I swear this in front of all of you," Justin continued, his gaze now fixed on Lafayette as well. "They bring that bastard Gates up here and I'll march all right, straight on York with a fixed bayonet, and I'll spit on any man who does not do likewise."

No one spoke, not even Harris, who put his own plate down and just stared off.

"I am sorry to have stirred such thoughts," Lafayette offered.

"No apology needed, sir," Harris replied.

"And yet you will all stay?" Lafayette asked.

"You heard what I said," Justin replied, anger still evident. "At least as long as he is in that headquarters building and not that damn Gates."

As he spoke, he pointed straight at the Hewes house. The men gazed at him but none now spoke, some looked warily at Lafayette, knowing the punishment Justin could face for having so openly expressed his opinion.

"My words and questions are ill chosen," Lafayette said, face reddening. "I know you will stay. It is just I am struck to the heart by your courage."

He seemed to fumble.

"My English, I am still learning. I meant no insult."

"None taken, sir," Harris replied quickly.

"I can offer no words of promise," he continued. "I would insult you if I did. I can only offer the wish that my countrymen will soon be at our sides with the supplies that your general has asked for. I cannot promise, other than to say that I have added my own words as well back to those in France who can help. But regardless if France does or does not, I too shall stay to the end. And I am convinced that regardless of outside help, that end will be victory as long as our General Washington has comrades such as you by his side."

"We thank you, sir," Harris offered.

"No, it is I who thank you."

He stood up, making a gesture for the rest of them to remain seated.

"I apologize if I have interrupted the pleasures of your repast," he said with a smile and a feeble attempt at humor.

Bowing slightly, he left the barn.

"Good lad, that Frenchie," someone said, and there was a chorus of agreement.

"I still think we should go and hang Congress," Justin grumbled. "And if Gates sticks his nose in here, well, I think we all know how we feel."

"Ah, shut up," Harris replied. "Work detail this afternoon. We're to start building some quarters and a shed behind the headquarters for staff and as a cookhouse and dining area."

"With what?" Justin asked. "Our bare hands?"

"If need be, damn it!"

"All right, Sergeant," Justin sighed. "A cookhouse, you say. Now, that sounds promising at least."

Justin pointed to his tin plate in the center of the group.

"Anyone for a louse race?" he asked.

Lafayette stood on the other side of the barn door, listening.

"Learn anything?"

It was Major Tilghman.

"You heard it, I assume."

Tilghman nodded, putting his hand on Lafayette's shoulder, guiding him away from the barn and the house and out into the field beyond.

"Most of it was soldier talk, soldier grumbling," Tilghman said. "The general's always said that as long as you can hear them grumbling there is hope. It is when they fall silent that it is time to worry."

Lafayette had heard the same words. And yet how strange was this world. In the armies of France, in the armies of any other nation, if such grumbling were overheard by an officer, a flogging or caning was certain, or a hanging in the Czarist and Prussian armies. How different indeed this America was. It had shocked him to the core the first time he encountered it. Even now, what the one private had said, not once but several times, about marching on York could be grounds for having a man lashed to death or hanged. The soldier had said it in his presence, and he wondered if it was an act of defiance or an echo of the disrespect more than a few first showed him when he joined this army. Or was it an echo of a new kind of army, an army of men fighting for their freedom, including their right to speak their minds as they saw fit?

Washington assured him that earning respect would come hard for someone who was as young as he was and who was French as well. Until recently, his France had been the traditional foe of all who lived here. He could try to force it by claiming a title, or by actions. The point of the advice was obvious, to earn respect by action, which he felt he had done. Even now, as he walked, the pain from the wound at Brandywine still troubled him, a reminder of what he was willing to do for that respect.

"I was stunned, though, by such open talk of mutiny," Lafayette finally offered. At least with Tilghman, a well-educated man, he could fall back into French, which was far easier.

"You handled yourself well, sir," Tilghman replied. "Instinct would have been to order the man arrested, which you could have done. So why didn't you?"

Lafayette lowered his head, not sure how to reply.

"Did you agree with him? At least as far as Gates is concerned?"

"If they remove our general and place General Gates in command, I shall resign and return to France," Lafayette said coldly.

"Ah, a fine point there," Tilghman replied. "A point of honor which we as officers have, but the enlisted man does not."

"And that is?"

"An officer may, without disgrace, resign his commission in protest at nearly any time, except when directly in the face of the enemy, when it is obvious that such a resignation is an act of cowardice."

Lafayette bristled slightly.

"No, sir," Tilghman offered, hand extended. "Perhaps my French is imperfect as your English can still be at times."

Lafayette relaxed a bit and smiled, the two falling into the American speaking English, the young nobleman French.

"The code of a gentleman and officer embraces you and me. We can resign in protest and be thought none the worse for it, something surely our general will do if in any way Gates is placed in direct command, either of this army in the field or in some new position he and his cabal can manufacture with Congress. This Board of War is damn near on that mark already.

"We can resign, but those men in there," and he nodded back to the barn, "what recourse do they have? Stand and endure it? Or go home . . . as a deserter and lose all honor, in fact face a flogging or hanging if taken in the act."

Tilghman sighed and shook his head. "God pity the common man. And that, sir, is what I believe this Revolution to be about. The right of the common man, even in uniform, to stand up and say no when a moral question strikes directly to his heart. It was Private Putnam, I believe, who spoke that way just now."

"I was not sure of his name."

"And you will not report him?"

"Of course not."

Tilghman nodded. "Good, thank you, sir."

"Why such concern?"

"He is a good soldier. He was part of the original regiment the general mobilized back in '75. His younger brother died during that winter in Boston. My God, the Virginians died by the score from the cold then. You heard him speak of his closest friend, a comrade engaged to his sister. He has stood the test. He'd be a sergeant, even an officer, if not for his damn loud mouth, but the men see him as their voice, even when they themselves lack the stomach to say anything themselves."

"So you agree with him?"

Tilghman smiled.

"Do you?"

"It is not my place to say."

"Come now, my dear Marquis, it is you and I, alone in this field. I swear to you my solemn oath that it goes no further. Do you agree with him?"

Lafayette looked at him, features grim.

"I already told you. If Gates comes, I resign."

"Even if Washington urged you to stay on?"

"The general is a gentleman and, yes, he would urge us all to do so. But sir, my oath of loyalty above all else is to him and always shall be. I will not stand for such a base betrayal of the one man who you and I know is the last remaining hope of this cause."

"Even though nearly all battles fought, except for Trenton and Princeton, have been defeats, perhaps even better defined as routs and debacles."

"And if our general had what he desired? Proper supplies for his men, shoes, dry uniforms, ammunition, and an army of long-standing enlistments, men of three years and not just six months or three months, there is no power that could stop him. I am sick of the fools that plot against him."

"As am I," Tilghman replied, shaking his head.

"We both see where this is going to lead," Lafayette continued. "You saw Wilkinson as did I, observing this morning's tragic drama. He is a good man in his own way, but he has fallen back into Gates's pocket. Even now he is riding at the gallop to York with the report that a quarter of the army disbanded this day. And does our general now just sit back and wait for the axe to fall?"

Tilghman smiled.

"Do not consider General Washington to have such naïveté. He is a general on the battlefield, to be certain, and under that quiet demeanor, he is as adept a fighter as any politician or lawyer in Congress."

Lafayette nodded, saying nothing. It would be nice to believe, but he wondered just how long a man such as Washington would survive in the court intrigues of Versailles.

"A dispatch rider is preparing even now, sir," Tilghman continued. "Letters of protest have already been written by Washington and signed, written before this morning's humiliation. They are addressed to those members of Congress he still feels he can trust. Sir, I approach you now with the request that you do the same. That when the rider departs, you send letters to all those whom you feel you can approach in Congress who will listen to your side of this issue."

"And you wish me to say?"

"In part what you said just now to me, but not as forcefully, of course," Tilghman smiled. "For, after all, before this all started, I was once a lawyer, though of the two I prefer the rank of an honorable officer, but believe me, I know how to fight as a lawyer, an art which at times in this war is just as important as my sword.

"The general is prepared and is acting. Major Laurens on our staff, son of the current president of Congress, is firmly on our side and has written nearly daily to his father. Generals Greene and Wayne have written to those whom they trust, making it clear that if Gates comes, they go. I am writing to my contacts. Your voice, sir, would be invaluable as well.

"Dare I suggest, sir, that if the implication is clear that you speak with knowledge of the mood of the French, that General Washington is the hero of the French Court in spite of the temporary setbacks before Philadelphia, and that you personally, sir, will seek withdrawal of support if His Excellency is demoted or forced out of command, it will play well for our side."

Lafayette took it in. Tilghman was asking him to join a conspiracy, and he smiled. He would die without hesitation for his general, who had become like a father for him, the father he had never really known. Little did Tilghman know that such letters had already been sent to France and, if not intercepted by the British blockade, should be at the court in a few more weeks. Well, at least it was out in the open now.

"Sadly, Benjamin Rush is out," Tilghman sighed. "Too bad, for I liked the man. A year ago, before Trenton, his efforts were crucial, and all know that, without him, Paine's articles never would have been published. I do not blame the man too much. He is, after all, a physician first, not a politician, and the sights he witnessed these last six months would shake the faith of any man whose heart is one of compassion, as his surely is. He is neither a military man nor a man of politics, and I pray that a day shall come when he shall awaken and return to our fold.

"John Adams is a stout, perhaps mule-headed New Englander. Gifted when it comes to the nuances of creating a government, but perhaps too caught up in the running of it. I heard last that he is now a member of twenty committees, and such a gadfly to some that they are shipping him off to your country to serve there with Franklin and thus get him out of the way. God save them both when they have to work together."

He chuckled at the thought of it.

"Hancock has gone home. Jefferson has gone home. Only a few of the original signers, even fewer of those who first nominated and placed our general in command, are still with Congress in York. What we have there, except for Laurens and a few others, are the second-raters. The type that slip in after the giants who created this Revolution have, for the moment, fallen by the wayside with exhaustion or disillusionment, or been seduced to abandon the cause or look to their own interests, or are filled with disgust for the entire project.

"Happy is the lot of a soldier who can clearly see the face of an enemy and, if afterwards Christian compassion prevails, offer to bandage his wounds and send him on his way.

"How I hate the machinations that are behind every war."

"Read Tacitus, Cicero, even that accursed Machiavelli," Lafayette replied. "Nothing changes in that regard."

"So you are with us, of course?" Tilghman asked.

"With what?"

"Our own dispatch rider to York leaves in the afternoon. Relays have been set up. With luck he should arrive ahead of Wilkinson or at least concurrent with him. One can assume that Conway is already back there, spreading his rumors. We must counter, and counter hard, if in a fortnight we are still to have our general, and with him an army, and with them a Revolution. If not, I would actually say defeat, at best, at worst a mutiny that could plunge all of us into a bloodbath."

"And as we plot this way," Lafayette asked, "what of those men back there? Will they eat tomorrow? Are there more tools for shelters to be built? What if the British should decide to sally forth from Philadelphia and march here tonight under the cover of the storm which seems to be approaching?"

Tilghman shrugged his shoulders sadly.

"The last first. Them marching on us? I doubt it. Morgan, Wayne, and their scouts, though roughed up these last few days, still have spies moving in and out of the city. There are no indications of a sally. They are too busy gorging, wenching, and now even preparing pageants and plays to entertain themselves, laughing that all they need do now is sit back and let us starve. Their spies are, without doubt, on to us as well, and are reporting with derisive humor our dire predicament. Why bother to fight us and shed more blood, and endure the discomfort of the field, when nature itself will deal with us? A week of blizzard and freeze or, worse yet, a week of icy rain will finish us once and for all. That is how precarious our hold now is."

"Food?" Lafayette asked.

Tilghman smiled.

"A herd of swine are being driven down from Reading——if the damn things don't run off, they should arrive here tomorrow afternoon. A hundred head, at least, enough meat for a few more days. Cattle coming in and, I heard, a dozen wagonloads of ground corn from the Reading area as well."

He ran the numbers in his head. A dozen wagons, a pound of corn or bread per man. No, a pound and a quarter or more, given the number that marched off this morning.

Crisis averted for a few more days at least.

How pathetic that we are down to counting days, Lafayette mused. Back home, the king's depots stored enough rations to keep an army of a hundred thousand in the field for at least a year, if need be, with proper roads and canals laid out to bring up more, from the border of the Netherlands clear down to the coastal plains facing Italy.

"Shall we go write our letters?" Tilghman asked, producing his pocket watch and flipping it open to observe the time. "The dispatch rider awaits, the general's reports are already signed, and I am certain a few letters from you would be heaven-sent at this point, my friend."

Lafayette smiled and clapped him on the shoulder.

York, Pennsylvania
January 4, 1778

Fuming, General Gates looked through the stack of correspondence. The report by Wilkinson, describing the departure of over a quarter of Washington's army, came as no surprise. His own agents had reported that probability to him long before the men paraded on the morning of the first of this New Year. Their reasons for not reenlisting were now laid out in his own report to the Board of War. Mismanagement on the field of battle, the utter failure of

Washington to attend to the most fundamental needs of those whom he was duty-bound to provide for, the useless deaths from disease, starvation, and exposure——it was now all in his report.

And yet it was the reports in the other letters that had arrived that now caused his simmering rage.

Though the exact copy had not been revealed to him, apparently the president of Congress had received an entreaty from his own son, serving with Washington, denouncing the Board of War, blaming them for the failure of supplies, containing in that report the veiled hint that if command was changed the army would desert en masse. A report as well that the French upstart Lafayette was spreading rumors that he was considering resigning, returning to France, and there denouncing before the Court at Versailles the entire war effort if the general he was a toady for was removed.

Conway was not helping matters at all. Upon his return, he stormed around the tavern and the courthouse that now served as the hall for Congress, bitterly denouncing his treatment at the hands of Washington. He demanded a letter of authorization from Laurens, signed by all members of Congress, reaffirming his promotion to major general. Washington must respect him, and all his recommendations as to the reorganization of the army per his orders as inspector general must be adhered to as coming directly from Congress, under threat of court-martial if Washington did not instantly obey.

"So what are you going to do?"

He looked up from the stack of papers at Dr. Benjamin Rush.

"What do you mean?"

"Precisely what I asked. He is calling your bluff. This confrontation was bound to come sooner or later. He is calling for a letter of endorsement from President Laurens. He is calling for a reorganization of the system of supply. He is calling for an endorsement that if need be, he may commandeer supplies as needed, based on promissory notes issued by him but sent then directly to Congress, for which we shall be responsible. Surely that is an action which the state government of Pennsylvania will object to in the extreme."

"That is outside his authority to do," Gates sniffed.

"He is not taking this lying down," Rush replied, and Gates wondered if there was almost a note of admiration in the doctor's voice, even though the man had affirmed after yesterday's meetings that he felt the commanding general's time, at least for now, had passed.

"He has made no response whatsoever to the letters of remonstration from Pennsylvania regarding regaining control of the west bank of the Schuylkill

River. Nor will he send troops back into New Jersey. He declares that such matters of military necessity must rest with him and not with Congress. He has denounced your ally General Conway, openly saying that the power of promotion finally rests with him, though he will consider the advice and consent of Congress during this time of war."

Rush gazed at Gates. "It is a direct challenge to your Board of War."

"My Board of War?" Gates retorted. "You voted for it, so it is yours as well."

"But you insisted upon being appointed head of that board, so the challenge is to you, sir."

"Do you think he must be replaced?"

Rush hesitated, and then finally nodded.

"You know I supported him in his desperate move against Trenton last Christmas, and then in the march around the British flank at Princeton, and on to the winter camp established at Morristown. But a year of unrelenting defeats since then, the horrors I witnessed at Brandywine, the state of our prisoners, the manner in which the British are far better prepared to treat their sick and wounded while we lack in everything, has turned my soul, reluctant as it was, to this decision. I have placed my trust in you, sir, and you are being challenged. What shall you do?"

Gates leaned back in his chair, looking at a half-empty glass of Madeira, motioning to it. The innkeeper came over with a fresh decanter. Without any pretense of gentlemanly behavior, Gates marked off on a tally sheet the charge of four shillings sterling, a practice he openly engaged in after Congress had failed to pay him the weekly charges, offering Continentals rather than Crown or Dutch silver. He refilled his glass and drained it.

"I shall face him down. I must. Laurens knows that Congress is increasingly behind me. I won at Saratoga. I have ultimately won on every field I commanded."

Rush said nothing for a moment. Gates had commanded on his own at Saratoga? If the other reports were to be believed, those written in the halting hand of Morgan, or the bitter denouncements of Arnold, still in convalescence from his nobly gained wounds in that fight, Gates had faced nothing short of mutiny from the other generals in the field. His fellow generals believed they had won Saratoga despite him, not because of him.

Though Rush did indeed fear the Caesarism that many whispered was the ultimate goal of Washington and those fanatical followers around him, such as Greene, Lord Stirling, and Wayne, he wondered now if he was indeed betting on the right horse. Disgusted as he was by the horrors he had wit-nessed on the battlefields and in the hospitals where he worked side by side with British surgeons, the flood of correspondence that had come in from General Washington and his supporters had caught him and the other members of Congress off guard.

He had spent the last few days examining the records of Mifflin, one of Gates's cronies, and his tenure as quartermaster. Tens of thousands of dollars had disappeared, the loss blamed on paperwork between state Commissary Departments and the Continental government. The arbitrary prices fixed by the different entities, often in conflict, were a source of endless confusion, and the losers were the armies, which were starving. That and the insistence that payment for supplies would be made in Continental scrip had played straight into British hands. What fool would accept five pounds Continen-tal for a full-grown sow when a British purchasing agent would pay half a crown sterling——and a full crown if the animal weighed three hundred pounds or more?

Page after page of such quotas and arbitrary prices for everything, from chickens and pigs to the paper and ink on which his own documents were writ-ten, had been created by Mifflin. And around it the taint that was buried in all the mountains of paperwork. There were the inflated charges for transport, for wagons to be commissioned by Mifflin with per diem charges that smelled of kickbacks to contractors for supplies, mules, and wagons.

No wonder the entire system had collapsed and even patriot families hid their stock away at the approach of Continental purchasing agents. And in the richest farmland of all the thirteen states, the realm west of Philadelphia out to Lancaster and north to Reading, land rich enough to support a hundred thousand men in the field for an entire winter, barely a sow or head of cattle could now be found.

He had thrown in with Gates and his side. He could not shake his truly Republican fear of Washington's proposed solution: long-term enlistments of three years or the duration of the war, along with payment to be forwarded to him in hard cash for troops and their supplies. It was anathema to any true patriot, he reasoned. The notion of men of three years' enlistment did indeed smack of the ancient Romans or the professional armies of Europe, which they now fought against.

The dream had always been that a yeomanry of free landholders, such as in the days of Rome before the Carthaginian wars, would be the backbone of this fight. History taught him that when Rome, under the so-called Marian reforms, had gone to a professional fighting force, Caesar and Augustus waited in the wings, to bend such forces to their personal ambitions.

And yet Washington, for so many the embodiment of all the ideals of a Cincinnatus, now argued the loudest for three years' enlistments, for a professional, well-trained army of the Continental Line, as he called it. Washington argued that a professional army that could stand volley to volley against Howe's professionals was their only way to victory.

Rush had thrown in with Gates because of his belief that this should never be the case. It had been the undoing of liberty in the English Civil War of the 1640s. Cromwell had insisted upon training what he called his "New Model Army," a professional force of long enlistments, the men drilled with ruthless proficiency, able at last to stand against the Royalists, and indeed they had won their war. But less than three years later, he had unleashed them against the very Parliament they were sworn to defend, putting their loyalty, as did Caesar's legions, to their general rather than to the cause to which they had first pledged themselves.

England then lived under a harsh dictatorship for more than a decade.

A Washington dictatorship? He knew that both Samuel and John Adams, though not vocal, had whispered concerns about such a possibility. Others had as well.

But this alternative? Gates?

He looked at the man closely. Gates would understand that the base of his power was in the support of Congress, which Washington by his own correspondence and that of his fanatical followers was all but openly willing to challenge, with blame for the debacle unfolding at Valley Forge.

Gates called for an army of militias——if need be, to disband the pathetic scarecrows encamped at Valley Forge. Send them all home to resupply, to nourish themselves in their own farms and villages. To put in their spring plantings——their families to sew new uniforms and fill their haversacks with rations——and then sally forth in the tens of thousands to drive out the invaders.

What good was enduring the nightmare of trying to keep the small band at Valley Forge alive over the next four months?

Send them home, except for a small, elite guard. Let them feed themselves off their own farms rather than the bankrupt public weal, and let them return in the spring.

And yet, as he looked at the man he had allied with, he wondered yet again if he had chosen the right path. His heart, so torn by the nightmares he had witnessed in the fall, said that he had made the right choice. His soul told him something different: that this war entered into a realm few had dreamed of in their worst nightmares of but a year and a half past.

How could he ever imagine that his own father-in-law, a signer of the Declaration, would be turncoat? That his wife, back in Philadelphia, would play upon that change as a means of negotiating protection of their own home, which at this very moment was filled with British officers. Fellow surgeons, to be sure——and, as such, they would extend to him a professional courtesy of protecting his property——but still he felt a deep twinge of self-loathing for having entered into such arrangements to protect his own.

He looked down at the stack of paperwork spread out on the table between him and Gates.

"It is obvious," Gates announced, his voice pitched loud enough so that others in the tavern could hear, "that our beloved General Washington has dismissed Major General Conway without the respect due to a man appointed by this Congress and approved by the Board of War, and I ask you, sir, what your intentions are in regard to this."

Rush leaned forward, feeling an inner rage building.

"Do not pressure me," he whispered softly. "You know you have my support; let us not make a public show of denouncing a man who served as he was asked to by the Continental Congress."

Gates swallowed hard and held his hands up in entreaty.

"I meant no such disrespect for General Washington," he offered smoothly.

"Then let us keep it that way, sir."

Others in the tavern had fallen silent, watching the two.

"Still, what we have learned of his secret correspondence with Laurens, the correspondence of that French upstart and his implied threats, and even the letters of Laurens's son, is that they are an attack on my character, sir."

"Did you expect less? Did you expect to attack Washington without some sort of response?" Rush asked.

"He is the commanding general. He should be above such low and base actions against my character and show all proper respect to his superior as director of the Board of War."

"Attack and expect to be attacked in turn, sir," Rush replied wearily, taking the decanter Gates had signed for and pouring himself another drink. "As to being his superior because of the Board of War, may I remind you that Congress has yet to rescind the authorization given to him as supreme commander of all forces now in the field of action."

"This, sir," Gates replied, "is a battle for the soul of this Republic, the authority of the Republic and the support of the Congress which I have come here, fresh from the battlefield of Saratoga, to defend with my life, sir."

"Yes, of course, I am certain of that," Rush replied coldly, as he drained his glass.

Gates fell silent, turning his attention back to the letters directed to him and to the fragments of reports of letters sent by others, including Washington, to Laurens and other members of Congress, spotted by agents of his on the desks of those men, with notes jotted down as to what they had seen.

Nothing was said for several minutes as the two sifted through the various documents.

Rush paused, picking up one of them and scanning it.

"Have you ever heard of a Baron von Steuben?" he finally asked.

"Who?"

"Some German. Claims to be a general who served under Frederick. He landed in Portsmouth last month with letters of introduction from Franklin and Deane."

Rush scanned the note.

"Hard to read, but states here that even now he is on his way to report to us in York."

"Another damn foreigner like Lafayette and Lee."

"Or Conway, for that matter," Rush replied dismissively.

Gates said nothing.

He put on his spectacles, and, holding the letter up to the candle that illuminated their table, he looked at it closely.

"States here he is some sort of drillmaster in the Prussian method of war. Served in the Seven Years' War, personally decorated by Frederick, and then served in the czarina's army against the Turks. Lieutenant general and a baron now, no less. Offering services without demand of rank or pay."

"That's a change," Gates sniffed. "No rank or pay."

Rush looked at him, making no comment about Conway and others demanding rank and pay before they were barely off the boat.

"He sounds interesting," Rush announced, tossing the letter back on the table between them.

CHAPTER SIX

* * *

Near Worcester, Massachusetts
January 14, 1778

Baron Friedrich Wilhelm Ludolf Gerhard Augustin von Steuben reined in his mount and looked at his thoroughly miserable companions, and the equally miserable countryside, as dusk settled upon them.

The day had started with a freezing rain and was now getting worse, with sleet, snow, and a bitter-cold wind out of the northeast. At least it was at their backs as they rode out of Boston, where he had lingered since his arrival in America a month ago.

Recruited by Franklin and Deane, he had tried to wrap his brain around English on the journey over through the stormy and nauseating Atlantic, but so far he had gained only a smattering of polite platitudes. Nevertheless, he had won over the former president of Congress, John Hancock, and the radical revolutionary Sam Adams, who had fired off letters to Congress announcing his arrival. They had urged Congress to take advantage of the vast skills of this well-respected professional, fresh from Europe, a man who, according to all documentation, had been a general with both Frederick of Prussia and Catherine of Russia.

But what he now confronted on this, his first day on the long journey to York, Pennsylvania, and a meeting with Congress, seemed to presage a bad start to his career with this strange new army on the far side of the world.

The weather had turned miserable, the storm driving them along as he and his companions took the post road out of Boston, heading west. His traveling companions for the long journey to meet with Congress were an amusing mix, a small band of young Frenchmen. Even his secretary and aide was

French, a pleasant enough lad, Pierre Du Ponceau, 17. He was a remarkable student of language in spite of his youth——he could at least converse in German and had already Anglicized or Germanized his name to Peter.

Several other young men rode with him, seeking office in the American Army, a couple of servants, and, most important to his morale, his ever-present and loyal Azor, a dog of doubtful pedigree but formidable powers of intimidation, larger than any mastiff or St. Bernard; if he felt his master threatened in any way, he stood by his side with teeth bared. It was something Friedrich found highly amusing, since at heart the big fool was a coward, and if the bluff didn't work, his dog would then quickly hide behind his human protector, leaving a wet trail in retreat.

"I think there is a tavern ahead," Peter announced. Throughout the day, he had dashed ahead in his youthful exuberance to explore and do reconnaissance, taking to heart John Hancock's warning, at their departure, to move with caution once out into the countryside, since bands of Loyalists were known to waylay and rob anyone they thought was a patriot. Once out of Boston, Peter and his companions had even expressed concern that perhaps Indians might be lurking, and Friedrich had teased that in such a case, they must forgo wearing a powdered wig in order to give their foes better access to scalps——a joke at which all had paled.

Inwardly von Steuben reveled in this new adventure. He had seen service for most of the Seven Years' War, been wounded and personally decorated by Frederick at Minden. When captured by the Russians, he had forged new friendships while being held prisoner in St. Petersburg, and was given parole that allowed him to visit the city during the day. He had been the first to inform his king that, with the death of the virulently anti-German Czarina Elizabeth and the ascent to the throne of Peter III, a slavish devotee of Frederick, the new czar would pull Russia out of the war. By that stage, Russia was on the verge of destroying Prussia. For at least a little while he had indeed enjoyed the position of a "Greek messenger" who had borne good news. And for a few years that had gained him a position on the Prussian general staff.

But postwar employment was difficult to hold, and eventually he offered his sword to Russia, under Catherine——after she had, according to rumor, murdered her husband, the late Peter III. He had fought against the Turks but then yet again found himself unemployed. He lacked the subservience needed for survival in the higher echelons of the armies and courts of Europe, particularly when there were no new wars to be fought.

This new adventure most definitely fit his taste, though there was a slight irony in that he was off to fight against the British, trusted allies during the Seven Years War; that he was riding with a gaggle of young French nobles, whose fathers he had fought against; and that if he were ever to go into action, he might very well face what the Americans called Hessians——actually men from half a dozen minor principalities, including his native province, with undoubtedly more than a few friends and comrades of old in their ranks.

Still, there was something about this adventure, this war, that caught him and held his attention. Gone here was the rigid system of court favors and lineage——though in Frederick's army, at least in time of war, an officer's rise was mainly through merit . . . as long as he had not made too many enemies on the way up.

From what he had studied of this war, the fact that the Americans had even survived for over two years against the hammer blows of the English, whose troops were second only to those of the Prussians on the battlefield, said something of their spirit. His month in Boston had been a time well spent in educating himself about this new cause and the new country that was growing from its passions.

The depressing side was that, as with all causes, this Revolution was torn by faction. As a survivor of the courts at Magdeburg, Berlin, St. Petersburg, and elsewhere, he knew how to survive. Until he had a firm foothold on the ground, he should listen, nod much, and say little in reply.

What he had gathered was that this Revolution was little better than thirteen independent states, gathered together for the moment. Like any alliance, it was prone to flying apart if not guided by a firm hand. It was torn by dissent: some, like Sam Adams, the firebrand, arguing that the war should be fought with short-term militias——that they had done well enough at Bunker Hill and in besieging Boston, and that Washington, besides being a Southerner, was bent on being the next Cromwell.

Many praised Gates as the man of the hour, the glorious victor of Saratoga, and both Adams and Hancock had written letters of introduction to that same general, couriered ahead to York.

Others whispered that Washington would still prove to be their guide to victory.

Twenty years of survival in the courts of Europe had taught him much. Coming to something of an understanding of the rather confusing chain of command for this nation and army, he had dictated three brief letters of introduction, to the current president of Congress, to General Gates as head of the Board of War, and to General George Washington. He had informed each, in turn, that as a matter of courtesy he was also in communication with the other two, and that first and foremost his goal was to offer his services to the cause they all shared and to the victory they all desired.

Hancock advised him to first report to Congress at York, and this he would do. Studying the maps, he could see that this journey of several weeks would take him within a few miles of where Washington was encamped. Protocol, he sensed, demanded he first go to Congress without paying proper respects to the general in the field. He sensed it was a waste of valuable time. But if he was to prove himself here, after years of languid inactivity, a few more weeks one way or the other should not matter.

Following Peter's lead, he pressed along the muddy road toward where the excitable young Frenchman said a tavern awaited. If this was considered a primary postal road in this country, he could well understand why no army here would venture forth on a winter campaign. Louis of France and all the kings of Prussia for generations had always placed an emphasis on building roads that were properly engineered and designed for drainage. Primary roads crossing rivers were to be spanned with stone bridges, and there were to be proper cantonments at regular distances to house troops and depots ready with food and supplies. This American wilderness was as bad as Russia, an absolutely appalling situation not even a day's ride out from one of their most important trading cities.

He spotted the tavern sign bucking back and forth in the wind. It was not a very promising looking place, shutters pulled tight, no light to be seen as darkness descended, a lone outpost on this miserable road with only a few outbuildings and a barn to be seen surrounding it.

They rode up to the door, dismounting, Peter leading the way. Peter tried the latch. The door was locked and he pounded on it.

A moment later it cracked open, a narrow, squinting face peering out.

"We seek lodgings for the night," Peter announced and gestured back to his half-dozen companions.

The innkeeper gazed at him coolly, eyes darting, noticing the uniforms.

"I'm filled up for the night. Ride on to Worcester."

"Sir, you see the weather. Night is falling. Surely you have room."

"Filled up, I tell you. Now ride on. Ten miles to Worcester."

Von Steuben, not understanding a word, stood with his back to the wind, and then wandered off a few steps to look around the side of the tavern. There was no sign of life, doors to the barn open, stalls empty.

He turned back as Peter continued to argue.

"What is wrong?" he asked Peter in German.

"The innkeeper claims he has no rooms for the night."

"Force your way in, damn him."

Peter nodded, obviously a bit nervous, but followed orders, putting his shoulder to the door, pushing it open, he and the others stumbling in.

Von Steuben, as befitting his rank in such matters, came last.

A warm fire crackled in an oversize fieldstone fireplace, but the room was entirely empty except for what appeared to be the owner's wife and a couple of servants, who stood nervously at the door leading from the tavern room back into the kitchen.

"Filled up, I tell you."

"I see no one here," Peter retorted.

"Are you calling me a liar?"

"Sir, I see no one here."

"They've gone out hunting and said they'd be back. Now, get out!"

Peter, stunned, could not reply, as the owner, backing around the long bar, produced a fowling piece. He didn't aim it toward them, just laid it on the bar.

"Now, James!" his wife exclaimed.

"Rebecca, shut your mouth. These are nothing but a bunch of damn Frenchie dandies, and I'll be damned if they stay in my place. I'm sick of all of them. Fought them in the last war and now they say they're on our side against the king?"

"What is this?" Friedrich asked of Peter.

"He hates us French and I think he's a Loyalist, sir," Peter informed him in German.

"What are you talking there?" James snapped.

Von Steuben ignored him, turned, and walked out of the tavern. Peter and the others looked at him incredulously, several of the young men turning—— ready to leave, retreat, and try to force their way on for several more hours through the storm.

Reaching his horse, von Steuben pulled out his favorite weapon, an old Cossack horse pistol, a massive thing with a barrel nearly a foot long and close to .80-caliber. Loaded with a one-ounce round ball and a dozen buckshot on top, it was a most effective weapon. Several times it had saved his life. He didn't bother to check the pan——chances were the powder was damp, and inwardly he knew he wouldn't pull the trigger anyhow. It would be a poor start in this country if, on the first day of his journey to meet with Congress, he blew the head off of a surly innkeeper.

Du Ponceau was in the doorway, assuming their leader had conceded. He was surprised to see him returning, and then grinned as he saw this German storm back in, right hand concealed under his cape. Von Steuben walked briskly up to the innkeeper, who stood there with a defiant smirk.

An instant later the pistol was out, cocked and pointed straight at his forehead. Azor was by his side, head high enough that he could see over the edge of the bar, hair on his back bristled, teeth bared in a throaty growl.

The man backed up, gaze shifting from the gun aimed at him to Azor, and back to the gun. He nearly stumbled over a chair as he tried to retreat toward the doorway into the kitchen, where his wife stood screaming.

"Pierre, translate!" von Steuben roared. "Curse for me, in English, at them. Then tell this man we are officers of their Continental army."

Du Ponceau began to speak hurriedly.

"Tell him we are tired, hungry, our horses spent. And say that I will send him straight to hell minus his head if he utters another word against our noble French allies."

Du Ponceau looked over at him with a sidelong glance and grinned.

"Thank you, sir, for that sentiment. May I curse at him some more as well?"

"Yes, damn him!"

Azor, sensing that the argument was going their way and that his master's opponent was absolutely terrified, stepped toward the cowering man, growling.

Von Steuben snapped a command and Azor stopped in place. Von Steuben almost smiled; he wondered what would happen if he ever did order his giant dog to attack.

"Some more curses, Peter, and then say that we are staying and add that we will pay him in silver."

Even before Peter finished translating, the innkeeper was nodding, hands held high. One of the young French officers, with a grin, reached over to the bar to take the fowling piece.

"Vogel, my purse," von Steuben announced.

His servant gingerly reached around to von Steuben's uniform pocket and drew out a small leather pouch.

"Ask this man what are the rates for all six of us, dinner, beds free of vermin, breakfast, and our horses properly tended to."

"Our bedding is free of vermin, I can assure you," Rebecca interjected nervously, as Peter translated, obviously insulted by the implication, but eyes now on the purse.

"No Continental money," James retorted.

"You are not in a position to argue," von Steuben roared, and Azor resumed growling.

"Fifteen dollars," he hesitated, "per man. Five dollars extra for each horse."

"My dog, meat and bones for free," von Steuben replied.

James nodded, not daring to argue, as if Azor might understand the negotiations and react if board was denied.

"Vogel, one silver thaler," von Steuben snapped. "And that is for all of us."

The heavy coin was tossed onto the bar. James looked down, snatched it up, and held it to the light of a smoking lantern.

"It's real silver," he announced, looking over at his wife.

The glint of avarice was obvious as James forced a smile.

"I thought you were the usual wandering thieves, begging your pardon, sir," he announced, all but groveling even as he clutched the silver coin. "We ain't seen real money in six months' time, and supplies round here is scarce. I meant no insult, believe me. It's just that I can't take lodgers in, get paid in Continentals, and then try and buy new vittles. That paper money Massachusetts prints up is absurdity, sir. Absurdity."

He was prattling, and von Steuben turned away as if bored.

"Vogel, pay him as well for one of those bottles of brandy behind him." After a brief but one-sided negotiation, they settled on an English shilling and sixpence. The bottle and glasses were hurriedly produced, Vogel sweeping them up and taking them over to a table by the crackling fire.

Von Steuben uncocked his pistol, turned and then made a formal nod to the landlady.

"Peter, inform her I meant no disrespect and that I would appreciate her seeing to a proper dinner as soon as possible."

She smiled, curtsied, and hurried into the kitchen, shouting orders to the servants, while Vogel went outside to lead their horses into the barn, the innkeeper even offering to help.

Von Steuben settled into a chair by the fire, casting off his thoroughly waterlogged cape and hat and stretching out his short, stubby legs. He gladly accepted a glass poured by Peter and smiled at the admiring glances of the young men. Azor came over, wagging his tail. Von Steuben affectionately patted his friend and pointed toward the floor, and the wet, foul-smelling dog settled down and stretched out before the fireplace with a contented sigh.

"That is how we negotiate in Prussian," he said with a grin, and they held their glasses up, standing, offering him and King Frederick a toast.

He stood when that name was announced, even though he would never voice, over here, the dissatisfaction he felt over how he had been treated after so many years of loyal service. As to his claimed rank of general . . . well, he had served on the General Staff, so that was equivalent, and he held fast to that, along with his claim to the nobility as a baron, though enemies countered that it was a title that had been falsely cooked up by his father.

Regardless, America was a new start and he would make the most of it.

The bottle was soon drained. The innkeeper was still out in the barn tending to the horses, so von Steuben went around the bar on his own, took down another bottle of brandy, and tossed another shilling on the table. He did not need to check what was left in his purse. Several more encounters such as this one would leave him penniless, except for a wad of Continental currency given to him by Hancock, but the show of bravado at the start of their long journey was the stuff that created respect and camaraderie for the long journey ahead. As a young officer, it was what his father and the army had taught him well. A good officer looked out first for his horses and then for his men, starting with the lowest private, then sergeants, and finally junior officers. In garrison, an officer knew when to buy a round for fellow officers even if it took his last pfennig, when to give a thaler to a sergeant to buy beer for the enlisted men if they had performed well on parade. Now, with these Frenchmen as his companions for a journey that would take weeks, his act of bravado would play well, and word of it spread. He could only pray that, in the future, they would pass through some towns where citizens would be eager to fete them at their own expense rather than his.

He uncorked the second bottle, filled the glasses of the others, and held his up.

He knew there was a political game that they were heading into, the waters murky, currents unclear, personalities maneuvering, factions forming and reforming. "To victory," he announced, and the others came to their feet, draining their glasses and grinning with delight as the first course, a venison pie, steaming hot, was carried out from the kitchen. Rebecca frowned at the second bottle but smiled graciously when she saw the shilling already on the table.

By the end of the evening, Steuben had gone through a crown of his English money for brandy and a jug of a vile drink that Peter said was corn whiskey, but it was worth it. His traveling companions laughed with delight as Peter translated his tales of adventure in the last war against their fathers and while in Russia, fighting Turks, Cossacks, and other rebels. The bonds were formed; these men would be loyal to him as he would be loyal to them as they made their way toward whatever awaited them in York and beyond.

Valley Forge
January 8, 1778

"Show General Wayne in," Washington replied. Standing, he acknowledged Wayne's salute. Once the door was closed, he came around from behind his desk, extending his hand, offering to help Wayne remove his snow-covered cape and hat. He motioned Wayne over to a chair by the fireplace and sat down in the opposite chair, Wayne extending his hands, rubbing them in front of the fire to take the chill out.

A snowfall of nearly a foot had blanketed the valley over the last few days, flurries still coming down, at least freezing the ground again, making it easier for his men to pull logs out of the forest and drag them in to build cabins. Labor was progressing, but, after more than two weeks, two-thirds of his men were still living under tattered tents and in lean-tos.

"I read your dispatch last night," Washington said, motioning back to his desk.

"I'm sorry, sir, but it had to be said. The force I took with me down to reinforce Morgan is gone, sir, totally gone, except for a few dozen men I left with Morgan's command.

"As I noted in the report, the men assigned to me from the other brigades were not the choice men you indicated was your desire, but instead a dumping off of troublemakers, village fools, men ready to desert, anyhow. By going with me, their desertions would not reflect on the muster rolls of their own regiments."

Washington extended his hand in a calming gesture.

"Anthony, there is no need to explain yourself. I trust what you reported."

"Still, sir," Anthony sighed. "Day after day, to see them, to see those damn . . ."

He hesitated.

"Sir, the same light infantry that attacked us at Paoli was there, and us not able to strike back. We'd try to position for at least some demonstration, some trap, even if just to sweep up a few wagons and their guards, but always they seemed forewarned. Word we got was that their General Grey let it be known that on whatever property his men were ambushed, the house would be put to the torch, but if we were betrayed, the owner's goods would be respected and purchased at fair price. I regret to say that I must report that most of the farmsteads lining the Schuylkill near Philadelphia are now either Tory or at least cooperate in some way to protect themselves. We've lost the countryside in that region.

"Some good souls secretly give our men food, a dry place to sleep if no British are across the river on patrol, but beg us to leave the area if even a rumor comes of another raid."

"Do you think there will be any more raids on the scale of what Howe did just before Christmas?"

Anthony shook his head. "Why bother? At least that is what our spies are bringing back from Philadelphia. They've gathered in enough food to see them through to spring. Their shipping moves freely on the Delaware, and all of south Jersey is open to them if they should wish. The word is that they've settled in for a winter of gorging themselves, that most of the daughters of the merchants openly dally with the officers, and I will not say what the lower-class women are doing."

Washington said nothing. The men around him knew that talk of issues of a bawdy nature was not acceptable in his presence.

"Sir, unless I am sorely mistaken, I think it shall be quiet until the spring thaws and dry roads are again ready to support an army on the march, with hay high enough to feed our horses and theirs."

Washington sighed at this report, stood, and went to the window, looking out across the frozen plain. A party of men trudged by out on the road, guiding several skin-and-bone horses dragging logs up the slope. Smoke drifted with the wind from the regimental cooking fires. A small convoy of food had come down from Reading the evening before, beef on the hoof, obviously not the choice stock, but still fresh meat.

The real haul, though, was over two tons of freshly ground flour, at least it was purported to be so, though weevils were found in more than a few sacks that obviously had been sitting for months, if not years.

He looked back at Anthony, who sat glumly by the fire. He knew the man expected a reprimand, perhaps even dismissal, for the utter failure of his mission to block the British light infantry at Darby, combined with his shattering defeat at Paoli three months before.

"Care for a walk?" Washington offered.

Wayne looked up at him in surprise.

"Sir?"

"I feel like a walk."

Wayne did not argue as he donned his wet, heavy woolen cape and hat, following his general out the door. The ground was frozen, with a goodly layer of snow upon it, providing a fair footing. Sergeant Harris, seeing his general come out, called for a squad of men to fall in as escort, Washington motioning for them to fall in at a discreet distance.

It was good to be out in the fresh, bracing air, snow flurries drifting on the wind, the snowfall of the previous days covering over, at least temporarily, the filth and squalor of an encampment of nine thousand men, so ill prepared for this winter. All around him men were hard at work, dragging in logs, cutting notches to fit them into place on the cabins, splitting shingles from dead cedars dragged up from the riverbank, mixing muddy clay in kettles over low-simmering fires and slapping the clay between logs as chinking, carrying in bundles of deadfall to use as firewood. The full meals of the last few days had worked wonders. Though, of course, the constant dread was that the larder for the army never held more than a day or so in reserve. If no food came in by this evening, it would be half rations tomorrow and no rations at all within three days.

The smells of it all he found comforting. There was always that pleasant tang of firewood, especially from hickory, maple, chestnut, and ash. Fresh meat was roasting over fires, groups of hungry men gathered around, carefully watching for the moment when they could line up and then play out the ritual of their sergeants dividing up the precious rations.

There were other scents as well, which as an old soldier he had long ago learned to block out: latrine pits poorly dug in the first muddy days and already overflowing, the scent of thousands of unwashed bodies. He heard distant cries from one of the hospital huts. Merciful God, it sounded like a surgery, as the victim begged and cried.

The first case of typhus had been reported to him this morning by Bodo Otto, the new surgeon general of the army, replacing the still absent Benjamin Rush. He had immediately ordered a quarantine hospital to be established several miles away for those stricken with the contagions of typhus, measles, and smallpox. The cases of dysentery and pneumonia and general complaints could still be handled by the brigade hospitals. A hundred men, in this case truly choice men, had been sent off with Otto to construct the necessary shelters for the dangerously sick, and an appeal had been sent out to neighboring communities for any surgeon or woman of good moral character who would volunteer for the dangerous task of seeing to these suffering men.

Duty required he must visit with the sick, a task to him far more painful than the prospect of any battle, and which he hoped to postpone for a few more days, until the buildings were completed and the sick and dying moved. The quarantine hospital, besides being good medical practice, as Bodo pointed out, was necessary as well to conceal from the rest of the troops just how many men were now falling victim to disease.

Yet in spite of all the unrelenting suffering, there seemed to be a positive air about the camp this day. They had enjoyed a full midday meal, a pound per man. More tools had come in as well. The pace of labor was picking up for their shelters. Though only a third were completed, still hundreds more were at least four or five tiers high, enough for a majority of the men still out in the cold to pitch their tents and lean-tos within to get out of the worst of the wind. A few regiments even had enough energy to stage a snowball fight, arrayed in battlelines, pelting each other vigorously to the point that officers finally had to break it up after a few teeth and bones were broken in the general melee, a small barrel of rum going to the supposed victors, men of the New York Line who then graciously offered to share the few ounces per man with the supposed losers, not so experienced in such melees, from the tidewater of Virginia.

"No fortifications yet," Wayne observed, and Washington did not reply. It was a terribly lax situation, but then again his report, which he trusted, indicated that at least for now there was no threat of a serious sortie out of Philadelphia. Shelter for the men, hospitals for the sick, sheds for the horses, warehouses for the supplies, if they ever appeared, must take priority now. What good were trenches, bastions, moats, and battery positions if there were no men left to man them?

He pressed on and finally Wayne raised his head, a flicker of surprise in his eyes.

"What's that I smell?"

Washington could not help but smile, feeling a bit foolish at the demonstration that was about to take place. Yet he felt that one of his most trusted generals, away for weeks on the most dangerous and frustrating of assignments, needed a boost in morale.

They crested a rise and there it was. A long, low log hut, thirty feet or more in length, and nearly as deep. It had four chimneys, smoke boiling out of each, a massive pile of firewood outside the entryway. A couple of men, stripped naked to their waists, emerged to pick up armfuls of wood, oblivious to their approaching commander. They dashed back inside under the rude doorway curtain of a tattered old blanket.

A large gathering of men waited outside. An officer yelled at them to wait their turn, and at the approach of Washington and Wayne he snapped to attention and saluted, the men gathered outside the doorway, nearly a hundred of them, coming to attention as well.

"May I ask your indulgence," Washington announced, returning their salutes. "An inspection tour for the benefit of General Wayne."

"Good ole Mad Anthony," one of the men gathered shouted, "I was with ya at Paoli."

Wayne sought out the man and offered a salute. "Next time it'll be the turn of those bastards, I promise you," he replied.

The others gathered around the man who had thus spoken, grinning and then laughing that he was a bootlicker as the two generals ducked under the blanket and went into the shed, though it was obvious they were delighted that one of theirs had been singled out.

The north wall of the shed was lined with brick ovens, the heat radiating from them as hot as a summer day. The scent in the shed was all but shattering in its power. It was a bakery.

The half-dozen ovens were made of nothing more than scavenged brick from the destroyed mill. There were no doors to the ovens or to the roaring fireplaces beneath them. Wooden hand-carved paddles were being scooped into the ovens, pulling out steaming loaves of bread. Even Washington felt his stomach constrict at the sight and smell of it. Along the far wall, dozens of men, crowded shoulder to shoulder, were mixing, pounding, rolling out dough. Before it had barely risen, into the oven it went, pulled out but minutes later at times not even half baked, so pressing was the demand from the men waiting outside.

"Second Maryland!"

A short, thick plug of a man stood with the curtain pulled back.

"Second Maryland, twenty loaves!"

"Damn your eyes, we need fifty," came a reply.

"You got a problem, you son of a bitch, General Washington himself is inside here, take it up with him."

There was a sullen, inaudible retort, but no further complaints as one of the bakers, like the others stripped to the waist, carried out a canvas sack filled with bread and handed it off to a captain and a guard detail who peeked into the bakery, saw Washington, hurriedly saluted, and ran off with their treasure.

The pluglike man turned back from the doorway, looking down at a sheet of foolscap.

"Third Maryland, ten minutes, twenty loaves!" he shouted, and let the blanket drop.

Cigar clenched between his yellow-stained teeth, the man smiled at Washington and saluted.

"General Anthony Wayne, may I present," Washington paused, "General Baker of the Army, Christopher Ludwig."

Ludwig, wiping his dough-encrusted hands on a tattered gray apron, extended his hand, which Wayne grasped eagerly.

"General, am I now? I was just joking, sir, when I said that should be my title."

"You feed the men and, by God, sir, you will draw the pay and honor of a general this winter," Washington cried.

"Care for a fresh loaf, General?" Ludwig asked.

Washington could not reply, thinking of the lines of men waiting outside.

One of his workers, with wooden paddle, fished a half-dozen steaming loaves out of an oven, shouting that there was room for more and, ignoring the presence of the general, cursed the wood suppliers, saying he needed more damn wood, and to be quick about it. The fire was dying down in his oven.

Ludwig, with a bit of a limp, stumped over to a rough-hewn table, where men were packing loaves into canvas and burlap bags, grabbed a steaming loaf, and broke it open. It was obviously still red-hot, but his gnarled hands, scorched and yet scorched again by a thousand flames, did not notice the discomfort.

He offered half the broken loaf to Washington, the other to Wayne.

"Sorry I can't offer you gentlemen a proper setting, with tea, fresh butter from the churn, maybe a spot of brandy to wash it down with," and as he said that he held an extended forefinger to his nose and winked, "but this is Valley Forge, you know."

The bakery fell silent as all eyes turned on Washington. He held the bread, suppressing the urge to just tear into it, instead properly breaking off but a piece. It hissed slightly from the steaming heat. He changed it from one hand to the other, the bakers grinning at his discomfort.

He took a bite, the men studying him as carefully as any battery of gourmet chefs standing by the side of a king.

It was, in fact, doughy, barely cooked through and only half-leavened, but the warmth, the near-burning heat, the taste of it, caused his head to nearly swim.

"Heavenly," he whispered with a smile.

Ludwig stood before him, arms folded across a chest as hairy as any bear's, and grinned with delight.

Six months ago he had been but a sergeant of militia, born in Germany, a pastry cook from Philadelphia by trade who supposedly boasted a shop renowned in the city and even patronized by the likes of Franklin and other members of Congress.

Two days after the army staggered into Valley Forge, he had barged his way past Tilghman and Hamilton, demanding an audience with "our general and, Gott, if you don't let me in, this damn army will starve, I tell you."

Without any niceties or preamble, he made his case clear. Give him a hundred men of his own choosing recruited from the various regiments——bakers, woodsmen properly armed with axes to make a bakehouse and able to bring in two cords or more of firewood a day, brick layers for the ovens and access to the ruins of the forge to salvage the bricks, and a ton or more of flour a day——and he'd feed this whole damn army or may a pox strike him blind.

Caught as much by the man's blunt-spoken audacity as by anything else, Washington had ordered Hamilton to draft the authorizations.

He looked over at Anthony, who unabashedly was wolfing the bread down in great gulps.

"Now, if only we had a spot of rum, even some whiskey to wash it down," Anthony sighed.

"I know a man who can turn corn into good drinking liquor," Christopher offered, but a stern look from Washington stilled that line of reasoning. Behind the baker he could see a bright, cheery grin from a man he suspected was from the frontier. He was long-bearded, arms sinewy but powerful, and had what looked to be a Seneca tattoo around his neck. His features had fallen at the rejection of the still.

"Twenty more," one of the bakers shouted, holding up a bag.

"Begging your pardon, sir," Christopher announced. "Got to do it myself, otherwise they'll be rioting out there."

He took up the bag, went to the door, shouted for the men of the Third

Maryland, handed them the sack of bread, dismissed their grumbling that they needed eighty loaves, and checked their number off.

"First New York Artillery next, four loaves!"

He stepped back into the steaming hot bakehouse.

"Told you, sir, give me two weeks and a hundred men and I'd have a proper bakery."

Washington could only nod with admiration.

Ludwig drew closer, dough-encrusted hands on his hips.

"Now, sir, what about flour for tomorrow?"

"I can't promise."

"Can't promise?" Ludwig snapped. "By damn all, sir, and begging your pardon, no disrespect. I got twenty men building an extension to this building to put in two more ovens, a separate room to let the loaves at least rise and leaven for a few hours, and now you say I'm out of flour after just one full day of baking? You see how many men are lined up out there?"

"I saw."

Ludwig just gazed at him.

My God, Washington could not help but think. Others would think this disrespect of the worst kind, but he could not. This man, whoever he was before the war, had decided it was his personal task to provide a pound of fresh bread a day to every man in the army, and damn anyone who got in his way.

"I promise you I shall see what I can do," he paused, "General Baker of the Army."

Ludwig puffed up with the announcement of that title, looking back over his shoulder at all those who had stopped in their labors to watch the confrontation.

"Back to work, all of you, damn your eyes," Ludwig snapped. "Five hundred more loaves and then you get your break and a loaf then for each of you, but not before."

Ludwig looked back at Washington, features reddening.

"Sorry, sir," he whispered, "but to keep 'em at their tasks, I promised each man a loaf for himself, begging your pardon."

"A fair enough trade for their labor and skills," Washington replied.

He looked over at Anthony, who was finishing his own half-loaf without comment. As for his own half, he wasn't sure what to do. Hand it back? He thought of his loyal adjutants back at the house and, a bit embarrassed, stuffed the loaf under his cape and into his haversack. No one said anything, but more than a few grinned.

"Next time you visit, sir, if you could only bring up a few dozen dairy cows and not slaughter 'em first, I'll promise you fresh butter and cream with your bread."

He could not reply. Such a balancing act. A score of such cows would be meat for another day for the army. Fodder to feed them, four to five hundred pounds per day? In return maybe eighty gallons of milk, a few gallons of cream, and a few dozen pounds of butter. He sighed. The trade was not yet worth it, no matter how tempting.

He would and must choose the meat rather than the butter, no matter how agonizing it was at this moment as the memory of such luxuries filled him.

"General Ludwig, I leave you to your labors," Washington said with a smile, "and my heartfelt compliments to you and your entire command."

There was a bit of a cheer as he left the bakery, the joy it created stilled by the sight of a hundred or more men, shivering with cold, delegates from the various regiments of his army, queued up in the hope of fetching back a quarter-pound of fresh bread per man.

He started back to his headquarters.

"Sir, I thank you for the repast," Anthony Wayne finally said. "Though a bit doughy, that bread was the most I've had in days."

They walked on in silence for a couple of hundred yards. Washington struggled with the thought of the warm half-loaf in his haversack but had firmly resolved it would go to Tilghman, Laurens, and Hamilton——and then he looked over his shoulder. His loyal guards kept pace, never really visible but always there.

"Sergeant Harris," he called, and the old man sprinted the few feet forward.

"Sir!"

"Were your men able to draw bread rations?"

"Sir, we have a detail up there but I fear they are at the end of the line."

Washington fished under his cape, drew out the bread, and handed it over.

"I'm sorry it is not more, Sergeant. For you and these men with you," he announced.

Without waiting for a response, he pressed on, looking back at Wayne, who was silent, as if consumed with guilt that he had so eagerly consumed what was offered to him.

"About what I wish for you to do next, General Wayne," Washington announced, now pressing to the core of the issue.

Wayne looked over at him anxiously.

"Sir?"

"I will speak bluntly, sir," Washington announced.

"But of course, sir."

"I am relieving you of the command of your brigade."

"Sir?"

Wayne stopped as if stricken.

Washington extended his hand as if to guide him along.

"Surely sir, my service . . ." Wayne's voice trailed off. "Sir, the court-martial regarding Paoli cleared me of blame . . ."

"Hear me out, General Wayne." He looked back over his shoulder to make sure his escorts were out of earshot. The men had slowed, carefully breaking up the bread, Harris as always insuring the doling out would be in equal shares.

"Perhaps I started wrong, sir. I am not relieving you of command, I am promoting you."

"Sir?"

"Your own report but an hour ago confirmed what I suspected. The English and their hirelings will not stir from Philadelphia. Even if we made a feint across New Jersey to threaten the garrison they left behind in New York, that would be futile as well."

He had not forgotten the sting of the letters of remonstration, demanding a sortie into New Jersey while at the same time splitting his forces to try to hold Pennsylvania west of the Schuylkill. To try to bring this army forth to seek engagement, even on ground of his choosing, was impossible. The men were no longer capable of fighting except in a defensive battle with, frankly, their backs to the wall, in this case the river behind them. To venture into Jersey would bring forth a riposte from the Philadelphia garrison, attacking him from the rear even as he struggled to close in on New York. Even if he could regain the Palisade Heights, how could he ever hope to cross the Hudson in the face of the Royal Navy? At the same time, Congress would be screaming that he had abandoned Pennsylvania . . . and them.

With Wayne's written report of last night, the report of spies still coming out of the city, the evidence that was before his eyes every day these last two weeks, he knew Providence had decreed that, this winter, the army must remain at Valley Forge. He hoped that the British, in their arrogance, would not sortie out to finish him.

What he needed now was not a general of fighting ability. Wayne was more than fitted for that title, in spite of his humiliating defeat. What was needed was a general of grit and determination for a task of critical importance. He sensed Wayne would fit that bill well.

He looked over at him.

"I am relieving you of command of your brigade, sir, at least until the return of active field service in the spring."

"Sir, I must protest."

Washington forced a smile. God, did it not seem that with every general under his command there was always the cry "I must protest," and usually over the pettiest of causes, right down to who would lead the order of march for the day and whose brigade would bring up the rear?

He remembered with great fondness one of Martha's favorite comments when ordering affairs at Mount Vernon: "George, this is more tiresome than trying to herd a parcel of cats."

"You heard our respected General Baker back there?" he asked.

"Sir?"

"General Baker Christopher Ludwig of Philadelphia, or wherever. Bring him two tons——better yet, three tons——of flour a day, and he can provide a loaf for nearly every man in this army. Four tons and some baking soda and we'll even have cake."

Wayne could not help but smile at the feeble joke.

"I will appoint you in command of the Commissary Department for the army encamped at Valley Forge."

"Merciful God, sir, please not that," Wayne cried, stopping in his tracks.

Washington stopped as well and looked over at him, forcing a smile.

"I can think of no better man for the job."

"Sir, this will be an everlasting disgrace on my name and honor. Sir, with all due respect, I shall offer my resignation rather than accept such a demotion."

Washington bristled and drew closer to Anthony.

"Damn it, sir," he hissed, "this is not a demotion. You yourself said that there would be no fighting till spring."

Wayne did not reply.

"Then I present to you, sir. What is the most pressing need of all for this army to survive to spring and be ready to fight?"

Wayne lowered his head.

"Answer me," Washington snapped.

Wayne looked up at him.

"Food, sir."

"Precisely."

"What about the system created by Congress to supply us?" Wayne offered as a feeble reply.

"You know better. You have seen the results," Washington replied angrily, gesturing with a sweep of his arm back toward the bakery and the line of men waiting for the meager handouts.

"I am not violating——nor will I ever violate——the mandates established by Congress, but they did give me last fall extraordinary powers to garner whatever supplies necessary in the immediate vicinity of where our armies passed.

"I need not educate you as to how the machinations of General Gates and his Board of War have complicated our supply problems. But my orders do grant to me the powers to gather supplies as needed, within the immediate reach of this army in order to sustain a campaign in the field.

"It is my intent, sir, to grant those powers to you."

"That, sir, will surely bring a crisis with General Gates and his confederates," Wayne interjected.

"What do you propose as an alternative?" Washington said bluntly. "Continue to let these men starve? No, sir, that is finished."

"Sir, I am a field commander, not a clerk," Wayne offered.

Washington drew closer, and it was evident that the reply was not to his liking.

"A clerk, sir," he said coldly, "at times is as valuable as any general. I am tasking you with organizing a special corps. A corps of supply for the army at Valley Forge. I give you free rein to find whatever is necessary to keep these men, these patriots, alive. This will be combat of a new kind, but it will be combat that is central to the survival of this army."

As he spoke he pointed back, yet again, to the bakehouse, his voice nearly choking with emotion.

"Our American Revolution has come down to this. A score of cattle a day, two, better yet three, tons of flour. A ton of other sundries and several tons of fodder for our horses if cavalry and artillery are to move next spring. That is far more important to me at this moment than any brigade capable of taking the field."

Wayne sighed, and Washington put his hand on the man's shoulder.

"You are the one I've chosen, Anthony, because I think you are the only man who can get this job done."

Anthony Wayne met his gaze.

"May I exact but one promise in return?"

"Name it."

"That once this crisis is past, you will return me to field command. For surely I will die of shame if, come the next fight, I am ten miles behind the lines counting barrels of flour."

Washington smiled.

"I promise that when we fight, you, my best fighting general, will be in the thick of it."

CHAPTER SEVEN

✳ ✳ ✳

Philadelphia
Evening, January 25, 1778

Lieutenant Allen van Dorn gazed one more time at the wavy image reflected back to him by the candle-illuminated mirror. He carefully adjusted the powdered wig, cautious not to let the flour mixture get on his hands. The uniform was new, having set him three months in arrears for pay, but General Grey had insisted upon its purchase and had even offered to pay for it. Van Dorn's pride of course prevented accepting that offer.

"Listen, Mr. van Dorn," the general had sniffed. "Not proper you being on my staff and in the uniform of a damn Loyalist.

"My lads won't much care for riding beside you when the bullets are flying. Those damn rebels always shoot at Loyalists first, even before our officers. And besides, if you are taken, your damn rebel friends might string you up. At least in the proper uniform of my staff, you stand a better chance of living."

Allen had not dared to reply that, if captured as a Loyalist wearing the light infantry uniform and identified as one of Charles Grey's staff, chances are he would be strung up anyhow. The memory of the Paoli Massacre marked any man with Grey, for the memory of "no quarter" remained bitter and strong.

A bugle call echoed from below, accompanied by three huzzahs, signaling that the evening's festivities had begun. It was followed then by a cry for a toast to the king. The toast was greeted with more lusty cheers, and then a lively reel started.

He took another look into the mirror, gazing at his long-drawn features. He felt a great sense of unease, as he did every evening at such events. The son of Dutch merchants from Trenton, he had never dreamed two years ago that he would be a soldier, let alone a soldier risen to the rank of lieutenant in His Majesty's army. He struggled yet again, as he did every day, with his new identity.

No cheering of crowds, no impulse to escape from the mundane life of running the shop and tannery, had driven him to this fight. His brother Jonathan had been influenced by the passions of the moment after the signing of the Declaration of Independence a few miles away in Philadelphia, and had left Trenton to run off to the rebel side . . . and now he was dead. His own choice had been far more pragmatic. With the rebels he saw only the prospect of the rule of the mob: Once this so-called revolution of the common man was done, demagogues would, as had always been the case throughout history, pervert it to their own reasons and desires. In spite of poor Jonathan's hero worship, Washington in the end would be nothing more than another Cromwell. Or, if not he, then someone else, such as Gates, would seize the moment instead.

And though General Grey had treated him well enough, admiring his bravery and openly praising it, he nevertheless was not one of them. Even the lowest-ranking officer from England had money behind him, education far beyond the one year he had taken at college in Princeton before returning to help run the family business. He described his parents as merchants, but never would he admit that their business had started as a tannery, a fact that would have left him open for smiling comments and derisive mockery as soon as he was out of the room. For British officers, a merchant was bad enough, but a craftsman or manufacturer would have been totally beneath consideration.

He took one last glance at his image, and then left the small room——a servant's garret before the occupation——and started down the stairs.

The house was richly appointed and tastefully arranged, for it was, after all, the home of the famous Benjamin Franklin, confiscated by the army and quickly seized by Grey as his headquarters when they took Philadelphia. Grey had ordered that the home be respected, even if it was the abode of a revolutionary traitor who had signed the Declaration. For before that dreadful fall, Franklin had indeed been one of the most honored men of the Empire. Franklin's fame as a scientist and writer was still intact despite his more recent, traitorous actions. Grey had ordered that they were to set the example as gentlemen and not deface or loot the house while occupying it.

The music swelled as he reached the second landing, a ceremonial flourish. There was a call for a toast for General Howe and his Lordship (and brother) Admiral Howe, and another cheer. He came down the last flight of stairs and turned into the parlor, which, during the day, served as a staff and map room, but in the evening was cleared of furnishings for their parties.

He had never been much for such things——the crowd, rich foods, the idle chatter. The war itself was supposed to be a topic forbidden at social events such as these, though at times that rule would be briefly ignored. Instead of practical talk, it was hour upon hour of mindless chatter about hunting, horses, the latest word of social doings back in London, what royalty was doing and who was having an affair with whom, and of course banter to charm the ladies in attendance.

He had also never been much for such doings. He was still a bachelor at twenty-five and, to add to his inner sense of insecurity, had virtually no experience with either the more courtly game of flirtation so easily practiced in these rooms or, for that matter, the far more earthy pursuits that many of the staff vigorously pursued and boasted about when ladies of breeding were not present.

He stepped into the swirl, the room already far too warm with so many packed in. He was drawn to the sideboard, almost sagging under the weight of offerings . . . roasted venison, partridges, pheasants and hares, thin slices of veal, pies of half a dozen varieties, rich, fresh bread that made him think of his mother's baking at home, all of it arrayed around a central ornamental display: a gaudy cake molded to the shape of a three-masted frigate. It was the excuse for tonight's party, to honor a frigate's captain who had just made port this morning, bringing in tow a captured rebel brig, taken with a hull full of French muskets, uniforms, flints, shot, and powder, enough supplies to outfit an entire brigade.

Pegged to the wall behind the table laden with treats was a hastily made sketch on a sheet of paper several feet square, a caricature of the French king and Washington on their knees begging for mercy, the captain of the frigate standing before them with saber drawn. It was a fairly good effort, the captain's smile one of disdain, as if debating whether to accept their surrender or lop off their heads.

"Obviously another work by John André," someone said with a chuckle, coming up to Allen's side, gesturing to the sketch.

Allen turned.

He could not remember the man's name. A quick look at his tabs told him that he was a captain with a foot regiment. He could see the captain scanning him, identifying him as an officer with Grey.

"Quite the talent, isn't he? Damn me, an artist, a poet, and the admiration of all the ladies," the captain offered, as he gestured to a decanter of wine, a private standing rigid behind the table nodding and pouring the sparkling claret into a fine goblet.

"Join me in a toast?" the captain said, looking over at Allen.

"But of course, sir."

The private poured a second glass and handed it to Allen, who nodded his thanks.

"Confusion to Washington and the damn French," the captain offered.

Allen held his glass up.

"Confusion to Washington and the damn French," he repeated.

The captain looked at him and nodded.

"Robert Youngman, Twenty-sixth Foot," he offered.

"Allen van Dorn, on the staff of his Lordship Earl Grey."

Robert looked at him, head slightly cocked.

"Colonial?" he asked.

Allen nodded in reply.

"Well, no bother. We're all on the same side here," the captain offered, voice now filled with condescension.

"Thank you, sir."

"Where from?"

"Jersey, sir."

"Where in Jersey?"

"Trenton."

The captain, obviously into his cups, sighed.

"Bad business there last year, but after all they were only Hessians."

"Yes, something like that," Allen replied in a neutral voice.

There was an awkward pause after they had drained their glasses, the captain motioning to the private to top off his glass again.

"Ah, there is the artist himself. My compliments, sir, on the genius of your work," Youngman announced with a grin, motioning back to the drawing.

Turning away from Allen, the captain had raised his glass to the approaching captain as if offering a toast, and drained it. The object of his attention, Captain John André, came up to the two, smiling, and offered a slight bow in reply.

Born of Huguenot parents, André could more easily have passed as a member of the French aristocracy than an officer of the British Line. He had a dark complexion. He was slender yet obviously fit, bedecked as he always was in a rich, well-tailored uniform from the finest shop in London, a uniform that without doubt cost ten, maybe twelve times as much as the twelve pounds Allen had paid for his. His features at first glance could be taken as melancholic, and yet his face was alight with a pleasant glow. If there was an officer on Grey's staff who knew how to enjoy and work a party, it was André. He was as much in his own element as Allen felt himself removed from it.

"Ah, Youngman, you devil," André grinned. "When can I meet you again at the playing table?"

Youngman held up his hands in mock horror. "And lose another sixty-three guineas to you? Not soon, I hope!"

There was a momentary pause, André smiling at Youngman.

"Sir, I spot a fine chase yonder," Youngman announced, gesturing with his empty drink to several women entering the room, "so if you will excuse me."

He bowed slightly to André, who returned the courtesy and quickly withdrew. Allen stood silent, searching inwardly for a way to politely excuse himself as well. André smiled at him while motioning to one of the privates to refill his glass and gestured for Allen to do the same.

"Fool," André whispered. "Lieutenant, if you need to fill your purse with a few pounds, sit down with Youngman. He is a most impetuous fool when it comes to cards."

André watched Youngman over the rim of his glass, now full.

"But do make sure he has money on the table. Those sixty-three guineas, I've yet to see it, though that is a debt from before we sailed from New York. A gentleman should not play with more than he has in his pocket."

"I'll heed that advice, sir."

André looked over at him and smiled. "Then again, Allen, you are Yankee-bred, and I've yet to meet one of you born over here who would play with even a sixpence if you did not see the same on the other side of the table."

André looked over at him and his features softened a bit.

"Sorry, Lieutenant, no insult intended."

Allen tried to smile in return.

André looked to one of the privates behind the table. "Two glasses of claret, young man," he ordered, taking the drinks and turning away.

"Come, Mr. van Dorn, I wish to introduce you to someone."

Allen, genuinely surprised by this positive attention, could only nod. André had had some hard luck. Rumor was he had left England to escape from the anguish of a broken love affair, buying a commission and joining his regiment. Only days later, the regiment had been surrendered, sending the captain into captivity at a remote camp outside Lancaster.

Grey, forever the collector of promising officers, had grabbed André as part of his staff after his exchange. He was supposedly fluent in half a dozen languages, something of a poet and playwright and even an artist, as demonstrated by his satirical sketch in honor of the frigate captain. He represented the beau ideal of a proper officer of the king: cultured, of at least some independent financial means, well spoken, and, as demonstrated on the battlefield, recklessly brave.

"I've been meaning to talk to you," André said softly.

"Sir?"

"We've not had a chance to converse since that night at Paoli."

Allen stiffened. He had hoped that this superior had forgotten that night, which he surely would never forget.

"You were right, you know," André whispered.

"Sir?"

"Just that. You were right. It was out of control. You know the other side did send a letter of protest, which General Howe refuted."

"Of course, we all know that."

"Well, I am shamed by what our men did. But understand, young sir, that in a fight like that, at night, with unloaded weapons on our side, a certain terror and then a frenzy takes hold of a man's soul."

Allen did not reply. All he could picture in his mind was that André's pistol was loaded. How he had pressed it to the temple of the man impaled on his sword and then squeezed the trigger. It was most certainly an act of mercy, and also freed Allen from the deadly embrace of his victim. But still . . .

"We'll talk more later, it is just that I wanted you to know I understood then how you felt and agreed with you. Sadly, there was nothing either of us could do. And, sadly, the result is that I fear it has filled at least some of our opponents with a terrible resolve."

André led the way from the packed room out into the foyer and into a room that had served as Benjamin Franklin's library, three sides of the room filled with bookshelves that reached from floor to ceiling. In quiet moments when off duty, Allen had found this to be a wonderful place of solitude and study. Philadelphia had offered him long hours free of any duties, and here was a place he could find solitude and repose. He was intrigued, especially, by the books on astronomy and philosophy, many of them filled with scribbled marginal notes surely made by the great Franklin himself.

The library was quiet, the party having yet to spill out of the parlor. At the moment it was empty, except for two women, both of striking appearance. One was seated at a bench before what looked to be a small harpsichord, leafing through sheaves of music resting atop it. The other stood behind her.

Both were dressed in the latest fashion of the year, dresses of finest silk, the younger of the two sitting on the bench in bottle-green, the other in pale blue, wigs not too high, both decorated with ribbons of the flag and, in honor of tonight, the royal ensign.

André set his own glass down on a bookshelf, took the two glasses of claret, and offered one to each of the women.

"Lieutenant van Dorn, it is my honor to introduce Miss Peggy Shippen," and as he spoke he held one glass to the young woman sitting on the bench, "and Miss Elizabeth Risher." He offered the second glass to the woman standing behind Peggy.

There were polite nods.

Allen stiffened, eyes meeting Miss Risher's. *Could it possibly be?* he wondered.

"Van Dorn of the van Dorns of New York?" Peggy asked with a bright smile.

Allen nodded, then shook his head.

"No, ma'am, of Trenton."

"Oh, I see," and her smile drifted away.

"Might your father be Emmanuel van Dorn?" Elizabeth asked.

A bit surprised, Allen nodded in the affirmative.

"My dear cousin Rebecca Risher is married to, let's see, I believe your cousin George. I think you and I met several years back at their wedding."

Startled, Allen looked at her closely, trying not to visibly react. She had indeed been at the wedding, a lovely vision he had wished to approach for a dance, though shyness prevented him from doing so.

She smiled in a friendly fashion, came forward and offered her hand.

"Well," André laughed, "one could say you are almost kin."

"I know your family well, sir," Elizabeth continued, "and can affirm they are of fine breeding, gentle manners, and loyal to our king."

She smiled up at him, and he wondered if she knew of his brother Jonathan and his fate.

He held her gaze and waited, as if almost ready for her to drop the next line——that his family business had been a tannery and leather goods, definitely not an acceptable origin for an officer of the British Army.

"I am delighted to see you in the uniform of our king," Elizabeth continued, and something in her gaze seemed to say more. Was it a surprise that he was in such a uniform?

"Elizabeth and I, for the life of us, cannot figure this thing out," Peggy interjected, and she turned and slapped the top of the instrument she was sitting in front of.

André laughed.

"Oh, it is one of Dr. Franklin's infernal devices."

Peggy drew her hands back, as if actually fearful.

André looked over at Allen with a smile.

"I often find you in this room, Lieutenant, perusing Dr. Franklin's library. Would you care to venture what it is?"

Allen, surprised by André's offer, finally smiled.

"It is a glass harmonica."

"A what?" Peggy asked.

Allen motioned to the device and to where Peggy sat. She looked at André, who motioned for her to move. She shot a quick glance at Allen but then surrendered the bench.

With Miss Shippen no longer sitting at the bench, he felt it proper to point toward where her feet would have been.

"The pedals beneath are attached to a drive belt," he announced, squatting down to point at them. Standing, he removed the sheaf of music on top of the instrument and looked around for an appropriate place to deposit the papers. With a smile, André took them.

Allen now opened up the main body of the instrument and the women gazed inside.

Instead of strings there were dozens of glass goblets of various sizes, mounted on a shaft. Sitting down on the bench, Allen began to push on the pedals. The end of the shaft holding the glass goblets moved and within a few seconds they were rotating rapidly.

"It really is some infernal machine," Miss Shippen cried.

André laughed.

"Demonstrate please, Lieutenant," André urged.

A crystal goblet filled with chalk rested next to the instrument. Allen dipped two fingers in, coating them, then lightly touched one of the rotating goblets.

The room was suddenly filled with a strange, unearthly sound, a humming vibration exactly like that emitted when the rim of a crystal glass is vigorously rubbed with a damp finger.

Peggy drew back slightly, and Captain André obviously was more than happy to put a reassuring hand on her shoulder.

Allen tried a few more notes, the tones shifting and then dying away as he stopped pumping the pedals. The glass goblets slowed in their spinning and there was silence.

"Wondrous," Elizabeth whispered.

"And Dr. Franklin created this?" she asked.

Allen nodded.

"Sounds like the cry of a devil to me," Peggy announced.

André chuckled.

"Go on, van Dorn, I've heard you tinkering with it before now. It's why I dragged you in here to explain this thing."

Allen closed his eyes for a moment, surprised that anyone had noticed his attempts. He had only dared to try to play this wondrous instrument when he thought the rest of the staff was out of the house.

He sat silent for a moment and then began to press the pedals. There was a faint whirling sound, like a lathe turning, which in fact was the principle Franklin used when designing this strange instrument. Allen had read that Franklin had a glassblower turn out dozens of sealed goblets of crystal of various sizes, testing each one for proper pitch, before then having them mounted on the rotating shaft.

He touched G-sharp, and slowly worked up a scale, the sound of each note overlapping. With some nervousness, he put both hands on the keyboard and played a short piece by Haydn, one of his concertos, just a few dozen bars. It pleased him that he had hardly made a mistake.

The sound was indeed unearthly——ethereal——something that only someone such as Franklin could have invented. It was, for Allen, soothing and gentle, so unlike the more strident tone of the harpsichord. If anything, it sounded more like a harp brushed by gentle hands.

"I've been loath to try it until now," André announced, "for after all, this is indeed a rare instrument. May I?"

Allen smiled and offered the bench.

André sat down, tinkered for a moment, working the pedals, playing a few scales.

What followed was, for Allen, like a call from heaven, ethereal as only this instrument could create sound, but something far more. The raucous laughter from the party in the other room intruded for a moment, but then seemed to wash away as André more vigorously worked the pedals, volume building, fingers lightly touching the rotating goblets. He at first used but one finger, then two. At one point, though he made several mistakes, he used four fingers.

With a sigh, André leaned back from the instrument, hands falling away, and opened his eyes.

"You've been practicing as well," Allen cried.

André actually seemed a bit embarrassed and could only nod.

"Sir, what was that?" Allen gasped.

"Oh, something by Mozart."

"The Austrian?" Allen asked.

"You know of him?" André replied, a bit of surprise in his voice.

"Yes, sir. Before the war, I was in New York with my father on business and I attended a recital. There was one piece, a concerto by Mozart that haunted me. I have tried to find out anything I could about him, but, with this war . . ."

He fell silent.

The distant haughtiness that characterized André was gone as he looked up at Allen and smiled.

"I actually heard him perform in Salzburg——let's see, it was perhaps four years ago. I was there that summer taking the waters.

"The Germans, their Bach, always Bach, far too heavy for my taste. Mozart is something different. You know what Haydn wrote of him?"

"Such talent comes perhaps but once in a century," Allen replied.

"Yes, exactly!" André cried.

"Sir, do you know anything else by him?" Allen asked.

André smiled.

"Lieutenant, it is John, not sir, this night."

Allen blushed with embarrassment and excitement.

"I have performed my triumph," André replied with a warm smile, "anything else I would surely fumble. But by coincidence I have actually ordered other pieces by him. If the wind is right and rebel raiders do not interdict, copies should arrive shortly from Petracci's of London. I will be delighted to share them with you. One was actually written for this new wonder of Dr. Franklin's. Perhaps we can master them together."

"Thank you, sir," Allen replied warmly.

"Allen, it is John."

And he then offered a most uncharacteristic gesture for any British officer: He extended his hand, which Allen took and shook.

André stood up and retrieved his glass of wine, taking a sip.

"You surprise me, Allen."

"How so?"

"Do not be insulted, but, how do I dare say it . . ."

"A provincial who knows Mozart?" Allen offered, and there was, even though he tried to control it, a bit of a defensive tone in his voice.

"No insult intended, but, yes, I must say yes. I am surprised that word of the Austrian would have reached here."

"Word of many things reaches here," Allen replied, and for the first time since joining Grey's staff he felt he could let his guard down. "Just because we are, as you say, colonials or provincials does not mean that we are an ill-educated lot of bumpkins."

André held up his hand in a gesture of reconciliation. "I did not mean insult."

"No, sir," he hesitated, "I mean John. No insult, but I will say that it could be one reason why I serve with General Grey."

"How is that?"

And as he asked the question, André took another sip of his wine, looking at Allen with an interest that had never been there before.

"Though the Atlantic is wide, and it might take two months or more for the works of Mozart to reach our shore, nevertheless, they do arrive here. And with his work also comes the *London Gazette*, which, in the years before this war, we read with increasing interest and dismay; the latest books from the publishers of London; and, dare I say now, even the writings of Voltaire and Rousseau. In some ways, we are no more distant from London by sail than Edinburgh by wagon if the wind is fair."

"And yet you Americans do seem so distant."

"How so?"

"Recall, I was a prisoner for a year out in the frontier wilds beyond Lancaster."

Allen could not suppress a bit of a laugh.

André bristled slightly. "What is so amusing in that?"

"Nothing, seriously, nothing. Maybe sixty years ago Lancaster was the edge of the frontier, but now? It is a region settled by the Germans who hold against war, the Dunkers and Mennonites, and our own English Quakers. Sorry to beg to differ, but the frontier wilds are now somewhere out near Pittsburgh, three hundred miles westward on the banks of the Ohio."

"I have never seen or been forced to endure such rude, ill-bred, foul-smelling bumpkins in my life," André replied, voice rising slightly, dark complexion reddening. "Barely one in five was literate, they drank to excess, and tobacco seemed to be stuffed into their cheek from the moment they were weaned until they fell into their graves. The promises made when my regiment surrendered under what I thought were honorable terms were ignored. They are a different race altogether and not Englishmen."

He hesitated, his anger showing, and he checked himself. "Not subjects of the Crown as I would know them."

"And yet I am a subject of the Crown, am I not?"

André smiled. "Yes."

"And yet the men who held you captive, are they not still subjects of the Crown?"

André shook his head. "Damn them, yes they are. Rebels, though, but, yes, they must be subjects of the Crown and conform to that."

He looked at Peggy and Elizabeth, who stood silent.

"My pardon, ladies, for my rude words."

"Oh, I do agree with you, though," Peggy replied. "When men like that would come to my father's office he would joke afterwards that he would need to bathe immediately afterwards."

Elizabeth laughed politely but said nothing.

"I agree with you, John," Allen replied. "But we must realize that most are men who fled Scotland and Ireland, or are the poorest of England and Germany. They came here to seek a new life. They did not come here necessarily to flee our king. If treated with fairness, I daresay, and I wish to believe, that many would renew their allegiance. That is why I stand on this side. Together England and this America, united, could reach to the Mississippi and beyond. Torn apart, though, it will be France, Spain, or others that shall rule here in the end."

"Precisely my point. But instead, these rude bumpkins and that turncoat Washington will lie in bed with the French?" André hesitated, looking at the two women. "Again my apologies. I fear that I do not hold my wine well this evening, and have let my passions take rein."

Peggy smiled at him.

"No offense whatsoever, Captain André. I most fully agree. The French are such detestable creatures and I am disgusted that neighbors and former countrymen of mine seek their aid."

"They have no recourse left," Allen replied somewhat heatedly.

"So do I infer that you agree with their courting the French?" André asked coolly.

"No, of course not. It is why I am in this uniform. I believe in a united British Empire just as much as you do, sir."

André forced a smile and nodded.

"I regret the treatment you received while a prisoner," Allen offered. "Do not assume for an instant, John, that such is the manner of all here on this side of the Atlantic. The rebels are but a small portion, a very small portion, of those who reside here. Most of us wish for an ending to this fratricidal war, a return of peace, and the king's fair justice." He hesitated for an instant and then continued. "A king's justice free of the manipulations of some who have created this tragedy."

"Who are you referring to?"

"I think we both know the answer to that," Allen replied.

"Would you put Benjamin Franklin in such a category?" Elizabeth interjected, and both turned to her with surprise at her sudden entry into the conversation.

"Dr. Franklin?" Allen asked. "All admire him as the greatest scientist and philosopher of our age."

"And yet he did sign the Declaration," Elizabeth replied.

"I would prefer to think the rashness of the moment informed that decision," André stated. "General Grey and Lord Howe have attempted repeatedly to extend the utmost courtesy and understanding to him, and yet even now he is in Versailles plotting against his rightful king."

"Perhaps we should ask why he is there, rather than here," and as she spoke, Allen felt her gaze lingering on him.

André laughed softly.

"At least we have the courtesy of his house," he said, forcing a laugh from the others, "and let the world observe we repay him by respecting his property and not despoiling it the way the French or Russians would."

Allen nodded in agreement.

"And I pray that my countrymen take note of that."

"Your countrymen?" Peggy asked, and now her gaze, rather than innocent, was sharply focused on him.

"Yes, our countrymen," Allen replied. "Yours as well, Miss Shippen."

There was a long pause.

"Oh there you are, André!"

The four turned. General Grey stood in the doorway of the library, beside him a captain of the navy who, from André's satirical sketch, Allen recognized as their guest, and the excuse for this evening's party.

"I've been looking all over for you. Besides your valiant effort at art in honor of our guest of the evening, I hear rumor that you have created a few lines of classical poetry."

André turned away from Allen and offered a formal salute to Grey and then the captain.

"Oh, champion of Britannia, thou son of Neptune," André announced. "Is it time for me to embarrass myself with that bit of doggerel?"

Grey smiled. "Your audience awaits."

André turned back to Allen. "My friend, and from tonight I think our love of fine music at least unites us, let us master this device of Franklin and I will attempt to teach you that piece by Mozart." André again extended his hand and Allen clasped it.

"Thank you, sir."

"John, from now on it is John. I must confess I have, shall I say, a certain antipathy for some whom I've met on this alien shore since this war began, but you, Allen, you are an Englishman at heart."

André next turned to Miss Shippen and extended his arm.

"Good lady, I would be honored if you would stand by my side while I attempt not to embarrass myself with this performance."

She smiled coyly, obviously pleased by the attention, and took his arm.

"Your audience awaits you, sir," Grey repeated with a smile. The small entourage left, Allen undecided if he should follow.

As André stepped into the parlor, where the party was in full swing, applause erupted at the sight of the frigate captain, Grey clasping him by the elbow, and André with Peggy at his side. Allen let them go, turning back to the glass harmonica. Sitting down, he slowly pressed the pedals, rotating the lathe so slowly that when he pressed C-sharp minor there was barely a whisper. From where he sat, he could see directly into the parlor, and could hear shouts of laughter and cheers as Grey called for a toast first for the captain and then for André, who had been convinced by a drunken major to stand atop one of the chairs, "putting your foot where Franklin's fat backside once rested." A momentary glance from André across the corridor to Allen suggested that André felt uncomfortable with the major's words.

Allen was tempted to join the crowd. They were, after all, his comrades, and though shyness at times crippled him, he knew that most of the men of Grey's command had come to accept him, not in any way as their social equal, but at least for his coolness and bravery under fire, his ability to inspire troops by his calm demeanor, and his open loyalty to Grey.

André began to declaim his hastily written poem:

Oh the crashing of thunder and of guns
When Britannia's brave sons
Sailed forth to smite traitors about to run . . .

Allen went to the library door and, standing behind it, let it slip nearly closed. He returned to the strange instrument created by Franklin, and pressed the pedals, feeling the slight vibration of the turning lathe. Touching a key, he tried to remember on what note André had begun Mozart's gentle piece. Finding it to have been C major, he let memory drift and picked out a few more notes, playing out the first few chords. Cheers and shrieks of laughter erupted from the other room. He half caught a bit of the poem alluding to the less than legitimate nature of the lineage of those whom "Britannia's sons" face upon the open seas.

"I thought you might wish for something to eat."

Startled, he looked up.

It was Elizabeth Risher, bearing a china plate in one hand, upon it a slice of steaming apple pie covered in cream. In the other hand she was balancing two glasses of wine.

Fumbling, he stood up, not sure how to respond as she offered one of the glasses to him and motioned for him to sit back down, setting the plate atop the lid of the glass harmonica.

"Am I interrupting you, sir?"

"Please, miss, just Allen is fine."

"And Elizabeth for me."

He nervously smiled.

She sipped her glass of wine and put it down.

"Too sweet, this claret, frankly, a bit of cider would be better," she offered and then smiled, "perhaps even some hard cider."

He could not help but laugh softly.

"You handled yourself well with the captain," she offered.

He could not reply.

"He really is a charming man. Typically English in so many ways, but beneath that a man of noble bearing, and if he has befriended you, he will stand by your side. Really he is a good soul. My friend Peggy, I think, is quite interested in him."

"He is a gentleman, to be certain," Allen offered.

"And so very English, if you know what I mean," Elizabeth replied with a smile. "Sadly, they come over here, can live here for years, but in the end never understand who we really are."

Allen grinned. "Yes, he is a noble soul."

"My friend is totally smitten with him."

"Oh, really?"

"As some folks say, I think she has set her cap for him."

He fumbled again, not sure how to reply, and Elizabeth laughed.

"So many of my friends have set their caps for the English and even the Hessian officers now with us this winter."

"Well," Allen offered, "they can be a charming, well-bred lot."

Elizabeth wrinkled her nose, and he found the gesture to be absolutely touching.

"And you, miss?"

"Sir, you are being impertinent with such an inquiry!" She said it with a laugh, and they both smiled.

"I do remember you from my cousin's wedding," Allen ventured.

"And I you. Why didn't you request a dance with me that night?"

He reddened at her brash directness.

"I feared," he stumbled.

"Feared what?"

"That you would refuse. Or that you would accept. Either would have been painful. I am not very good at dancing. And the end result would have been embarrassment for both of us. I did not wish to subject you or me to that."

She laughed and he found that thrilling. Shaking her head, she let her hand rest on his forearm for an instant. "I have, as they say, two left feet. Peggy can dance all night long and charm the entire room. But not I. That is why it is convenient for me to hide here while she holds forth over there." She gestured to the next room.

"If you had asked me to dance, Allen van Dorn, we would have been a good match."

She chuckled softly and, as if embarrassed, motioned to the pie, but he was too taken with her to wish to eat now.

There was a long moment of silence, the two looking off in different directions.

"Yet you play music well. With such a refined appreciation of music, surely you can dance as well."

"You have yet to see me dance," Allen offered with a nervous smile.

"My cousin and yours were a handsome couple, were they not, when they were wed?" she offered, a wistful note in her voice.

"Yes. I know he loved her dearly."

"I know she adored him."

She hesitated and then lowered her voice.

"How is he?" she asked in a conspiratorial whisper. "Have you heard from him at all? She is in agony wanting to know if he is safe."

"Not since the war started. Last I heard he was with a Pennsylvania regiment."

"Those poor boys," she sighed. "Rebecca last heard of him before the fighting at Brandywine, not a word since."

"She shouldn't worry too much," Allen offered lamely, "the post now rarely carries letters through the line."

If he had survived Brandywine, surely he would by now have written a reassuring letter to her.

"We all hear rumors, though. What the," she hesitated, "what the Continental army is enduring up at Valley Forge."

"Perhaps his regiment was sent elsewhere," he offered. "It's reported a number of regiments from Pennsylvania were sent to garrison Lancaster, Reading, York, or even out toward Pittsburgh. We have word many of them left the ranks at the start of the new year. Maybe he was discharged and simply cannot return home now until this war is over."

"I've heard the same, but it is small comfort for her. She is due in another month."

"Really?"

She blushed slightly.

"Yes, really."

"Where is she now?"

"Back here in Philadelphia, with her parents. They insisted she return home from Trenton, saying she needed proper care. She's had a difficult time of it, and they feared she might lose the child, and that she is in danger as well. Her family knows Dr. Rush, who they hoped would be with her when her time came, but he is off in York, so they are frantic with worry as to who will attend her."

Allen was thoroughly abashed by the turn of the conversation and could not reply.

"Damn this war," Elizabeth sighed.

He nodded, still unable to speak, not surprised or taken aback at all by her sudden bitterness or choice of words.

"Your family, are they well?" he finally asked.

"My parents, yes." She hesitated. "I recall a brother of yours."

"James?"

"No, your youngest, Jonathan. A sweet lad." She smiled.

"He did ask me to dance even when you would not. All flustered and blushing when he did so. He must have stepped on my toes a dozen times. He was such a sweet, innocent lad."

"He's dead," Allen said, voice barely a whisper.

Sitting by his side, she reached out, resting her hand on his arm. He could feel her hand trembling.

"I heard rumors, but wasn't sure if they were true," she whispered, voice suddenly choked. "Rebecca said he was sick and died after the battle. I'm so sorry, Allen, I didn't want to believe it. You know how it is with this war——so many rumors, and you are not sure what to believe."

Allen lowered his head.

"He was with the rebels. They never should have put him in the ranks that day," he said bitterly, as he fought for control of his emotions. "He was still a boy. So sick that when they pulled out of Trenton after the fight, I helped to carry him back to the ferry and across the river. He died that evening."

She squeezed his arm again, leaning closer.

"Go on, I would like to hear if it does not pain you too much."

"He actually took me prisoner," and he shook his head, sighing. "He joined the rebels and I joined the Loyalists. What more is there to say? When the Hessians occupied Trenton, I was assigned to be on the staff of Colonel Rall since I can speak a bit of German. I hoped I could bring my village and the German soldiers to an understanding with each other. I saw that as my duty to the Crown and also to my family and neighbors, and to this day I do not regret it.

"After the battle, Jonathan actually was the one to take me prisoner, along with his comrades. Maybe you recall young Peter Wellsley?"

She shook her head.

"One of his comrades."

He sighed. "They found me in my parents' house. I was taken prisoner. I gave my parole so I could help tend to him. I didn't go with the Hessians into captivity but was allowed instead to go with the rebel army as they crossed back over the river. He was dying even as we marched, but they wouldn't let us stop. Jonathan was never all that strong. The march to Trenton and back killed him that day, but that didn't stop them from using him. He was gone an hour after we crossed back over the river."

His voice trailed off.

"I'm so sorry, Allen," she whispered. "I regret asking now."

"The following day, Peter Wellsley," he continued, as if not even hearing her words of sympathy, "went to General Washington and asked for my release without terms or condition."

"Washington actually heard him?"

"Yes, he heard me, too."

"Tell me?" And there was suddenly a curious light in her eyes.

"I did not ask for release. I was willing to go into captivity with the Hessians. I had signed to serve and felt it my duty to go with them. I told Washington that. He replied that in exchange for the service and sacrifice of my brother, he was willing to sign my release without exchange if I agreed to honor the conventions of war and not reveal anything that I saw. I did not see that as a violation, so I agreed. I went back to Trenton to see to my parents and tell them about Jonathan, but when the Continentals returned there a week later I went to Princeton to join with Cornwallis. It was there that General Grey took notice of me and I was recruited to be his liaison for working with the Loyalists in Jersey. He asked me about what I saw while with the rebels, I told him I was honor-bound not to reply, and he actually smiled, then asked me to join his command."

She squeezed his arm again and then pulled her hand back as if she had overstepped propriety.

"I am so sorry about your brother."

"He was a noble soul."

"Yet he died fighting for the rebels."

"He was still a noble soul," Allen replied softly, looking straight into her eyes, and she did not lower her gaze.

"Why, then, are you fighting on the Loyalist side," she asked, "if you feel that way?"

"Because this is where my duty calls me."

"Yet Washington treated you justly, even with compassion."

"That is the tragedy of all of this," Allen sighed. "We are not that dissimilar. Take Captain André. Until tonight I felt a distance from him that could not be bridged. And yet we did find common ground here in this room." He touched Franklin's invention as he spoke. "We share the same blood and heritage. If we fracture apart, if the rebels join themselves to the French, what then? Some say Washington is another Cromwell or Caesar in the making. I cannot believe that. But those around him, perhaps yes. If we stay with the king we can be a nation secured. The waters my brother was willing to wade into are driven by passions. Perhaps his dream will come true if they win, but I fear not."

"But if your fears are ill founded?"

"Then that will be a miracle," Allen replied.

"Don't you believe in miracles?"

He looked back at her and smiled.

"Do I detect something of the rebel in you, Miss Risher?"

She arched her back slightly and looked at him defiantly.

"And so what if you do?"

He laughed softly.

"Your secret is safe with me. For after all, it could be said we are kin by marriage, are we not?"

She relaxed and smiled.

"So my secret is evident?" she offered.

"I think more than one lady here tonight is at heart a rebel."

"More than a few," she replied. "And still more than a few will cheer for the winning side when all is done."

"And you?"

"The Shippens are family friends, which is why I am here. She is only sixteen, and her parents insisted that a friend must attend to her. So this old spinster of twenty-four is here as a result."

"You could have stayed home."

She laughed softly.

"My parents have been Loyalists from the start. I have a brother with the Royal Navy. But, if I might be so bold, Allen, there is a bountiful table in the next room and my parents did urge me that a meal in exchange for a few dances was not degrading for a lady and might help insure her position if this army is here to stay."

She looked at him, eyes suddenly cold. "Or do you see that as the selling of myself?"

"Never," Allen cried, "I meant no insult."

She forced a smile.

"Well, that pie is good," she offered.

"I'll try some later. But you did not answer my question. Are you a rebel at heart?"

She laughed softly.

"What do you think?"

"I think you are."

"That is bold of you, sir, to think you know a woman's heart, and when we have been but barely introduced."

He blushed and she laughed softly. He dared to look back at her. Her blue eyes were radiant, her figure slender, and he remembered that at his cousin's wedding, wisps of blonde hair had peeked out from beneath her wig. He did not dare to admit how the memory of her had haunted him afterwards, how he had cursed himself as a fool for not having the bravery to ask for a dance, while his innocent, fumbling brother of but fifteen had gone up to her, she at least five years his senior, and begged for a dance.

And now to see her again, tonight, years later.

"Do you think less of me for staying with the king?" he asked nervously.

"No, of course not. You went where you felt duty called you. But, still, is it not all so tragic, after all? Your brother gone. My cousin with child not sure if the father of that child is alive. Even those officers in that next room, laughing, cheering——so many of them are torn from families and loved ones."

They paused as if listening. André had finished with his poem of praise for the naval captain, and a lively dance was now taking place.

"And more than a few of them, as well, absolute rakes, I dare say. A woman can barely walk on Market Street without being accosted."

"Has anyone been trouble for you?" he asked protectively.

"Would you fight a duel for me if I said yes?"

He was flustered, but nodded his head, and she laughed.

"Oh, Mr. Allen van Dorn, you really are a provincial."

He was not sure how to react.

"Now eat that pie before it is too cold. I daresay there are thousands up in Valley Forge tonight who would give a month's pay for such a repast."

She took the plate and offered it to him. Unable to resist, he did as ordered. As he ate, she sat silent, watching him. He was too embarrassed to stop until he had carried out her order.

Finished with the pie, he set the plate back and looked over at her.

"So tell me about this Mozart that you and Captain André so admire."

He rambled on for several minutes until sensing that she was simply being polite. But he was now somewhat lost as he launched into the brilliance of the mathematics of the works of Bach, which lacked this new soul of music that Mozart was creating.

"Think you can play it?" she asked.

"Mozart?"

"Yes."

"I'm not sure. Let me see." He straightened himself, turned back to the instrument, pressed the pedals, and, feeling that Franklin's device was ready, pressed a key. Again that soft, strange sound.

"Can I try?"

"But of course!"

He continued to press the pedals as she randomly touched the keyboard, exclaiming with childlike delight at what she created.

A bit of a tune started and he was surprised by her audacity. It was "Chester," the marching song of the rebels.

She played but a few bars and then sat back, looking at him with a smile.

"So you are a rebel!" he said softly.

"Perhaps. Or perhaps I just like the tune. Now to the Mozart," she said.

Trying to remember what André had played, he gently touched the keyboard, worked out a few chords, and began. After a few attempts she joined him, the two playing together.

They were so absorbed in their joint effort that neither of them noticed John André, who had been standing in the doorway ever since she had played the few chords of "Chester." Nor did they see his sad smile as he turned and went back to join the party in the other room.

Nor did André see Allen's right hand and her left brushing together as they played, Allen trembling with a thrill of delight as they touched.

CHAPTER EIGHT

✳ ✳ ✳

"Do we all clearly understand General Washington's orders?"

Anthony Wayne paced down the line of men. They were ragged, filthy. They stank and looked like scarecrows, but most of them were grinning as Mad Anthony continued down the line.

"It's about time. We're with you, General, now let's go!" someone cried, and a cheer went up.

Wayne grinned, stalked back to the front of the column, and mounted, motioning for them to follow his lead. When the dozen wagons in the column, each pulled by a team of four bony horses, bogged down in the mud of the road within a hundred yards after they set off, the hundred infantry accompanying him put their shoulders to the wheels and tailgates of the wagons to force them along.

A typical late January thaw had set in, temperature well into the forties. Fortunately, with the sky clear and no threat of rain for at least the next few days, they could yet move forward. Rain now would render the roads entirely useless. Wayne's first target had been carefully chosen. He had set a goal for this command, a command he had never wanted, but now, stuck with the task, by God, he would fulfill it.

They dropped down into a gentle hollow, a bit of morning mist clinging above the muddy, swollen creek. Men had to push and shove the wagons through the mud on the opposite slope and back up the hill. Still he heard little complaining, the troops seemingly feeling as if they were almost on holiday.

Gaining the crest, Wayne looked back. After more than five weeks, the encampment at Valley Forge was taking on the semblance of an actual military post and not just a gathering of beggars. Regimental streets lined with cabins were spread across the upper plain. Orders for this day were to save on firewood and to let fires in each cabin die down until dusk.

The last of the shelters were supposed to be finished by the end of the week. Men focused their limited energies on corduroying roads with saplings and brush. Those not assigned to firewood duty or excused by illness——which now afflicted more than a third of the men in the ranks——were to fall out for fatigue duty to build the fortified lines guarding all approaches, the battery positions atop Mount Joy and Mount Misery, and the bridge to their rear across the Schuylkill, which would be their bolt hole if ever attacked.

The prospect of that threat, at least for the next several days, was nil. At daily officers' call this morning, at dawn, the general had, as was his custom, reviewed the reports of the day before. He had included, in general outline—— for he never revealed his private sources——the latest intelligence from Philadelphia, New York, and elsewhere. There were no indications of any planned movement. No reports of officers in Philadelphia calling for last-minute repairs of equipment, unusual movements of their patrols, or the telltale preparation of three days of marching rations, reshoeing of horses, and the issuance of fresh cartridge and ball. The latest intelligence was about a party hosted by General Grey to honor some Royal Navy captain who had brought in a captured American ship laden with much-needed supplies for the Continental Army, now to be used or simply burned by the British in Philadelphia. The mere mention of Grey's name of course triggered a grumbling reaction from Wayne, who had personally sworn to face the man one on one before this war was over and cut his heart out. Outrage at British atrocities in Paoli by Grey's command still rankled that deeply in Wayne's mind.

Besides, given the thaw of the last few days, it was one thing to move a dozen wagons and a hundred men in this quagmire. But an army? They'd bog down into utter chaos and collapse in less than three miles. The first troops to pass would make the roads impassable for the rest of the army.

The wind blew fair on their faces, providing even a touch of warmth in the air. More than a few of the men had stripped off their foot wrappings, which would otherwise have turned into heavy, clogged weights, and ventured ahead barefooted in the mud, one of the men exclaiming with a certain joy when he hit the warm droppings of the horses laboring ahead of the wagons.

After a steady hour of marching, they reached the banks of the river, passing through the small village of Phoenixville. Word of their approach had spread before them; the houses of more than a few farms they passed along the way were boarded up tight, owners having fled, taking with them their cattle and supplies, leaving behind but a servant or two to keep an eye on the place. In Phoenixville the few shops were boarded shut as well, except for a tavern of a known patriot, who stood outside his doorway, waving to Wayne at his approach. A couple of the tavern keeper's sons rolled out a few small barrels of beer, and the gesture was met with huzzahs from the men and a promise from Wayne to those marching with him that, at midday, when their task was completed, they could each have a fair portion. He did a quick calculation. The barrels looked to be about ten gallons total. At a gallon per ten men, it would be just under a pint per soldier, and that would be fine. They would avoid the trouble that might have been caused if it had been rum instead.

The road ahead was fairly level, bordered by orchards, pastures, and fields of corn stubble and winter wheat that shone green in the morning light. Farmers watched apprehensively as they passed. Most of the men stood stoic and silent. A few, though, came down to greet the troops. A woman came down bearing a large basket heavy with warm biscuits, but not enough for all. Wayne ordered that the offering go to the lads who needed it the most, and the woman received three rousing cheers as they passed.

She beamed with delight, tears in her eyes. "My son, Jimmy Ferguson, is with the First Continental Foot, and you tell that rascal to come home and see his mother," she cried. "Can you do that, General?"

Wayne nodded, and made a pretense of turning to one of his aides, telling him to note the boy's name, find him, and give him a pass for three days. With that, the woman burst into tears of gratitude and came out from behind the gate. She made to kiss Wayne's hand.

"Madam, it is I who should kiss your hand in gratitude for your son's patriotic service," he replied solemnly, averting his eyes.

He rode on, noting the farm, marking it for later. He recalled the boy's name and had not the heart to tell her that her son was on the roll of the dead, the flux having taken him a week ago. He would send one of his staff back later to break the news to her.

They pressed on, along the banks of the Schuylkill, gently rolling farmland, perhaps the richest in all the Americas, fertile with topsoil six feet deep in places. The river in the spring ran full with shad; apple trees bent nearly double in the autumn with their offerings. Connecticut had been good land, well tended by hardworking Yankee farmers, but here, all one needed to do was cast seed upon the ground and, four months later, bring in the bounty.

And that bounty is what he now sought, the first target in his new command.

Boys came out from houses, circling the men, laughing, playing at being soldiers. The men tolerated them with smiles. More than a few of the older ones in his ranks, thinking of sons——even, for some, grandsons——were visibly moved. A couple fought tears as they patted the boys on the heads, allowing them to play with their equipment for a few moments, to carry their heavy muskets or to wear a bedraggled cap.

The boys were indication enough to him of what he should do next. Excited boys could spread word faster, it seemed, than any mounted courier. Wayne now ordered his few staff and the small detachment of mounted dragoons to gallop ahead, outracing word of their approach if it were still possible to do so.

The men clattered off with delighted shouts, mud spraying up from their mounts as the rest of the column of infantry staggered on behind them. A couple of the men began to grumble that they had been marching for nearly three hours without a break, but a look back by Wayne stilled their complaints. There was really no serious complaining, though, just typical grumbling, for they all knew the reward ahead.

The day slowly increased in warmth——another five to ten degrees and it would be springlike. The warming breeze out of the southwest blew at their backs, the sun baking away a bit of the moisture on the road so that the going became easier, though the deep frost from earlier in January was still working its way up out of the ground.

At last he saw his goal for today. His half-dozen mounted dragoons and staff were out on the road, one of the men with sword drawn. As ordered, the rest were waiting for his arrival. He nudged his mount and cantered ahead of the column to join his advance guard.

It was Johansson's mill, one of the most prosperous on the midreaches of the Schuylkill River. He and several of his staff had ridden up here several days earlier, as if heading toward Reading, and had studied it carefully in passing. But they had not stopped——to avoid arousing suspicion. Careful inquiries at a tavern just south of Pottstown, six miles farther on, revealed that, though not an overt Tory, old Johansson kept his cards close as to his loyalties.

Millers were men with whom all farmers had a relationship of both love and hate. For grinding the farmers' wheat and corn, millers traditionally charged one-tenth of the crop. If he had enough clients, in a month or more in the autumn a miller could garner far more from twenty farmers than all their hard labor of plowing, hoeing, weeding, harvesting, and threshing would provide for any one farmer in a year. Every one of them doubted a miller's weights when it came time to measure back the ground corn, wheat, barley, and rye. None had ever seen a penniless miller, and more than a few farmers were forced to turn to them for loans of cash when times were hard. This was not to say that all millers were bad sorts——more than a few were held in esteem as men of Christian charity. If a farmer had had a bad year, the miller would keep but a fraction for himself, and what he did keep would usually then go to a local pastor to be given to the poor.

Johansson, though, was spoken of in the tavern as a man known for a hard bargain. It was said that if you turned your back while he was measuring out the grain and held up a mirror, you'd see his thumb on the scales.

However, there was no denying that he was a hardworking man, having built his mill nearly forty years before. The enterprise was now largely run by sons and grandsons. A sluice into the Schuylkill fed water into a millpond, which had enough drop via a wooden pipe made of barrels cobbled and tarred together to feed two overshot wheels.

As he rode up and dismounted, Anthony could hear the workings of the machinery within. Waterwheels connected to drive shafts, which in turn rotated two stone gristmills. Raw corn, wheat, whatever was to be ground that day would be unloaded from wagons via an upper ramp, shoveled in by Johansson's ever laboring sons and grandsons, down into a chute to the grindstones, with a near endless stream of flour raining out to be bagged and loaded aboard wagons at the lower level. So powerful were the headwaters of the mill that in the off-season, when flour was not to be made, mechanical gears would be shifted and power diverted to operate a sawmill to turn out clapboard for house siding and floorboards. It even had a fine-toothed saw that could cut chestnut and walnut into wainscoting for paneling.

It was quite a prosperous industry that Johan Johansson ran. For lack of a better choice for this morning's operation, given the rumors of his, at best, neutral leanings, Anthony had decided he would start here with his task, heading out far into the countryside beyond Valley Forge rather than beginning closer to home.

As he rode up, the old man was outside his mill, glaring defiantly at the dragoons whom Anthony had ordered to do nothing more than surround the establishment until his arrival.

Gray beard quivering, Johansson stormed over to Anthony.

"What, sir, is the meaning of this?" he cried. "These ruffians ride up, they even drive off one of my customers in a panic! What is it you are doing?"

He pointed up the road toward Pottstown, where a heavily laden wagon was retreating, the farmer aboard standing, lashing his horses onward. The back of the oversized wagon was piled high with unground wheat.

"Sergeant Olsen, fetch that wagon back here," Wayne announced calmly, and with a grin the sergeant galloped off. Then he turned his attention back to Johansson.

"I am General Anthony Wayne of the Continental Army, currently encamped at Valley Forge," he began.

"Mad Anthony, is it?" Johansson sniffed, looking up at him defiantly. Anthony forced a smile.

It was a nickname he rather liked, and if that was how this miller wished to address him, so be it; it would help in the dealings he was now embarking upon.

"Yes, I am Mad Anthony Wayne, and I am here to requisition supplies for the Continental Army."

"The devil you say," Johansson snapped, though Wayne could see the man looking nervously back down the road toward the approaching wagons.

Anthony dismounted, brushing the mud off his legs, and approached the man, who towered above him. He looked to be in his midsixties, but his shoulders and neck were those of a bull. Clearly a man who had labored for years at his mill, shouldering hundredweight bags, carved out his own grindstones, built the dams and sluices to divert the river both to and away from his mill, so that in those times of flood that so often wiped out many a miller, he could be up the following morning and, just by cleaning out the sluiceways of mud and flotsam, back at work. He had every reason to be proud of his life's work, and in a way Anthony pitied him for what had to be done. But pity would not stay his hand when he thought of the men back at Valley Forge.

"Your coin, sir?" Johansson said coldly.

"A voucher signed by General George Washington himself, payable in hard cash when presented to the Congress or a legal representative thereof."

"Damn, is that the game today?" Johansson roared. "I knew it would come to this!

"Jacob, Ebenezer, Jeremiah!"

At his call, three men, obviously his sons, all of them bearded as well, all with powerful shoulders and thickset bodies, came out from the upper entryway to the mill, one of them carrying a shotgun.

The dragoons behind Wayne instantly reacted, drawing their carbines. Several of the men cocked their weapons and raised them.

"Stand at ease, men," Wayne snapped, not looking back but with his gaze still warily fixed on the three giants approaching.

He stepped closer to the old man.

"Look down that road," he hissed, pointing to the advancing column of infantry and wagons.

Johansson gave a quick sidelong glance.

"We can settle this one of two ways. Either you comply or you fight. I admire your grit, sir. I would react the same if all was reversed. But there are nine thousand starving soldiers back at Valley Forge, and by General Washington and the great Jehovah I am tasked with feeding them. And I shall feed them. Do I make myself clear?"

Johansson, bristling, began to reply, then looked again at the approaching column now less than a hundred yards off, at the dragoons behind Wayne, and then back at his three sons.

"We fight them, father?" one of his sons asked, obviously more than a little frightened at the display of force. His shotgun was no longer leveled but now pointed at the ground.

Johansson threw out his arms in a gesture of exasperation.

"Put the gun back inside, Jeremiah," he sighed.

His son seemed more than happy to comply.

"When can I have this voucher?" Johansson asked.

"You can stand beside me and count every pound loaded. I will countersign it. Given the current situation, I regret to say you must carry it to York for payment, but your troubles are but a single drop in an ocean of woe at this moment, sir. This is war. If I do not do this, nine thousand men will starve tomorrow."

"Damn your war," Johansson snapped.

"It is your war, too."

Johansson sniffed derisively.

"Fellow countrymen, weapons pointed at me. Is this your idea of liberty?"

"For the moment, it is the necessity from which liberty will spring, yes, sir," Wayne replied coldly.

The head of the column was up, the men slowing at the sight of the dragoons, weapons still leveled. The men at the front of the column were now unslinging muskets and holding them half ready.

"Shall we begin?" Wayne asked, but it was most definitely a statement now, and no longer a question.

Johansson muttered a curse, stepped aside, and gestured to the open door of the mill.

"You are the highwaymen now, Mad Anthony, but, by God, I will count every peck that you take."

Wayne turned back to the men with the wagons.

"One at a time, to the lower level."

He looked over to a barn slightly upslope from the mill.

"Two wagons up there as well. Sergeant Travis, you were a miller, were you not?"

"Yes, sir," Travis grinned. "And had a damn sight better mill than this on the Housatonic, I can tell you."

"Sons of bitches," Johansson cried, "robbed by New England Yankees, no less."

Travis laughed as he came up to Johansson's side.

"You stay with Mr. Johansson here, make sure the count is fair," Wayne ordered. "And no miller's count, damn your eyes!"

Travis handed his musket off to a comrade.

"Come along, old man," Travis said with a grin. "I'll make sure you aren't cheated, and I'll even help you cheat them a bit if you work with me."

Wayne saw that bringing Travis along had been a smart move. Johansson seemed to find some comfort in a fellow of the same trade. The two went inside, Wayne following behind.

Within the mill there was a cacophony of noise. The mill was in full operation. Both wheels were turning, wooden gears rattling, drive shafts turning the millstones on the lower floor. A farmer, wagon half off loaded and caught by surprise, stood silent, glaring at Wayne, who made mention that he would be compensated and then stepped past him rather than hear yet more complaints.

Since boyhood he had been fascinated by such contrivances, machines that, once constructed, could do the labor of a hundred men. With the temporary thaw, the Schuylkill was running at full flow, some of the rising waters diverted by sluices into the miller's upper pond. Cold water flowed in a torrent over the twin waterwheels, which, during the freeze of the previous weeks, had most likely been locked solid.

Now was the time for grinding down the late fall harvest, and he had timed this raid to match that. A few weeks ago this place would most likely have been idle. Now it was in full, flourishing operation.

The farmer with the wagonload of wheat looked sullenly at Wayne, saying nothing as Wayne inspected the clanking gears, the turning grindstones a floor below. Off to the left in the work area below, the mill-powered saws stood motionless. Beyond them was a stack of several thousand board feet of fresh-cut lumber, planks ten feet long, a foot wide, and a couple of inches thick. He marked them. If the bounty of sacks of milled flour, corn meal, rye, and barley did not fill his wagons, he would round out the rest with the lumber. A few hundred planks would help with the corduroying of the roads or would serve as siding for one of the hospitals to keep out dangerous drafts. Gearing was also hooked to a bellows for a forge, and there was even a small drop hammer for fashioning iron and the cutting of nails, several barrels filled with them.

He climbed down a ladder to the lower level, where his men were already eagerly at work, hoisting up fifty- and hundredweight bags of flour and ground meal and carrying them out to the army wagons.

"Those are not really mine," Johansson protested. "Their owners will sue me for certain if they come back here and I have nothing to show!"

"Sergeant Travis, make proper note."

Travis, log book open, simply nodded, offering a few words of condolence to Johansson as he meticulously checked off each bag and its weight when the men dropped the bags on scales, waited for a measurement, then hauled them out and tossed them into the wagons.

Each bag had already been stenciled with the name of the farmer who owned it, and Wayne felt a moment of pity for the miller who would have to explain to dozens of clients why their ground flour and corn had disappeared. Lawyers in nearby towns would be delighted for months to come with the suits that would most likely follow.

"Hey, General, you gotta see this!"

One of the men he had sent to the upper barn was standing excitedly before him, shifting back and forth from foot to foot with excitement.

Wayne smiled and followed. It was Corporal Garner, one of the best foragers of his old command. If any man could smell out supplies it would be him.

He followed Garner up to the barn. Inside was indeed a treasure trove that made Wayne's mouth water. Dozens of hams hung from the rafters, well smoked, more than a few of the men having obviously already cut off a slice for themselves——strictly against orders, but, frankly, he could not blame them. Half a dozen dairy cows on the hoof were in the barn, looking wide-eyed at the new arrivals and, if filled with any sense of consciousness, fully aware of their fate before the day was done. Sacks of ground meal lined the wall of the barn.

In the upper loft rested hundredweight upon hundredweight of mown hay for the cattle, fodder that his starved horses would greet as eagerly as he would a well-seasoned whiskey or rum.

Garner excitedly led the way to the back of the barn, where a couple of men, armed with spades, were hard at work, having already unearthed a fifty-gallon barrel.

Oh, God, Wayne sighed. A barrel of corn liquor. With much heaving and grunting, they pulled it up from its place of concealment.

The men looked expectantly at the general.

"Well, Garner, find me a cup to test this. It could be a wicked Tory plot to poison us."

Garner unclipped his own cup from his haversack belt and offered it, even as the men tilted the barrel, one of them taking the cup and holding it under the spigot.

All stood silent as Wayne took a sip.

My God, he sighed inwardly, this is good. Most likely aged in this oak cask for at least several years.

He took another sip and then looked at the men.

Fifty gallons, a hundred men. Come tomorrow he would face a court-martial before Washington if he let this brew loose to his command.

He looked at the grinning Garner and his three confederates.

"Listen carefully, you bastards," he snapped, forcing himself to make a deliberate show of emptying the rest of his cup on the ground.

"When I leave here, a quarter gill apiece to each of you and, damn you, not a word to the others. And I mean that. If any of you even remotely appears to be drunk, I'll have you all flogged through the camp.

"Do we understand each other?"

"But of course, General," Garner replied.

"Garner?"

"Sir?"

"This liquor is for the sick and injured only."

"Of course, sir."

"Garner, when the surgeons took off your nephew's leg for the frostbite and rot last month, what would you have done to give the poor lad a sip of this to ease his pain before dying?"

Garner stiffened.

"Yes, sir," he whispered. "Of course I'll see that it is taken care of properly."

Wayne came up to the corporal and patted him on the shoulder.

"Get this safely back and dropped off at the hospital and it is Sergeant Garner, starting tomorrow, and a gallon of this brew for you and your men."

"Thank you, sir," Garner replied huskily, then paused. "No need to bribe
me, sir, like that. I'd of done it anyway now that you made me think of poor
Jamie, and bless you, sir, for remembering him."

Wayne clasped his old comrade on the shoulder and left the barn, head
swimming slightly from the kick of the corn liquor, concerned that others
might now smell it on his breath.

The loading was going apace. Half a dozen wagons, each burdened down
with half a ton of ground meal or flour, were drawn to one side of the road. A
dozen or so curious onlookers had gathered, some supportive of Johansson,
most just smiling that it was his misfortune rather than their own. They
chatted away with the soldiers, asking for news of how the war was going. The
farmer with the wagon who had tried to flee was protesting vehemently——
that he was a good patriot, with two sons in the militia——even as his grain
was off-loaded and fed into the mill.

Sergeant Travis seemed to have reached some sort of understanding with
Johansson as they examined each bag of flour going out, noting down the
weight when it was first tossed upon a scale. Wayne assumed that of course
Travis was making Johansson feel better about this affair by adding more than
a few pounds to each bag on his tally list.

It was past noon and Wayne ordered a halt in their labors. The reward for
venturing out on this task was now offered. Two thick smoked hams were carried down from the upper barn, along with a couple of bushel baskets of dried
apples. Sergeants lined their men up and played out the ritual of "Who shall
have this?" but today there was no bickering, for each slice was at least a pound
or more, rich with fat and seasoning. Some of the men decided to build small
fires by the side of the road to roast it first; others just ate it cold along with
the dried apples, and handfuls of sauerkraut hauled down from the upper barn
as well, all of it washed down with near on to a pint each of small beer given to
them by the tavern keeper in Phoenixville.

It was the most the men had eaten in better than a month. A reward but, as
Wayne also feared, too much for some: Even before they were finished, they
had to run off to the privacy of a nearby woodlot. Several of the men became
ill from the rich and unaccustomed fare as well. As to the barrel of corn liquor, Garner kept close guard on it, and stood by the wagon upon which it was
loaded.

Miller Johansson and his sons and grandsons watched them all with sullen dislike. The miller kept circulating around, Sergeant Travis solicitously by his side, scribbling notes as to everything taken: pots of sauerkraut; corn liquor; dozens of bushel baskets of dried apples; the smoked hams; six cows on the hoof, all of them giving at least two gallons a day of fine milk and cream. The fodder from the barn was put before the horses of the dragoons and wagon teams. There was even tobacco from a neighboring barn, a rare find this far north, hung up to dry in the rafters. Men stuffed wads into their cheeks, filled their pipes after their feast, or stuffed whole leaves into their haversacks to share later with comrades.

It was hard to drive the men back to work. Most of them lay in the sunlight along the side of the road, drifting off to a few minutes of sleep. Exceptions were those whose innards the feast had unsettled after so many weeks of privation.

The last of the heavy bags of ground meal and flour were finally loaded aboard the wagons, smoked hams carried out of the barn along with the remaining baskets of dried apples, destined for the hospitals as was the sauerkraut, to combat the scurvy that was rampant within the army. The poor farmer who had been caught trying to flee found himself holding a voucher, signed by Washington, to be certain, but now minus the wagon, two mules, and half a ton of wheat, except for a hundredweight that Wayne told him to take back to his family, loaded aboard a wheelbarrow that Johansson agreed to rent to him for a pence a day.

Wayne looked over the receipt that Travis had laboriously filled out and shook his head. If paid fairly with real coin and not Continentals, the miller had made out well this day, overcharging by a good 20 percent or more.

But it was all part of a tragic game. It was doubtful at this moment that Congress would ever honor the voucher issued by Washington and countersigned by him. Those surrounding Conway, Gates, and Mifflin would denounce it as not following proper channels and tell the poor miller to go to hell. They would then forward the bill directly back to the general with a terse letter of reprimand that he had not followed proper procedure and that, beyond this, he had agreed to overpay the miller, a charge that might bring an investigation. If the war was lost, the miller would lose. If the war was won, even then it might take years for Johansson to press his case on the Congress, while in turn he would be facing the lawyers of many an angry client of his mill.

But that was not Wayne's problem now, as he took the receipt filled out by Travis, scanned it, smiled, and asked for proper ink and quill.

Three tons of flour of fine grade,
One and a half tons of corn meal of medium grade,
One half ton of ground barley, fine grade,
Four hundred weight of rye, fine grade,
Thirty-one smoked hams, each of fifty pounds weight,
Six head of dairy cows,
Seven crocks of sauerkraut each of twenty pounds weight,
Seventeen chickens, thirty-one bushel baskets of dried apples, three of
    dried peaches, three thousand two hundred board feet of cut
    lumber, one fifty gallon barrel of corn whiskey, four bottles of port,
    six barrels of hard cider ten gallons each, twenty one bushels of
    potatoes, three hundred pounds of hay, three sows of two hundred
    pounds each . . .

He tallied up the figures, telling the miller to assign to each the current going price once he was gone, which he was certain the man would inflate another 50 percent.

He signed and left the office, the miller, his sons, and grandsons following, joined by the farmer who had lost his wagon, mules, and half a ton of wheat ground while they had looted the place.

He ran the figures in his head.

One day on the road and they had enough flour to keep Baker General Ludwig busy for at least two days, at one pound of baked bread per man. Meat, if the cows were fat enough, along with the smoked hams: barely enough for a day.

The kraut, apples, and whiskey: not even enough for the thousand in the army hospital, let alone those who were ill but still languishing in huts with their comrades.

Before leaving, Wayne had the audacity to suggest that the miller concentrate on cutting lumber for the time being. He told him that the army would pay a fair price for the wood, to be used in construction and road making. No sense in suggesting that he entice the local farmers to bring their grain in for grinding. News of today's expedition would keep all of them away from any miller in the region. In a few days' time, news of this new policy of confiscation by the Continental Army would sweep the countryside.

He pointed his column back east, the day now so warm that men marched with blanket capes removed, barefoot in the mud that was almost warm, in high spirits with full stomachs except for those stricken sick by the repast and riding in the wagons. One of them, an old comrade of Wayne's command from the beginning of the war, had been so stricken with an attack of the flux that he lay prone and semiconscious in a wagon, crying feebly, anxious comrades to either side of the wagon. Wayne had of course relented and ordered that the poor man be given all the corn liquor he might desire to ease his passing. Chances were he would be dead before they reached the hospital. He looked the other way when several of his comrades dipped into the cup of liquor as well before passing it on.

As they marched back, as before, many of the farms were shuttered: gates closed, except yet again for the few patriots who stood by the roadside. The tireless mother, anticipating their return, had baked enough biscuits so that each man would have two. And of course she reminded him yet again to please let her son have leave to visit her. He could not bring himself to stop, go inside with her, and break the news. He could face battle without flinching. But a grieving mother? He felt himself a coward as he rode on, whispering to one of his staff, who was horrified with the assignment, to stay behind and tell her the truth . . . that her son would never come home.

CHAPTER NINE

* * *

York
February 8, 1778

It had been a long three weeks on the road, and the end was finally in sight. Baron Friedrich von Steuben and company had crossed the Susquehanna River via ferry shortly after dawn, and now, after cresting a low rise, finally saw the town of York, the current capital of the United States. It was a most pitiful, god-awful sight, he thought.

"Merciful God," he heard Du Ponceau whisper. "Just what have we gotten ourselves into?" The sentiment of his interpreter was echoed by the others.

Von Steuben tried to maintain a calm, dispassionate exterior, not reacting openly, but inside he wanted to scream in agreement. If they were approaching the capital of the cause they had pledged their swords and careers to, they had most certainly joined the losing side.

Frontier outposts in the wilds of Russia had looked better than what he now gazed upon. The road, if anyone could call it that, was a frozen, slippery track, covered now with nearly half a foot of the snow that had begun falling during the night. At least the snow gave their horses some traction. The storm had parted for a moment to give him a glimpse of the alleged town ahead. It contained nothing more than what he assumed was some sort of town hall or courthouse of clapboard at its center, a few taverns, a broken-down, abandoned-looking stockade with a few sagging log cabins within, and not a sentry in sight. In the center of the town was a cluster of shops and a few churches, some of them of rough-hewn logs.

It was definitely no Berlin, nor Paris, and certainly not St. Petersburg. The pettiest princeling of the lower Rhine or the Balkans could claim a court a hundred times more splendid. It looked like the last refuge of a dying cause, and his heart sank. This was the destination he had ventured all upon, had been traveling to since boarding a ship in October in France, running the dangers of the British blockade and the storm-tossed Atlantic. This was the destination he had traveled to for three weeks on horseback from Boston, staying at more than one tavern with beds filled with bugs, eating bad food, and drinking wretched, watery beer while greedy innkeepers demanded hard currency or told him he and his men could instead sleep in the barn. If ever it looked like his career was truly at the end of the line, it was here at this moment, as he reined in to look around for his dog. He was close to giving way to cursing despair when he spied Azor over by a fence rail, claiming more territory. Azor finished, tore up some snow with his hind legs, shook himself, ventured to the next fence post, sniffed it, gave a snort of disdain, and then repeated the ceremony of conquest.

His loyal dog broke the glum mood he had fallen into.

"He has claimed enough territory between here and Boston for an empire greater than the czarina's," he exclaimed in French.

His jest broke the melancholic mood of his companions, Peter Du Ponceau throwing back his head and laughing and then, with a flamboyant gesture, dismounting, and going to the same fence post to relieve himself.

"Now see here, dog, this land is now mine!" he cried, and the others laughed and applauded.

Azor looked at him disapprovingly with his massive head cocked to one side, and once the Frenchman was finished, he went back and laid claim to the same spot yet again, causing the others to laugh.

"Someone is coming," Vogel, von Steuben's servant, announced, pointing toward York.

A lone rider was coming up from the village, a man in uniform riding a rather fine mount.

Pulled from the merriment of the moment, von Steuben assumed a serious demeanor as the rider approached, reined in, and saluted.

"Baron von Steuben, I presume," he asked.

Von Steuben nodded, returning his salute.

"I am Captain Rutledge, of General Gates's staff," he announced in a halting attempt at French. "I have been sent to guide you and your comrades."

"Lead on, Captain Rutledge," von Steuben replied.

Rutledge turned, his horse slipping on the snow- and ice-covered road. The man, maintaining his saddle well, broke into a trot, the others following. As they came down off the slope and into the village, von Steuben was surprised and pleased that there was something of a turnout for him. Apparently a fair number of the citizens of this outpost had been rousted out, in spite of the storm. They stood by the side of the icy track, waving their American flags, a few even holding up homemade Prussian and French flags, a couple calling out greetings in German, which he smiled and acknowledged with a bow.

Rutledge led the cavalcade into the village square, a patch of open ground, rutted, covered over with snow, and already trampled down. A company of rather well-dressed infantry was standing at attention, fifers playing a tune which he was coming to recognize as their "Yankee Doodle." Several officers in rather well-trimmed uniforms awaited with a handsomely dressed civilian delegation around them, which he assumed were members of their Congress.

He reined in and with a flourish saluted the American colors, an action that drew cheers from the small crowd, and was greeted by salutes in return and a ragged volley fired by the infantry company. He could not help but note that a number of the muskets misfired, the men not having kept their locks properly covered in the storm, something that, if given authority, he would most certainly see to. It was a display of amateurism that would certainly have drawn, afterwards, the wrath of any proper officer of the Prussian or even the Russian army.

Orderlies came up to hold the reins as von Steuben and his entourage dismounted. Azor, a bit frightened by the volley, was by his side, looking around nervously. He whispered for the dog to sit and stay, and the animal obeyed for once, but then slowly crept up behind von Steuben as he stepped forward to meet the delegation.

"Baron von Steuben," Rutledge announced, "it is my honor to introduce you to General Horatio Gates, chairman of the Board of War."

Von Steuben made it a point of coming to attention first, clicking heels together, and saluting by bowing and removing his hat, a gesture that he saw pleased Gates and the others.

They shook hands, and Gates, speaking through Rutledge, introduced him to the president of the Congress, Laurens, the other members of Congress present, and the officers of his staff. It took some minutes for the ritual to be played out, Rutledge's French so pathetic that after several introductions von Steuben was completely lost as to who was who. Throughout, the storm renewed its fury. Most of the civilian crowd fled back into their homes or the taverns.

Von Steuben introduced each of his traveling companions and was pleased when at least one of the members of Congress———he believed it was the doctor he had heard about——did not hesitate to approach Azor, whose sheer size normally intimidated most. He gave him a playful pat on the head and a scratch behind the ears, which immediately earned him Azor's affection, the dog rearing up and putting his muddy paws on the doctor's shoulders, ready to lick him in gratitude.

Von Steuben snapped a command and the dog went back on all fours, the display breaking the formality of the moment and causing the group to relax.

"May I suggest we retire within?" Gates announced, and von Steuben nodded his agreement.

The honor guard fired another volley. This time barely a third of the muskets discharged. Fifers broke into a shrill-sounding piece and the unit marched off. Once clear of the village square, all broke ranks and dashed for the shelter of the broken-down stockade and the warmth of the fires within the dilapidated cabins.

In the tavern, servants helped von Steuben and the others as they struggled to pull off their heavy, ice-encrusted jackets and capes. Azor trotted over to the oversize fireplace and settled down before it, as Gates gestured to a table around which were a dozen chairs, tankards of hot buttered rum quickly placed before the group as they sat down.

It was a difficult moment for von Steuben——he didn't know who should sit where——but, fortunately, Du Ponceau and the others who traveled with him already understood the game, and did not move to take any of the chairs, contenting themselves with going over to the long, rough-hewn bar, where the innkeeper had set out rum for them.

Before sitting down, Gates gestured for von Steuben to sit by his right side and then offered a toast to him and his companions. The toast was returned by von Steuben with a call, in halting English, for a blessing upon the American cause and confusion to its enemies, which was greeted with something of a cheer.

The others sat down and he suppressed a sigh as he did the same. It had been a long three-week journey from Boston. He had barely slept the night before——so voracious were the bedbugs that he had finally abandoned the cornhusk mattress and simply sprawled out on the hard, drafty, cold floor by Azor, next to the fireplace. Proper hosts would have understood the needs of a traveler. In Europe he would have been met by his host but then quickly handed off to servants for a light repast, a warm bath, a good shave, and a proper nap, while his uniform was cleaned and brushed down, wig seen to, shirt boiled——and then only in the evening would come the formalities.

These Americans struck him as a curious lot indeed: British in certain ways, but a mixture of other qualities as well. On the road from Lancaster to here he had even stayed in a tavern owned by a German from Magdeburg, where he had been born, and though obviously of peasant stock, the innkeeper proudly rattled off the names of the nobility he had served as a cobbler and officers he had known. He was even fairly current on gossip from the Fatherland. The man claimed to have fought at Minden, slapped his left arm, and rolled the sleeve of his shirt up to show the scar of a saber slash.

In fact, his knowledge of the names and doings of court were so good that von Steuben felt a bit uncomfortable that the man just might know a bit too much about himself, his family, and the fact that, though he was indeed a baron, it was a title that had been purchased and was not of long lineage . . . or some of the rumors as to why he was no longer in service to Frederick. But if the innkeeper did know it, which he suspected from a couple of veiled comments, as a fellow countryman he had kept mum as they drank themselves into happy oblivion. In the morning he had left his last silver thaler on his bed and a brief note of thanks for his hospitality and what he hoped would be respectful silence when it came to a fellow countryman making a new way in this new world.

Du Ponceau, who had a fairly good grasp of English, had pointed out the distinguishing characteristics of people they had met along the way: the very proper residents of Boston; Scots Irish refugees living along the frontier boundaries; the Dutch of the Hudson Valley and north Jersey; the familiar countrymen from Germany; the various Anabaptist sects that populated the region from Lancaster to here, known as Dunkers; Mennonites and Amish from the Rhineland who had fled here for religious freedom. He could not understand their staunch sentiments against war of any kind (resembling in their pacifism the English Quakers he was told had founded Pennsylvania), but the orderliness of their fields, their homes as big as barns, their barns as big as churches, their neatly arrayed orchards that stretched for acres were to him a touch of home. It filled him with pride and it was good to speak German again as they passed along the road.

Such a strange nation indeed, he thought, as he looked around the table, the dozen gathered here returning his gaze with open curiosity.

Their greetings having been offered, it became obvious that they were expecting him to say something.

He had been inwardly preparing himself for this moment for weeks. His long conversations with John Hancock and Sam Adams were warning enough that he was wading into the perilous seas of a revolutionary government on the edge of defeat and sharply divided against itself. He had a sense that this strange land presented to him an opportunity that was now forever closed back in Europe, and that he must tread with utmost caution. If not for America, he would eventually have wound up either a drunkard or a suicide.

Gates smiled at him and began to speak, von Steuben motioning for Du Ponceau to come over and stand by his side. He whispered for him to translate directly into German.

"I trust your journey was not too toilsome," Gates started, and von Steuben offered the usual pleasantries in reply. Even as they spoke, Du Ponceau doing an impressive job of rapidly translating, he carefully scanned the others. From several he detected bored disinterest. The excitement of the day was over, a storm was raging outside, the tavern was warm, the rum hot, and one man was already motioning for the innkeeper to bring the pitcher over and refill his mug. As he watched Gates intently, nodding with the completion of nearly every sentence, he shot sidelong glances at the others and noted who was paying attention. In the background he could hear Vogel chatting with the innkeeper, who, by good fortune, spoke German, and Vogel was already adroitly at work, casually asking who each man was, their rank and titles, so he could give him a detailed report later on each.

Gates, not too subtly, finally drew the subject around to more direct questions.

"You are aware, sir," Gates announced, "of the dire straits the army has been placed in this winter after the disastrous defeats before Philadelphia and the loss of our capital as a result."

"Temporarily lost," one of the congressmen sniffed. "Come spring, with proper leadership we shall take it back."

"That is why I rushed here as swiftly as possible," von Steuben replied. "Upon my arrival, I heard of these events. When I departed from France, the latest news then was from early in the summer, of the hard fighting in the north. Needless to say, General Gates, I was delighted upon landing to hear of your glorious, hard-fought victory at Saratoga and the proper credit you have received for that triumph."

Gates, smiling broadly, looked around at the others, some nodding. He took it in. A Prussian would have taken such bald-faced praise and flattery without a flicker of a smile.

"And your opinion, sir, as to how news of this victory, which surely has arrived in France by now, will likely be greeted by the court there?"

"Sir, I am not in position to say, not being in the service of His Most Catholic Majesty."

He looked up at Du Ponceau.

"Peter, perhaps you could render an opinion?"

"I am certain, sir, it will be greeted joyously," he responded in English.

"It better," one of those on the other side of the table grumbled. "They certainly are taking their damn time about helping us."

Von Steuben did not understand the man's words but sensed the tone. Du Ponceau flushed slightly but did not reply.

"We fear that the setbacks suffered before Philadelphia will negate the positive gains achieved at Saratoga," Gates announced.

"I am certain, sir, that the capture of an entire British army, unheard-of in any campaign in Europe across more than several hundred years, cannot be compared to what is but a temporary setback here," he replied.

He watched the Americans carefully as Du Ponceau translated. Who nodded, who did not react, who did not seem to care what was being said.

"And your opinion of the setbacks here?" one of the congressmen asked——who, he was not certain.

"Sir, they transpired while I was in transit. I have not had time to study them."

No one responded for a moment. He remained erect, returning their glances, smiling affably.

"Saratoga occurred while you were in transit, yet you apparently know of it," someone else offered.

"But of course, sir. However, news of it traveled to Boston faster than events this far away. And of course being a glorious victory it was the talk of the city when I arrived."

"And the reaction in Boston to all the news?" Gates asked. "Of both victory and defeat. What did Hancock, Samuel Adams, and others say to you?"

"Sir. I cannot speak for Herr Adams or Herr Hancock and their innermost opinions. I should add, sir, that even if they did share something with me in confidence, as an officer I am trained to keep such confidences."

Du Ponceau translated, and he watched as there was some shaking of heads.

"Let me add, gentlemen, that in the same vein, I consider conversations with men of position such as you to be in confidence as well, and upon that I give my solemn oath as a German officer who is offering you his sword. A Prussian officer never betrays the trust and confidences of a fellow officer or of those whom he serves."

He kept his attention focused on Gates now, as a conversation broke out among the Americans for a few minutes.

Gates glanced at him even as he spoke with one of the members of Congress on the other side of the table. Du Ponceau was obviously listening but felt it inappropriate to translate. He did recognize the name of Washington being mentioned several times.

Finally Gates turned to him, eyes narrowing.

"And of General Washington. Have you formed any opinion of him yet, sir?"

Von Steuben smiled openly and, he hoped, disarmingly.

"How could I? I have not yet met him. It would thus be unfair for me to even begin to offer an opinion other than to say that in the courts of Europe he is spoken of highly."

He hesitated, then quickly added, "Of course, sir, recall that I left before word of Saratoga had winged its way across the ocean, so I am certain, sir, that your name is as well known now as his."

It was bald flattery and nearly stuck to his tongue as he uttered it. He could see Du Ponceau looking at him with a bit of surprise. In nearly a month of traveling together, the two had transcended the differences of age, rank, and nationality and now knew each other as friends. His flattery was out of place, but Peter did not hesitate to translate.

He had learned enough along the road to know what was now transpiring. These Americans all held an opinion, and above all else seemed to cherish the right to repeat that opinion loudly and often in every inn, tavern, and taproom, from Boston to this rude outpost at what seemed like the end of the earth.

It was Gates versus Washington. And before much longer there would be only one or the other. Of course there was pragmatic self-interest behind his words. That was part of the game of survival he was playing at this moment.

It would either be Gates or Washington, and he was being boldly sounded out on it before the chill of the journey was even out of his bones. A true gentleman, a more adroit player, would have at first beguiled him with hospitality rather than grilling him. Let him relax for several days; ply him with choice wine and casual conversation concerning everything but the central topic before at last closing in.

The way Gates now gazed at him told him so much. This man was not a gentleman. If he was to survive and bring some meaning to this journey of four thousand miles, though, he would have to master dealing with him. A true confrontation was about to explode between this man and Washington, who as yet was an unknown except for what others had told him.

The prospect, however, of riding clear back to Boston, penniless and without a commission or employment, was terrifying. The game was here. It had to be played here, and he offered a bland smile as the others talked for several minutes among themselves in English. He knew Du Ponceau was gathering in every word, while in the far corner of the room Vogel was listening carefully as the innkeeper translated in hoarse whispers.

Gates finally turned back to him.

"We understand, sir, from your papers that came by post ahead of you, that under Frederick you were actually a lieutenant general."

He looked straight into Gates's eyes and did not blink, and just merely nodded, not saying a word.

"That, sir, is a rank higher than even mine," Gates finally said.

He did not respond for several seconds, then leaned back in his chair, took a sip of the buttered rum——which was rather tasty, far superior to the vodka of Russia, though never a match for a good cognac——and smiled good-naturedly.

"Sir, such ranks and titles I left behind when I took ship to offer my sword here. Choose what rank you will for me, in order to avoid resentment from junior officers, native-born, who have won their spurs by hard fighting, sir. I would prefer to simply be a volunteer, to have time to prove my merit and then let you gentlemen decide my appropriate rank."

Du Ponceau translated that smoothly enough.

"But according to our current rules and regulations," Gates pointed out, "it is General Washington who nominates for promotion to the higher ranks. A privilege he guards most jealously."

Von Steuben juggled that for a few seconds.

"And yet I must assume, as it is in Europe, that such nominations in the end are submitted to the supreme authority of the ruling powers."

Nods greeted his reply.

"So you would agree to serve as a volunteer without any demand of rank and accept that ultimately your commission comes from this Congress?" Gates asked.

"Of course," he replied quickly.

"And your pay, sir?" one of them asked, and he guessed it might be Laurens.

He found that almost amusing. It would be the equivalent of the czarina or king of Prussia debating the pay of but one officer and then looking into a private purse. But then again, in the darkest days of the last war, Frederick was most likely reduced to that more than once.

"If I have no defined rank, how could I, as a gentleman, demand a certain pay?"

He laughed softly, and as his reply was translated there was laughter from the others as well.

"But of course there are the harsh realities of this world, gentlemen," he continued quickly, and the laughter was stilled.

"I think it would be fair though to at least submit my expenses and be compensated in that way."

No one spoke for a moment, and the one he suspected was Laurens finally nodded. He felt it time to press the next point, which was a serious point of honor for him.

"Also, I do hold these young gentlemen with me as indispensable," and he gestured to Du Ponceau and the others of his retinue. "All of them offer their swords as well, as volunteers, and wish to serve as members of my staff. They are young and, as with all youth, somewhat naïve as to the world. Surely we can talk about their expenses as well along with some junior rank——say, captain——and reach an appropriate agreement."

He could see the visible relief in Du Ponceau's eyes as the young man translated. Though of a well-placed family back in France, his purse was now as light as that of the man he followed, and the other young men were just as desperate.

Besides, having several captains as his aides-de-camp would establish his proper position, even if his own rank was not defined.

"So we agree, then, to cover expenses, rank and posting to be discussed later," Gates replied, bargaining like a shrewd merchant, "and that you will accept the position assigned to be subordinate to the authorities here."

Ah! He smiled inwardly and yet held his contempt from being visible. By "authorities," Gates clearly meant himself.

"Sir, I offer my skill as a trained staff officer of the Great von Steuben where it is most desperately needed at this moment. When you gentlemen decide where my skills as an officer and as an inspector general can be of greatest effect, there I wish to therefore embark in your service."

"Inspector general?" Gates snapped, and in that instant von Steuben knew he had misstepped.

"Sir, this army already has an inspector general in Major General Conway."

He had heard nothing of this and hesitated.

"Perhaps our guest means to serve in some capacity with the command of the inspector general's office," came a reply, the man speaking being the doctor.

Gates looked over at the doctor and a hot debate ensued for several minutes, von Steuben silent, knowing better than to interfere.

"Within the structure of command under General Conway," Gates finally announced.

"Of course, as you define it," von Steuben replied quickly. He hesitated. "Of course I would like to assume my duties as quickly as possible," he finally replied.

He had no intention of lingering in this godforsaken place a day longer than necessary. Wherever the situation was most desperate, that is where he wanted to go. Most certainly there would be expenses——plenty of them, of course——but, by his honor, he expected to earn those expenses and not spend the rest of the winter languishing at this place, trading pleasantries with and being subservient to Gates, a man for whom he was already developing a distaste.

"In due course," was all that Gates said in reply, and his heart sank. He wanted to go as quickly as possible to the center of action. Surviving the politics of court, be it imperial or this ragtag group, was not his forte. He feared now that until he could somehow persuade Gates of some sort of loyalty, he would be stuck in this dreary outpost for months to come.

Valley Forge
February 8, 1778

He could no longer contain himself! She was here!

General George Washington bounded down the steps as the carriage door opened, and with a radiant smile Martha stepped down. Snow, now nearly a blizzard, swirled around them as he came down the walkway with long strides. From the corner of his eye he saw his guard company lined up to either side at present arms in salute, their normally fixed demeanor breaking, many of them grinning as he raced by and, once he was past, looking sidelong at each other and nodding.

"Extra rations tonight and maybe a gill of rum," Peter whispered to Putman, who was standing next to him, and smiled in agreement. A poke came from behind from Sergeant Harris, reminding them to remain at attention.

Washington came up to her, his staff officers already gathered around, hats off, offering their greetings, looking up as he approached, stepping back, all of them smiling.

"My dear, thank God you are safe and you are here," he gasped, taking her bare outstretched hands into his, pulling her closer as if to kiss her.

"George," she whispered, looking up at him, "remember, they're watching."

He caught himself, a quick glance around. Lafayette was openly grinning; of course the French would be far more demonstrative at a time like this. General Greene and his wife, by his side——she had arrived only yesterday——were both smiling. Tilghman, Laurens, and Hamilton, as always the proper staff officers, tried to appear dispassionate. Hundreds of troops had come streaming down from their cabins, pouring out in spite of the raging storm to see the general's wife.

There was a scattering of cheers, a wag crying, "Go on and kiss her, sir, we ain't watching."

She looked up at him with a smile, seeming almost diminutive as she stood before his towering height.

He leaned over.

"George," she whispered, smiling mischievously, "later, when alone."

Sighing, he took the formal approach, removing his hat, bowing, and taking her right hand and kissing it. Then, ever so lightly, he kissed her on the lips.

He straightened up, taking her hand.

"Three cheers for His Excellency the General and Mrs. Washington," someone offered, and rousing cheers went up from the men lining the street. She stopped, turned with a smile, and offered a formal curtsy in reply, which drew forth more cheers as she took his hand and together they walked back into the headquarters house, followed by officers and staff.

Once the door was closed Sergeant Harris stepped out onto the walkway. Merciful God, there were several hundred men. He had been hoping the howling storm would have kept them in their huts; thankfully, the last of the huts had been completed only a few days ago.

"Lads, by order of His Excellency, in celebration of the arrival of his fair wife, a bit of a treat out behind the barn, so get out your cups."

There was no need to urge them on. The men were already vaulting the fence, Peter and the honor guard breaking ranks to join in the rush.

"Don't tell anyone else!" a cry went up.

At the far side of the barn, two ten-gallon barrels of corn liquor rested on a table, wooden bungs already driven into them. The men guarding the barrels, Harris could see, had already taken a liberal sampling.

"All right, boys, no shoving. Line up, at least a drop for each of you, and for God's sake don't go running back to camp to tell anyone else, or there'll be nothing but a lick of the tap for each of you."

It was hard to see in the storm, but he figured at least two to three hundred and ran a quick calculation, maybe a quarter gill per man at most. Peter was by his side and he nodded for him to man the other tap.

"No shoving, now, no shoving!" Harris cried, half a dozen tin cups and mugs being pressed under his tap. He opened it.

"One potato, two potato, that's all!"

Peter did the same ritual, more than a few cursing that he had held back.

The men, laughing, surged around, holding up their cups with the precious few ounces, toasting Washington and his wife, damning the British, damning the cold, blessing Mad Anthony for having dug these barrels up from somewhere. It was soon quite the party, for after so much deprivation, even a few ounces of corn liquor went to the heads of many.

As the last of the well-wishers of the staff withdrew, Martha Washington closed the door, then looked out the window, watching the celebration out behind the barn, occasionally obscured by the swirling snow so that the men seemed almost ghostlike as they danced around.

She turned and looked back at her George. He was thinner, far thinner than when last she saw him. With his wig now off, his hair was visibly grayer, as were his features, cheeks hollow, eyes deep-set. Though he was smiling broadly, she sensed a deep inner sadness.

This time she did let him kiss her and kissed him back. She held him tight for a long moment.

"Thank God you are here," he sighed. "It has been agony without you."

"And nothing but worry for me," she replied, breaking his embrace and stepping back to look into his eyes.

"And what is this I heard about you riding about the front line at Brandywine, getting more bullets in your jacket? You promised me you'd never do that again. I was sick with anguish, dreading the arrival of every post rider who came in."

He smiled that great self-confident smile she recalled so fondly and which had won her heart so many years ago.

"Passion of the moment," he replied.

"Save your passions of the moment for me, dear husband."

He laughed softly and tried to step closer.

"Just a moment, General Washington," she announced, holding him back. "I must look a fright, and, besides, you know they are all just waiting in the next room."

"Mrs. Greene has planned a dinner in honor of your arrival," he sighed. "Nothing fancy, to be certain. Plain fare, just salted pork, mixed with some dried apples and sauerkraut. It is all that we've scavenged of late."

He hesitated. "Better than what they have out there." He nodded toward the frost-covered window.

The storm, the worst of the season so far, was rising in fury, a regular nor'easter, as the New Englanders called it, again a reminder of a year ago before Trenton. But no marching army this time.

"I've heard rumors," she said, and returned to the window to look out.

He didn't reply.

"How many are left, George?"

"Just over eight thousand by this morning's muster roll, of which near on to four thousand are listed as unfit for duty. We have over a thousand in hospital."

"You've lost weight, George, a full stone or more," she announced, looking at him appraisingly.

He shrugged, drawing closer to stand by her side.

"General Wayne is starting to bring in food. We have almost a three-day reserve at the moment, thank heavens. For a while there, it was down to watery potato soup and not much else."

"We'll soon see to that," she replied a bit defiantly.

He laughed softly.

"So tell me. You concealed some smoked hams and sausages, plenty of greens, perhaps even a roasted lamb or two inside your carriage? Perhaps several bottles of my favorite Madeira?"

She shook her head and could see that he had actually been half serious with his statement and was now disappointed.

"George. We had to skirt around Philadelphia, pass near where you fought at Brandywine, and then go up to Lancaster before doubling back here. The poverty in the countryside is heartbreaking. Barely a farm that has not been despoiled by the armies. Word is, though, that at least the British are offering hard coin, and therefore most are hiding their food until enemy purchasing agents or foragers arrive. I heard the state government of Pennsylvania and its militia have been particularly harsh in reply, confiscating all goods if the family is proven to be Tory. Not even you have been doing that."

He did not reply. It was about what Wayne was doing right now, ranging farther afield every day with his foragers. If the family were known to be patriots, particularly if a son or father was with the army, they would only "purchase" half of what was in their barn, root cellar, and smokehouse. If Tory, it was nearly everything except their seed stock and enough food to get them barely through the winter.

Wayne had to plan his raids like full-blown military exercises. If word leaked ahead of him as to which direction he was going that day, farmers would drive their cattle, pigs, and sheep into distant woods, clean out their smokehouses and bury the contents, and then stand there straight-faced and swear that thieves and raiders had hit them the day before. The warm spell of the last few weeks, though, usually left clues for Wayne's trackers, who could follow the muddy paths left by the animals and the signs of freshly turned earth.

Wayne would send scouts out several days in advance. One was particularly good at posing as an itinerant Methodist preacher. Once the "preacher" scouted out a likely source, a squadron of dragoons would ride ahead, blocking the roads, and then he and his wagons would sweep out before dawn. Every day they needed nine thousand pounds of meat on the hoof or smoked and cured; two tons of flour, be it wheat, rye, or oats, for the General Baker; any dried fruits and pickled vegetables; and vinegar and sauerkraut for the hospitals. Tools, especially shovels, were still desperately needed as the men turned to finally building the fortifications.

Fall behind by even a few days and the army would again starve.

"How are you feeding this army?" she asked.

He sighed.

"We're getting by."

"As I came into the camp, George, I noticed quite a few women about, even some children," and as she spoke she looked at him a bit strangely.

Camp followers for armies were as old as history. But she and more than a few other wives of officers had preached that this was to be a new kind of army, an army of a new Republic, and if God's blessings were to be sought, there must be at least some attempt at morality within the ranks.

"They are all entered properly into the muster rolls. Nearly five hundred of them."

"On the muster rolls?"

"It is all proper, my dear. They help in the regimental cookhouses and the army bakery, mend clothes, and nurse the sick."

"I should like to help, then, as well."

"Martha, the sickhouse . . ." He sighed. "It isn't safe."

"If it is smallpox, I've had my inoculation."

"No, it's worse. Typhus, galloping consumption," he paused, "dysentery, and the flux."

"Still, come morning I shall do my part. I will. I must set an example here. Surely the other wives of officers are doing the same."

He didn't reply. Some indeed already were helping with the most menial of tasks. More than a few, though, held themselves far aloof, seeing it as beneath their station. The thought of Martha tending to an infantry private dying of the flux——he did not like the idea in the slightest.

"And the children. Isn't it dangerous for them to be here?"

He could only shrug.

"Martha, for some, the entire family is here, husband and older son in the ranks. If the wife and younger ones stayed home they would starve; their homes already have been swept over by the war. I've ordered that women in the camp who do proper work are to receive half-pay. More than a few families with homes inside the British lines have been driven out by their Tory neighbors. They have no place to go but here. Children who help by bringing in firewood, tending to fires, or helping in the bakehouse, thereby freeing up a fit man to work on the fortifications, are receiving quarter-pay and rations."

"Proper work," she finally said in reply, looking straight at him and then letting it drop. "I think I shall take a look about tomorrow and see where I can start to help."

She went up to a small mirror and gazed into it as she took off her winter bonnet. He helped her remove her cape, then motioned for her to step over to the fire, where she gladly extended her hands, rubbing them vigorously to take out the chill.

"A cold ride this morning," she said. "As you know, we had to swing wide by back roads to avoid Philadelphia. Lancaster was swarming with patriot families that had fled the city——there was barely a room to be found. These last ten miles were a nightmare, George. Empty farms, some of them burned-out, were looted clean. The guards you sent down to meet me said it was best not to identify who I was as we rode on."

She sighed, reaching around to rub her lower back.

"I just wish I could get out of this awful corset. It is near to killing me."

"Later," he said with a smile, which she returned.

"But, as you said, they are waiting for us."

"They can wait a few minutes more. We have waited for these many months," he replied.

He opened a bottle of wine, warmed by the fire. It was a hearty port——a gift from Greene, whose wife had brought it along with her. They sat side by side, gazing at the fire, sipping quietly.

It was such a flood of emotions for him. For at least this moment, all that was outside the room could be forgotten, the cold, the death, the defeats and misery. She was here by his side, her lavender scent filling the room.

They sat alone for almost a half hour, just gazing at the fire as Martha told him all about Mount Vernon. How good the crops had been, the births, marriages, and deaths of the slaves at their plantation, and the wishes they had extended to him. He thought of Billy Lee helping in the next room to prepare their dinner. Away now from his family since the start of the war. Of course his wife could not come to join him for this winter. Again the vexing questions of what they were fighting for, and yet again the unintended duplicity of it, with those few simple words "all men are created equal."

His great fear when the British fleet had entered the Chesapeake was that they would at least send a few ships up the Potomac to raid, gather supplies, and of course burn out the plantation and home of the military leader of the Revolution. It was curious Admiral Richard Howe had not ordered that to be done. He could only consider it to be an act of civility on the admiral's part, and he was thankful for it. So strange was this war. He was forced to fight it with every fiber of his being, to stand by, dispassionate, at least outwardly, as he watched his army disintegrating from starvation and disease while his enemies feasted and enjoyed the winter warm and safe in Philadelphia but twenty miles away. Wayne still seethed, and would forever seethe about what he and the survivors called the massacre at Paoli, though even General William Howe, Richard's brother, had agreed to an investigation, pointing out through an envoy that the attack had gone on at night, with unloaded muskets, at bayonet point only, which rarely left room for surrender in the mad panic of such a fight. He added that very many men had indeed been taken prisoner and shown mercy.

And yet those same men, shown compassion on the battlefield, were reportedly dying at the rate of upwards of a dozen a day for lack of food, heat, and medicine, locked up just a few short blocks away from where General Howe and Admiral Howe made their headquarters.

Strange and cruel this war is. My farm is spared, and yet men starve. Officers exchange pleasantries and salutes under flags of truce, but in a vicious fight at night the wounded, begging for mercy, are bayoneted to death. On one day civilians, showing proper passes, are allowed to pass back and forth freely through the lines, and yet a day later their farms might be ravaged and destroyed, and in more than a few cases the owner whipped, tarred and feathered, then driven off his land if believed to be on the other side.

He sighed, and Martha, knowing his ways, saw that he was lost in thought while staring at the fire. She fell silent, just reaching out to take his hand and hold it tight.

He looked at her, smiled, and stood up.

"God, how I have missed you," he sighed, and this time she did melt into his embrace, the two sharing a passionate kiss, Martha then sighing and leaning against his chest.

"We heard so many terrible things. Battles lost, rumors you were dead or captured, then this ugly gossip about Gates, Mifflin, and Conway trying to have you removed."

"You heard of that?" he asked, a bit incredulous, stepping back slightly to hold her at arm's length.

"George, the countryside is alive with the rumors."

"Those . . ." His voice trailed off. Martha could not even tolerate a "damn" coming from him, let alone what he was about to explode with.

"I would have thought they were gentlemen enough to keep it private between us. If the countryside knows, then most assuredly the British know. If they know, it is only encouragement for them to wait us out rather than seek an engagement, as I hoped."

"Then it's true?"

"Yes," he sighed, "it's true."

"How dare they!" she announced indignantly.

"Of course they dare. The facts are plain enough, my dear. Gates allegedly wins at Saratoga. He showed himself to be a poltroon last year when he refused to cross the Delaware in support of my attack and instead fled with Congress to Baltimore, there to lobby for position. He finally wrangled a command in the northern theater and laid claim to the victory that came but weeks after his arrival.

"Colonel Morgan and others tell me that if the victory belongs to anyone, it is to our loyal friend, Benedict Arnold, who saved the battle at a crucial moment and, in so doing, was wounded in the leg so severely it was thought at first he would lose the limb. He is now recovering back at his home. Gates actually had him arrested for insubordination before that fight, but Arnold broke arrest and galloped to the front just at the moment Gates was ready to retreat. He rallied the men and led them to victory.

"But it was Gates who wrote the reports and all but galloped back to Lancaster and then York claiming the victory, glory, and praise."

He shook his head.

"He is now head of this contemptible Board of War and had the audacity to send his lackey Conway to, as he said, 'evaluate this army,' which had all but been abandoned by Congress to fend for itself. Of course, all fault was laid here."

"Will they remove you, George?"

He smiled.

"We do have allies, my dear. God bless the Marquis de Lafayette. You will like him. He is like a son to me."

Feeling awkward, he fell silent after saying that. Martha had given birth to two children from her first marriage. But there had been no children for the two of them, and the reason for it was therefore obvious. It was a burden and disappointment that haunted him, and thus, some rumored, why he formed such close bonds with young men of promise, who in turn looked to him as if he was their father.

Lafayette, it was clear to her, was obviously one of them.

"Why do you bless this young Frenchman? I heard the armies are all but overrun with adventure seekers claiming high rank, and Congress is all too ready to hand out those ranks."

"This lad is different. He offered himself to me directly as a gentleman volunteer for my staff. He was everywhere and anywhere, almost a nuisance at times with his eager rushing about, but in time he proved himself. At Brandywine I gave him temporary command of a brigade and he led it with such élan and valor that the men and mind you those men were tough veterans, some in the ranks since Boston cheered him.

"Now he is fighting a different battle. Perhaps one just as crucial, or even more so. He and others, of course, supposedly without my knowledge"———he paused and looked at her coolly as if to emphasize his point———"or yours, have embarked on a letter-writing campaign. He went so far as to write President Laurens directly, that if there was a change in command he feared that friends of his in France might construe such a move the wrong way and urge the king to withdraw all support. I am told that, reading between the lines of that letter, it was clear he would be the one to write to the king of France and then personally deliver what he'd written. Generals Greene and Stirling are doing the same. There has even been a petition from several Virginia companies."

"You seem to be getting told a lot about the activities of others, George." She looked up at him with that understanding gaze of a wife who knew her husband far too well. "And your hand in this?"

"It would not be proper, of course, for me to engage in such activities or urge others to do so."

"Wars are not just won on the battlefield, George. I recall reading one of your books, by that Italian, advising princes and such."

"Of course, I have no idea what you are referencing, Martha."

"Oh, of course not, George."

He smiled.

"Is it true about Dr. Rush joining your critics?"

He nodded his head sadly.

"Yes, I trusted him. A good man. His encouragement was crucial before Trenton. That he would go over to their side is saddening. I have heard the same for both of the Adamses. Of John I would have thought better."

"Is there anyone on your side?"

"Some of the Virginia and Carolina delegates, but last report I had, there is barely a quorum left in York——the rest have fled or gone home for the winter. So there is little Congress can do.

"As for the Board of War led by Gates. They can file their reports. But with whom? As to their mad idea to rely solely on an army of militia and disband any troops of longer service? I dare them to come to this place, line up these men, and tell them so. I daresay half the men will grab their blanket roll and go home, most likely never to return, but as for the rest?"

His voice was cold as he spoke and she could feel the tension in him.

"Not likely. I daresay that perhaps that was a hidden intent all along when we arrived at this place, found not one day's food, not even a single ration waiting for twelve thousand hungry exhausted men. Not one tool, not one shelter prepared."

His anger became clearly evident.

"Perhaps that was the intent all along. To let this army disintegrate, melt away, and go home. I would then be dismissed, and Gates would take command in the spring——that is, if he could rally any army at all to stand beneath the flag once more."

He broke away from her side and went back to the window to look out at the rising storm. A few men trudged past the headquarters, leading a pony cart pulled by a skin-and-bones mule, the wagon piled high with firewood.

Outside he could hear axes ringing. Men of the headquarters company were busily chopping up more firewood for him and for their own shelter in the barn, where they had rigged up several of Dr. Franklin's stoves, parts of which had been salvaged out of the ruins of the forge down in the valley.

A soft knock on the door interrupted them.

"Enter."

The door cracked open and it was Billy Lee. At the sight of him Martha broke into a smile.

"Billy Lee, how are you?"

"Just fine, ma'am, and it is a joy to see you."

"As it is a joy for me to see you. But I must have a word with you."

"Ma'am?" and he looked at her nervously.

"The general has lost weight. Far too much weight. I told you to take good care of him, didn't I?"

"Yes, ma'am. I'm sorry, ma'am. But you see the vittles, it's been hard to find a proper meal of late."

She stood up, laughed, and went to his side, though she did not take his hand.

"Your wife, Janie, sends her love to you and orders you to keep safe. She knitted a new scarf, mittens, and wool cap for you. I have them in my luggage."

"That is kind of you, ma'am, and her. Ma'am, is she safe? We heard there was fever there some months back."

"Just the usual summer complaints," Martha lied. The smallpox epidemic had at last reached their rather isolated home; four slaves had died, two of them children, and over a score of others had fallen ill. Janie had been one, and out of loyalty to the man serving her husband in the field Martha had insisted that Janie be brought into the main house and nursed there by her personal servants. The girl had recovered but was terribly scarred. She would tell George of it and let him find the proper time later to break the news and arrange for a letter to be sent back to Mount Vernon from him.

"Ma'am, General, dinner is ready."

"Thank you, Billy Lee." Martha said, and this time she did reach out and touch him lightly on the shoulder. "And, Billy Lee, thank you for keeping my beloved general safe. We've heard rumors of your heroism and I am grateful to you for it."

"Thank you, ma'am. I will tell them you shall be joining the party shortly."

He closed the door, and she looked back at her husband, who was smiling.

"That darn fool," he sighed. "At times the British must think I am an African. Whenever the bullets begin to fly, he somehow finds a way to get between me and them."

She went back to the mirror, checking her hair one more time, forgoing the formality of a wig for this occasion. Brushing some lint from the wool cape off her shoulders, she looked back at him.

"Am I presentable?" she asked, almost girlish with concern.

"Forever presentable," he replied with enthusiasm, "and I am so glad you are here to be presented."

He took her hand, led her to the door, and opened it.

In the room across the hall the table was set. His staff, generals, the wives of Greene and Stirling, all of them were waiting, the room crowded, extra mismatched chairs pushed in around the table.

As they entered, General Greene and his wife, acting as hosts, greeted them, the general bowing, Mrs. Greene offering a curtsy. The two women embraced, for they were friends from the winter before at Morristown. All gathered around the table broke into applause, George and Martha assuming the place of honor at the head of the table, which was so small that they were pressed almost shoulder to shoulder.

The plates had already been set. No fine china, just plain pewter. In the center of the table was a repast of boiled and fried salt pork, though there were some very thin slices of smoked ham as well. The bowls of sauerkraut and dried applies were filled to overflowing The Greenes again acted as hosts, doling out equal portions as the plates were passed around. Two bottles of wine for more than a dozen around the table had already been uncorked, companions to a jug of sweet cider for the second glass set before each. When all were served, Nathanael Greene stood, glass held high.

"For Martha Washington and her beloved and honored husband, His Excellency General George Washington."

The others stood to join in the toast. Martha smiled broadly but Washington remained unmoved, merely sipping from his glass, waiting for the others to drink and sit down.

He then stood.

"Gentlemen and fair ladies," he said softly. "There is a tradition we must never forget, no matter what the circumstances."

He held his glass up.

"For these United States of America. For the Congress which guides and governs it, for the Declaration of Independence which defines us, and for those who serve honorably as their sworn duty directs them to serve."

The others stood, looking one to the other, and raised their glasses, repeating the toast and then sitting back down.

As he settled into his chair, he looked over at Martha. She had tears in her eyes.

"Bet they're having roast beef, suet pudding, kidney pies, plum duffs, the works in there," someone growled.

Peter Wellsley looked over his shoulder at the complainer. Of course it was Putnam. The others joked if he didn't have a complaint by the end of a day it would surely mean the coming of the end of time and the Day of Judgment.

"Ah, shut your yap and take your ration," Harris growled.

The daily ritual of their company had just been played out. The finest choice of some actual smoked ham had been the last to be doled out, along with a handful of dried apples and a cup of kraut. Harris, betting most likely that the best would be the next to last, had called his own name, only to wind up with the ham bone to gnaw on, while Putnam had received the prize. Harris immediately declared that he would boil the bone later to get the marrow out.

Over the last month they had managed to make the barn a rather cozy place to live. Extra boards had been salvaged from the wreckage of the forge and hammered over any cracks. Fresh hay and straw were still up in the loft and had been forked down to be turned into bedding, though after a month they were crushed flat and increasingly filled with vermin. Dried horse manure had been moistened and troweled into cracks between the boards to keep out drafts, what was left of their tenting strung together to form enclosures around the Franklin stoves, parts of which had been found in the ruined forge, carried back here, literally on the backs of the men, then bolted together. Fortunately, two of the men in the company had been blacksmiths before the war. Tearing out boards from the animal stalls, they had even managed to make rather comfortable benches circling the stoves. Each man had his claimed spot. Many of them had prowled around, found old grain sacks, and stuffed them with straw, dried moss, and leaves for cushions. Fights as to who owned what had been avoided by Peter, who concocted some ink from lampblack and a bit of linseed oil, stenciling the names of the owners on each.

The stoves only used a fraction of the wood of an open fireplace. As the headquarters guard company, they had hung on to their possession. In many a regiment, some officer would have laid claim to the precious find and carted them off to his own cabin. There had even been some concern when a colonel of the Massachusetts Line had spotted the arrangement, but Harris had simply told him to take the matter up with the general, and the precious stoves had stayed in place.

The storm outside was in full blast now. In spite of all their efforts to insulate the barn, the wind thundered through the eaves of the upper level, icy gusts eddying down into where they were gathered, the ragged tents strung together to form their inner shelter fluttering. Flakes of snow melted and then dripped upon them in moist droplets.

Harris made a suggestion that after their meal they take a half hour or so of what he called "the plastering detail," scraping up more manure from the pigpen and cattle stalls, cooking it up into a paste to try to seal off the cracks in the walls of the upper level, but there were no volunteers and he let it pass.

Peter, who had assumed something of the task of firekeeper for the stoves, given that he had first found them while prowling around the ruins of the forge, put on a heavy canvas glove, gingerly pulled open the door to the firebox of each, and shoved in more wood.

Putnam's foraging party had hit upon a real trove earlier in the day before the storm settled in. A quarter-mile out toward the east, they had found a couple of dead ash trees and a birch, down in a tangled hollow that others had not yet ventured into, the trees apparently knocked over in a storm a couple of years before and then covered over with vines and brambles. The wood was well seasoned, not as green as what so many of the men were trying to burn to keep warm. They had fallen upon the treasure with a will, fetching several two-handed saws and then bringing each log back to be split inside the barn. After some democratic debate, which had lasted all of about thirty seconds, they all agreed that this was their find alone, Putnam and company not foraging for the general but simply out prowling about on their own in search of wood or the few hares or pheasants that still survived in the area——thus all the wood was theirs. Fortunately, the storm had shadowed their efforts as they smuggled a good half-cord into the barn to be split.

It was heaven-sent: dry ash and birch that was easy to cut and split, burned hot, and left a good bed of hot ashes to warm them through the night.

In spite of the cold gusts, Peter had his uniform jacket off, the vest, such a lovely gift from Mrs. Hewes, unbuttoned. As others finished their meals, some drew off their jackets, removed their shirts, and began the ritual of louse hunting, carefully going through the seams, a find greeted with a loud exclamation of delight, the victim then crushed between dirty fingernails.

The Robinson twins, each stripped to the waist, were examining each other, poking through each other's hair and armpits, their efforts greeted by more than a few ribald comments about where else they should search for the ever-elusive foes.

Putnam, putting a plate down in front of one of the stoves, suggested a louse race, but he had no takers, men now too intent on their own labors after a hard day, some already taking their cushions, fetching a raggedy blanket from their kit hung up by their sleeping stalls, and just simply flopping down near the stoves and quickly falling asleep.

A few took out crumpled sheets of paper from their haversacks or jacket pockets and, beneath the flickering light of a couple of tallow lamps, read yet again letters that had already been read a hundred times or more . . . for no post had arrived other than those bearing official dispatches since they had come to this place more than six weeks ago. Others fetched a precious sheet of paper for which they had paid two dollars Continental, a fifth of a month's pay, and, using the ink Peter had concocted, laboriously set to work with letters for home, a couple opening small diaries to note down the events of the day: "Mrs. Washington arrived. We got a quarter gill of corn whiskey to celebrate. Storm today, much snow. Still no word of home and if Barbara and the baby are safe from the smallpox . . ."

Others drew out small pocket Bibles or a bit of newspaper and began to read, while off in a corner the gamblers were at work with a tattered deck of cards.

Peter sat silent before one of the stoves, the sides glowing with a soft, shimmering heat, as darkness settled outside, the storm still howling through the eaves. He was lost in thought.

Home. What day is it? Friday? He wasn't sure. Maybe Saturday. Oh, if Saturday, that was the night his mother would always bake some pies and lay up food so as not to have to cook on the Sabbath. In autumn and winter there would always be an apple pie or cobbler drenched in fresh cream. Father would then go to the parlor to read the Bible or, if the post had arrived in time, the latest news from New York and Philadelphia and the world beyond.

Jonathan would often come over, and they would sit on the floor by the fireplace playing chess when boys, though as they got older sometimes the Olsons or even the van Broklins would be having a social, and if so they would be given permission to go. Sometimes there was a songfest at the Methodist church, which his parents didn't hold with; but they turned a blind eye because the entire village knew he was more than a bit smitten with Sarah Treadwell, daughter of the preacher. Of course, he would have to return home before nine. He and Jonathan . . .

Jonathan. Jonathan was dead.

He stared at the glowing stove.

Just a day of rest here, warm, dry, a day of full rations . . . you would be alive, my friend, my beloved friend.

He sat silent, staring at the glowing stove. Jonathan sleeping in his grave in the cold ice- and snow-covered ground at McConkey's Ferry, and yet I am still here.

I am here. I could be home in Trenton now. Hell, nearly everyone else on this night was home except for us few fools. Jonathan's brothers? James, damn him, was most likely grown fat by now, warm by his fireplace——laughing, most likely, at the thought of our misery. Allen? At least he had the stomach to stay on the side he had sworn loyalty to, damn him. Several months back, a letter had come from Sarah, all formal, of course, since her father had without doubt read it before allowing it to be posted, but she had said that there was rumor that Allen had been promoted and was now on the staff of a British general named Grey.

The implication was obvious. Her father was a Tory. If only she had set her cap for Allen, she could perhaps be receiving the attention of a proper officer, one most likely safe and warm in Philadelphia this night.

Allen, my God, Allen, you actually threw in with the butcher of Paoli? He found it hard to believe that Jonathan's brother would have sunk to such an extreme.

And I sit here. Trenton not a day's walk away, or the same as Philadelphia, where it was reported that if a man turned his coat, came through the lines, and signed the oath of allegiance to the king he would be given a warm meal, the king's shilling, and a warm uniform free of vermin.

"Peter?"

He looked up. It was Sergeant Harris.

"Didn't you hear me, lad?"

"What?"

"I told you five minutes ago, change of the watch."

"Oh."

Harris was holding his cartridge box and musket.

Reluctantly standing up, extending his hands for a few more seconds over the blazing heat to warm them up, he buttoned his vest, pulled on his jacket, buttoned it tight, then ducked out under the awning of tents. The temperature on the far side was already below freezing as he went to his stall, where he put on his blanket cape, the dampness in it frozen solid. He inwardly cursed himself——he should have thought to dry it out by the fire earlier. Too late now. Putting on his broken-down hat, he took a strip of canvas and tied the hat down tight under his chin, the canvas covering his ears and cheeks.

Harris was over by the door of the barn, handing him his cartridge box, checking to make sure the outer and inner flaps were sealed tight.

"I checked your load and the pan is dry," Harris said, as he handed the musket over, an oiled cloth wrapped around the lock.

The sergeant cracked the door open and quickly slipped out, closing the door so it would not let in too much of the wintry blast.

Peter took a deep breath. It was painful. Freezing cold, wind driving the snow into his face as he followed Harris to the front door of the headquarters house, where a lone sentry stood. Since no one was watching, he was hunched over against the blast, stamping his feet, musket resting against the doorsill, slapping his hands together to try and keep out the frost.

"Private Sanders! Is that any way to keep watch?" Harris roared.

The poor sentry looked up at him, grabbed his musket, and tried to assume a position of attention.

Harris went up to him.

"Your report?"

"Nothing, Sergeant."

"That's not the way to do it and you know it!"

"Sergeant of the guard. No one has entered or departed since I assumed watch," Sanders announced, teeth chattering. "All quiet, Sergeant."

"That's better. Now dash inside. Unless the boys stole it while I've been out, there's salt pork, and even some warm cider."

Sanders made a feeble gesture of salute and shuffled off for the barn.

"You think you can stand it?" Harris asked. "It is your turn, you know."

"Yes, Sergeant."

Harris patted him on the shoulder.

"Just two hours, lad. I'll keep a spot open for you by the stove."

"Thank you, Sergeant."

Harris patted him again and then wasted no time retreating to the barn, its outline dim in the driving storm, which blasted full into Peter's face.

Peter stood silent. After a few minutes the cold had seeped into his damp boots, each blast of wind in his face sending shivers through him.

He could, at times, hear laughter from within. Snatches of a song caught his attention. It was a hymn. Then another. In the past, before Mrs. Greene and now Mrs. Washington arrived, if there was singing it was usually the songs of soldiers. That had changed and the sound of it warmed his heart.

Jonathan was dead. Sarah was in Trenton. Allen was most likely in Philadelphia, warm and content this night while I freeze out here.

But at least, for the moment, the echo of the hymn warmed his soul.

The evening's entertainment passed with warmth and friendliness. Martha was back by his side, and he could see the delight in the smiles of his young staff and older comrades for his happiness. At least here, at this moment, the world felt at ease.

The meal gradually broke up, Martha insisting that she help General Greene's wife with cleaning up alongside Billy Lee. The house was warm, his stomach full, and he now felt a great unease.

Excusing himself from the last few well-wishers, he went into the foyer and drew on his cape and hat.

"Sir?"

It was Laurens.

"Just going out for a walk."

"Sir, should I call the guard detail?"

He shook his head. Laurens was obsessed with the fear that a British agent, an assassin, might be lurking somewhere, and he was always on guard. Washington himself had long ago taken something of a Presbyterian view of such matters . . . if fated to die that way, that was fate, and he would not live in constant fear of it.

"May I go with you, sir?"

He smiled.

"Stay here in case any dispatches arrive. I just need to walk off the meal."

Before Laurens could argue further, he opened the door and stepped out into the storm. The private guarding the entryway roused himself and snapped to attention.

He looked over at the lad, hat rim bent down with the weight of wet snow.

"It is Private Wellsley, isn't it?" he asked.

"Ah, yes, sir."

"All quiet."

"Sir. Yes, sir. All quiet."

"Good work, soldier, stand at ease," he replied and walked on.

Closing the gate to the barnyard, he walked up the snow-covered road to the main encampment area. Snow swirled about him, all but obliterating the world, carpeting it in pure clean whiteness. Storms like this were rare along the Potomac, but often, out on the frontier, especially in the western Virginian mountains, a blow like this would come on. He and his companions would quickly pitch a camp and sometimes wait for days for it to clear. And when it did, all was blanketed in purity of white.

As he reached the outer ring of encampments and company streets, he slowed. He knew his form was hard to conceal, for he was, after all, one of the tallest men in the army. He hunched his shoulders down, and pulled the brim of his cap low over his brow, passing a picket, who simply saluted after he replied with the password for the day.

The air was rich with the scent of burning wood. He could see the reflected glow of fires from the wattle and daub chimney tops of the cabins. There were snatches of conversations, laughter, the sound of a violin playing a jaunty air. Everyone except the forlorn sentries was inside——out of the storm. He stood silent, listening for a few minutes in the middle of a company street. There had been full rations today and the men were relatively content. With the storm upon them, the instinct was to huddle together close to the fires within, and only to venture out for the most pressing of personal business.

An officer passed, hesitated, asked for the password, looked closely at him as if not sure.

"Cold night, sir," he finally ventured.

"'Tis."

"Can I get you anything, sir?"

"How goes it with your men?" he asked.

The officer seemed to hesitate.

"Hard day, sir. One of the regimental pets died."

"Sir?"

"Our drummer boy. Only fifteen. Lung sickness. He had a father and three brothers in the ranks. Everyone is taking it hard."

The officer nodded to the cabin they were standing near.

Unlike the others, from within this one he could hear crying.

On impulse he turned and went to the cabin, the officer nervously following.

"Sir, they are Irish; it's a wake."

"I feel I should make my condolences," he replied. Slowly moving back the blanket that served as a door, he bent low and stepped in.

It was indeed a wake. They had yet to bury the boy, his still form stretched out on a bunk, gray face exposed. A man he assumed was the boy's father sat on the bunk, holding the hand of his dead son. The cabin was packed with men so that it was actually warm within. Those sitting stood when they saw who was standing in the doorway. The father looked up at him but didn't stir.

"Please, all remain at ease," he offered, suddenly feeling a bit embarrassed for intruding thus.

"I was just told of your tragic loss, sir," he said to the father, "and may I offer my condolences."

The man did not speak, just gazing at him.

"I am so sorry . . ." His voice trailed off. What could he offer here? A speech of encouragement? Hollow-sounding words that the youth had died for a gallant cause. The boy's feet were sticking out from under the blanket, black from frostbite and rot.

If anything, he wished at this instant he could grab every corrupt contractor, every member of Congress who dawdled with committee reports, and bring them before this corpse and the father and let them explain.

"I am so sorry," was all he could say yet again, and he started to back out of the cabin.

"Tell that to my wife, sir," the old man snapped, looking at him coldly. "Will you go to her and explain why our youngest died like this?"

He did not reply, as there was no reply to give. He stepped back into the storm, the officer following.

"I apologize, sir," the officer offered.

"None needed, sir. After the boy is buried, give the father, or one of his sons, a furlough home so they can break the news to that boy's mother."

"Thank you, sir."

He sighed, back turned to the storm.

"Sir," the officer ventured, nervously clearing his throat.

"Yes?"

"There's a rumor that we are on half-rations again come tomorrow."

It was true. If this storm did not abate, freezing their wagons and Wayne's foragers in place, it would be half-rations tomorrow and then either no rations or quarter-rations the day after.

"Pray the storm relents and General Wayne can bring in supplies," he sighed, and walked off.

He felt he should turn back——Martha was waiting——but he continued on, shaken by the gaze of the mourning father. He passed more regimental encampments, barely noticed, like a ghost drifting by. In one street a bonfire was burning——a waste of firewood, but there seemed to be some sort of entertainment, a fifer and drummer playing a tune, some of the men and women of the camp dancing in spite of the storm. In another street there was an altercation, and he was tempted to step in. Two men exchanged blows until he saw that it was a fair "soldier's fight." Men were ringed about, cheering the two on, both men stripped to the waist, a sergeant moving in to break them apart, at one point shouting, "No kicking, wrestling, or gouging——fists only." He watched for a minute until one of the pugilists, the bigger of the two, was knocked flat, the sergeant jumping between them, shouting that the fight was over and that the two were to shake hands.

He smiled when he overheard that the two were brothers and the brawl a nearly weekly affair between them. Still, he was a bit surprised when the man who was knocked nearly cold stood up, the sergeant helping him don a captain's jacket, his brother in the ragged uniform of a private.

He crossed an open field, the parade ground, rarely used, and then saw ahead the low, squat cabins of one of the hospitals. He got up the nerve to step into the nearest. Soldier or not, the stench was near to overpowering. The room was dimly lit by the fireplaces blazing at each end. Bunks were filled to overflowing, the bunks pegged four high above each other from nearly the floor to the ceiling. A woman was carefully feeding broth to a young soldier whom she was holding as if he were a child. Another woman sat by the fire, reading aloud from a Bible. At first no one noticed his presence. It was hard to breathe, and he just stood for a moment, then caught the eye of a soldier in a bunk at shoulder height to him.

"General Washington?" the man whispered.

He nodded and stepped to his side.

"You will soon be well," Washington offered, again feeling awkward, his words lame, for the man was little better than a skeleton. From the stench it was obvious he was in the final throes of the flux, body wasting away.

The man extended a hand, which Washington grasped. The man tried to force a smile as if to reassure him.

"You will soon be well," Washington whispered.

The woman reading the Bible had stopped and looked at him. Standing, she came to his side.

"Now, Vincent, the general is right. Rest easy."

The soldier looked to the woman but this time shook his head, tears welling up.

"You wrote my letter home," he whispered.

She nodded in reply.

He let go of the general and rolled on to his side, facing the wall.

She pulled the single filthy blanket up over his bony shoulders.

Feeling as if he was an intruder, Washington went out the door, and the woman followed.

"Sir?"

He turned to face her.

"The rumor about food, are we out again?"

"For the hospitals, no," he replied and at least this was true.

"But medicines? We have nothing."

"I know. I am trying."

She leaned forward and began to cough. A deep rasping wheeze with each indrawn breath.

"You are sick, you should not be out here," he paused, "or in there, either."

"What else am I to do then?" she announced, forcing a smile.

"I could order you to rest."

"Thee can order as thee pleases, sir. And I shall disobey. This is the duty God gave me."

He stared at her intently, bracing her as she was seized by more shuddering coughs.

She stopped, wiping her mouth with the back of her sleeve, and in the darkness the splotches of blood looked black.

"I should go back. Vincent has not much longer. I should be with him."

He nodded, squeezing her shoulders.

"God be with——with thee," he hesitated, adopting the Quaker manner of speech.

"And with thee."

She returned to the hospital hut. He stood alone for long minutes in the storm.

He walked alone thus most every night. It was the time to gauge the mood, the sense of his camp, his army. The suffering was beyond any he had ever imagined this war would bring. At times he felt it would indeed break him.

And how would General Gates handle all of this if he took command? The thought haunted him. He had long drilled himself since early manhood to think not of himself. A gentleman, a leader, did not bring personal considerations into such equations. But these men and now these women?

One ill-chosen response, one flash of temper, of self-serving behavior or blame-casting, one day of failed leadership could shatter the fragile core that held this army together. And in humility he knew that he was the center, the core of what was holding this last fragment of an army, of a Revolution, together.

He turned and started the long walk back to his headquarters, facing into the eye of the storm, hat now pulled low, not to conceal but to keep the icy gusts out of his eyes.

At last gaining the gate, he paused for a moment to catch his breath. That was disturbing. He was no longer a man of twenty, he was going into his forty-seventh year——by the old calendar it was only a few days off. He at last opened the gate and approached the house. The same sentry was in place. Not seeing his general approach, Peter had rested his musket against the doorsill and was vigorously beating his arms around his chest and stamping his feet. At the sight of Washington's approach he quickly grabbed his musket and came to attention.

"Your relief should be along any minute, Private," Washington offered. "'Tis a bitter night."

"Sorry, sir," he offered.

"You are doing your duty well, son. I hope a warm fire awaits you."

"Thank you, sir."

He went to open the door for the general, but Washington took the knob himself and opened it, then quickly closed the door behind him as an icy gust blasted around him.

"George?"

He was delighted to see Martha standing on the staircase, wrapped in a heavy blanket.

She hurried down to help him off with his wet cape and hat, hanging them up. His staff, in the kitchen, stood up, ready for orders.

"Any news while I was away?"

"No, sir. Nothing."

"Fine, then, gentlemen," he hesitated, looking over at Martha for a moment.

"Time to retire, then."

He felt a bit self-conscious going up the stairs with Martha following. It felt strange to have her in the bedroom, where he had slept alone for over a month. She had set out a pitcher of warm water for him to wash his hands and face. He thought of the hand he had grasped of the man dying of the flux, wondering if Dr. Rush's theory might be true that such contagions could be spread by touch and just by breathing the same air.

He scrubbed his hands thoroughly with the rough cake of lye soap. Martha helped him doff his uniform jacket and vest and then insisted upon helping him with his ice-caked boots, setting them close, but not too close, to the crackling fireplace.

He felt suddenly shy as he removed his breeches, which she took as well and hung up by the fireplace while he slipped between the covers. Merciful heaven, the sheets were warmed by several bricks she had set in the fire earlier, fished out, and wrapped in towels. It was a comfort Billy Lee never thought of.

She blew out the candle by the washbasin, dropped the blanket she had wrapped around herself, and settled in by his side.

It had been far more than half a year since they had been alone. And yet now? This moment?

He thought of the Quaker woman, the icy chill of the hospital cabin, barely touched by the fires within, the father with his dead son, the rough-hewn cabins filled with men shivering on this cold winter night, knowing their stomachs would be empty again come morning.

She snuggled in by his side, his arm around her.

"My dear," he finally sighed, "I need to think awhile," he whispered, embarrassed.

"I understand," she sighed, drew closer to his side, and then drifted to sleep.

Long after she had gone to sleep, he stared up, the flicker of light from the fireplace dancing on the ceiling while outside the cold wind rattled the shutters, windowpanes frosted over. And thus he would still be awake with the first light of dawn, lost in thought and prayer.

CHAPTER TEN

* * *

Philadelphia
February 12, 1778

It was a glorious Sunday afternoon, the weather almost springlike, with a warming breeze wafting over the city from the southwest, such a welcome change from the storms of the week before. The dark skies of the previous days were gone, replaced with a deep, warm blue, more like an April morning than a winter day with spring still far off.

Most of the officers of the army were engaging in the weekly ritual of the Sunday promenade along the Philadelphia dockside, joined by those citizens of substance who wished to show their loyalty and comradeship with the higher ranks in service to the Crown.

But Allen van Dorn was unaware of those strolling by, other than keeping a wary eye out for superior rank and offering the proper salute, which could be tiresome since it seemed on this day that nearly every officer, British and Hessian, was out and about, enjoying the fine break in the weather. He was lost in thought, pausing to gaze up at the forest of masts of the dozens of ships that lined the wharf, some of them heavy oaken frigates, along with brigs and sloops of the Royal Navy. Beside them were transports, supply ships, merchantmen, and even a few whalers, their crews Loyalists. Having fled their home ports in rebel New England, they were now based here.

The excitement of an hour or so ago had caused a crowd to gather as a fast packet from London, bearing the latest dispatches for the army, had tied off at the Market Street wharf. Word was already sweeping the streets about the news from France. He had stood at the edge of the crowd. Far too many officers of superior rank were pressed up to the gangplank demanding that their personal letters and packages were to be handed over before all the others. Near fights and challenges of duels had erupted when some young earl took umbrage that a mere colonel of infantry had pushed ahead of him.

"Lieutenant van Dorn! I say, van Dorn!"

He turned and saw that it was Captain André, with both Peggy Shippen and Elizabeth Risher in tow. He felt a thrill of delight, not having seen Miss Risher since the party. André had chided him more than once: He had by all reports repeatedly shown bravery on the battlefield, thus why not venture a frontal assault, go to her dwelling, and see what came of it, or at the very least pen a note to thus convey his interest.

He had not pursued either suggestion. Philadelphia was a city seething with intrigue, and though he trusted Miss Risher, he knew her parents as well. How would they react to his attempt? They would never see him as the proper sort of suitor. If victory in the end should go to the English side, then without doubt they would hope to make a proper arrangement with a proper officer, and not a Loyalist from a provincial village. And if the British side should eventually lose? Many parents with an eye toward the future were keeping watchful eyes on their daughters, cautioning them to wait until the campaign was resolved before extending any kind of serious attention. Besides, they did know his family, the fate of his brother Jonathan and the role he had played at Trenton, and were the type that would spread rumors about his own loyalty even though General Grey had dismissed such speculation when he put him on his staff. Of course, part of the reason Grey had taken him on was his intimate knowledge of the land and its people, from Trenton to the Jersey coast, which he had often traveled over with his father on family business. And that, as well, would stand against him with the Rishers, for he was the son of a tanner.

But at this moment, he pushed those concerns aside as André approached, his normally sanguine features aglow with delight.

"They came!" André announced, holding up a sheaf of papers.

Others were turning to watch as André came up to Allen and, as if presenting an award, handed the package over to him.

The package and wrapping were torn open, and within . . . within was a treasure.

He scanned the first sheet——it was the music by Mozart!

Scanning the lines, he translated the notations, in his mind, to the sound of Franklin's glass harmonica.

Good heavens, though, it was most difficult——on the second page, a fugue ran for a dozen stanzas that required all ten fingers. At most he had mastered four fingers, a few brief moments of chords using six fingers . . . but this would demand quarter- and eighth-notes, with all ten fingers at play.

On a harpsichord he might have been able to do it with a little practice, but on Franklin's magical instrument?

And yet, when he tore his gaze from the pages and looked up at André, and particularly Miss Risher by his left side and Miss Shippen at his right, what could he do?

"Give me a few days," he announced, trying to force a smile of confidence.

That was something he had quickly learned by serving in this army. At times skill and true ability did not count in the slightest. It was the front, the bluster, the forward show that counted for so much here. André, though still a mere captain, exuded that. He had a certain flair, a self-confident tone of voice and manner that equaled and could trump that of any nineteen-year-old earl or duke demanding command of a brigade because of his lineage and connections to the king.

"So, Lieutenant, think you can master some Mozart in time for our party come Saturday?"

Considering his musings about having the right flair, he looked back down at the incredibly complex sheet of music, studied it for a moment, then nodded gravely.

"Consider it done, sir," he replied. It would mean committing himself to long nights of practice without sleep in order to be able to give a halfway decent performance and not embarrass himself or André. At least with the harmonica, unlike the harpsichord, volume could be controlled by applying just the lightest tough to the rotating glass, so that he did not have to fear awakening the staff and General Grey over the next week.

"Splendid, my good fellow!" André cried, clapping him on the back while taking the precious sheet music back.

"Amazing talent, this Mozart," he waxed enthusiastically, holding up the package. "I scanned it briefly, letting it play in my heart——and to think this composer is younger than us! To have such talent."

"But would you trade it for the ability to command a regiment in the field?" Miss Shippen asked, smiling boldly.

André looked over at her.

"Which would you prefer?" he asked.

She smiled coyly.

"I think . . ." She paused, and the display caught Allen in the wrong way. It was obvious she was playing the flirt. "I think a soldier is more to my liking. These musicians are such flighty types, almost as bad as writers. Did I tell you I actually was forced to eat dinner once with that detestable Thomas Paine?"

"Well," André offered, "he does have a certain talent with the quill, even if it is claptrap and treasonous rot that he writes."

Allen said nothing. Her mention of Tom Paine struck him like a bolt. The memory of his brother Jonathan, clutching the waterlogged, tattered pamphlet as he died.

"Paine can go to hell. Thousands have died because of what he wrote and he is still alive," Allen snapped.

André looked at him and smiled, Peggy laughed at his exclamation, but Elizabeth was just silent.

"Oh, enough of him, he'll be dead from drink within the year, I hear," André announced, stepping away from the group and motioning for them to follow along, leaving the growing, clamoring crowd around the packet ship behind.

They stepped around a gang of laborers off-loading a light sloop with steeply raked masts, André explaining that it was a prize ship, yet another French smuggler captured with a load of powder, a dozen fieldpieces, and other assorted accoutrements for the rebels.

"Captain of the frigate that took her, the *Hermes*, is a cousin twice removed. His share of the prize money should fetch a thousand pounds or more, I hear." He sighed. "Perhaps I should have gone for the navy after all."

"And missed wintering here with us in Philadelphia?" Peggy asked.

He pressed her hand in closer against his side.

"Of course I chose to serve where my king might need me," he replied, and Allen looked over at him, seeing the touch of a sarcastic look as he gazed back at the booty being off-loaded.

A man with proper connections could, of course, buy his way into command even of a regiment, but far more sought after were high postings with the Royal Navy, for there indeed was the prize money. But that took, in turn, money and proper connections, unless one was willing to enter as a mere midshipman and endure years of danger and hardship in order to rise. André had neither the time for one nor the money to purchase position other than where he now was.

There was, of course, the prospect of quick promotion offered by war, as voiced in a favorite regimental drinking toast, "to a long war or a bloody plague."

André gazed back longingly at the captured sloop and then pulled his attention away.

"So, have we all heard the news?"

"Only a few odd bits," Elizabeth replied. "Everyone was so excited and jostling about."

"And you and Miss Shippen saw that jostling crowd as your opportunity to slip off from your chaperones," André retorted with a grin.

"Something like that," she replied, smiling.

"And thus I found them," André announced. "Two fair maidens, tossed upon a lonely sea of rude majors, gouty colonels, and coarse civilians clamoring for news. I of course rescued them. And having spied you out earlier, upon receiving my long anticipated package I thought it might interest you." He reached into his breast pocket and drew out a folded sheet of paper. "The *London Gazette*, dated the fourth of January this year," he announced. They slowed as André held the paper up and turned so that the warm afternoon sun was over his shoulder. He scanned the paper for a moment as if withholding some great secret, Peggy leaning up on his arm to catch a glimpse.

"Oh, the usual deaths of barons and kings, some sort of trouble in the Maldives and India, the usual things. Oh heavens, a plague reported in Persia. I do see that Coleridge and Sons are offering the finest silks newly arrived from China . . ." His voice trailed off as he played out his game of indifference. "Hmm, no really fresh news here."

His features, so light a moment before, finally turned grim as he scanned what everyone on the street was already talking about.

"Though there is something about Saratoga."

"That's the first report out of London, isn't it?" Allen asked.

André looked over at him, no mirth in his eyes, and nodded gravely.

"Poor Johnny. He will never live it down. A good man, Burgoyne. The blame is not all his by any stretch."

Allen found himself looking around, hoping that no one had heard such a cavalier response. Few in this army would dare to put the blame for the disaster anywhere other than at the feet of General "Johnny" Burgoyne. Though all of them, including General Grey, were struck incredulous back in August when the army had boarded ship in New York, not to sail up the Hudson to meet Burgoyne in a grand pincer movement that would have shattered the rebels' northern army and sealed off New England, but instead to sail in the opposite direction to seize Philadelphia.

The campaign south instead of north had struck many a young officer as absurd: sailing all the way down to the Virginia Capes and the entry into the Chesapeake Bay, then turning north to sail all the way back to near Wilmington. It had taken nearly a month, while all knew that Burgoyne, in the northern wilderness, fully assumed that the Howe brothers would appear any day, drive off the bedeviling enemy surrounding him, and achieve a stunning victory.

Instead, their action, though giving them Philadelphia, had given the rebels Saratoga.

André scanned the report, lips pressed tight, features suddenly grim.

"Parliament is demanding an investigation. Report that Whigs in Dublin celebrated by dancing in the street and hanging Burgoyne in effigy, damn them."

He sighed and shook his head.

"What of France?" Elizabeth asked.

"Oh, yes," he replied rather absently, all merriment of but moments before gone.

"A report that at Versailles a grand illumination was ordered by the king, with fireworks and numerous salutes fired in honor of the rebel victory and its glorious leaders."

He scanned further.

"Our ambassador to the court of Louis XVI has returned to London in protest. The correspondent reports that the king has formally acknowledged the presence of Mr. Franklin at a royal reception," he paused, "and that a recognition of the rebel government and with it a declaration of war are expected within the month."

Muttering a foul curse, he crumpled up the precious paper and threw it down on the pavement. A street urchin swept in and snatched it before it hit the cobblestones and was off with his prize, which would surely fetch sixpence or even a shilling this day.

André turned away from his friends and walked down to the edge of the street and docks, stopping at last to look out over the Delaware, which was tossed by whitecaps from the southwesterly breeze. His arms were folded across his breast, head lowered.

Peggy went up and slipped her hand back under his arm. He looked down at her and forced a smile.

"My apologies, my dear," he said, and looked back at Allen and Elizabeth.

"Apologies, most ungentlemanly of me."

"Understandable," Allen replied.

"It could have been ending by now," André said, voice filled with bitterness. "We should be back in New York at this very moment, having sallied northward to first relieve Burgoyne, seize the Hudson Highlands, and then, with Burgoyne's army swelling our ranks, the northern rebels shattered, New England would be entirely cut off. Then time enough in the spring to march on this city, take it, and end the war before summer."

Yet again Allen looked around cautiously, nervous that someone might overhear his friend's lament. It was, of course, the complaint of nearly all when sitting together late at night over a bottle of brandy and cards, but most undiplomatic to be voiced out on the streets of the former rebel capital on a Sunday afternoon. If one of Howe's staff overheard and marked André down, any hope of advancement for him would be shattered, even if his assessment was indeed true.

"Not now, sir," Allen whispered. "What is done is done. We'll talk of it later."

"He's right," Elizabeth offered. "Please sir, moderation is best at this moment for you."

André looked over at her and smiled.

"Thank you, Miss Risher. Good counsel, even from someone who I suspect is a rebel at heart."

Her features did not change in the slightest, nor did she reply.

He laughed good-naturedly.

"Please do not take offense, Miss Risher."

"Well, I am certainly not one of such persuasion," Peggy announced.

He looked down at her and smiled.

"Oh, of course not, my dear."

André looked over at Allen.

"What do you think?"

"Not my place to say, sir."

"Allen——it is Allen, isn't it? At least last time we talked I recall that being your given name," he announced with a smile.

"Yes, sir."

"And out here it is John, so drop the sir."

Allen did not reply.

"What do you think, Allen?"

"Do you really want my opinion?"

"I wouldn't ask otherwise. Let's call this our little conspiracy, Allen." As he spoke, he motioned for him to draw a little closer.

Allen stepped closer and noted, for the first time, that there was the hint of brandy on André's breath. Was he drunk? If not, he was without doubt being indiscreet.

"It is hard news."

"Oh, really? War with France, it is inevitable. Every twenty years or so we have a war with France, and maybe once every hundred years we ally with them for a time. So no shock there. Might as well have at it again——after all, we are soldiers and war is our trade. So business will be good come summer."

Allen nodded. "It troubles me that my own people would ally with the very enemy we fought less than twenty years ago."

"Political necessity. But then again you Americans seem to favor some notion of war being a moral question rather than one of political reality. So it might be distasteful to some to ally with a former enemy against your fellow Englishmen, but then again, such is war."

Allen could detect the bitterness in André's comment.

"I want this absurdity to be over with, Allen. Why your Washington and company hang on in Valley Forge is beyond me. You've seen the reports—— as have I, from our scouts and spies. They are dying by the score every day. They only built the last of their so-called shelters within the last week. They sustain themselves on a ration a day that we would sneer at and throw into the gutter for the dogs. When will they just give up?"

"When they are beaten and not before," Allen said quietly.

André turned to look at him, and now there was a glint of anger in his eyes.

"When? Poor Johnny and his men, but one small part of our armies. Yes, I denounce this move here rather than going to his aid, but, good God, man, we've beaten Washington in every battle except for a few minor skirmishes a year ago."

Minor skirmishes. He looked over at Elizabeth. She said nothing, but he sensed that she was thinking of Jonathan and his death.

"You want my honest opinion, sir," Allen asked.

"It's John, remember, Allen. For the moment it is John."

"Then I will tell you."

He hesitated, looking at Peggy, wondering for an instant if this night she would share every word she heard. He could see curiosity in Elizabeth as to where he truly stood.

"You will have to put this Revolution in the grave," Allen said. "No more coy games of march and countermarch and then settling in here for the winter and hoping that the rebels will just melt away."

Frustrated, he looked back to the southwest, into the warming breeze. Out in the countryside this breeze was wiping away the last of the snow of the week before. Another day or two and the roads would be dry enough to support light infantry; a day or two after that, the entire army.

"One forced march could put us in front of Valley Forge. Then if it snows, rains, freezes, whatever God sends, we are in front of Valley Forge. If need be we endure what they are enduring within sight of their lines. If the weather turns foul we endure it as they have endured it. Then the first fair day after that we sweep them away in one hard push and end this damn war rather than sit out the winter here swelling our bellies, drinking ourselves senseless, and playing our games."

André shook his head and laughed softly.

"My, you certainly do sound like a Frederick, or even a czarina."

"I had an uncle who fought on the frontier in the last war, not like my father, who just sat in a garrison for a few months, but out on the edge of the Ohio Valley. He was out there for two years. I've heard Washington did the same. They learned from it, and if I dare to say it, if my uncle was still alive today, he would be at Valley Forge and laughing at us."

"As your brother would be if still alive?" André replied, and Allen stiffened.

He was not sure how to react, and André, realizing he had overstepped, extended a hand in a calming gesture.

"Of course General Grey knows. He shared it with me because he knows you and I are friends, but I swear to you, upon my oath, that no others with the brigade know. It is safe with us."

Allen still could not reply.

"I meant no insult, though your words just now were harsh."

"They are how I see it. You asked me, sir, and I am telling you. Do not underestimate the capacity of the rebels for suffering. They will not melt away with the next winter storm. If anything, that will toughen them and make us weaker."

André shook his head.

"You give too much credence to this Washington and his rabble."

"I saw them, sir. I was their prisoner, as were you. You know how tough they can be."

André shook his head, and Allen could sense he had hit a raw nerve.

"Rabble, I tell you," André said coldly. "My friend, do not be insulted by what I say. There is a profound difference between you and me."

"And that is?"

"I have been on both continents, you have not."

"So I am a provincial?" Allen let slip.

André laughed softly and shook his head, putting a reassuring hand on Allen's shoulder.

"You Americans and your pride. No insult intended."

"Nor taken," Elizabeth interjected, and André offered her a courteous nod.

"You Americans take such pride in your heartiness, in this frontier of yours, which you claim shapes men such as Washington, Wayne, and Morgan. I will admit that, man for man, one of your yeomen, matched against some poor devil swept up from the streets of London or Edinburgh and pressed into a uniform because there is no alternative left . . . well, there indeed is a match. But what can be found in our army and not the rebels' is discipline."

He warmed to his subject, and Allen noticed that some of those strolling by slowed, taking in André's heated words, more than a few of them officers out with their ladies, or what they attempted to pass off as ladies, by their side this sunny afternoon.

"I will not deny the courage of the rebels, at least at Germantown, or the year before at Trenton and Princeton. But in the moment of crisis, they lack discipline. They lack officers of character and breeding in whom they can trust. The rebels, an order is given and, good God above, the privates are ready to form a committee to debate it even as the cannonballs fly about their ears!"

He chuckled softly, shaking his head.

"Our men can march fifteen miles in a day with eighty pounds on their backs, knowing that if they drop out there will be a damn good flogging unless they show a pass. The rebels, we've seen how they march, the roadside littered with cast-off equipment, every woodlot filled with their deserters running off. They are drunk when they should be sober and, by God, sober when they do have a right on occasion to be drunk as any soldier would be.

"Our army and the Hessians have been drilled on the battlefields of Europe. More than a few of them veterans of the Seven Years. And, yes, more than a few of them veterans of the last war here. Thus they know the ways of the wilderness and how to fight in it when need be. I daresay if poor Johnny had our brigade of light infantry with him to sweep ahead of his main body as he marched from Lake George to Saratoga, the damn newspapers in London would be printing a different story today."

André had touched on the pride of the brigade he now served with, and Allen could not help but nod in agreement. In his heart, though, he suspected that in the end they would have gone into captivity as well. A brigade of light infantry, no matter how brilliantly trained for fighting in rough terrain and wilderness, would collapse if cut off from rations, ammunition, and resupply, as Burgoyne's men were.

"Our men can fire four volleys a minute and sweep the field before them, even if they are hollow-chested consumptives from the streets of London. The rabble? After the first volley, all they know how to do is run when they see the solid red lines of infantry advancing toward them with bayonets lowered."

He finished with a flourish. A number of those passing by, slowing, heard his statement and offered polite applause. A few cried out, "Hear, hear! Well said, Captain!" and then moved on.

André, the touch of the showman in him, realizing he had gathered an audience, smiled and nodded in reply.

Allen stood silent. The mention of bayonets conjured the memory of Paoli, the wounded on the ground screaming for mercy. This army dismissed it, even held an inquiry, exonerated Grey, and praised him. But the rebels? He could imagine that the memory of it still seethed and that there might someday soon be a terrible reckoning, especially if Wayne and his men ever received a chance to square off against Grey and the light infantry in an even match.

André looked straight at him and shook his head.

"You disagree."

"I wish for nothing more than a final victory of our arms and an end to this bloody war."

"But you do disagree?"

"Suppose this winter they learn discipline."

"What?"

"Discipline, sir. What are they doing up there at Valley Forge?"

"Starving and freezing, though maybe today they are sitting outside their huts, and while we enjoy this afternoon promenade they are picking lice out of their shirts and beards."

He looked to the two ladies and nodded. "Forgive me for such coarse references," he said with a smile.

"But suppose they do learn discipline this winter?" Allen pressed. "Maybe not matching us volley for volley, because that takes years of training, but discipline enough to hold their lines, take casualties, maneuver, and keep on fighting. God help us if they do master that."

"Then it shall be a most interesting fight come spring," André replied, still smiling.

"No insult intended to any of you," André sighed. "I am carried away by the moment. Come, my friends, let us return to Dr. Franklin's house and see what this latest work by Mozart sounds like on his amazing instrument."

André led the way, turning back southward along the dockside. They passed the captured sloop with its equipment. So desperately needed by the rebels now, it would just sit in a warehouse, for the army was bloated with such supplies. They pressed around the edge of the crowd that was still gathered around the packet ship, officers and even some enlisted men lined up, calling out their names and regiments, hoping for a cherished letter or package from across the wide sea. André and Peggy were a bit ahead by now, Elizabeth falling in by Allen's side.

He could see she was looking around warily, and then relaxed once clear of the crowd.

"Guess your father gave up on you and went home," he offered.

She laughed softly.

"Peggy's family is all but throwing her at the good captain, but my parents . . . ," and she sighed, smiling but shaking her head.

"I will vouch for your safety and honor," he offered.

"Precisely the point, Allen van Dorn."

"In other words?"

"You know as well as I do how my parents stand."

"In other words, I'm just a provincial, not a proper officer?"

She came closer to his side and to his amazement slipped her hand under his arm.

"Precisely, good sir."

He looked at her and saw the blush coming to her cheeks.

Dare he hope?

"Why did you not call upon me? Or at least write?" she asked in the most forthright manner.

Caught off-guard, he could only stammer, "I thought you would . . ." and his voice trailed off.

"May I ask a question?"

"Anything."

She hesitated, looking over her shoulder and to either side.

"Why are you in that uniform?"

"Miss?"

"You heard me."

"I think it is obvious, isn't it?" he finally offered, his voice barely a whisper.

"I know you well enough to know you are not a turncoat. That you believe in what you are doing. But still, Allen, I was amazed when I met you at the party last month, though I did hear of your capture and release."

"So you are a rebel?" he whispered.

"Of course I am."

"And Miss Shippen?"

She gave a snort of disdain. "Loyalist if the uniforms in town are red, patriot if they are blue or homespun."

He could hear the cool dislike in her voice.

"You seem friendly enough with Captain André."

She laughed softly.

"Allen, you really are a provincial. A lady can be charmed by a true gentleman regardless of uniform, but that does not mean she will set her cap for him. He is a noble soul and I wish he was on our side."

"Rather than mine?"

"Yes, rather than yours."

"And your feelings about my being in this uniform?"

"Oh, Allen, didn't you hear me? I can be charmed by a gentleman regardless of uniform. Though in your case I just might set my cap for you."

It felt as if his heart would stop. She sensed his reaction and laughed softly.

"And, no, I am not some flirt such as Miss Shippen. I speak my mind as I see things."

"Why me?" he blurted out.

"Maybe I like Mozart," she said, raising her voice slightly, for they were approaching the front door of Franklin's home, a servant holding it open. André, hearing her, looked back and smiled.

She drew closer. "My parents at times are out of town visiting my mother's family. I will send word when they are. My servant is African. His name is David, and he can be trusted."

He stammered, unable to reply.

They were at the door. Some of the windows were open in the warm air. It was time for tea, and there was an informal gathering within. All talked of the latest news from London and the prospect of open war with France. Boasts were offered that such a prospect would surely bring promotions to all of them by the time the war was finished.

André guided them into Franklin's study, hurriedly going over to the harmonica. Several other officers and their companions were in the room. André announced that there was to be a concert. Two of the couples withdrew, but one of them stayed, a captain who sniffed that surely they were not going to crank up such a machine made by a damn rebel.

A sidelong glance from André stilled the protest. A comment in French and the captain stiffened, glared at André, and withdrew.

"What did you say?" Allen asked.

"Oh yes, forgot. You know German, not French. Rude of me."

"What did you say to him?" Peggy asked.

"Just being rude, that's all," he laughed, and opening the package he set the composition on the stand by the side of the harmonica, eagerly motioning for Allen to sit down.

He looked at the sheets of music. At least thirty pages or more. Good heavens, this was not some simple piece for a harpsichord, it was the length of a concerto. Knowing André, the captain would be boasting about a concert for next weekend. There was many a sleepless night ahead.

He began to work the pedals, the drive belt turning the shaft upon which were mounted the crystal goblets, each one marked with a tracing of colored ink: yellow for C, dark yellow for C-sharp, light blue for G, and so on up the scale.

Unfortunately, the sheet music before him was not marked with colored inks. He would have to talk with André, to at least dot each note with the matching color on the harmonica if there was any hope of him mastering this piece in less than a week.

He dipped his fingertips into the bowl of chalk, studied the first few measures for a moment, took a deep breath, extended his hands, and lightly touched the spinning orbs of crystal.

He tried only six fingers. The second and third finger of his left hand were off by half a note, and he adjusted. Another deep breath, the next notes, another breath——far too long, of course, for Mozart opened this piece with his usual vigor. He slowly worked through the first few measures, tried a second time, and then nodded.

"Here goes," he whispered, and at half-time at best, he managed the first line.

It was wonderful, absolutely wonderful. All else of this world was forgotten as Franklin's machine turned notations of ink on paper and his feeble attempt to play them into a sweet, melodious blend of heavenly chords.

All was forgotten, the war, what they had just spoken of, even, for a moment, the presence of Elizabeth and her bold offer of a rendezvous.

"What is that god-awful wailing, I say?"

Startled, Allen stopped and looked up. The captain that André had shooed off was standing out in the hallway, several others gathered around him, shaking their heads.

André made no pretense now. He strode to the door and without comment slammed it shut, then turned back, smiling.

"Let's forget about the rest of the world this afternoon, my friends. Pray, sir, please continue!"

Allen could see genuine excitement, even affection in André's eyes, and indeed, all was forgotten for the moment as he turned back to the instrument, spindle whirling, glass orbs mounted on it a blur, casting rainbow patterns on the wall from the sunlight streaming in from the west-facing windows. He noticed something he had never taken in before, that this instrument was like one of Newton's prisms, turning light into rainbows.

He let his fingers brush against the turning orbs, and this time played the first line as Mozart had intended it. And yet, even as he played, all else forgotten for the moment, he could not help but notice Elizabeth's hand resting on his shoulder, squeezing it tight. He looked up at her to smile and noticed, to his astonishment and delight, that there were tears in her eyes as she gazed at him; and it seemed to him that, in that moment, she saw not a merchant's son and soldier but his very soul.

CHAPTER ELEVEN

* * *

Valley Forge
February 28, 1778

He had started the morning ride from near Morgantown, a pleasant region of rolling hills and what had once been prosperous farms, obviously tended by Germans, as witnessed by their neatness and apparent wealth. This new country did indeed hold promise, if they could ever win their independence. The land was rich. Here a peasant could own a hundred acres if he had the strength to clear it, and in a generation his sons could live like gentry if they worked hard enough and were frugal. The war, however, had reached this far westward. The barnyards looked empty, houses were shuttered, the few farmers about watching warily as his party rode past. No young men were in the fields, and the muddy lane that passed for a road was devoid of any traffic.

The day had turned warm——the snow on south-facing slopes, fallen several days ago, had melted away by midday; the ground was heavy with moisture. The road was barely passable due to the mud, and at times they had to turn off to trot across open fields. Turning a bend in the road, he was pleasantly surprised to be confronted by outpost riders, concealed within a woodlot that the road passed through. A barrier, concealed inside the woodlot, was across the road, and as he drew closer to the outpost a couple of rough-looking riflemen came out of the woods behind them, looking warily at this cavalcade of finely dressed officers in the uniforms of France and Prussia. Both of the sentries were dressed in their traditional dark brown hunting frocks, broad-brimmed hats, and ankle-length trousers, moving silently as if one with the woods.

The attitude of the young officer manning the barrier changed as soon as

L'Enfant presented their papers, informing him that they were from York, with orders to report to His Excellency General George Washington.

The young Pierre L'Enfant had been loitering at York for weeks, and it was Dr. Rush who suggested he join the baron's staff. He seemed pleasant enough, spoke of his training as an architect whenever the opportunity presented itself . . . and von Steuben wondered if he was in fact a spy for Gates.

The fact that von Steuben had even made it here was something of a miracle. For several days it appeared that it was the intent of Gates and his War Board to keep him reined in tight. Only the assurances of his loyalty to Congress——and also the more pragmatic point that, if assigned to at least look around Washington's camp, pay vouchers for staff and his own expenses would come from Washington's purse rather than Congress——had helped sway the argument.

Day after day, adventure seekers had arrived at York, some with real credentials, others with crackpot schemes such as making fleets of ships that could sail underwater to run the blockade. The total swamped Congress. All of them had to be fed, housed, entertained until the wheat could be separated from the tons of chaff. Thus pushing the baron and his half-dozen retainers out the door had finally resonated with Rush and then Gates.

"Remember, sir," Gates had insisted. "Your commission comes from here, your loyalty is here. I want a harsh and direct evaluation of the deficiencies that you see in Valley Forge and recommendations to Major General Conway as to their remedy."

He had of course agreed . . . anything to get out of the bedbug-infested inn they had quartered him in.

The day's ride had been pleasant, spirits were high with his lads, and now it seemed the adventure would truly begin.

"We've been expecting you, gentlemen!" one of the sentries announced, and he passed the word to a dispatch rider, who mounted and galloped off eastward, kicking up a spray of mud. The officer had obviously been ordered to delay them a bit, so von Steuben dismounted, calling his dog to heel. Azor was curiously sniffing the nervous young man. Von Steuben took him off into the woods so that he could relieve himself.

He returned to find the dozen enlisted men around the officer looking at him a bit wide-eyed, several vaguely offering salutes. He merely smiled in return, muttering "Good day, good day," in English, and mounted.

"And these are soldiers?" L'Enfant asked in French.

"Let's not judge yet," von Steuben offered, though his impression was the same. Only a few were clean-shaven. Even in the czarina's army, men were expect to shave twice a week——beards were viewed as a sign of slovenliness, fit maybe for a Cossack or a Turk but not a proper soldier. Other than the officer, who had an epaulette on one shoulder and wore what appeared to have been, at one time, a uniform of brown with red facings, the rest were dressed in assorted castoffs, or just the ubiquitous brown or tan hunting frock. Several were barefoot. Only a couple wore what could be considered proper boots . . . and all of them stank like an open latrine. He did note that the musketmen shouldered weapons that were well tended, polished and with good flints. The riflemen toted long-barreled weapons, nearly as long as their owners were tall, and even on this mild day the locks were covered with oiled cloth to protect them from the damp.

They might be filthy and smell filthy, but they looked lean and tough, especially the riflemen, and he would think twice about challenging them to a fight in the woods that were their element. All reports indicated they were steady when combat was in backcountry and wooded terrain. But an open-field volley match with the British and Hessian line regiments supported by artillery, cavalry, and light infantry?

That was why he was here, and it was something he said little about to Gates, so intent was the man on his swarms of militia who would turn out for a month or two of service, win the war, and go home. That was barely time to teach just a company of men how to load and fire in unison, a technique essential if ever the British were to be met in an open-field fight.

A messenger returned, telling them they could proceed. As they approached the encampment area, a gentle breeze arrived, carrying with it the promise of a developing storm from the east, bearing with it the smoke from hundreds of fires. The first scent of it was pleasant, as it would be for any soldier: wood fires burning at midday as dinners were prepared. But other scents were on the wind as well, and even though he was a well-seasoned soldier, he still wrinkled his nose as they drew closer. The place smelled unhealthy, and he soon saw why as they trotted past a burial ground. Hundreds of mounds of earth dotted the hillside. Some were individual graves, but there were also stretches of ground of thirty feet or more that looked like filled-in trenches, with a couple of dozen wooden boards or slabs of wood poked in atop them. Sickeningly, it was obvious that more than a few of the graves had not been dug all that deep, for dogs and wild pigs had obviously been rooting into them, and thus the stench of decay hung in the air.

A party of men was standing around an open trench, several men standing in the open grave dug not much more than chest-deep, while corpses were being off-loaded from a two-wheeled wagon, carted over, and then handed to those in the grave, who unceremoniously put the bodies down and reached for others. No coffins, not even a winding cloth or blanket was there to cover the dead. The faces of the dead were locked in the rictus of their final struggles, some pale, emaciated, some pox-covered, others swollen and distorted. One of them hauled out was missing both his feet, the stumps from the amputation obviously fresh, blood dripping from the body.

Behind him, he heard L'Enfant gag and then vomit.

Some of the burial detail looked over at them, a couple nudging each other at the sight of the splendid Frenchie vomiting, joined a moment later by two more of his cavalcade.

"This is war, too, gentlemen," von Steuben announced in French. "Get used to it, by God. Now show respect. They are watching us."

An officer with the burial detail shouted for his men to continue their work but shot a dark glance at von Steuben, who remained motionless and then solemnly took off his hat, lowered his head, and put his hat to his heart, remaining thus until the last of the dead were pulled from the wagon.

A minister offered a quick prayer, and a ragged volley of but three muskets was fired over the open trench and the interment of nearly thirty men. The daily total of dead from the hospitals was finished. Those gathered around picked up shovels to fill the mass grave. Slightly upslope, others were already laboring on the trench for the next day's business.

He put his hat back on.

"Ride on and look straight ahead," he hissed.

Those following him did as ordered. L'Enfant came up to his side.

"I'm sorry sir," the boy gasped, "the smell, and the sight of that poor man."

"If you wish to be a soldier, lad, you'd best acquire the stomach for it. After Minden we buried five thousand like that."

"Yes, sir," he replied weakly.

"First time you've seen something like that, son?"

"Yes, sir," he gasped and von Steuben was afraid the boy would vomit again.

"Think of something else. Breathe deeply, the air here is good now," he whispered, "don't shame yourself in front of them."

A few battles or months in camp would harden him, or kill him, but he knew the talk around campfires tonight would be about how the new foreigners vomited. It would not reflect well on him.

. . .

Past the graveyard, they rode alongside half a dozen log huts, each nearly thirty feet long, with wattle and daub chimneys at both ends. The blanket covering into the one nearest the road was open, but he didn't need to be told it was a hospital area. Dozens of pale, sickly men were outside, leaning against the south wall to soak up the feeble heat of the early afternoon sun. Several rested on crutches, minus a foot or leg. No one spoke as they rode by. Rough-hewn beds of planks covered by some fir branches were on the ground, men huddled on them. All the nurses were women. One——well dressed, middle-aged, gray hair tucked up under a "plain cap," wool cape over her shoulders——looked like a woman of some distinction. She sat on a camp chair, holding a book that looked to be a Bible and reading aloud in English, more than a few of the sick turned to her, listening attentively. She caught his gaze for a moment, and he bowed from the saddle and she returned the salute with a nod of her head, but did not interrupt her reading.

The hospital area left behind, the party continued up the slope, no one speaking. The journey of over a month was nearing its end, but there was little enthusiasm in his group, the young French officers sobered by what they saw. Even his hound Azor stayed close to his side, obviously disconcerted by the alien scents and sights.

The low crest ahead was cut by earthworks, very rudimentary works, a sagging line of tossed-up earth and cut sod. L'Enfant sat up in his saddle to scan them.

"Amateur works," he sighed. "No revetments, no bombproofs, no secondary line nor *cheveux-de-frise*, it is pathetic."

"This is a new army," von Steuben announced, "we are here to teach, not to criticize. For right now, remember we are their guests."

He looked over at the young Frenchman, who was obviously filled with disappointment and more than a little disgust at what he was seeing.

Von Steuben forced a laugh.

"When I was in the service of the czarina, you should have seen me among the Cossacks loyal to the empress! Try to teach them how to dig a fortification? This will be easy, lad."

L'Enfant did not look encouraged.

"It is either that or you can ride twenty miles to the south and see what the British might offer." Now his voice was cold.

L'Enfant looked at him, a bit startled, but his cold gaze stilled any reply.

He turned and looked back at the rest of his companions.

"Remember, my friends, we have crossed an ocean and ridden our backsides raw this last month to come here. Here. This is where God has called us, and we might now say God help us all. But this is our lot. You do not win allies by berating them and showing them their shortcomings. You win them by offering your hand. It is either that or I suggest you turn about now and ride back to York and play some more politics.

"Now, do we understand each other? All of us?" And he said the last words in German, his servant Vogel quickly translating.

No one spoke.

"I will have no complaining. No saying they are doing everything wrong, because, by God, they have indeed stood against the British and my cousins from Hesse for two years and are still in the field. Do we understand each other?"

This time there were nods of reply.

"Good, then," and he turned, pointing to the crest of the hill where a group of horsemen awaited.

"I think, gentlemen, that is our new commanding officer. If now or in the future any of you fail to show the utmost deference to him and those ranked above us, I will break you from my staff.

"Do we understand each other?" And again he lapsed into German.

"Yes, sir," was the universal response.

"Good, then, my children, let us go and meet our new leader." He spurred his tired mount, who on the mud-caked road could barely manage to break into a canter.

A lone officer broke away from the group and came down to meet them, reining in and stiffening at their approach.

"Baron von Steuben?"

He smiled and nodded, the officer greeting him stiffening even more.

"Monsieur, I am honored," he replied in French. "I am the Marquis de Lafayette, and we, the entire army, are delighted with your arrival. My General Washington awaits you."

He was startled for an instant by the obvious youth of the officer——the lad could not be more than twenty at most, and yet his name was known on both sides of the Atlantic.

His staff, excited to meet a fellow countryman, broke into their usual flourishes of introduction while he simply removed his hat in salute, a gesture that Lafayette immediately returned with all the proper panache of a wellborn nobleman. It was indeed strange for a brief instant. *I fought against the*

French for how many years? he wondered. In the last war the British were our allies. Now I am four thousand miles from home, a stripling of a French marquis greeting me in this new adventure against my former allies.

Such is war.

The marquis fell in by his side, chatting amiably, inquiring as to his health and the comfort of his journey as they rode the last hundred yards up the slope.

It was easy enough to pick out the man he had crossed an ocean and ridden half a continent to meet. As described to him, he was half a head taller than any who were around him, strong-shouldered, features calm and composed, though heavily scarred by the smallpox. Uniform well tailored, but not anywhere near as finely trimmed as Lafayette's or even that of his new aide-de-camp, L'Enfant. There was a dignity to him, though, that bespoke a man who was aware of the role he must play before others as their commander, and he immediately liked that. With the warmth of this almost springlike afternoon, he did not wear a cape. His blue and buff uniform was clean, though obviously threadbare from time in the field. He kept his mount well, a horse of superior breeding. Behind him was a black servant, well dressed in brown broadcloth and astride a horse nearly the equal of the general's. That must be the legendary Billy Lee, he thought. Half a dozen other officers were arrayed behind him.

He slowed as he approached and came to a respectful halt, removing his hat, as did the rest of his staff, as Lafayette offered the formal introductions. Washington and Billy Lee he had figured out, the others were not obvious. He would have to rely on Vogel later to tell him again which man was this Anthony Wayne, and Greene, and Stirling, and in turn their various aides and followers.

The uniforms were a hodgepodge, as if every man had decided for himself how he should dress for a war, a situation that could be most confusing in the smoke of battle, for even with Cossack chieftains and Turks, their rankings could be told by the richness of their dress and the trappings of their horses.

But his first impression was a strong one. Washington struck him at first nod as a leader, the deference shown by the young marquis obvious.

A small honor guard was drawn up on the side of the muddy road, and at the conclusion of introductions, the company came to attention and presented arms.

He winced inwardly. If this was their best, then heaven help me, he thought, though his features remained fixed. No two men wore exactly the same uniform jacket. One was wearing a long, drab civilian cloak that was mud-splattered. At least they all appeared to be wearing shoes or boots. Several fifers and a

drummer broke into a piece he could now identify——"Yankee Doodle"——
and all looked appropriately solemn as it was played, though he could not help
but remember the rather ribald verse that had been taught to him by Vogel
while they were still in Boston. At the conclusion, seven of the honor guard
stepped forward and offered a somewhat decent volley, though one of the
muskets misfired, the sergeant leading the men obviously displeased. He suppressed a smile, for any good Prussian sergeant would most certainly make
the rest of the day difficult for the young malefactor who had not checked his
pan and flint before marching out.

The ceremony finished, General Washington turned to face von Steuben.

"I am pleased to see you, sir," Washington said in English, Lafayette translating to French. "I trust your journey was easy and your health is good?"

"It is an honor to at last meet you, sir, and yes, the journey was interesting
and my health is good. I thank you for inquiring. We are glad to be here and
look forward to serving under you."

There was a momentary pause and Washington gestured for him to fall in
by his side.

"Let's ride together as we talk," Washington announced. "I understand
you speak French, and I hope you will accept the services of my friend General
Lafayette to help us speak together."

A respectful gesture, von Steuben thought. Etiquette allowed for a man to
request his own interpreter, and Washington indirectly was making that offer.

He nodded his approval, and Lafayette fell in to von Steuben's left, so as
not to be between him and Washington as they rode. Behind them, a couple
of dozen paces back, the rest of his staff fell in alongside those of Washington's staff who had ridden out to meet them, and he could hear conversations
start, some in French, with Vogel laboring to go directly from English to
German and back again.

The three up front rode on in silence for a moment, Washington letting
him take in the view of the encampment site. Clusters of rough-hewn huts
lined up in company streets were obviously grouped by regiments and brigades. Not much work appeared to be going on. Some were already standing
around cooking fires at each regiment where a hog or sheep had already been
slaughtered and was being butchered for the cook pot. The fare did not look
all that good. The men waiting seemed to be doing so with some anxiety, as if
rations were short and they wanted to insure their fair share of the day's vittles. A cattle stall with a dozen animals within was well guarded by a detail of
half a dozen men, the animals a miserable-looking lot, with little flesh on

their bones. There was, however, the scent of fresh bread baking, and they rode past a large hut, the size of a small warehouse, a dozen brick chimneys lining one wall. A wagon came out the far end of the building, steaming loaves of bread piled high. A guard detachment kept careful watch as the wagon slowly moved along a muddy track toward the center of the camp.

"I trust you ate well while with Congress in York?" Washington asked, breaking the silence, his gaze still fixed on the wagonload of bread.

"Yes, sir, the food was more than adequate."

"Today my men are lucky. Nearly a pound of meat per man will be doled out this afternoon, and a fresh loaf for every two men. For tomorrow a dozen cattle are all we have so far, and just enough bread for one loaf for three. I had asked to set aside half a dozen cows to provide milk for the sick but fear they must be slaughtered as well."

He now looked over at von Steuben.

"I have heard of your difficulties while traveling here, sir."

Washington nodded.

"I am reduced to foraging under my own authority," Washington announced. "At best we have reserves of but three to four days of food on hand. Today we are down to two, though I am promised a delivery of fifty head of cattle from Reading by this time tomorrow. That and what General Wayne's men will bring in by the end of the day."

Von Steuben did not reply.

"What authority did Congress give to you, sir?" Washington now asked.

"My servant is carrying my papers," von Steuben replied. "I will present them now if you wish," and he motioned as if to turn back.

Washington shook his head.

"In your own words sir."

"Authority here, sir?" he asked diplomatically, "or as given by Congress?"

"Congress first."

"I am under orders to General Gates, reporting through General Conway."

"And here?"

Von Steuben gazed intently at the man. Everything he had heard before arriving at York seemed to bear witness. "Sir, whatever task you wish to assign to me, without rank, as a volunteer I will accept from your hand."

Washington looked at him but, said nothing.

"All I have asked all along," von Steuben continued, "is that my staff receive some form of commission, captains even, to defray their personal expenses. As for myself, sir, I am at your disposal without expectation of rank or pay other than to defray expenses incurred. If I prove worthy of your trust you may decide later how to employ me."

"And your reports to Generals Conway and Gates."

"Sir, I am here now under your direct command." He drew a deep breath. "Any reports filed, as I was trained long ago, will go through proper channels first, which means you as direct commander in the field."

Taking that in, Washington finally smiled.

"This is different," Washington said in English to Lafayette, who did not interpret, the young Frenchman smiling and nodding in reply.

"I understand you are a baron and served on the general staff of Frederick the Great?"

He looked straight at Washington and simply nodded.

"Your duties while with Frederick?"

"I have come through the ranks. In the German armies an officer cadet often first serves a time with the enlisted ranks in order to better understand how to lead them. I commanded a company and a regiment in battle during the Seven Years, was decorated for valor by the Great Frederick and promoted to his staff. I was captured near the end of the war by the Russians, was treated well by them, served as an advisor to their Czar Peter when the war ended and he switched alliances to Prussia, and was later employed by the Czarina Catherine in the Ukraine and against the Turks."

What he said was all true; what he left out, he did so without a blush. There was no sense in dwelling on some of the "difficulties" that now drove him to this distant place. An unemployed career officer at this stage in life should be expecting a comfortable billet as a colonel of a garrison or even a general on staff.

They rode on in silence for a moment. As they did so they passed a parade field where a regiment of several hundred was drawn up in two ragged lines. Von Steuben slowed to watch, Washington and Lafayette by his sides.

The colonel of the regiment stood with his back to the three and apparently was delivering a sound chewing-out. Some of the men were leaning on the muzzles of their muskets, though as they realized that Washington and others were watching, they started to come to attention, some shouldering their muskets, others awkwardly just holding them in front, butt still on the ground.

The colonel slowed in his harangue. Several of the men were nudging each other, grinning, and nodding to their colonel like schoolchildren having fun tipping off a friend that an elder was watching.

The colonel, a slender, hawk-faced man with pinched cheeks, turned, saw who was watching, and fumbled to attention, shouting with a high voice for his regiment to present arms.

Washington and the others returned the salute.

"You may carry on with your duties, Colonel," Washington announced.

"Thank you, sir."

But the colonel did not move for a moment, as if not sure what to do.

He finally made an exaggerated turn, ordered the men to shoulder arms, and then just stood there.

"General, an indulgence?" von Steuben asked.

"Yes?"

"Might the marquis run these men through a little drill for a few moments?"

Washington looked at him and just nodded.

"Marquis?"

"With pleasure."

"Would you be so kind as to order them to about-face and then march, keeping their line as if advancing to attack?"

Lafayette looked over at Washington, who nodded.

Lafayette rode up beside the colonel and passed the order.

"Battalion, about-face! Forward march!"

Von Steuben leaned forward on his mount, watching intently. Most of the men executed their about-face correctly, though more than a few turned left about rather than right about. A drummer picked up a beat, a fifer joining in after a few steps; it sounded like the ubiquitous "Yankee Doodle." If it could be called a "step," at least the majority were conforming to it to a certain degree, though one man had already tripped over his unraveling foot wrappings and tumbled out of the rank, a sergeant stopping, standing over the man, and looking up at the watchful gaze of Washington. He hissed at the poor soul to get up, the gawky youth fumbling with his musket.

The ground was uneven, a cut hayfield, but still open and smooth enough not to interfere with alignment, but already the line was bowing, the flag-bearer at the center keeping pace with his colonel, who was taking huge steps rather than an even, measured, and identical-length step timed to the beat of the drummer——who in turn was not doing a very good job of staying steady and methodical.

"Order them to stop, please," von Steuben announced, riding out into the field to join Lafayette.

The command was given, the men coming to a halt, the colonel now running up and down in front of the ranks, shouting for the men to dress on the flag, some of them already half a dozen paces behind the center.

"If I may please?" von Steuben whispered, looking over at Lafayette, who was facing him, a bit red-faced.

"Sir?"

"May I suggest a few orders? I just wish to observe the results."

"Of course."

"Order them to fix bayonets, then charge bayonets."

"Half of them don't have bayonets."

"I can see that, sir. Please indulge me, though."

"Battalion, fix bayonets!"

More than a few looked back at Lafayette in confusion.

"We ain't got bayonets!" someone shouted from the ranks.

"Well, make believe you got them, damn it!" the colonel shouted.

There was a ripple of laughter from some. Sergeants began to curse, and some officers drew swords. Others just looked around as about half the men complied.

"Charge bayonets!"

A few of the men started to run forward rather than properly follow the command, which was for the first rank to level their weapons with a shout, the rear rank shouldering their weapons high. In a proper Prussian or British line three files deep, the second rank would hold their weapons high over the shoulder of the front rank while the third rank shouldered arms.

The line was now in confusion.

"Battalion, at the quick time, forward, march!" von Steuben cried in German, forgetting himself for a moment, Lafayette translating in his high, clear voice.

The men started forward.

The regiment lurched forward, within seconds nearly all semblance of formation gone. There was just a surging mass of men. Von Steuben was silent, watching, trying to keep his features emotionless.

"Battalion, by the right wheel, at the quick time, march!"

As he expected, the unit disintegrated. Some men simply continued straight ahead; others turned right on the spot and went off in that direction. The company on the far right did try to wheel, but no one followed them. The drummer didn't even know the proper beat to signal the command. The fifer just kept blasting away with the only tune he apparently knew.

Without comment, von Steuben turned from the field. He kept his features composed, almost cheerful, but shot an icy glance at L'Enfant and the others of his staff for them to remain absolutely silent, though most of them were looking on either with bemusement or outright horror.

"We're all dead men," Vogel whispered in German.

Von Steuben rode back to join Washington, who had remained silent, unperturbed, though General Greene had ridden over, a bit red-faced.

"Sir, it's a fairly new regiment of replacements from Connecticut," he offered. "Most of the veterans went home at the end of last year."

"I understand, sir, do not apologize," von Steuben offered with a smile.

"Shall we continue on?" Washington offered.

"Of course, sir," and now Lafayette was back beside them.

"The display was rather disconcerting," Washington offered. "I can assure you some of my regiments do behave better, significantly better."

"I am certain they do."

"But . . ." Washington's voice trailed off, von Steuben not replying.

"It is not what you expected, is it?"

He shook his head. "It is what I expected, sir."

Washington eyed him carefully and wished, at this moment, that von Steuben's command of English were better. He feared that an inflection or a wrongly chosen word would now convey all the wrong meaning.

"How so?" Washington asked.

"I have read the reports, sir," and Lafayette provided the translation. "First, I do not doubt the valor of your men, of those men out in the field just now. They must have valor to have volunteered to be here."

He paused, fearing there was an implied insult.

"I rode past the burial ground as I came here," he said quickly. "I know that hundreds, perhaps a thousand or more have died since you've come here, and thousands more have either gone home because enlistments are up, or have simply deserted."

Washington nodded, saying nothing.

"Those that stay in spite of that are men of valor. Though by the accounts I read you did not win at Germantown or Brandywine, nevertheless the men fought hard, and some of them did fight to victory at Trenton and Princeton."

"And precious few of those men are now left," Washington replied, and von Steuben could detect the sadness in the man's voice.

"In the Prussian army we say that it takes three years to train a man from being cannon fodder into a soldier who can march, follow orders, and fight on a battlefield. The discipline of the battlefield is the hardest school to master."

"And you are saying we do not have that?"

He looked straight at Washington. "There are many kinds of battlefields, General. I understand you yourself have experienced a number of them. How you Americans might fight out on the frontier, as you did with Braddock, or how the northern army fought in the forests of upstate New York, will be vastly different from how you fight in the the farmlands, villages, and towns down here along the coastal plains. Vastly different."

Washington nodded, saying nothing.

"Perhaps that is where I might first be of service to you, sir."

"How is that?"

"Training. Traditional Prussian school of training."

Washington looked at him in silence.

Von Steuben smiled and shook his head.

"I already understand that you in this New World see many things differently. This is not an army of drafted peasants, or men that my old commanders stole from farms in Poland, or swept up out of the gutters of every city in Europe. These are free yeomen, landholders themselves, men who fight for a reason, and they must be respected as such. But they must all learn to pull the same rope at the same time."

"Same rope, sir?"

"To work as one, in discipline. One regiment, trained to march in order, fire in volley three times a minute, to hold its line in defense, advance, charge, or retreat, must act as one. Give me one regiment such as that in an open-field fight and they can stand against five regiments that do not fight in unison and maneuver as one. I think you will agree with me on that, sir."

Washington offered a smile and nodded.

"I do. We have all witnessed the power of disciplined British and Hessian professional units."

"Perhaps that is where I can be of best service to you, sir."

"You've thought about this already, haven't you, Baron?"

He could not lie here. "Yes, I have."

"Why?"

"I read the reports. I had the accounts in the British papers read to me. They dread encountering you in forests and mountains, but here, in this region, where you must fight to hold open farmland and villages, they find themselves invincible. The moment their disciplined lines advance at the double, bayonet points gleaming, they know they have won, and indeed up to now they have won. But now we can change that.

"General Washington, when was the last time you witnessed a battle, fought in the open during the daytime when bayonets were actually crossed?"

"A few moments at Trenton, Long Island . . ." His voice trailed off as if the memory was too unpleasant to recall.

"And at Paoli," one of the officers riding nearby snarled.

He looked back, nodded, and saluted.

"May I presume you are General Wayne?" von Steuben asked.

"The same," and his voice was taut.

"Sir, what would you give to use the bayonet on their light infantry after first beating them back with disciplined volley fire?"

Wayne gazed at him coldly, but then just merely nodded.

"Perhaps I can help you, sir. I have fought in the fields of Germany and the wilds of Russia not unlike this. Each terrain requires a different method. I am certain you have mastered one. I would be honored to help teach your men the other and gain the vengeance I hear you have sworn yourself to."

Wayne did not reply, just continuing to gaze at him.

"I think General Wayne can attest it is the sight of the bayonet that breaks lines, not the actual touch of the blade. It is the sight of a disciplined line that is doing one of two things: either advancing, en masse, shoulder to shoulder, unrelenting, bayonets poised, or holding its ground in the same manner, also unrelenting, sweeping the field with volley fire to break a charge. It is the look in each man's eyes, the feel that they are unstoppable, that they will not break, that carries the battle at its climax. It shows that the will of the one is stronger than the other and will not be broken."

He sighed and looked back over his shoulder at the disorganized battalion that was still trying to sort itself out, the colonel now bawling the men out at the top of his lungs.

"General, I do not for an instant doubt the worth of those men. Combine that with proper drill, drill, and yet more drill. Drill so that rather than one time a minute they can fire two to three times a minute——that alone will make it seem as if you have fifty percent more men on the field of battle. And, yes, I know the British can fire four, and some of my fellow Germans can fire five, times a minute. We do not have to match the very best. We only have to become good enough to stand against them. Even just that modest increase in disciplined, reliable firing will mean much to our men's morale."

Washington could not help but smile as Lafayette translated "our men." This Prussian seemed to have the right attitude and the right identification with the cause of American freedom.

"Then add in drill and yet more drill, to march in line, wheel, turn, charge, hold, fall back in proper order . . ."

His voice trailed off. He realized that he had warmed so much to his subject that he was now as excitable as a reckless lad. Lafayette was struggling hard to keep up with the translation, and those riding behind them were silent, trying to listen in.

"I am sorry, General, if I spoke out of turn," he concluded woodenly.

Washington rode on, looking straight ahead, taking it in. He said nothing for a moment. Von Steuben was now worried that he had tried to oversell himself and his view of discipline, drill, and warfare.

"I have heard it said that with the Great Frederick, his drills are near on like battles, and his battles at times are nothing more than bloody drills," Washington responded.

"I have heard that, too. I have lived it and know it to be the truth."

"I must remind you, sir, that this is an American army. I demand discipline and respect from my men and do not broker with insubordination, drunkenness, and desertion, but still these are Americans. A year ago I would have told you they were still men of thirteen different states, but at least here, some semblance of oneness is taking shape. I pray that this army will be a model for the entire nation by the time this war is won."

The way he forcefully said the last four words, "this war is won," caught von Steuben. It was the way Frederick the Great would have said it, even in the darkest days after Berlin had been taken and the alliance was closing in from three sides. It was far more than he had ever seen with Gates, and at that instant he was glad he had refrained from the game of politics in York and held out for this posting with the real army.

"We are making a nation here," Washington announced, speaking louder, so that the rest of the entourage could hear.

"I do not wish to see, nor would they tolerate themselves, the type of mindless discipline instilled by the British army with its troops. I want an army of men who can think, I want officers who can seize the moment and lead without cowering and looking over their shoulder for direction the way that poor colonel back there did. But at the same time I want an army of men who can stand toe-to-toe with the British and their Hessian allies, fight it out, and hold the field. I know, sir, we have all been lacking in training for that type of fight. I want an army that can fight, Baron, and beat our professional opponents at their own game."

Then I am your man, sir, von Steuben was tempted to say, but he remained silent, for it sounded far too self-seeking.

Washington reined in his mount and looked directly at him.

"Can you help me with that?"

He lowered his head in reply, nodded, saying nothing.

"And you do so as a volunteer without seeking rank or pay?"

"That is my offer, sir," and he paused, looking over at Vogel and the others with him who were watching anxiously. "Though, sir, I would restate that at least expenses be covered for my personal servant and that some sufficient rank of your own choosing be provided for my staff. They have ventured far to join this cause and have not the independent means that I might have."

Washington looked past him to the anxious, hopeful faces of the half-dozen others behind him.

He forced a smile, looking like an overworked father who was suddenly confronted by yet more mouths to feed.

"I am certain billets can be found according to their ranks and skills, sir."

There was an uneasy silence.

"You will join me for dinner, Baron, and afterwards we can discuss this in greater detail. I have a task in mind for you that I believe you shall find interesting, as will your staff."

He offered a polite nod and then a formal salute that signified dismissal. Turning his mount, Washington rode off, followed by the other generals, though Lafayette stayed behind.

"Gentlemen. We cannot offer accommodations befitting you at this time, but a cabin has been set aside for you," and he motioned to the side of the road, where a log cabin without a door awaited them. Dismounting, Lafayette led the way, von Steuben and the others following. Pulling aside the blanket that served as a door, he motioned for them to enter as if he was a servant at a grand palace, and von Steuben detected the hint of a smile.

It took a few seconds for his eyes to adjust to the gloom. The fireplace was cold, though kindling and wood was stacked up for them. The bunks were nothing more than saplings pegged into the walls, no mattresses, just rope loosely woven and covered with a blanket, pine boughs, and some straw.

"Palatial for some of us, if not quite like home," Lafayette announced, and von Steuben could hear the hint of humor in the young man's voice.

"This will serve," von Steuben replied, stilling any protest from the others.

Azor sniffed around the room, picked a lower bunk, and immediately climbed into it, the bunk sagging beneath his weight. With a sigh, he settled down.

"He has made his claim," L'Enfant offered, and the others laughed.

Vogel, ever efficient, was already kneeling at the fireplace, breaking up kindling, producing flint. Within a few minutes a fire began to flicker to life.

"Gentlemen, you may take dinner with me tonight," Lafayette offered. "Not much, I can assure you: boiled mutton, some cobs of their Indian corn, and sauerkraut. Baron, when you hear the evening salute fired, that will be the signal for dinner with the general. If an aide is not sent to fetch you, you will find the headquarters but another two hundred yards downslope, a small stone house."

He looked around the small cabin, smiled, bowed low, and left.

"So this is it?" L'Enfant asked.

"Certainly not Versailles," Du Ponceau retorted sadly.

Von Steuben threw back his head and laughed.

"You lads wanted war and an adventure. Well, you have found it. Now see to your horses. Remember, a good soldier always sees first to his mounts and then to his men before his own comfort. Time enough to complain later."

They did as ordered, leaving him alone in the cabin with Azor, Vogel going out to tend to the baron's mount.

He reached back into his breast pocket, pulled out the flask of cognac, un-screwed the cap, and offered a toast to Azor.

"Well, my friend, here begins our new life," he announced with a sardonic smile. Azor did not reply, just looking at him forlornly, for there had been nothing for him to eat this day.

"First I must learn to curse well in good English, for I shall need it," he sighed, emptying the rest of the flask.

The evening salute and tattoo echoed across the fields as Martha Washington trudged along the muddy track back to the headquarters. It had been a long, trying day. Three of the lads she had been tending to had died, two from what was now feared to be typhus, the other from exposure and an attempt to amputate his feet, both of which had developed frostbite in the last storm as he had stood sentry. The doctor had forbidden her to attend to him during the surgery and inwardly she was grateful that he had done so. He had forcefully argued that he could never face General Washington if he should find out that his wife had witnessed such a thing.

And yet so many of the other women working in the hospitals had wit-nessed such things every day, and held up without complaint, some never leaving the place. More than a few of them were now sick as well, two of them dying in the last week.

As mistress in charge of a plantation in which hundreds lived, were born, worked, and died, her duties had never been as romantic as some might think. She had helped with the borning, had held more than one of her servants as they prepared to die, and prayed over their graves. Death was nothing new to her, but the conditions here, this winter, were indeed a trial to the soul, with no end yet in sight. Her husband had argued with her nearly daily that there were places other than the hospital where she could be of help, but she felt it her duty, at least for a few hours each day, to visit there, if only to sit with some of the sick and read to them. Since her arrival, she had shamed more than a few officers' wives to take on more of the burden that hundreds of other women already were bearing.

As she approached the headquarters home, she saw her husband out with several of his officers slowly walking back after attending evening parade. As if sensing her approach he turned, looked over his shoulder, smiled, and excused himself from the informal meeting. He came toward her and extended a hand, which she gladly took.

"You're cold," he announced anxiously, squeezing her hand tight, and she smiled.

"My hands are always cold."

"Well, there is that saying about it meaning a warm heart," he offered and she smiled, falling in by his side.

"Your day?" he asked.

She did not reply for a moment.

"How many did we lose?"

"Over thirty, George. One of them a boy of only sixteen. Frostbitten feet. Dr. Otto tried to remove them . . ."

Her voice trailed off.

"You weren't there, were you?" There was a bit of a harsh tone to his voice.

"No, he forbade me, but I felt I should have been."

"It is not your place."

"It is my place," she replied forcefully.

He looked down at her.

"Let's not have this argument again, dear. With typhus now loose I would prefer you not to be in the hospital at all."

"Then order out all the other women who labor there and perhaps I'll follow."

He shook his head.

"Such insubordination. And to the commanding general," he said with a rueful smile.

"You would expect nothing less from me."

"Still." He sighed. "You know I would prefer otherwise."

"If you want me here with you, then expect this."

He finally held his free hand up in a gesture of surrender.

"Can I order you not to be in the front line when there is a battle?" she continued. "We've had this argument before. You say it is your duty, but at times I think you actually seek out the thrill of it."

"You can't say that being in the hospital is in some way exciting," he offered back. "It is a reckless danger and I worry about you."

"You stop leading from the front and I will stop going to the hospital, and no," and now her voice was harsh, almost bitter, "believe me, it is no thrill."

"A duty, then."

"Yes, as I see it. Yes," she replied firmly and intensely.

He shook his head.

"So how is this new German?" she asked.

"You heard he is here?"

"No. But I saw him ride by. More European officers looking for rank?"

He smiled and shook his head.

"This one is different, I think."

"How so?"

"Something about him. He is not asking for rank, though I sense that is simply a game for the moment. But, still, a refreshing difference. Apparently he survived York and the Gates crowd untainted, offering his sword directly to me as a volunteer, with the position to be chosen by me."

"It could be a ploy," she offered.

"No, I have my sources, and what he said confirms their reports."

She laughed softly.

"You and your sources, George."

He laughed.

"You seem merry this evening. I think you like this new man."

"I do. One senses that he has a few cards he is not showing, but then again who doesn't? I just have this feeling about him that he is the man I've been waiting for."

"For what, pray tell?"

"To shape this army into a new kind of army, an army that will win."

CHAPTER TWELVE

✳ ✳ ✳

Valley Forge
March 4, 1778

"My God, what a muddle it all is," von Steuben whispered under his breath.

"Sir?"

He turned to the entourage that had taken to following him around the camp. Du Ponceau was a step behind him on one side, carrying a plank of polished wood with a sheet of paper pegged to it, ready to take notes, struggling to keep up with translations from German to either French or English. Joining him on what was now his daily inspection tour were a number of young staff officers who had found him to be a fascinating new addition to an encampment already replete with more than its share of eccentrics.

Young Alexander Hamilton was one of them, his command of French solid enough to allow him to follow some of the discussions without need of translation. As one of General Washington's most trusted aides, his presence was an obvious political boon, but far more important, a gangly young lieutenant colonel on Washington's staff, John Laurens, was also with him today.

Von Steuben had finally abandoned his horse and was now tromping about on foot along the line of field fortifications, staff and the others following to see what he might do next. And what he was doing was turning the encampment upside down.

The day was cold, blustery, a sharp wind out of the northwest after a frigid day of snow, which eddied and drifted about them as von Steuben continued his inspection of the fortification line on Mount Misery.

"Look at this, just look at this!" he announced, as he stood at a parapet and pointed to his left. The others gathered around, not sure what he was saying or pointing at.

"My God, there is defilade there below us," and he pointed downslope to a fold in the ground.

"Defilade?" Laurens asked, trying to follow the translation. "Is that French? What does it mean?"

"It means cover for an attacking enemy," Hamilton whispered urgently.

Von Steuben set a sharp pace along the shallow entrenchment, heading to his left to a point fifty yards off that jutted out along the natural crest of the hill.

"Now look again at the same place," he announced, "defilade!"

He said the word as if it was an obscenity.

They all gazed thoughtfully at the fold in the ground between the two points below the wall of the fort as if they were looking at some monstrosity that had crept into their camp, though few were sure why they were looking at it.

"You there!" Von Steuben turned to where a lone sentry stood, wrapped in a blanket cape, face all but concealed by a scarf. At least when the entourage had approached, he had stopped slapping himself to try to ward off the cold. He was standing with shouldered musket.

"Me, sir?" the sentry asked nervously.

"Yes, I not talk to the sky," von Steuben replied in broken English, "damn, yes, you."

The sentry nervously approached and made an attempt at coming to attention and saluting.

"Look at that ground down there," von Steuben barked, pointing with his walking stick to the low hillock that he had suddenly found so offensive.

The sentry did as ordered.

"Now, what you do if English there?"

The sentry nodded thoughtfully. He was chewing on a wad of tobacco, jaw working hard, staring at the ground in question.

"Me and the boys thought the same thing now, standing out here like we do," he finally replied. "If we was charging this fort, we'd go for there, hunker down, wait for a volley to fire, then jump up and come the rest of the way. Don't like it one bit if you're asking me, sir. Whole bunch of places around here like that where they can gain on us and we can't shoot 'em."

Du Ponceau offered a translation, and von Steuben smiled and slapped the sentry on the shoulder.

"You are a good soldier. By Gott, I think you should be a general," he announced in German. It was quickly translated.

The sentry grinned.

"Forget the promotion, I've worked this chew out, you got another?" And as he spoke he spat the wad over the side of the trench.

Von Steuben looked at him, eyes narrowed. All were silent at what was obviously an impertinent act, and then the baron broke out laughing.

"By God, I like you. Anyone got a chew, as he calls it?"

Laurens, a good son of South Carolina, fished around in his breast pocket and pulled out a small block of tobacco, gazed at it longingly, then finally broke it in half and gave a chunk to the sentry, who grinned with gratitude and bit into it with a smile.

"May I offer a suggestion to His Excellency," von Steuben announced, looking back at Hamilton.

"It is what I am here for, sir," Hamilton replied, fishing a scrap of paper and pencil out of his breast pocket, hands trembling from the cold.

"Once the thaw comes, either level down that hillock for a clear field of fire, or cover it with abatis."

"Abatts, sir?"

"*Cheveux-de-frise.*"

Hamilton looked at Du Ponceau nervously.

"I'll explain later," Du Ponceau offered.

Von Steuben looked back at the private.

"Your name?"

"Billy Butterworth, sir, Third Pennsylvania."

"You say there are other places like that defilade?"

"Don't know what the hell that is, sir, but if you mean cover, well, hell, yes, all along the line we're guarding."

"Colonel Hamilton," von Steuben offered with a diplomatic smile. "May I pass a suggestion that with the approval of His Excellency the General, an order be passed to this Third Pennsylvania, that this soldier be promoted to sergeant and given a detail of men to work in front of the lines with proper tools to either level down or fill in places of cover for an attacking force, or build abatis or entanglements thereon."

Hamilton hesitated as the request was translated.

"Sir, I will pass along the suggestion, but our officers with engineering appointments might have a differing view."

Von Steuben sighed, tapping his walking stick atop the low wall of the fort, which at this place was barely waist-high.

"I wish no disrespect, of course, and I am merely an advisor," he replied with a smile. "But His Excellency did give me leave to examine the camp and make suggestions."

"I'll try, sir. But as for the promotion of the private here?" And his voice trailed off as the candidate for promotion fixed him with a baleful gaze.

Hearing the translation, von Steuben nodded.

"Translate clearly," he said to Du Ponceau.

"Colonel Hamilton, no disrespect, sir, and you have a correct point of protocol. I am only an advisor and mindful of that at all times. But I have always been of the school that a good officer will find that a private sees far more than an officer at times, because he is forced when on sentry to stare at the same place day after day that an officer just passes by. It is good for an officer to listen to his men when they make proper suggestions, though do not confuse what I have just said when it comes to the battlefield.

"In the heat of action, a private"——he looked back at Butterworth, his features now serious——"a private or even a newly promoted sergeant must obey the officer without question. Discipline in battle must always come first. That is how we shall win."

As he spoke, he knew that the private was listening, which was exactly what he wanted. The promotion might never come, but this man would tell everyone this evening how the "sauerkraut general" had offered to promote him, that he had urged officers to listen to their enlisted men, and that obedience in battle must be given unflinchingly. Tonight he would thus win over yet more of the enlisted men for the plan he would launch tomorrow.

He slapped the private on the shoulder.

"You smell like a dying dog, but you are good soldier," he announced with a laugh, and moved on.

Leaving the fort by the rear sally port, he remounted, the others following his lead, and they continued across the field back toward his quarters. One of the army's generals had gone home on leave, and Washington had offered him the man's small, two-room stone house, which he had gladly taken after a couple of freezing nights in the log hut.

The quarters of the men were appalling. If the weather turned warm during the day, the dirt floors turned into clinging mud. When it rained, the rough-cut shingles of the roof leaked like an open sieve.

After but a day of wandering around the camp, asking questions and observing, he had come to the conclusion that the conditions were the fault neither of the general nor of his men. The problem was above all the lack of tools.

The men openly complained that for the entire army there were only several hundred axes of dubious quality, only a handful of them with properly tempered steel blades. Adzes and froes to shape the logs and to cut shingles for roofs were even scarcer. The hundreds of cords of firewood that should have been cut last summer and set aside to season properly had never been laid up, so the men were forced to try to keep warm with green wood that barely cast a flame. Any dry deadfall for miles around had already been scooped up, the best of it set aside for the hospitals. Several forges had been constructed for the making of tools, but getting a good supply of charcoal to provide the higher level of heat for forging iron into steel for tools was next to impossible.

In a proper winter camp, as he was used to seeing in Russia where weather conditions were, of course, far more severe, the army would have gone into winter quarters in a proper fortress or town. If not, provisions would have been made early on to construct cabins tight against the winter blasts.

As to sanitation, that was a total nightmare. He had learned on the first day to carefully watch where he stepped. Sanitary discipline was nonexistent, and once night fell, few men took the trouble of hiking all the way to the latrine pit when just behind their cabin was sufficient. For many poor souls, the flux that was afflicting the camp made even a dash of a few dozen feet impossible. As a result, a freeze was welcomed, and any thaw turned the fields into little better than a stinking cesspool.

It was now even worse because of the decision to enforce the inoculation of all soldiers who had not yet suffered from smallpox. Few had taken this order gladly; some had even deserted rather than undergo the ordeal. More than a few preachers in the camp railed against inoculation as an act that went against God's will. But out of sheer necessity Washington had ordered that all who could not clearly show that they had endured smallpox were to be inoculated.

For the majority of men, the symptoms suffered in the weeks after were fairly mild, but hundreds living in the harsh conditions had fallen seriously ill, and scores had died. It was not nearly as bad as a real epidemic, but for the time being it had laid low nearly every tenth man with the army, and another one out of ten was in hospital with other complaints. In Frederick's army, at least half of these men, von Steuben concluded, would be declared unfit for duty, with a fair percentage of them discharged as no longer being fit for any kind of service other than as reserves in a warm and dry garrison fortress.

A thousand things should be seen to, he thought as he rode through the camp. However, diplomacy required that he hold his tongue, and as for blame, if there was any, it was not, in his eyes, for Washington. The general in chief spent most of his time writing, making appeals to Congress and to the strange hodgepodge of state governors and legislatures to which many of the militia units answered, appeasing local inhabitants who bombarded him with complaints, and yet at the same time trying to keep this army alive both physically and with the spirit needed to survive and fight.

He needed a proper inspector general to see to such things. On the staff of any army on the continent the inspector general was tasked with taking care of what he was now observing, leaving the general in command free to see to the broader issues, and to plan both for defense and any forthcoming campaign.

But with no tools, creating proper flooring for cabins, well-sealed doors, leakproof roofs, and split logs for corduroying the roads and walkways was impossible. Without funds, obtaining proper rations for these pathetic scarecrows was also impossible unless, as Washington had now been forced to act out of necessity, a general simply seized what was needed for his beleaguered forces, offered scrip in payment, and prayed that the local population did not rebel in turn. Without money there was no medicine for the sick other than home-brewed remedies.

Without . . . without . . . without . . .

He sighed and yet forced himself to keep his good-natured smile as he rode past a column of infantry that was attempting to simply march by column of fours and properly wheel.

He paused to watch for a moment, trying to conceal his dismay as the men floundered about. My God, that they had survived this long in and of itself both off the battlefield and on it was a miracle. He rode on and did not bother to pain himself by looking back as he heard an exasperated officer shouting orders that were met by grumbling, cursing, and even outright laughter.

Tomorrow he would see if they still laughed!

He caught sight of his modest dwelling, smoke pouring from the chimney.

"I am hungry, my friends," he announced, and he nudged his mount to a canter, the others following eagerly. This evening was special. He had offered a fete for the junior officers on the staffs of Washington and some others. It was an obvious political move, but already he had grown fond of the lads. With a bit of proper training, boys like Hamilton, Laurens, and others could be the match of any staff in Prussia. What they lacked in proper training they more than made up for in their youthful enthusiasm and——something that was indeed lacking in nearly all the armies of Europe——their passionate belief that transcended mere national pride, a belief in a revolutionary cause and devotion to an honest leader of that cause.

When in Catherine's service, he had seen such fire in some of the Polish and Cossack prisoners. They were fighting for a losing cause, and they knew it, and yet they fought on, believing in a free Poland and Ukraine. These Americans had that same fire——even more so, in a strange way, because it transcended mere national identity. Hamilton was the illegitimate son of an island planter who had come to this country to strike out on his own. Laurens, the son of a plantation owner who was now president of Congress, openly talked about his idea that, if they were to hold to the truth of their Declaration, then they must offer full freedom to all slaves and immediate emancipation to any who would take up arms and fight for that freedom. Lafayette, the child of French aristocracy, spoke of bringing back to his country the ideals of the Revolution, planting it on that soil and, if need be, fighting for the equality of all men.

He was not yet sure if he himself could believe such things, but nevertheless, this was fertile human soil to work with and from which perhaps to shape an army of a new and different kind. One that would bear his stamp.

They drew up to his modest dwelling and Vogel came out to meet him.

"All is ready, sir," Vogel announced, taking his horse.

He sniffed the air.

"Good God, what are you cooking in there?" he whispered.

"Horse."

"Horse?"

"It is one of the artillery horses with the battery over there." Vogel motioned to where a two-gun section from New York was camped. "I learned they had a dead horse. So I traded your extra pair of dress shoes for twenty pounds of meat."

"Not my silver buckled shoes?" he gasped.

"I took the buckles off and replaced them with the pewter buckles after polishing them to look like silver," Vogel whispered.

He thought about it for a moment.

"Good man," he sighed, patting him on the shoulder. "How dead was the horse?"

"They found him dead this morning. No disease. Just starvation."

"I hope."

Vogel looked at him indignantly. The man was an old campaigner and knew an edible dead horse from one that needed to be burned or buried.

"I got some of the liver, and mixed it in with some potatoes that were being issued to the troops."

"Can you feed all of these?"

He pointed to the staff that had followed him, along with half a dozen other young officers who, having heard that "the German" was offering dinner, were now just standing conveniently nearby.

Vogel shrugged his shoulders.

"I'll thin out the soup a bit before you bring them in."

Von Steuben stalled the gathering for a few minutes while Vogel dashed back inside, commenting on the beauty of the sunset, though as it approached the temperature was quickly dropping. It promised to be a cold night.

The evening tattoo echoed from the general's headquarters, picked up by drummers with the various brigades, the signal that evening supper, whatever it might be, was now to be served, guard details were to be changed, and the camp was to settle in for another cold night.

"Gentlemen, it would be my pleasure to share supper with you," he announced, looking back for a second through the open doorway and seeing Vogel waving him in after having poured a gallon or more of water into the soup pot.

Acting as the gracious host, he stood by the door, as Hamilton, Laurens, various staff, and, to his delight, even Lafayette came riding up to join them. Cloaks and hats were laid out on his bed, and all retired to the kitchen, which was delightfully warm, almost stuffy. Several rough-hewn tables were set end to end, nearly filling the room, with split log benches to sit on, the men joking as to who would pick up a splinter and by camp tradition thus be entitled to a free drink before the others.

A various assortment of plates, some pewter, others china, in various states from fine to badly cracked and chipped, were set out. Vogel, with the help of a couple of servants from Lafayette's staff, maneuvered the kettle of soup to the center of the table and then, acting as if he was at a state dinner, ladled out bowls full of potato soup leavened with horse bones and liver. There were good-natured jokes that here was a meal fit for a French king, since all believed that as the English adhered to their kidney pies and plum duffs, the French preferred anything made of horse.

Next came a platter covered with blackened and curled slabs of horse meat and roasted potatoes. It was at this point that von Steuben stood and hurled a good-natured round of German, English, and French invective at Vogel: that he was holding back and keeping a treasure for himself. His servant hurried into the bedroom and came out with a heavy jug filled with the ubiquitous corn liquor of the Continentals. That had cost him two pounds of precious salt and a silk vest in trade with a Pennsylvania militia sergeant, but for this night it was worth it.

This was greeted with a round of cheers as Vogel poured out a gill for each of the men, von Steuben watching with a smile even though he inwardly sighed. There would be precious little reserve left, especially if the rules of hospitality required that he offer a second round.

There was no dessert to offer, nor coffee other than the usual chickory blend, and of course tea for such an occasion was not a proper political statement. An officer drinking tea, especially a foreign one, would be viewed as suspect for not understanding one of the legendary causes of this war, with many a man pledging he would not drink tea again until victory was achieved and it could be purchased freely, without a British tax, and then only from the Dutch.

With the gill of corn liquor, the usual toasts were now offered to His Excellency the General, to the Declaration, to confusion to the British king, and even one for the horse who was now their dinner, having died in service to his country. To his dismay, after the last toast more than a few of the young officers slammed their mugs down emphatically, a polite gesture that it was time for a refill. Vogel looked over at him stricken. He merely nodded and smiled, and his servant made another round, carefully doling out what was left of the jug.

Lafayette broke the embarrassing moment by turning to one of his servants helping Vogel. He whispered an order and the man dashed out. Minutes later he returned bearing two bottles of brandy and was greeted with a rousing cheer.

Von Steuben caught Lafayette's eye and ever so subtly nodded a thanks. The young Frenchman grinned at him, as if silently saying that he understood the predicament, and at that moment von Steuben's love for this man redoubled. Chances were that in the midst of this abject poverty, he, as a proper French noble, quietly managed to insure that his own larder was well taken care of, and yet chances were that perhaps these two bottles of brandy were the last of it, for the blockade by the Royal Navy was ever tightening.

Another round of toasts now resounded to good King Louis XVI, to Frederick, king of Prussia, and even to Catherine, though for propriety's sake von Steuben was glad that none of the several Polish volunteers serving with this army were present, for such a toast would have prompted something of a problem, and just maybe a fight.

As the table was cleared of the empty platter of horse meat and the kettle of soup, he felt it was time at last to turn to business.

Everyone stood to stretch, some going outside to relieve themselves, and he went into his small bedroom, drew out the papers he had been working on, and returned to the kitchen. Vogel had managed to snatch one of the bottles of brandy, half-empty, and by watering it down a bit and mixing in some nutmeg and other spices was now heating it to serve as an after-dinner cordial.

Nearly all the young officers returned, though a few begged off, obviously intent on the hope that they might be able to scrounge up some additional food at another headquarters, or simply because the flux was upon them and dinner had not set all that well. But the key individuals he sought were still with him, Hamilton, Laurens, Lafayette, and several of the aides for Greene, Wayne, and Stirling.

He opened up his leather case, drew out a sheaf of papers, and looked over at the ever-present Du Ponceau, who, though a bit into his cups, was still ready to serve as interpreter.

"Gentlemen, I have been in this camp more than a week and have learned much," he began, "and I thank you for the kindness and friendship you have shown me."

There were nods of approval and indeed he could see that these men really had taken him to heart. He had criticized what he saw when his sense of duty had required it but had always done so with the proper amount of praise for the obstacles so far overcome. The balance of praise and criticism had won them over. He had learned as a young company officer many years earlier that some officers could only lead by the flogging cane across the back. Such officers never rose to superior rank. Praise mixed with discipline and criticism when required worked far better.

"I wish to be of service and have cast about for how best to do that," he continued.

Hamilton leaned over to look at them and, taking a sip of the cordial set before him by Vogel, finally shook his head and forced a smile.

"I can imagine whatever it is you are writing, sir, is indeed genius, as befitting a lieutenant general of Frederick, but I must confess my ignorance, sir. I cannot read German."

When translated, there was a round of laughter.

"Perhaps I should have written it in Russian," von Steuben offered with a smile, and the others laughed.

Lafayette studied one of the sheets intently.

"This looks like a manual of drill for the battalion," he said. "This sheet is deployment from column of companies to line of battle."

"Precisely," von Steuben replied. "Very good, General."

Lafayette beamed like a schoolboy, which in age he almost was.

"I am proposing a manual of drill for the entire army. It is how I was trained. It is why Frederick prevailed on so many battlefields in spite of the odds. It is, I must say with all humbleness, the issue that should be foremost at hand with this army."

The papers were picked up by the others and handed back and forth. He had, in fact, been working on it even while in transit from Boston to York. There were dozens of pages of sketches of unit formations, from a single company up to brigades and divisions, encamped, on the march, and, most important, maneuvering from column on the road into battle formations.

Some nodded in eager agreement; others sat polite but silent.

He looked around the room, carefully scanning responses.

"Colonel Hamilton, pray, sir, what is your reaction?"

"I can't read German." But he said so with a smile and not as rejection.

"Nor I English," von Steuben replied in English.

"Sir. We have tried to drill our army in the manner of the British. It has been an abysmal failure."

"Why, sir?"

"Some argue that we do not need to do so. That the rigid discipline of the British line marching in tight formation is not befitting the nature of free men who would better fight as individuals."

"And your personal opinion?" von Steuben offered.

Hamilton smiled.

"I think it is known already, sir."

"Pray, go on, though."

"I was with the army at New York and watched them break and run. I have been in every battle since. When we catch them by surprise, as we did at Trenton and Princeton, the valor of our men will indeed prevail. We break them before they can organize and form ranks. But in a stand-up fight, such as at Brooklyn or Brandywine, we will lose every time."

"Then we avoid such fights," a young officer, an aide to Wayne, offered, his voice edged with hardness. "Avoid such fights the way we did at Saratoga, draw them out beyond their supplies, and cut them off. They have yet to dare to march out here to meet us, and I say, if need be, we just keep pulling back, extending them out, then cutting them off from behind until they give up."

Von Steuben looked around the room and saw several nods of agreement.

"This," and the young man pointed to the sheaf of papers, "this looks like the British way of fighting, and I must ask: Why?"

"Why do we keep losing?" Hamilton replied coolly.

"Because . . ." The young man trailed off into silence.

"And if I hear but one word against His Excellency," and now it was Laurens who spoke, "I will take that as a personal insult, sir."

"I did not even remotely mean to imply that," the young man replied quickly. "I would follow him to hell as surely as you would, sir."

Von Steuben extended his hands in a calming gesture.

"My friends, we are all on the same side here," he offered.

There was silence for a moment.

"What are you proposing, sir?" Hamilton asked.

"A new model of drill for this army," von Steuben replied.

"How so?"

"It is said that it takes three years to make a proper soldier."

"Rare that a man stays in the ranks for more than a year," Laurens replied sadly. "Many are with us for only ninety days, then go back home until next year."

"I understand that," von Steuben replied, "and have thought on it long and hard before I arrived here."

"Are you proposing a long-service standing army?" Laurens replied quickly.

Von Steuben smiled. He sensed already that this young man was solidly behind General Washington, who was calling for just such a measure, against the revolutionaries such as Gates, and even men such as the Adamses, who by instinct mistrusted a standing army and instead called for swarms of militia.

"I will leave policy to those who make policy," he replied with a smile. "I hope my task shall be to form what is provided for the time it is provided into an army that can drive the English and, yes, my German cousins from these shores."

"Hear, hear!" Hamilton offered, raising his glass and finishing the cordial. With a sigh, Vogel offered a few precious ounces as a refill.

"What I am proposing is a model of drill for the army that I pray, within ninety days, can transform it into a force that can meet the British in an open-field fight and then hold that field, in fact drive them from it."

The young officer with Wayne sat back, shaking his head. Hamilton and Laurens smiled, and the others just sat silent, staring at von Steuben. He wondered if they thought he was mad.

"Gentlemen, we must agree on this. In an open-field battle, in terrain such as is found along all the coastal plains, from Savannah to Boston, the British, and I must announce with regret my former comrades from Germany, reign supreme. In a land of gently rolling hills, of rich open farmland sprinkled with woodlots, they will always hold the field.

"In a land of what passes for good roads"——he paused, not wishing to denigrate what these men called roads but which he could only define as mud tracks——"there is currently no force on this side of the Atlantic that can beat them."

"Get them into the forests of upstate New York, or the way Braddock went wandering off toward Pittsburgh, and it is a different story, though," Wayne's young loyalist retorted.

"And, yes, my friend, I will readily agree with you," von Steuben replied. "But the war will not be won at Saratoga, Pittsburgh, or some other wilderness outpost. It will be won in front of Philadelphia, New York, Charleston, or in the tidewater of Virginia. It will finally be won by what His Excellency calls a Continental Line, of disciplined infantry, backed with artillery, horse-mounted troopers and dragoons, and well-supported logistics. But most of all by disciplined infantry. Infantry that can stand and fight the British to a standstill and then drive our opponents from the field."

He was now warming to his subject, and as he spoke he slapped the table with his hand.

"Fabian strategy will no longer work in this war," he continued.

"Who was Fabian?" Wayne's staffer asked.

Lafayette interjected, "He was a Roman leader who believed Hannibal could only be defeated through a long war of attrition while avoiding pitched battles until the Carthaginians were worn down."

"It worked for him, didn't it?" came the reply.

"Gentlemen," von Steuben interjected, fearing that——so typical of these Americans——a heated debate was about to unfold, "putting aside two-thousand-year-old Romans, who in fact built a new model army in Spain under Scipio, let's focus on defeating today's British. What I believe is needed is a new model army. Like those which William of Orange, Cromwell of the English, or Gustavus Adolphus of the Swedes developed in the last century."

Lafayette nodded enthusiastically, but von Steuben saw he was losing the others around the table with his references to the great generals of the past.

He reached out across the table and gathered back the scattering of papers, silently cursing himself for having forgotten to number each page. It would take a while to sort them out. He went through the papers for a moment, fearful that he might be losing his audience, but they remained patiently focused on his next words, while Vogel poured out the last few precious drops of the watered-down cordial.

He finally held several sheets up.

"This is where I propose we"——he hesitated, fumbling for the right word, while looking at Du Ponceau——"where all of us should start.

"It is a school of infantry for but one company of men."

He pointed to the sketches on the sheet. Though he prided himself on at least having a passing ability with watercolors, sketches on cheap foolscap with a quill pen were not his forte.

"I propose starting with a hundred men, one company in strength. The men are to be picked from every regiment with the army. And please, gentlemen, I am a soldier and I know how when a call is given for a levee of several men from each regiment, the tendency is to pick out those that an officer wishes to get rid of, the malcontents, slackers, and cowards.

"That is why I ask you now for your help."

He fixed each man in turn with his gaze as if making a personal appeal.

"I want the best of each regiment. Enlisted men only of proven character and leadership. I beg you, my friends, if this plan is to work, I need your help. For General Washington to have an army worthy of his leadership, I need your help."

Again the look of appeal, and he saw nods from nearly all, including the man with Wayne who had so openly questioned him.

"I will then personally drill this company in a manner which I deem appropriate for your army."

"And that manner is?" Hamilton asked.

"I shoot the first man who disobeys."

There was a moment of stunned silence as Du Ponceau translated. He remained stone-faced for long seconds, then broke out laughing at their looks of disbelief.

The tension in the room broke, and he knew he was winning them over. A well-placed joke at the right moment always worked with soldiers.

"I will start with the most basic of basics. How to stand at attention, how to dress a line, how to salute, how to break ranks and then in an instant reform ranks with one sharp command."

"Good luck on that," Laurens sighed. "It is almost a matter of pride that the men take their own time."

"Then we show them reasons not to."

"How, flog them the way the British do?" the officer with Wayne asked.

"No," and his reply was a bit heated, "we give them pride in a task well done. Americans cannot be driven and beaten into obedience, but I believe they can be reasoned with and educated into a system that will help them defeat their enemies."

There were nods around the table, and he could not help but be pleased with himself.

After thirty years, he knew well the workings of an army. It was one thing to present a plan to the general in command. It was another game altogether to first go to the junior officers, to win their confidence over a good meal, or at least what would pass for a good meal, to be as liberal as possible with spirits, and then appeal to them as brothers in arms.

"I will personally drill the men," and then he quickly added, "with your help, of course."

That was part of the plan as well. If Lafayette, Laurens, Hamilton, and others were there and joined in, it would encourage other officers to observe and to participate as well.

"I will drill them first as individual soldiers, starting with the most basic of things. Once I am satisfied, I am certain they will feel a sense of pride in their bearing and deportment.

"Then to the next step, which is to drill them as a company. We will start with the simplest of maneuvers, to march in column of fours."

"They already know that," Laurens offered.

"Yes, they do, but perhaps not as we would wish to see it done," he replied with a grin. "There should be a precise measure to their step, exactly twenty-eight inches."

Laurens looked at him, a bit confused.

"Trust me, good sir, it goes all the way back to the Romans. First you must train your men to an exact step, all the same: left, right, left, right . . ." As he spoke, he beat out a tattoo on the table.

"And it must be exactly seventy-five steps a minute for normal march. That is regular step. Then to quick time, double-quick, and so on."

"Why?" one of them asked.

"Ah, please bear with me, my friend."

The room was silent now.

"Marching in column of fours is easy; I plan that it can be mastered in half a day at most. March at standard pace will be a bit harder but they will learn, encouraged by you and others."

He stood up, moved to the side of the room, and began to march in the standard measured step, counting off the time as he did so, marching the twenty-foot length of the room, turning about, marching back, and gradually doing it in an increasingly exaggerated manner so that the others began to laugh.

"See, even half drunk I can do it!" he exclaimed.

He sat back down.

"Vogel, more brandy!" he announced.

His servant looked at him with an absolutely stricken expression.

There was a pause and then Lafayette, to the cheers of the others, motioned for his servant, who ran off yet again, Lafayette making a most French gesture of exaggerated despair. The men broke into conversation, and minutes later the servant returned with two more bottles and was greeted with cheers.

"My brothers, truly this is the last of it," Lafayette exclaimed, "but I can think of no better friends to share it with and no better time to drink to our victory over tyranny."

The two bottles of brandy were uncorked and there was no pretense of watering it down as they were passed around the table, each man receiving a glass full.

Von Steuben nodded his thanks to his newfound friend. It was obvious that Lafayette knew the subtlety of the game von Steuben was playing and was fully part of it.

"Now, as I was saying," he continued, first holding up his glass to Lafayette and offering a nod of thanks for the last of his brandy, the others joining in. "Once our good men have mastered the proper march and pace, we then deploy to that most difficult of formation, the line of battle."

There were nods of agreement now, and no protests.

"It shall be two ranks deep."

"Two ranks?" Lafayette queried. "Every army of Europe deploys into three ranks to provide maximum firepower."

"I have pondered long on that, my friend," von Steuben replied. "There are a number of reasons why I suggest two rather than three. Deploying from column of fours to files of two is easier, for one thing; each file of four on the march breaks into two files for the line of battle. Second, it will extend our line farther, which in an even match will overlap their flanks. That will allow us to bring more fire to bear on them. It is also easier to train men for in the time allotted to us."

He looked around the room. The tactical nuances of a line of three versus two were lost on many. But this was indeed something he had pondered for a long time. It made the line weaker, to be certain, but, given the limited time to train these men, it did make for an easier formation to maneuver in battle, and no one now objected. On a volley line, a file three ranks deep required a lot more training when it came to actually firing volleys, or firing by line, than did a battle line only two ranks deep. Without proper, extensive training, many would be the man in the first rank shot in the back of the head by a nervous soldier in the third rank, a guaranteed destroyer of morale. There would be time enough later to explain these finer details.

"Once they have mastered marching and holding their formation, we will then graduate to learning how to wheel, to change front, to go from line to square against cavalry, how to charge at the double-quick time and hold formation."

"All of that in how long?" Hamilton asked.

"I propose that within a month our model company will have mastered all such things. Beyond that, as we conclude the month of training, they will do it in simulation of actual battle, with officers suddenly being taken from them, sergeants, even corporals, then having to take command because of battle losses. Every private will learn the role of a corporal, a corporal a sergeant, and so on up the line of command."

"A month?" Lafayette asked, and even he had a note of doubt in his voice.

Von Steuben forced a smile.

"Do we have any alternative? It is already March. If the weather is good, the campaign season might start as early as May."

And inwardly he prayed it would rain and snow until June.

Lafayette did not reply.

"Plus, I know the standard is to expect the men to fire no more than two rounds a minute. I propose that this model company be trained to three rounds a minute."

Now there was a murmur of discord again.

"It can be done," he said quickly. "I have seen the most ignorant flat-footed Rhinelander peasant, who never touched a gun in his life, be trained to three rounds a minute in a month's time. Surely Americans, who it is said come from their mother's wombs gun in hand, can do the same?"

Again there was a round of laughter and the protests died.

"Once our model company is properly trained they will return to their regiments, all of them bearing the reward and the rank of sergeant."

He looked around the room and all saw his point. The promotion and with it the extra pay, even if it was but five dollars a month Continental, would be incentive for most, if not all, of the recruits to endure the endless drill.

"Then, in turn, these new sergeants will drill each of their regiments as they were drilled. It will become a competition, and you Americans certainly love a good competition——"

He smiled.

"——as I learned in more than one game of cards and chance while trying to make my way here." And though he did not admit that he had won most of the card games he played, his comment was greeted with laughter.

"If we can succeed, then a month hence a grand review would be held. I would pray that perhaps His Excellency the General would preside, with special honors and awards to those regiments that excel in the new model of drill I propose."

There were nods of ready agreement.

"Once that is mastered, regiments would then master the higher arts of maneuver by brigades in mass formations."

"You do make it sound easy," Laurens said. "But in this army some regiments are of but forty men, others of four hundred. Organization as you propose and which I think I see in your sketches would mean a radical reorganization of the entire army and its command structure."

"Perhaps regiments could be combined to form the proper regulation strength, which I would propose as at least two hundred men per regiment. The strongest regiment holds its name and the others form under its flag."

His suggestion was met with a shaking of heads and even outright laughter from every native-born officer present.

"Oh, I could just see McDonald from South Carolina and his precious command of thirty-eight men being told to relinquish his precious rank of colonel," Laurens announced, and the others laughed in agreement.

Von Steuben sensed this was definitely a losing fight for now and held up his hands in a gesture of surrender.

"We can worry about that later. But for now, do I have your support?"

The room fell silent and finally there were nods of approval and muttered, "I'm with you, sir," and "Aye, it's about time."

"Perhaps it was impolite of me to share it with you gentlemen first, rather than going straight to His Excellency, but enthusiasm got the better of me," he announced.

It was little short of a bold-faced lie. He had already mentioned his scheme to General Washington, who had suggested this exact maneuver, since he was most certainly treading on the territory of every regimental commander in the army. Winning the junior officers over was crucial, and though an order from the top down would have won their required respect, it would not have necessarily won their support.

"Fine, then. I shall submit this report in the morning to the general, and I pray, gentlemen, that I shall see you shortly upon the drill field."

Alexander Hamilton, who was in on the scheme, stood up, signaling that the dinner and conversation were at an end.

"General von Steuben, I think you are taking the necessary steps we have all been praying for," he announced, and the others joined in with their congratulations.

Von Steuben went to the door, and as each of the young officers departed, he warmly shook their hands while Vogel fetched their hats and capes. The weather outside was turning far colder, wind backing around and carrying with it the scent of a storm, perhaps snow by morning.

Finally, only Lafayette and Hamilton remained. A subtle gesture on his part had conveyed to them that he wished them to linger for a few more minutes.

He turned to Lafayette and offered a bow.

"Your sacrifice of brandy, sir——I hope someday to redeem it."

Lafayette smiled.

"To a worthy cause, though heaven knows when my family shall be able to smuggle another case through. Let us pray it is soon."

Von Steuben looked at the two, took a deep breath, and then finally delved into what he had been dreading for months but knew had to be faced.

"Sir, you addressed me as General," he finally said, looking at Hamilton.

Hamilton's response was polite but obviously a bit confused.

"Well, sir, that is the rank you did hold under Frederick the Great."

"Well, sir, how shall I venture this?" he replied, now nervous.

"There is a concern?" Lafayette offered.

"And that is?" Hamilton offered.

He cleared his throat.

"General might not be the exact term applied to me when I served with Frederick."

The two were silent as they gazed at him.

"Well, you see . . . ," and his voice trailed off.

He had deliberately let Laurens, now so enthusiastic a follower, leave the gathering before venturing this delicate point. He had played the game well enough with Gates, the buffoon, and ever since arrival on this shore, but sooner or later, rumors of the truth would dog him. He had never been a general; he had served on the General Staff in Berlin for only the briefest of times before being sent off; even his title of baron was a purchased one by his grandfather. His service with Catherine had come about solely because he had been a prisoner of war, and at war's end, when released, had briefly served her addled husband the Czar Paul. After she had murdered Paul, she had found it convenient to employ an unemployable German officer to try to whip her army into shape.

He knew that sooner or later the rumors would follow him across the ocean. He had debated it ever since arriving in Boston, where, to his surprise, the American agents in France, Deane and Franklin, had inflated his resume to the highest of ranks. In the boiling pot of American politics, sooner or later the rumors and charges would catch up. In just the last week he had come to respect Washington more than any officer he had ever served. If von Steuben were attacked after given a place of confidence, it would be an embarrassment to Washington and could only be answered in turn by a single action, resignation on his part.

Best to venture at least some of it now and then hope for the best.

"Your rank?" Hamilton ventured. He looked at him hopefully.

"I think, sir, no slight upon their honor, sir, but I daresay that in their enthusiasm for our cause, certain, how shall I say, exaggerations have been made on my behalf by your American agents in Europe before I took ship to this shore."

Hamilton did not reply; Lafayette stepped closer, looking straight into his eyes.

"Are you saying, sir, that your commissioning papers with the Prussian and Russian armies might be not as they first seem?"

He did not reply.

"Nor your rank of nobility?"

Again he did not reply.

Lafayette remained silent and then threw back his head and laughed.

"I am a marquis. But where else in this world at the age of nineteen can I be a general?"

Hamilton, who understood French, shook his head and laughed softly.

"Welcome to America. I'd like to think we check such things at the border and count more on what you know and what you can do rather than who your great-grandfather was. Claim what you will, General Baron von Steuben. But, by God, if your plan to remake this army works, for all I care you could have been a bloody sergeant in the service of the Khans. Just make it work."

Von Steuben actually felt tears cloud his eyes as he looked at his two new-found friends.

"When I think the time is right, I will broach this with General Washington," Hamilton offered, "but first let's see how your drill works out."

He could not help but clasp their hands.

"It will work," he reassured them intensely, voice choked with emotion.

CHAPTER THIRTEEN

* * *

Valley Forge
March 7, 1778

"My God, you look like starving sons of bitches!"

Peter Wellsley understood just enough German to at least think that was what this man pacing before him was saying, though the translator pacing behind the German rendered it "starving dogs."

A flurry of laughter ran through the ranks, especially from the Pennsylvania men who fully understood German.

"But I do see that you are soldiers," he announced loudly.

There were now murmurs of approval.

Rumors had swept through the encampment that this man was setting up some kind of training school, and that only the best would be picked from each regiment to attend. It would mean relief from fatigue duty working on the fortifications, an extra ration of meat, and the promise of promotion. There were more than enough volunteers.

To Peter's delight, General Washington had insisted that his entire headquarters company was to attend as well. There were a hundred men from the various units of the army, and fifty from the headquarters.

The day was cold and blustery, with occasional bursts of snow falling to the frozen ground. Briefly, weak sunlight would shine through the drifting clouds for a few minutes before another snow squall descended around them.

"We will train together every day for a month," von Steuben continued. "We shall do so from eight in the morning until I tell you we are finished, and, by God, if that means marching in the dark, you will do so."

His gaze now became determined.

"And I break my walking stick on your head if you do not listen right," he announced, holding the stick aloft.

A few men muttered under their breath, but others laughed, seeing that he smiled as he made his threat.

"Now show me a proper line, two ranks deep."

The men looked about, not sure who to form on. Several young officers with von Steuben began shouting orders, pointing to where two poles had been set in the ground, about forty yards apart, topped with dirty rags. The men shuffled over, forming up into lines as ordered, von Steuben watching, pacing up and down in front of them.

"That is a line?" he finally cried almost in anguish.

Many of the men leaned forward slightly, looking up and down the line.

"Stand at attention!"

They braced themselves. Von Steuben gazed sternly at them, shaking his head.

"First I want shorter men in the front rank, taller in the second. Then with each line I want shortest at the end, tallest at the center. Now do it!"

Peter looked around, not sure where to go.

The baron's assistants stepped forward, walking down the line, pulling men out of the rank, moving them around like playing cards being reshuffled. It took a good ten minutes of sorting, some of the men complaining that they wanted to stand next to an old comrade or brother, but their protests were ignored. One of them announced he was quitting and began to stalk off, but was kicked back into the line by a sergeant. Finally they were properly arrayed.

Peter found himself near the center, in the front, with Harris by his right side.

"That looks better now," von Steuben announced. "Now, I want you to say hello to the man to either side of you and shake his hand."

He made an exaggerated gesture of shaking an imaginary hand, which drew some laughter. Peter nodded to Harris and turned to his left. A young man, features deeply pitted from smallpox, looked at him and offered a smile.

"Rob Boers of the Third New York," the boy offered and they shook hands.

"Count off from the right by fours," von Steuben ordered, and the count came down the line, Peter a number three, Boers a four.

"Good, we are all friends now," von Steuben replied. "You may fall out and gather round me."

This seemed easy enough, Peter thought, and he stepped out of the line with the others and walked toward von Steuben.

"You did not say thank you!" von Steuben roared. "Now fall back in line exactly where you were!"

There was a scramble, men bumping into each other, and the line reformed.

"No one move!" von Steuben shouted. "Now count off with exactly the same number you gave last time."

It was a shambles. Peter was embarrassed to realize that he and Boers had shifted places.

The count-off finished, von Steuben walked slowly down the line and with his own hands shifted each man back into place, then ordered them to stand at attention.

"Now, my children, can we remember who our neighbors are?"

"Hell, Johnson here made the mistake, not me," someone in the back rank complained.

Von Steuben eyed the protestor.

"And I break my stick over both your heads if you make the mistake again," he announced.

"Now, again, fall out and gather round me."

Several of the men sarcastically muttered thank-yous, but all knew the game, anticipating a shouted command to form ranks, though this time he did not play it as they thought. They gathered round and he smiled.

"Much will seem strange as we start," he announced, "But there is reason for everything I do to you. It is like building a house. First we make foundation." He gestured as if digging. "Without foundation the house will tilt and fall. Except for the mason and those who dig the holes, no one sees the foundation, but it is there and it will make the building strong. Do we understand?"

There were nods of agreement.

"Now, my children," he said softly, "fall in and come to attention."

The men scrambled back as ordered, and this time only two were out of place, the others around them cursing under their breath.

He had them fall out and do it again, and this time it was done right and he nodded with satisfaction.

"First lesson learned. From now on, you will always fall in exactly the same place in line. Always! That way, even if it is the middle of the night and there is an alarm, you will know where to stand."

He ordered them back to attention, and for the men to shoulder arms. This done, he gazed along the line, then turned away, motioning for his staff to gather around. There was a whispered conference for a moment, the others nodding their heads in agreement, and he turned back to face the line.

"Fall out to the rear and stack muskets by sections of four."

There was some confusion as the men were shown where to stack arms at the end of the drill field, and then a shouted command for them to fall back in at the double time.

The line reformed, Peter feeling slightly strange without a musket in his hand. Nor did he like stacking his weapon with those of a group of men he didn't know. As a member of the headquarters company, he took special care of his weapon, always insuring it was well oiled and polished, with not a speck of rust or dirt. More than one man, stacking arms, might return later to find a rusting flintlock in its place.

"First you will learn drill as you should learn drill," von Steuben announced. "Everything in its proper time and place."

"Company, attention!"

He kept them like that for nearly an hour, insisting on what Peter thought was absurd——that each man's feet must be placed just so——shouting that they looked like mules and sheep otherwise. Hands were to rest on the crease of their trousers, if they had trousers, with fingers extended no matter how damn cold. Men to the left of the regimental flag-bearer, in this case one of von Steuben's assistants holding a Continental flag aloft, were to have their heads slightly turned in his direction, so that the left eye was aligned with the row of buttons down the center of his uniform, if he had had a uniform, let alone buttons. Those to the right of the flag-bearer were to do the opposite, looking to their left with right eye aligned to the center row of buttons.

Throughout, von Steuben would offer comments, alternating between praise and then at times turning to one of his young French officers, shouting, "Curse at them good in English, damn it!" The comments that followed always drew subdued laughter.

As each man was checked in turn, commands were alternated between standing at ease, coming to attention, eyes front then toward the flag-bearer, the baron explaining that every man must learn to keep his eyes to the center, where the flag could always be seen, marking the position of the regiment in line, and with it the officer leading the way.

Just mastering these few things took up most of the morning. Finally, von Steuben was satisfied with the men breaking ranks, falling out, then returning to their position and coming to attention with heads turned properly.

Next he ordered them to remain at attention and take one step forward.

The resulting confused result caused another explosion, with him yelling at Du Ponceau to curse them again in English.

"I guess I shall have to be your father and teach you how to walk," he shouted, and this time he did seem a bit exasperated.

"The proper step for a soldier in this army will be twenty-eight inches, not one inch more or less."

As he paced up and down the line, his assistants to either flank stepped off a pace, hammered stakes into the ground, then took another pace, hammered stakes into the ground, and so on for five paces.

"With each step, I want this line to be perfectly straight. Now do as you are told. Forward one step!"

The line moved forward, men bumping into each other, stopping, leaning forward to see how they stood relative to the marking stake, von Steuben slapping the ground with his walking stick, pacing back and forth, glaring at them.

"Step!"

The line lurched forward.

"Step!"

At the end of five paces the line was still curved and bowed.

"About-face!"

Now, more confusion, with some turning to their left, others to their right, von Steuben launching into more invective, shouting that all the men were to turn the same way.

There was grumbling in the ranks, some whispering that a man should at least be able to turn the way he felt like it as long as he got himself faced about correctly.

The weather was turning colder, wind picking up, and von Steuben gazed at them, shaking his head.

"Go over to the fires, warm up, there's soup waiting." He pointed to where several large fires were burning at the edge of the parade field. The men gratefully broke ranks, Peter sticking with Harris and making his way over to the warming blaze.

"Damn crazy Dutchman," someone muttered, "if I had known it was going to be like this, I'd of gone on sick call instead."

"He's got a point," Harris offered.

"How's that?" the complainer retorted, while they stood in line, pulling wooden bowls or tin cups out of their haversacks, each man receiving a ladle of soup thick with potatoes and even some thin slivers of meat, though which kind of meat was purely a matter of speculation.

"Hell, we can barely march, let alone keep a line in a fight."

"I joined this here war not to march around like a toy soldier. I joined it to fight."

"That's what he's teaching us," Harris replied.

"Still beats digging latrines or burial detail," someone else muttered.

"I got seven weeks left," another retorted, "and then be damned to all of it, I did my part and I'm going home."

There were mutters of agreement from more than a few.

Peter said nothing, draining down every last drop of the soup and then using his finger to scoop out the last droplets and lick them clean before stuffing the bowl back into his haversack.

"Hey, we better look sharp," Harris suddenly announced, and nodded to where von Steuben was standing.

General Washington was now with him.

"Well, damn it, maybe he can talk some sense into this German. We're Americans, damn it, not Hessians."

"How are you faring, Baron?" Washington asked, returning the drillmaster's salute.

Von Steuben grinned.

"As is only to be expected, sir."

"And that is?"

"Meaning no insult, sir, but they will need work, much work."

Washington nodded thoughtfully.

"You may proceed, Baron, and if it will not discomfort you, I would like to observe."

"By all means sir, it is an honor."

Washington rode off a discreet distance to the edge of the field and remained mounted, as von Steuben gave the command for the men to fall back into line.

Thankfully they did so without much trouble, each man finding his proper place, then automatically dressing on the center.

This time he detailed them to form squads, in columns of four.

"Perhaps if we dance in small groups we can learn the step quicker," he announced, as it took several minutes for the men to shift from line into seven columns. He detailed off his assistants, who took over, moving the columns off in various directions so commands to one would not confuse another standing nearby.

Von Steuben shouted the beat, "Step . . . step . . . step!" until his voice was nearly hoarse. There was some stumbling and confusion to start. One of the men caused a column to break down in confusion because one of his foot wrappings unraveled and the man behind him stepped on it, tripping both of them up. The unit broke down in gales of laughter, and von Steuben humored them by issuing a volley of good-natured curses, keeping the language toned down because the general was watching.

He slowly increased the beat to sixty steps a minute, holding out his watch, a new, expensive one that had a second-hand sweep. After a while he stopped counting and let his assistants maintain the pace, with poor Du Ponceau, whose voice was hoarse from repeating the baron's commands, following by his side.

He knew Washington was still observing and slowly walked over to his side.

"The pace seems slow, is that your intent?" the general asked.

"Yes, sir, for now it is just to master the length of step. The standard for the army in line of battle will be seventy-five paces a minute. Standard march. One hundred and twenty at the quick time."

Washington nodded, saying nothing.

It was now past noon and von Steuben could feel his own hunger pangs growing.

But before he allowed them to break, he shouted for the columns to halt, the men to fall out and at the double time form back into line.

"You do this right now and we eat, by God," he announced as the last of the men pushed their way into the line and found their proper places.

He stepped to one side of the line.

"Do it right and you eat. If not, you don't eat. Company at my command."

Several of the men started to take a step forward. He said nothing. He'd overlook it this time.

"Forward, march . . . step! . . . step! . . . step!"

The line held formation. It was only ten steps, less than thirty feet, but the alignment held.

"Now my lads, without moving, stand at ease, then look to your left and right."

They did as ordered and there was a ripple of comments.

The hundred and fifty men were perfectly aligned, with barely a bulge in the center, where the tallest men, by nature, would continue to take slightly larger steps. For a Prussian parade formation, the response would have been hours more of merciless drill. But this was different, very different indeed.

"Excellent, my boys. We have had a good start. Now get some food, fall in again in a half hour. Dismissed."

The men broke ranks and headed for the cooking fires, where half a dozen women had been at work, with kettles of boiled mutton.

He ventured over to where Washington had remained motionless, with Lafayette by his side, watching for more than an hour.

"It is a start," von Steuben offered, with Lafayette translating.

The general nodded.

"I had often heard it spoken that the Germans were the hardest taskmasters of all upon the drill field. I have seen evidence of that when facing the Hessians. I expected a stricter manner from you, sir."

He was not sure if Washington's words were meant as a reproof or not.

"I have only had a few months in this country but can see much difference between the training of free landholders such as serve in your ranks and that of the peasants and street sweepings pressed into the service of European kings. The men need discipline, yes, much discipline. But they also must be shown and have the reasons why explained, and, yes, at times they must be cajoled. Much I plan to teach will seem strange to them, to any American, but I think, Your Excellency, it is the key to victory in the next engagement, for the enemy will not expect it."

Washington simply nodded thoughtfully.

"Carry on," he finally replied and turned to ride off.

The half hour passed too quickly for some, several of the men, obviously ill with the flux, asking to be relieved of duty before staggering off. When von Steuben reformed the line, he had the men count off again and acquaint themselves with the new comrade who might be by their side.

He then put them through the drill, several times, of falling out, and then, at command, springing back to form line of battle. Next it was simply taking ten steps, going about-face, then ten steps back. Ever so slowly he picked up the pace of march to the seventy-five beats a minute he sought, a drummer, a young black soldier from North Carolina, whom he had personally picked and trained the day before, keeping the tempo.

Next he had them march twenty paces, thirty paces, and then finally the length of the field, so that by midafternoon they were marching with precision and obvious pride as they covered the entire length of the drill field and back again, keeping alignment. Von Steuben responded with fulsome praise. The temperature continued to drop, the wind picking up, and it was obvious that the men, especially those barefoot or with wrappings, were suffering, and he did not chide them when, even while standing at attention, they stamped their feet to try to keep circulation going.

Just when they seemed well puffed up with what they had already accomplished, he felt it was time to pull his next move and knock a peg or two out from under them.

He called his assistants over, and then detailed them off, the young officers spreading out in front of the line.

"Forward, march!" he shouted, the drummer picking up the beat.

After just several steps the young officers moved in, blocking a man. "You're shot! Lie down!"

After less than a dozen paces, gaps were opening in the line. A few of the noncommissioned officers in the marching line knew what they were to do and shouted for the men to "dress on the colors!"

Von Steuben ran in front of them, shouting for them now to quicken their pace to the quick time, the drummer picking up the beat. All the time, his assistants kept pulling more men out of the line, a near fistfight breaking out when Du Ponceau picked on a particularly large sergeant from Rhode Island who roared out that he would be damned if he would fall out even if he were shot.

He was glad Washington did not witness the shambles the line had disintegrated into after barely fifty yards.

"Halt in place! Don't move!" von Steuben roared.

The men came to a stop. The line was curved back, in places completely broken, men just a loose mass. Those pulled from the line stood about, some moving to rejoin the ranks, others just sitting down on the cold ground, glad for the break from routine.

"All right, my lads, fall in around me," he called.

The men, many now deflated from their pride of but minutes before, gathered in around him.

"You know what it is I was doing?" he asked.

No one spoke.

"How many of you have been in a battle?" he asked.

About half of them raised their hands.

"Where?"

"I was at Germantown," one of them announced. "Paoli," another said. "I've been with this damn army since Boston," another cried.

He looked at the man, as Du Ponceau pointed him out. He had a deep furrow across his left cheek, the scar a slash from a blade or musket ball.

"Your name, soldier?"

"Sergeant Harris, headquarters company of His Excellency General Washington."

"That wound?"

"Princeton," Harris replied coolly.

"And what do you think?"

Harris looked around at the others.

"It's one thing to march about like parade soldiers out here," he announced, "another thing when the bullets and grapeshot fly."

"Precisely. You are a good man," von Steuben responded, and he reached out to slap Harris on the shoulder.

"You men have done well today and I am proud of you."

He looked around at the gathering. A few grinned, most were silent, nearly all of them shivering from the cold.

"It is March. In two months the campaign season will again be upon us. In those two months, by God, I will teach you everything I know. You are good men and I know you will learn.

"We will start tomorrow with the same thing. Marching in line by step at regular time, then quick time. That shall be easy after what you learned today.

"Then it shall be marching by column, and, in an instant, the blink of an eye, you shall jump quickly and go from column into line."

As he spoke, he held up his hands to demonstrate.

"Then it shall be marching in column at regular time, quick time, and at the run. Then it shall be forming line in any direction commanded, marching, and now shall come the hard tasks of keeping that line while wheeling about, changing fronts, and continuing to advance."

He was warming to his subject now.

"You will learn to do so and then more. How to withdraw while under fire, how even to form square against cavalry or go to open order against artillery and then back again in an instant.

"And that is even before I will let you shoulder your muskets again."

There was a murmur from the crowd.

"I know, I know you pride yourselves that you can shoot, but how many of you can claim with certainty that you have ever actually shot an enemy you aimed at?"

He looked around at the group, several dozen hands went up, there were some comments back and forth, a few boasting, others taunting, some of the hands were finally lowered.

"Oh, I must have shot a hundred Turks myself," he offered with a disdainful wave, "and that was with a pistol at a hundred paces."

Some of the men laughed and a few more hands went down.

"It is disciplined fire, concentrated on a single point, that wins the fight in an open field," he announced sharply. "All of you firing together, at my command. First one rank and then, as you reload, the other, and by God you will fire at least two rounds a minute, every one of you. That means every fifteen seconds you will sweep the field before you . . ."

He gestured to the open field, now bathed in the slanting light of a cold late-afternoon sun, the flurries of morning and midday having cleared. It promised to be a cold night.

"Fifteen seconds. That means never again will you shoot and then before you reload the enemy can be upon you with bayonets. For as one line reloads the second stands ready to smash down any attempt for them to charge. Do you see that?"

There were some nods of agreement, especially from the veterans of previous fights.

"I still prefer to do my fighting hunkered down," one of the men replied, "nice and safe behind a wall or tree. This is foolishness."

Von Steuben looked at the complainer and nodded.

"How many fights have you been in?"

"I was at Paoli," the man replied tensely.

"And how many of your comrades were bayoneted to death while trying to lie down behind a wall?"

The man glared at him.

"If in those first seconds of surprise you had formed a battle line and even in the dark opened fire, how many of the enemy would have been left standing?"

There was no response.

Von Steuben stepped closer to him.

"I understand what you feel. Believe me, I do. I fought in the Seven Years' War. I faced enemy lines at fifty paces and had to stand firm and not flinch. If we broke, if we lay down, they would have slaughtered us like sheep. In such a fight there is only one way to fight back. To hold your line. Hold your line!"

He nearly shouted the last words.

"Hold your line, and then give back to them as hard as they hit you. Then it becomes a battle of nerves," and as he spoke he clasped his two hands together as if they were wrestling, "nerves and endurance."

"Let one hand feel that it is the stronger in courage, in firepower, in its will to stand and deliver, and I promise you, men, the other hand will weaken, collapse, and run away."

He gestured now with one hand going limp and the other hitting it.

"Stand with me for a month, men. Let me teach you all that I know. You have already mastered much today, there will be more tomorrow. Stand with me, and then when you are ready, go back to your own regiments and in turn teach them as I have taught you."

"I'll do my teaching in good American," one of the men announced, and there was open laughter, von Steuben joining in, then calling on Vogel to give the man a good curse in English, which he did, to even more laughter.

"In one month you will be ready. Then in the next month you will teach your comrades. Once they have learned we shall bring you together not just by regiments but by entire brigades and learn yet more new things. How to march in brigade column and then deploy to line of battle with all possible speed. How one regiment can support another on the line, and turn an enemy flank while others hold them in place. There is much to learn, much to learn."

He looked around at the group.

"You are good soldiers, though I will say standing close to you hurts my nose and I fear for how many lice I now shall have." He made an exaggerated gesture of plucking one off his sleeve and crushing it with his fingernails.

Again, laughter.

"Fall into line!"

The men sprang back to their position, line forming, still far too slow for his liking, but nevertheless, forming up far better than they had in the morning.

"Attention!"

They did as ordered, heads turning slightly to face the center, where he now stood.

"If after today you do not have the stomach for this, or think it folly, tell your commander tonight and he will send someone else in your place. For, by God, tomorrow, though we have laughed today together as comrades, I will tolerate no lack of discipline. If you waste my time, starting tomorrow, I will have you driven out of the ranks and break this stick over your back or head.

"Do we understand each other?"

Caught off-guard by his sudden change of mood, the men were silent.

"We now have one month to teach you what a Prussian soldier takes a year or more to master. I think you are of sterner stuff than the Hessians whom I know some of you fear to face. In a month you will be ready to face them, in two months' time you must train your comrades to do the same. In three months' time, if you prove to be the men I think you are, you will see fear in the eyes of your enemies and know true victory on the battlefield, and I swear I will stand in the line with you that day.

"Think upon what I have taught you and what I have said today. You are dismissed."

He turned and stalked off, his staff falling in around him.

My God, he thought inwardly. What a tangled mess this all is. He actually pitied those poor men. With the temperature dropping, the chill was even striking into his bones, and he had on his heavy wool uniform and cape. Some of them indeed were little better than scarecrows.

Of course after but a day of drill they could march in line, on a parade field, but the last maneuver, when he forced some of the men to act as dead and wounded——within seconds all semblance of formation disintegrated. At Minden he had seen entire companies swept away in the blink of an eye by concentrated blasts of grapeshot from batteries of the enemy's six-pounders. Assaulting a fortified line, covered with heavy twelve-, eighteen-, and twenty-four-pounder guns, entire regiments could be cut in half in a single salvo. Yet still they were expected to continue to press forward at the double, dressing line as they did so, keeping formation and ready to fire or press in the charge on command.

His young staff was silent, walking to either side of him. None of them had ever actually been in a fight. They knew their drill, of course, but the reality of a battle, the man next to you decapitated, his brains splattering into your face and you were expected to keep control, to lead and not become unnerved?

They were nearly as green as the men he was training.

He looked around at them and smiled.

"My lads, you did well today," he offered with a smile, hiding all his inner fears.

His few words of praise caused grins of delight.

"Vogel, what is the suggestion for dinner tonight?"

They had managed to hire one of the women working in the camp to cook their meals and tend to their small headquarters house. She had gone into the army with her husband, who had died the week before from the flux, and one of Lafayette's staff had recommended her as someone of good character who needed the work. Besides, she could speak German.

"Mrs. Wismer said it will be boiled mutton, that was what was issued."

"Ah, my favorite," he lied. He detested mutton, but if that was all that was available, for the moment it was better to claim it was his preferred dish, and he led the way across the field.

Peter, legs numb, raced to where the muskets were stacked, and was glad to see that no one had tried to run off with his weapon, though a few arguments did break out between men of the headquarters company and those of other regiments when a few of the preferred second-model Brown Besses were supposedly grabbed by mistake, and battered Charleville or the detested Dutch muskets left in their place.

Harris settled the arguments, backed up by the others of the company before they set off as a group back to their barn.

"Tomorrow we stack weapons together, boys," Harris announced, "and one of the men detailed off as sick can keep guard on them."

There was a chorus of agreement.

"What do you think of all this?" Peter asked.

"That German?" Harris asked.

Peter nodded.

"It's one thing to do what he says marching around out here. But with a grenadier company coming straight at you, covered by light infantry?"

"Like he said," Harris replied, forcing a smile, "we got thirty days for him to teach us, thirty days for us to teach the rest of the army, and then thirty days after that we face the bastards again."

Peter looked around at his comrades. All of them had lost weight, some a stone or more, their faces drawn, haggard. As a headquarters company they were expected to be clean-shaven, which only served to reveal how thin and malnourished most of them were. Seven of the men of the company had so far died, three from the flux, one from smallpox. One had just simply collapsed and another had frozen to death while on sentry duty one night. Two more had deserted. They were faring a little better than most companies, at least, but still one out of six who had been with the ranks when they marched here were gone. And now the starving time was truly beginning to set back in again, for the countryside for miles around had been stripped clean by Anthony Wayne's foraging expeditions. Food was running short and disease was taking an ever-increasing toll.

Ninety days and it would be nearly summer, and he wondered how many of them would be alive by then.

CHAPTER FOURTEEN

* * *

Philadelphia
April 9, 1778

In the crowded room, with candles lit only around the stage itself, they were in near darkness, pressed in on all sides by the audience, intent on the play before them. The actors were arguing how to spell "declaration," two of them trying to duel with long quill pens. The audience was laughing good-naturedly at the farce.

"I didn't know you were here," Allen whispered, leaning over. His attention barely focused on the play . . . Elizabeth having just slipped up to his side and taken his hand. Contrary to the custom when it came to evening fashion, she was not wearing a wig, but had her natural hair piled high, adorned with the first flowers of spring. The scent was intoxicating.

"How did you get here?" he whispered.

"I walked."

"No, I mean . . . your father?"

She giggled like a schoolgirl.

"He's off to New York to meet his business partners, and Mother is 'taken with the vapors' and asleep. I swore the servants to secrecy and just walked here."

Her boldness startled him. They stood silent for a moment, hands clasped, acting as if they were watching the play. A character lampooning Thomas Paine drew loud hisses from the audience as he waved a sheet of paper attempting to sing his lines——that his "common sense" should rule them all. A captain in the front of the audience, more than a little drunk, climbed up on the low stage and snatched the piece of paper, made an exaggerated gesture of using it to blow his nose and then wipe himself, which drew gales of laughter, as he bowed and returned to the audience.

Allen knew it wasn't part of the play——his friend André would not have written something quite so crude. The actor playing Paine fumbled for a moment, then shrugged, held up an imaginary sheet, and kept on singing, his efforts greeted with mocking cheers. Allen, a bit embarrassed, looked over at Elizabeth, who made no attempt to let go of his hand to offer applause.

"Have you read his work?" she whispered, while the forced hilarity lampooning Paine and now Jefferson waving his "Declaration" focused the attention of the rest of the audience.

The memory of Jonathan clutching *The American Crisis* in his dying hands flooded over him again. And yes, he had read *Common Sense*, and found himself torn when he did so. Always pragmatic, he had agreed in some ways with the argument presented but saw, as well, that it was a document that, in the end, would be drenched in blood. Its ideas were now tearing the country apart, and history had always shown that such revolutions, filled with high promises, almost inevitably ended in yet more tyranny, violence, and suppression.

"Yes, I read it," he said softly.

She looked up at him inquiringly.

"And?"

"I think it has caused more anguish than hope. Jonathan read it, he believed in it with all his heart and soul, and now?"

He paused.

"I doubt if I can even find the grave where they buried him."

"I'm sorry," she whispered, "I didn't mean to bring back painful memories."

"It's not your fault," he replied.

The character of Jefferson broke into a duet with Paine, the two of them dancing a hornpipe, the audience laughing and booing good-naturedly.

"It was in this very room," she whispered, and he could sense her anger. "I stood outside this building when the Declaration was read for the first time. It was such a moment . . ."

The two characters on the stage finished their song and then the taller actor playing Jefferson, one of Grey's staff, leaned over and embraced Paine, played by a short, rotund sergeant of the light infantry, the act triggering ribald laughter and comments.

She let her hand slip from Allen's and left the room, no one noticing her leaving.

He followed her out onto the front steps of the meeting hall.

She looked back up at him.

"I didn't come here to argue politics and the war with you, Allen," she whispered.

"Then why?" and there was a touch of nervousness in his voice.

She smiled at him.

"I'd like to think there was a certain fondness between us, long before this war ever started."

She stood on tiptoe, leaned into him, and offered a gentle kiss on the lips.

He let his arms slip around her and held her close, kissing her again and then again.

They stood thus for several minutes. More than a few couples were outside doing the same, or wandering off into the darkness together.

"Perhaps when the war is over?" he finally whispered.

"What after the war is over?"

"Your father would accept me, for having served the Crown. I can return to my family's business. Perhaps then we could . . ."

His voice trailed off, and he inwardly cursed himself for being so tongue-tied.

"Yes, I would like that," she replied, and he could feel her begin to tremble as she drew him in closer. "But there is tonight as well . . ."

"What?"

He was shocked beyond words.

She looked up at him, smiling, and then jumped with a start when the muffled report of a gun, and an instant later a second one, echoed from within the meeting hall.

He laughed softly.

"End of the play," he whispered. "John Bull just shot Thomas Jefferson and Tom Paine."

"Fitting behavior to be expected," she said, stepping back slightly.

"It is only John André offering some satire," he offered.

She didn't reply.

"We were saying," he offered, trying to bring her in closer again. She accepted his embrace but did so stiffly.

"Would you marry me?" he blurted out, voice beginning to choke.

She looked up at him.

"When the war is over we'll talk of such things," she said.

Their semblance of privacy disappeared as the double doors into the meeting hall were flung open. The audience began to throng out, some heading for other parties, others for more private rendezvous, couples going off alone into the night, the few unfortunates whose battalions were on watch for the night reporting back for duty.

"Capital, John, simply capital! Good old John Bull at the end like that!"

Allen turned to see his friend in the doorway, accepting congratulations from General Howe, John politely inclining his head as the commander praised him. With his current mistress on his arm, General Howe started down the steps. Allen released Elizabeth from his arms and came stiffly to attention, the general nodding to him and passing on, followed by his entourage of staff and their ladies.

Elizabeth did not offer a curtsy, remaining stock-still, and as the group passed she sniffed.

"Well, I see Beatrice Walker has succumbed," she whispered under her breath.

"Who?"

"Beatrice, she's with that fawning major of Howe's staff."

And then she laughed softly.

"And she will be certain to tell my father she saw me with you, the gossip."

He couldn't help but smile.

"Perhaps not——the question might be raised of how did she see you?" he offered, and she laughed softly.

"What did you think?"

It was André, beaming with excitement, coming down the steps to join them, Peggy Shippen clinging to his side.

"Afraid I missed the ending," Allen offered, and then smiled "but the reports from within were rather thunderous."

André laughed.

"Double-loaded the pistols with powder and I told that big oaf playing John Bull, Lieutenant Harrison, to point them high so no one would get burned. Instead he aimed it straight at poor Lieutenant O'Brian's chest, burned a hole clean through his jacket. No love lost between the two, they had a falling-out over a woman, you know."

He stopped for a moment, looking at Elizabeth, and decided to say no more on that subject, since the woman in question was notorious for her lack of virtue of late.

"No one hurt, thank God, but it scared the hell out of O'Brian. Rather than fall down dead, he just stood there patting at the flames and cursing

Harrison like an Irish washerwoman. It was rich." He sighed. "Pray, it doesn't turn into a real duel later."

He turned away for a moment to accept the congratulations of others who were leaving. Apparently the near-tragic mistake at the end was actually the high point, and he accepted the compliments concerning the humorous ending as if it had been planned thus all along.

"Have you heard?" Peggy whispered loudly to Elizabeth.

"Heard what?"

"About General Howe! The room was all abuzz with the rumors."

"And that is?"

"He will be relieved and ordered back to England to report on his failure to finish the war."

Allen looked at her, startled.

"Is the rumor true?" Elizabeth asked out loud.

"Which rumor?" André asked. "You are curious, my dear, aren't you? That Howe has a second mistress? That his brother the admiral has the pox? That the king of Prussia has started an affair with the czarina of Russia?"

"You know what I mean," she replied with a smile.

"Oh, General Howe? Has this fine lady been talking? I told her not to say a word!"

He looked good-naturedly at Peggy and then gave her a playful swat on her backside. She looked up at him, grinned, and replied with a slight tap on the cheek with her closed fan.

"I am, sir, a lady and will not brook such crass behavior."

"My apologies, *mademoiselle*," he replied with exaggerated courtesy.

"Just rumors," André offered and then he drew closer. "So my dear Miss Peggy, please do not attach my name to them."

The party inside was growing louder by the minute.

"They're celebrating," he sighed. "Couldn't wait for the old man to leave." He shook his head. "My theater company can clean up and see to themselves. I'm played out for the evening, and enough congratulations have been said. To hang about for more would be boorish. And a gentleman should never be boorish.

"Shall we retire to our quarters? Miss Elizabeth, please do come, your secret is safe with me, as I am certain it will be with Miss Peggy."

Elizabeth hesitated but then nodded in agreement.

The two couples walked the few blocks to Benjamin Franklin's former residence, still the headquarters for General Grey and his staff. Elizabeth hesitated at the doorway for a moment, furtively looking around to see if anyone might notice her entering a private dwelling with only one other couple, who, it was rumored throughout the city, were already engaged in an affair.

André took her by the arm and led her in, motioning for them to go into their favorite room, the library, while he fetched a bottle of claret. Wine poured for his guests, he settled down in an overstuffed leather chair, stretched out his legs, and sighed.

"The king, Howe, and Clinton," he said softly, raising his glass, the others following suit——but Elizabeth, without fanfare or overt display, did not take a drink.

"Clinton?" Allen asked.

"My young friend. It is all rumor," André said, and now he looked pointedly at Peggy, who blushed slightly but returned his gaze.

"Dispatch ship, as we all know, arrived this morning. Very fast passage, under four weeks. The London papers are filled with the news that France has declared war in support of the Americans. Bitter denouncements in Parliament, statements as well that General Howe had utterly failed to properly support poor old Johnny Burgoyne in upstate New York, thus the defeat at Saratoga was not Burgoyne's fault but that of both General Howe and his brother the admiral. His critics in Parliament argue that rather than move here to Philadelphia, he should have ventured up the Hudson to relieve the beleaguered northern army. Thus Clinton."

"Why Clinton?" Elizabeth asked softly.

André looked at her for a moment, then shrugged his shoulders.

"It's no secret now. Last summer he argued vehemently for the army to move with all possible haste to relieve Burgoyne. General Howe, instead, ruled that we take Philadelphia and that Burgoyne could take care of himself. He did allow Clinton to venture with a small force up the Hudson, but by then it was too late. Burgoyne was cut off and Clinton was forced to turn back in frustration."

André looked into his now empty glass and then refilled it.

"And what do you think Howe should have done?" Elizabeth ventured.

André looked at her and forced a smile.

"A proper officer never questions his superiors," he replied, a bit of a chill in his voice.

"Maybe at times you should," Elizabeth replied, and Allen looked over at her with surprise.

"Yet again, Miss Elizabeth, your spirit strikes me as rebellious," André announced.

"And if I am?"

He smiled.

"Your secret is safe with me, as I am certain it is with Miss Peggy."

"I have said nothing against the king or those who serve him," she replied coolly, and André, ever the gentleman, nodded to her.

"Even if you had, your secret is safe with me, though I daresay that if you wish to continue to associate with our good Lieutenant van Dorn you should be cognizant of his career."

She looked at Allen, blushed, and then lowered her head in acknowledgment.

"Van Dorn and Clinton do have something in common," André offered.

"And that is?" Allen asked.

"Clinton is also colonial by birth. He was born in Newfoundland, came of age in New York, and actually served in the colonial militia before taking a regular commission, returning only then to England and rising through the ranks. Of course his family in England was of help with that, but born a colonial nevertheless."

"And thus some might say he understands the war here better than most," Elizabeth offered.

André nodded.

"Exactly, and thus the rumors. He has a strong faction behind him in England. Some are saying he was right all along and that, if his advice had been followed, rather than a defeat at Saratoga, the rebel army there would have been trapped between two forces and annihilated. With the Hudson thus secured, the full strength of our army could have been turned against General Washington this year. That with our victory at Saratoga rather than that of Gates and his rabble, France would definitely have remained neutral."

He sighed.

"It's going to be a long war."

He refilled his glass yet again and looked at Allen.

"Your thoughts?"

"As you said," Allen replied, "it is not my place to question my superiors, especially when it comes to who commands."

"Well, I think you can guess my thoughts," André said, his features now impassive.

"Do you think we'll start the new campaign soon?" Allen asked.

"Campaign?"

"Against Valley Forge?"

André returned his gaze to his glass, drained it, refilled it, and then shook his head.

"No."

"Why not?" Allen asked. "The weather has been good for the last week, the frost is out of the ground, the roads are drying out. Now would be the perfect time to strike."

"Not now. Not with the scent of a change of command in the air. Not with France declaring war. This is now the largest army we have in the Americas, but with France in the war, orders might come any day diverting us from what should have been done months ago."

"And that is?"

"Finish it, rather than sit here, growing fat and lazy and making up plays. We could have finished it in December with a forced march on Valley Forge, but our leaders said it was over, and besides why fight when we could spend the winter in warmth and comfort, our bellies full, while that rabble in arms starved and melted away?"

"But they didn't melt away. They are still out there, ragged and starving, it is true, but they are still out there and we still just sit here."

There was a bitter edge to his voice, and, realizing he had said too much, he waved his hand in dismissal, as if trying to wipe away what he had just said.

"Come, my friend, your turn to entertain us," he announced, pointing to the harmonica. "I've done enough entertaining for tonight."

Allen hesitated, but, with Peggy and Elizabeth now both urging him as well, he sat down in front of the instrument, pushing on the pedals to get the lathe turning. Dipping his fingertips into the bowl of fine powdered chalk, he finally touched one of the spinning crystal spheres, producing a single haunting note. Then, delighted to be able to show off how much he had been practicing since his barely adequate performance of the previous month, he applied four fingers, then six, and began the Mozart.

He concentrated on it intently, barely making a mistake, caught finally in the rapture of the sound. When at last he had finished he sat back with a sigh, the last chord drifting away.

There was no comment or applause. He looked around and was startled to see that only Elizabeth was in the room, standing behind him, looking down at him, a hand going lightly to his shoulder.

There was no one in the adjoining room across the hall and the silence was startling.

"They went upstairs," she whispered.

He looked up at her. There was no look of shock or disdain. She was actually smiling. It was the way she was smiling, though . . .

"Would you walk me home?"

Barely a word was spoken as they walked the few blocks back to her home. For Allen it seemed like an eternity. The way she had looked at him. What did it portend?

As she approached the corner of her home, she slipped her hand into his and guided him down the carriageway to the back of the house and the servants' entrance. The house was dark except for the glow of a lantern in the kitchen.

She did not stop at the door, as if to turn to say good night. He felt as if his heart would burst as she held his hand tight, squeezed it, looked to him with an almost childlike, mischievous smile, and put a finger to her lips to signal for him to be quiet.

She led the way in and for an instant his heart froze. Someone was standing in the kitchen, one of the family servants.

"David, this is the young man I was telling you about. David, this is Lieutenant van Dorn."

"Sir," and he nodded slightly.

Allen, inwardly shaking, could only nod in reply.

"My mother?" she asked.

"Asleep, missus. The doctor gave her an opiate so she could sleep."

"The other servants?"

"This is their night off, missus. I am the only one here and they will return and go straight to their quarters, missus."

"Thank you, David."

"Allen, would you care for something to drink?"

"Miss Elizabeth?" There was indeed a trembling in his voice.

She laughed softly.

"A bottle of my father's port, David. You choose the bottle."

The man smiled and left the kitchen carrying a candle as he ventured into the basement.

Still holding his hand, she led the way out of the kitchen through the dining room and into the parlor. The room was dark, illuminated only by the glow of moonlight.

She sat down on the sofa, nearly pulling him down by her side. He sat nervous, silent, coming to his feet when David returned, bearing a silver tray upon which was an open bottle of port, two crystal goblets already filled, and a candle.

He set them down, smiled, and nodded.

"I am retiring, miss," he announced.

"Thank you, David."

"Good night to you, sir."

He nodded, still not sure how to reply.

"And don't worry, Mrs. Risher, she is fast asleep until dawn."

Allen wondered if the man had actually winked at him.

David bowed again to the two and withdrew.

Allen stood dumbfounded and actually stepped away from the sofa, going over to the harpsichord as if to examine the sheets of music.

"If you play one note on that thing, you know it will wake my mother," Elizabeth announced.

He looked back at her.

"Ah, Miss Risher, are you sure you are . . ." His voice trailed off as she laughed softly and patted where he had been sitting.

"Lieutenant van Dorn, surely the British army has taught you how to behave like a gentleman. Now come sit by my side and share some port with me."

He did as ordered, draining off his goblet a bit too hastily while she sipped hers.

"You must think me a woman of terrible virtue to behave like this," she finally said, breaking the nervous silence.

"No, miss . . ."

"For heaven's sake, Allen, it's Elizabeth. I wanted to dance with you and kiss you the first night we met back in Trenton. I've sat in my room alone night after night waiting for you to work up the courage to come call, so I resort to this."

He looked over at her. She had her glass resting on the tray and ever so gently took his and set it down as well.

"Now, for heaven's sake, young man, kiss me."

He did as ordered, the sweetest order he had ever received, and was startled how she melted into his embrace.

She finally leaned back slightly, breaking their embrace.

"Allen van Dorn, forgive my boldness, but you have never done this before, have you?"

He wanted to lie but could not.

"With a lady, Elizabeth? Never."

"Ah, but with someone not a lady?"

He thought of the few fumbled attempts in New York before the war, when he would go there with his father and slip off with friends to stews, as they were called.

He thought it best not to answer.

"You must think I am horrid and will never call upon me again after to-night, or should I say now, this morning."

"Elizabeth . . ." His voice trailed off.

"And, no, don't ask me again, Allen," she sighed, but continued to smile.

He could only shake his head.

"With that understood, does it bother you?"

"I love you, Elizabeth."

"But does it bother you?"

"No, of course not."

"Swear? Cross your heart?"

"I swear," he whispered.

She leaned forward and kissed him lightly.

"If not for this damn war, Allen, I would not behave like this. But who knows how long," she hesitated, "either of us have. I could not bear the thought of you going back into the war and my not having at least one night with you."

"Nor I."

"Then we understand each other?"

"I think so."

She smiled, leaned forward, and kissed him again, this time without restraint.

Valley Forge
April 9, 1778

Ever so rarely would he let emotions show, but at this moment George Washington sat silent, eyes clouded.

The entire room was silent except for the actors on the stage and the crackling and popping of the banked-down fires. The bakehouse this night was their playhouse, rough-hewn benches serving as seats for himself and the invited ladies. The long length of the rest of the room was packed, doors open, more gathered outside for this performance of Joseph Addison's *Cato*.

General Baker of the Army Christopher Ludwig had objected most strenuously to his bakehouse's being converted into a playhouse for the evening, but he now sat in the corner, openly weeping, as were many in the audience.

All knew it was Washington's favorite play; he had memorized nearly every line years ago, and it was considered by many to be "the play" of the Revolution. Patrick Henry all but quoted it with his famous cry, as had the martyr Nathan Hale just before he gave his life.

And now, in this final act, Cato, implacable foe of Caesar, defender of Republicanism against Monarchy, was dying. After Caesar's victory at Thapsus and the crushing of the last resistance by those opposed to his seizure of power from the Senate, Cato had chosen death by his own hand to life under the tyranny of the usurper.

The actor playing Cato, a lieutenant with Anthony Wayne's staff, a survivor of Paoli, saber scar on his face a fierce reminder of that night, slowly lay down.

> *Portius come near me——are my friends embarked?*
> *Can anything be thought of for their service?*
> *Whilst I yet live, let me not live in vain.*

Some could not conceal their weeping as Cato hoped that his death might divert Caesar so that his beloved sons and the few followers who had stayed loyal to him could still escape the wrath of the dictator.

> *Whoe'er is brave and virtuous, is a Roman——*
> *——I'm sick to death——O when shall I get loose*
> *From this vain world, th' abode of guilt and sorrow!*

Washington could feel Martha's hand tighten in his. He knew her deepest fear. It was not his death on a battlefield of victory . . . it was what she knew he would do if he realized that indeed all was lost . . . that he would seek death on the field of defeat, the last man to die for the cause, never to surrender. Though he had not spoken of it, he had so resolved on the night march to Trenton. And when the campaign of spring came, if indeed after this eternal winter of suffering, and now of at least some hope, if defeat became inevitable, he would chose the path of Cato rather than fall into the hands of the enemies of his country.

On my departing soul. Alas! I fear
I've been too hasty. O ye powers, that search
The heart of man, and weigh his inmost thoughts,
If I have done amiss, impute it not!

He closed his eyes even as Cato, on the stage little more than an arm's length away, slumped down and closed his eyes. The man did not perform in the style of nearly all professional actors, declaiming his last lines loudly, arms flung wide, crying out as he swooned and death took hold. There was not a man in this room who had not seen death. Nor was there barely one who had not held a dying comrade, struggling to ease his final moments, leaning close to hear his last whispered words for loved ones, wives, children, parents, and then whispering a prayer in reply.

The actor portraying Lucius, Cato's closest friend and ally, knelt down by the side of his comrade, holding him close, actually crying for a moment. The actor was an elderly sergeant with a Massachusetts regiment. He had begged for the part when Hamilton had first suggested a performance, reciting every line flawlessly at the very first rehearsal. His passion for it now showed.

Washington could not help but wonder what inner woe this man carried from the war and now poured so fervently into his performance.

There fled the greatest soul that ever warmed
A Roman breast; O Cato! O my friend!

He paused for a moment and then looked straight out at the audience:

From hence, let fierce contending nations know
What dire effects from civil discord flow.
'Tis this that shakes our country with alarms,
And gives up Rome a prey to Roman arms,
Produces fraud, and cruelty, and strife,
And robs the guilty world of Cato's life.

The room was silent. No applause, only silence, except for those who could not control their tears. For the play was of them, about them, about the ordeal they were now enduring . . . and ahead, fate might still lead them to this moment.

There was no curtain to draw closed, the stage illuminated by half a dozen lanterns only. Hamilton and Laurens stood up and, stepping forward, bent over and blew out each lantern, darkening the stage.

No one spoke, and Washington could sense that all eyes were turned toward him, the actors in expectation of some praise. He squeezed Martha's hand and stood up, but he did not ascend the few steps to the stage, instead turning and facing the audience.

He struggled to clear his throat.

"This——" He paused. "Keep this in your hearts. Cato's death was not in vain, for it inspires us to this day. The death of our comrades must not be in vain. Let their sacrifice be our inspiration in the days to come.

"God be with you all, and may God forever bless this Republic, which we hold so dear."

He had not prepared any speech, had not intended to speak at all. His delight in agreeing to the production of the play was the hope that it would serve as inspiration. He sensed it had done far more this night than he had ever hoped for, and his few words could not add to the experience but only detract from it if he continued.

"Good night, comrades."

He extended his hand to Martha. She stood and together the two left the bakehouse, those gathered in the doorway drawing back respectfully as they left.

The full moon cast a light nearly as bright as day. They walked together in silence, her hand tightly clasping his. He looked down at her.

"Martha."

"Yes."

"If," he hesitated, "if our cause should not win through, you know what I must do."

She didn't speak.

"In the end, we cannot, we will not, lose. Others will follow afterwards, a generation hence, maybe a hundred, two hundred years hence, but in the end it will triumph. Caesar and those after him did believe they had won for the moment, but in the end tyranny will always destroy itself as long as good men and women stand against it."

He sighed.

"I am sorry for what I have put you through, Martha. I did not want this."

"Do you think I would love you more if you had not chosen this path, George?" she replied, and there was the slightest touch of reproach in her voice.

"It is because you are who you are that I love you."

He squeezed her hand tightly.

"Thank you, my dear."

"I'll invite the actors to sup with us tomorrow as a thank-you."

He smiled at her suggestion. Leave it to her to find the proper thank-you he could not find a voice for tonight.

"I want them to perform this again and again, until every last man and woman with this army has seen it."

"I think, George, they are eager to do so."

"When this war is over, we will go home, Martha, there to live in peace."

"Of course, George," and she sighed. "Of course your duty will be done when this war ends. Like Cincinnatus."

He looked down at her and laughed softly.

"Yes, like him."

"Before or after he was called back to serve his country yet again?" she whispered, as she turned and buried her head against his chest, struggling to conceal her tears.

Philadelphia
April 10, 1778

"David?"

"I'm ready, missus."

She looked down at her letter. Allen had left more than an hour ago. It already seemed like an eternity, and her hands trembled as she folded up the letter and handed it to David. He slipped the note into an open seam of his coat. He already had needle and thread ready and in little more than a minute she deftly sewed the seam shut.

David had already tucked into his vest pocket a second note, the cover letter for his journey: a plaintive appeal to an alleged lover, a Methodist minister living out beyond Darby whose child she was carrying. The letter demanded his acknowledgement of her and his responsibility to marry her. If he were to be stopped by pickets or roving patrols, they would find only this second letter.

He had indeed been stopped once, and the discovered false note had triggered a derisive response. The sergeant of the patrol had sent him on his way with ribald comments that his owner should choose someone other than a Methodist preacher to have a liaison with.

Of course, a thorough examination by someone who knew the tricks of the trade would soon uncover the resewn seam. If discovered it would mean death for David and, most likely, imprisonment for her, and an inquiry would soon trace its way back to Allen, who had talked far too openly in the hours that had just passed.

Finished with the sewing, and biting off the end of the thread, she looked into David's eyes.

"God be with you, my friend," she whispered.

"With His protection I will be safe, missus."

She hesitated.

"David."

"Yes, missus?"

"David . . ." Her voice trailed off, tears filling her eyes.

With an almost fatherly touch he put his hands on her shoulder, and held her as she cried.

"I know, missus, I know. You truly do love him."

"I do," she whispered. "I feel so terrible. I feel like . . ."

"Hush now," he whispered, but his voice was sharp, insistent. "When this war ends, the two of you will be together."

"If he knew, he would spit on me."

"Oh, missus. Believe me." He chuckled. "If every man knew every secret within a woman's heart. May I humbly suggest that this little secret is between us and I shall carry it to my grave?"

"Don't talk like that," she replied, looking up into his dark features.

"Sorry, a wrong choice of words. Now don't you fret. Go to bed and sleep. I will be back by midday."

"Please be safe."

"Remember, missus, I have a wife and children to return to. And someday . . ."

Her father had not purchased his family, who were still slaves in New York, though he promised often enough he would . . . someday.

"When this war is over, David."

"No promises, missus. But, bless you, I know you will honor them if you can."

"It is the least this country can do for you."

He did not reply.

She stepped back, taking his hand. "May God protect you on your way," she whispered, lowering her head in prayer, "guiding your footsteps along the way, to safely return to this home and family."

He drew back and was out the door and gone.

She blew out the candle in the kitchen and went back to the parlor, where she and Allen had been little more than an hour ago. She stood silent, gazing about, making sure no evidence of his stay was present.

It was hard to hold back the tears. When she had approached Dr. Rush, months ago, asking how she could serve her country when it was evident that the British would take this city, he had smiled and then innocently suggested that all she need do was keep her ears open, act charming, and nothing more.

Her friend Peggy had pointed the way, openly flinging herself at one of the most eligible bachelors with the army, Captain André, but she was so flighty, and now so in love with him, that to enlist her in this conspiracy was foolish, if not outright dangerous. Besides, she was more than eager to spill every secret she learned to prove her powers over the captain.

But never had she contemplated doing what she had just done. Peggy was source enough of information, but to so use the innocent love of Allen as she had tonight left her feeling cold——soiled, even. David had not hesitated when she had nervously queried him about the prospect of Allen and her having a rendezvous in the house. He had covered for her before: A young officer from New York who had died last summer of the fever had slipped in more than once while garrisoned in the city, so it was no shock to this loyal family servant.

And yet what of Allen?

If he had not been an officer on Grey's staff and a friend of André's, would she have lured him here tonight?

There was at least that reassurance. She would have because she loved him regardless. The rumors and news aside, in a few short months at most he would be gone. Win or lose, if this war did not end soon, chances of his living were slim at best. At least that logic helped to calm her soul a bit. If by using what he had said, she could help to insure a swift ending to this war, she might thereby spare his life. Then indeed she would marry him, and only David and she would know the full truth: that she had betrayed him even as she loved him in the hope of somehow saving him.

CHAPTER FIFTEEN

✳ ✳ ✳

Philadelphia
June 10, 1778

"Gentlemen, we shall evacuate this city and return our base of operations to New York City."

A murmur of voices greeted this bold, straightforward statement.

Sir Henry Clinton, the new commander of His Majesty's forces in the Americas, let his officers speak among themselves for a moment. Of course they knew it was coming; all of Philadelphia had been seething with rumors. What he was calling a movement of his base of operations was in fact a retreat, and he had been saddled with doing it.

He held no real animosity toward the Howe brothers; they had treated him well enough, had given to him the lion's share of honor and glory for the battle of Long Island, the battle that had won him a knighthood. Nevertheless, it was they who had created this situation, and now they were gone. General Howe had been ordered to return to England to receive proper recognition, as was said in the official dispatches, but in reality it might very well turn into a court of inquiry for his utter failure, after two years, to crush this rebellion once and for all.

For heaven's sake, Clinton thought sourly, as he looked around the room at his brigade commanders and staff. The men he was losing to garrison islands in the Caribbean because of France entering the war were some of his elite troops, seasoned to the climate of this place after two long years. Half the poor buggers would most likely die of malaria and yellow jack before the summer was out in Jamaica.

If they were doomed to die, the real enemy was here, only twenty-two miles away. With those five thousand veteran troops, he would be more than a match for Washington and could finish this war as it should have been finished six months ago. There at Valley Forge was the true heart of this war. Something that London did not see. It was, at this moment, Washington and his ever-growing army alone that mattered. The American ranks were swelling every day, and there were disturbing reports of a German drillmaster who was changing the main corps of that ragtag force into something different, a trained army.

"Why don't we attack now instead and be done with it?" General Grey snarled, and there was a chorus of agreements.

"I have to follow orders from London," Clinton replied, and there was a touch of sarcasm in his voice. "You only have local knowledge of the real situation. You do not appreciate the subtleties of our masters looking at a world stage."

It was obviously not how he felt; each word was spoken with bitterness.

"Hang the damn orders!" Grey retorted, and now there were even louder assertions of agreement. "Win the victory, then write back and ask them if you should let the prisoner Washington go with apologies even though we've already hanged him."

There were snickers of laughter around the room.

"I want Washington as much as you do," Clinton snapped, slapping his fist on the table.

"Then let us take him. I beg you, sir, we could do this within the week and the war will be over."

Grey looked around the room to the other brigade commanders for support. Most were nodding yes.

"Their Lordships are attempting to manage a war from a distance of four thousand miles. We are here, twenty-two miles away. Seize the moment, seize the moment, sir. How often did Caesar ignore the orders of the Senate when in Spain and Gaul?"

"To his everlasting infamy," Clinton replied softly.

"Or one could say his greater glory," Grey replied.

He could not admit it to this audience, but in his heart he agreed with Grey. The Howe brothers had made a bungling mess of it all and now London was going to compound their mistakes. Why can't they see that you can't run a war from such a distance?

Yet he had weighed the odds. Five thousand men were, this day, beginning to take ship for the Caribbean. They would have to make a long and arduous voyage to the south, running contrary to winds and currents. It could take six weeks, perhaps two months, before they arrived at Jamaica. And only three months hence, when the hurricane season began, no admiral would dare to venture his fleet on open waters to stage an attack in that region. Across two hundred years, countless fleets had just simply disappeared or limped back to port, shattered by the late summer and autumn storms that raked the tropics.

If only I had those five thousand at my disposal today, rather than going down to the docks to see them off.

He inwardly sighed.

Or am I using that as an excuse? he wondered.

It was one thing to be second or third in command and to then second-guess your superior, who was bearing the kind of weighty responsibility now entrusted to him.

If I venture battle, perhaps against superior odds, and lose, I will be forever cursed, another Admiral Byng.

He thought of the words of a French philosopher contemplating the tragic fate of Byng: *Dans ce pays-ci, il est bon de tuer de temps en temps un amiral pour encourager les autres.*

Disobey, but I do not win a full and total victory? Hanged, then, for the encouragement of others not to take risks?

Besides, New York is exposed. The garrison there is less than five thousand strong, most of them second-rate troops left behind last summer. There is little clear intelligence as to how much of the Americans' northern army, victorious at Saratoga, was still in the field in the Hudson Valley.

Though he had gone through the mental exercise repeatedly since word had arrived of the transfer of command, his calculations always came out the same. A daring thrust to Valley Forge could just possibly win the day. Yet the victory might not be a Blenheim or a Quebec, a blow effectively assuring victory. It could be a standoff, or, as he advanced on Valley Forge, Washington could decamp, strike across New Jersey, and attempt to grab New York City by a quick, daring assault. There was even the fear, expressed by Their Lordships, that rather than strike in the Caribbean, the French might venture to land a force on Long Island, in conjunction with a strike by Washington from New Jersey, and seize New York while he dallied here.

And yet with all of these dangers, they take five thousand of my best from me.

He had been silent for a long moment, Grey gazing at him with anticipation.

"We retire to New York as ordered," he said softly.

Grey exhaled noisily, sitting back in his chair, making a dramatic show of picking up his glass, filling it with brandy, downing the drink in a single gulp and then with a muffled curse throwing the empty glass into the fireplace.

"I understand your frustration, sir," Clinton replied calmly. "And yet, think of my chagrin if I ordered you to do something and you failed to do so."

"You are here, sir, not four thousand miles away."

Grey looked around the room.

"At least please release my light brigade for a raid in strength——at least that, sir."

Again Clinton shook his head.

"The army is to be reconstituted to its original order of battle. Light infantry companies are needed with their original battalions. The brigade of light infantry will be disbanded and you will reassume your original command."

Grey blustered, but now the other brigade commanders did not support him. They had complained bitterly of being stripped of their light infantry companies. It was not their ox being gored; on this Grey would have no support.

"Our regiments will need their light companies since we shall move overland through New Jersey."

"Why not by ship?" O'Hara, commander of his Guards Brigade, queried.

"Not enough transports, for one, what with the ships being used to carry the men we are losing to the Caribbean. Second, we have an additional concern. Numerous good people of this city have openly demonstrated their support. We must offer them protection in return. There will not be enough shipping for them and their goods, nor could we expect them to try and venture across Jersey to New York on their own."

It will be like Boston all over again, he thought, remembering the wretched state of the refugees, begging to go with him when he was forced to abandon that city and retreat to Canada.

"Damn all rebels," Grey whispered. "My God, if we leave those people behind they will be shot or hanged."

"I would prefer not to think so lowly of General Washington," Clinton offered, "but at the hands of their neighbors they might suffer, and the king himself has expressed concern that all those loyal to him must be protected."

"We should fire the city as we leave," Grey replied, and now again he had the support of the others. "After all, it was their capital."

Clinton looked at him in surprise.

"We are not barbarians, sir. This city is still the realm of the king, even if we must temporarily leave it."

"They burned New York when they evacuated."

"That is not proven, sir. Sometimes cities do burn by accident, even in war."

It was obvious his words were not accepted by all, and he looked around the room coldly.

"These orders must be made clear to every man, down to the lowest private and camp hanger-on. There will be no looting. We will come back to this city some day, to stay permanently. If we burn Philadelphia now it will only serve the rebels as a great propaganda victory and give them yet more foul accusations against us. Any who violate my order shall face the full weight of military justice."

Even Grey had to nod in final agreement.

"I plan for us to leave this place within a fortnight. Prepare your troops for marching with all accoutrements and supplies. We will put out rumors that we are planning to take the campaign into the hinterland in pursuit of their Congress."

"That should cause their politicians to wet their britches," O'Hara interjected, and there was general laughter.

"We will cross the Delaware and, within three days' march, gain either Amboy or to a point just south of Long Island at the Monmouth Heights. There our army will be transported by ship back to Staten Island and New York City."

"And after that?" Grey asked.

"We await further orders from London," Clinton said dryly.

No one responded.

"You are dismissed."

The officers stood to leave, all but Grey and, standing behind him, one of his staff, the popular young André.

"Come now, Henry," Grey offered informally, now that they were alone. "Surely you will not go along with this. Tell me, you have a card hidden up your sleeve. I never knew you to back away from a fight."

Clinton shook his head.

"Charles, I wish I could say differently. You know as well as I do that our forces are now split into three components, the garrison here, the garrison in New York, and the third part being sent on this wild goose chase down to the tropics. At least back in New York I will have a unified command of two-thirds of the forces and can act accordingly at that time."

"I still believe Washington might yet be vulnerable," Grey continued. "I

NEWT GINGRICH and WILLIAM R. FORSTCHEN

begged Howe for months to exploit Washington's weakness. I know you supported me all along on those requests. We've scouted him nearly every day. I have even had men, disguised as herders, bringing in cattle inside their camp."

"That was three months ago; this is now," Clinton replied forcefully. "I fear there is something different stirring up at Valley Forge, and you know as well as I do that if I were to try to venture up and did not win a complete victory . . ."

He forced a smile.

"Their Lordships would break every bone in my body."

"Damn all of this," Grey replied with a weary shake of his head. "I hate when politics gets in the way of good simple soldiering."

Clinton patted him on the shoulder.

"You still have your old command back, my friend. At least it isn't you heading down to those damn islands."

Grey nodded in agreement.

"I hear Anthony Wayne swears he will personally turn me into a eunuch if ever we shall meet in battle. Can't disappoint giving him the chance," he laughed, "though it will be he going to Italy to sing opera instead."

André, standing behind Grey, laughed.

"I shall write him a piece for a castrato beforehand, sir."

The two generals grinned.

"See to your men," Clinton ordered.

Grey saluted and turned to leave.

"Remember, only commanders of regiments are to know the truth of it. The men are to think we are just preparing for a spring campaign in Pennsylvania. I'll string up the man who breathes a word, that"——he paused—— "that we are pulling back."

"Yes, sir."

"Sir?"

"Next time, if you are in the mood for throwing fine crystal into the fireplace, use your own, Charles. My wife sent me that set from England, along with the brandy."

Valley Forge
June 11, 1778

Washington's heart swelled with pride at the sight of them. The head of the column was still a hundred yards off, but already he and those gathered around him could hear the rolling of the drums, the shrieking call of the fifers.

A pavilion tent had been set up for the invited ladies of the camp, to ward off the heat of the afternoon sun, and what now was the threat of an approaching thunderstorm. He alone remained mounted to receive the salutes. His officers and staff and the wives, including Martha, stood under the canvas.

The army approached in column by companies, each rank ten men wide, the brigades of Generals Greene, Stirling, and Wayne, men who had been drilling in the school of von Steuben for nearly two months now. At the front was the Guards Brigade of General Lafayette.

It was obvious Wayne was in his glory. What was to him the onerous task of bringing in supplies was at an end. The army was about to march and Washington had returned him at last to his old and beloved job in field command, allowing him to seek restoration of the honor he felt he had lost at Paoli.

Arrayed on the other side of the parade field were the ranks of militia regiments that had joined the army in recent weeks. The purpose of the parade, now a twice-weekly ritual, was twofold: to instill pride and boost morale in those training, and to demonstrate to all coming into this army what was now expected of them. This was a new army, and it was essential that every volunteer learn he was joining a real army and not merely a mob of untrained, undisciplined militia.

Lafayette's brigade approached, the command given for the men to march at the quick time. They presented a grand sight. The first shipment of new uniforms from France had arrived at last, complementing the earlier loads of muskets and ammunition. They had either been landed in New England and hauled down by wagon or, for the more daring ship captains, run in along the Delaware and Maryland coast, aboard swift-moving privateers able to dodge the Royal Navy's blockade.

The uniform jackets were blue and buff, as Washington had requested to Benjamin Franklin more than a year ago, as if placing an order with a fine tailor overseas, and most definitely not surplus castoffs of the French Army; their absurd white might be fine in Europe but was nearly impossible to keep clean. The French Army might devote hours a day to such tasks, but not an American army. The uniforms were made of heavy wool, designed more for winter use, and would have been like manna from heaven if they had arrived in December. On this warm June afternoon he could see sweat streaking the faces of the men wearing them, and chances were they would shuck them off once back in camp, but by autumn they would again be grateful to have them.

And besides, with the lead regiments dressed thus, the men actually did look like and, at least on the parade ground, march like an army.

The young French general astride a spirited white horse that appeared to be prancing to the beat of the drums raised his sword with a flourish to salute General Washington, who returned the salute along with the assembled officers, the ladies breaking into applause. Even the militia on the other side of the parade ground appreciated the display, New Englanders letting loose with three huzzahs, the men from the backwoods of Virginia offering up a spine-tingling cry that sounded almost like the baying of wolves.

Lafayette shouted the command for the Guards Brigade to advance at double-quick time and the men sprinted past, muskets at the shoulder, keeping fairly good alignment, the air filled with a sound that Washington always thought to be melodious, the steady rhythm of men's feet, the clattering of tin cups and canteens, the slapping of cartridge boxes on hips. In the long years of peace after the Indian Wars, how that sound would, at times, haunt his dreams, as he remembered the disciplined ranks of Braddock's doomed regiments on the first days of the march inland to their rendezvous with grim disaster.

The left and right wings of the Guards Brigade swiftly passed in review. A hundred yards past the reviewing pavilion, the column wheeled ninety degrees to the right, slowed its pace, and started the march back to their camps.

Lafayette turned aside from the lead and rode at a swift canter to come up and join the entourage, dismounting to stand behind Washington, just as Greene's regiments came into view.

The new uniforms had yet to be supplied to these men. Most were still dressed in their winter rags, cleaned up as much as possible, though many at least sported new French cartridge boxes, the leather strap buffed white. These were men of North Carolina, Maryland, and Virginia, and, deliberately selected by Washington, the New Hampshire brigade to leaven out the southern unit with a mix of men from the far north. His blending together of regiments into brigades always was done with an eye to insuring a mix from different regions, to reinforce that these were United States soldiers, sharing a common struggle.

The Virginia and Maryland regiments had tried to keep some semblance of their uniforms, brown with red, blue, and buff, and had actually protested when similar uniforms were issued to Lafayette's brigade. Their uniforms were threadbare, the knees of nearly all of them patched and patched again, once-white trousers a dingy gray and black. Most of the tricorner hats were long since battered down to broad brims, and some of the men went bareheaded . . . but they marched with élan, eyes left to their general, whom they claimed as uniquely their own. The last regiment of the brigade, men from North Carolina, most of them in homespun hunting jackets, marched proudly, some carrying octagonal-barreled long rifles rather than muskets.

Next was Stirling's command, men of Pennsylvania and Massachusetts. It had not been an easy unit to create and was made up of stiff, prideful Yankees, more than a few of whom still seemed to feel that this Revolution was their creation and still spoke of how, when they fought in their home territory, victory had always been theirs. The Pennsylvania regiments were led by the First Continental Regiment of Foot, the men proudly claiming the title since they had enlisted for a full three years, the first to do so. Though their uniforms were still homespun, they had also been beneficiaries of the issuance of new muskets and cartridge boxes from France and carried their new weapons proudly.

Last of the infantry was a small detachment of Anthony Wayne's, men who had been tasked during the winter to bring in forage or to keep picket watch along with Morgan's men down on the lower Schuylkill. Many were light infantry, carrying an assortment of weapons of their own choosing, and rather than pass in review at the quick time, they did so nearly at the run, rifles and muskets not shouldered but carried in one hand at their sides, Wayne proudly riding ahead of them. Loud cheers greeted them as they sprinted by.

Few of Wayne's proud fighters had participated in von Steuben's new training. They had been employed elsewhere and, as light infantry, knew their own way of war.

As they wheeled left and cleared the parade field, the small detachment of army dragoons thundered across the field at a gallop. The few horses that had survived the winter were at last fattening out on the rich pasturelands of the Schuylkill Valley and were again capable of bearing a rider at something better than a slow walk, at least for a short distance. They were by no means even remotely a match for the well-bred and well-fed horses of the British and Hessians, but at least the army could again field a small detachment of mounted troops for scouting and skirmishing.

A battery of Knox's guns, six-pounders of the First Continental Artillery, took up the rear. The four horses pulling each gun and limber wagon were beginning to fill back out as well. Two months ago Knox had reported that the horses were so underfed that, within the entire army, he might only be able to put a single battery on the road for a full day's march, but with each passing day their condition was improving.

A thousand or more horses with the artillery, cavalry, and supply train had died during the winter, the army so in need of food that each death was greeted by the men as something of a gift, as they quickly butchered the skeletal animal for what little meat could be salvaged, also claiming the heart and liver, and boiling down the hooves for broth.

The survivors now pulled the six pieces as they came abreast of General Washington, and Knox shouted a command, the veteran crews wheeling the pieces about, gunners lifting the trailing prologue of each gun off the back of the limber wagon, setting the piece down, drivers of the horses then leading their limber wagons twenty paces back from the gun.. The loaders were already opening up the lids of the wagons even as they moved, drawing out serge bags filled with a pound of powder. In less than a minute the charges were rammed home. Gunner sergeants, who had been carrying lit linstocks, waved the staffs that held burning tapers of saltpeter-encrusted rope, the tips glowing brightly, each waiting as his assistant, using a brass pick, stuck the wire down through the breechhole to pierce the serge bag of powder. A thin trickle of priming powder was poured down the breechhole from a powder horn, the assistant then stepping back, hand raised to signal all was ready.

"Battery, on my command!" Knox shouted, swinging his mount in directly behind the six guns, spaced across the open field, pointing downrange across the open slope facing south. Many of the militia spectators at the far end of the field refused to budge, some of the wags shouting from the artillery to go ahead and fire, knowing, of course, that the weapons were loaded with blank charges . . . at least they assumed so.

Knox grinned and brought his sword down with a flourish.

"Fire!"

The six gunnery sergeants stepped forward and turned their heads to one side while touching the lit linstocks to the breeches. Five of the six guns leapt back with a roar, the sixth was silent for a second, and then a spark finally caught and it leapt back as well, the gunnery sergeant looking back at Knox with embarrassment through the smoke.

"Limber up!" Knox shouted, barely heard above the applause and shouts of approval, and the distant playacting screams of the militiamen down range who pantomimed that they had been hit.

Washington looked toward them for a second, tempted to shout an order of reprimand. They were obviously green militia who had never faced artillery before, because if they had, by heavens they would not be joking about it now, not with memories of a man next to them being decapitated, or both legs blown off by a six-pound shot, or an entire line going down from a blast of canister and grape.

But all were looking toward his reaction now, Knox waiting expectantly like a youth awaiting a nod of approval. He stood in his stirrups and offered a salute as the gunners, who had already hooked their fieldpieces back on to the end of the limber wagons, turned those wagons about and, at least able to coax their horses to a trot, set off down the field. The parade ended.

Washington felt that a final gesture was needed.

He rode out several paces, turned, looked across the assembly of officers gathered under the pavilion tent, saw the baron, and rode over toward him, reining in. Before von Steuben could offer a salute he did so first.

"Sir, you have been heavensent to us. As my inspector general of the army you have fulfilled your duty as a professional"——as he spoke, Lafayette whispered a translation——"but, sir, as a drillmaster, all I can say is that when next this army goes into battle, the laurels of the victory shall indeed be yours."

Von Steuben looked up at him, and his eyes clouded with tears. He bowed from the waist, unashamedly wiping his face as he looked back up at the general.

"Sir, I beg to differ. The victory shall be that of this army of brave, gallant men, led by you, sir, and no other."

Lafayette all but shouted out the translation, and wild cheering erupted. Washington dismounted and, in an uncharacteristic gesture, shook von Steuben's hand and those of the other officers who had led their troops in the grand review.

Under the pavilion, tables had been set for the evening meal. With a flourish he pointed to them and Martha took over as hostess, a role she so superbly played, whether at Mount Vernon or in the roughest army camp.

Though not yet plentiful, at least there was more variety to the food, now that summer approached. All craved any kind of greens and fruit. Peaches planted on the south slopes of hills were not yet ripe——even down in Virginia it would still be several more weeks——but with some careful picking, and cooking, passable cobblers awaited. Several spring lambs from a nearby farm had been brought in. For some reason, the sight of lambs being killed had always bothered Washington, so he made it a point to ride off while Billy Lee and the officers' mess cooks saw to the task. There was fresh cream, even real coffee smuggled in by a venturesome Dutch captain, fresh bread baked by their General Baker, and all settled down for the repast.

The seating was a bit awkward, for Martha refused to sit anywhere near General Lee, Washington's second-in-command and senior officer, who by tradition should be near his right side.

Lee, after more than a year and a half of imprisonment, had finally been exchanged and returned to the army a month ago. His first night, actually the following morning, had proven to be an unmitigated disaster.

Washington had personally seen to the hosting of a special celebration to honor the return of the captured general. There had been rumors that his behavior while in the hands of the British had been less than honorable. Captured British officers joked that Lee had offered them advice and at one point his sword if he would be allowed to turn coat. Lee, when gently prodded on this by Lord Stirling, acting, of course, on Washington's request for information, had protested vehemently, and even implied that if such a line of questioning continued, a duel might be the result.

The man had gotten too far into his cups. The embarrassed gathering finally let him withdraw for the night to a small bedroom, adjoining what had become Martha's private sitting room. It was here that she entertained the wives of other officers and even of enlisted men that she had befriended in the camp.

All had awaited for Lee to awake in the morning, but the man did not appear until nearly noon, when Washington finally sent Hamilton to knock on his door and request his presence for breakfast. Hamilton had returned a minute later, obviously embarrassed, followed by Lee, who looked disheveled and still more than a little drunk. And from his small room came the loud, drunken laughter of a woman. General Lee had smuggled her into the camp. She was the wife of a British soldier who had trailed along with him when he rejoined the army.

Martha was outraged. Of course she had to turn a blind eye to some of the goings-on of soldiers, but she expected the most upright Christian propriety of her general, his staff, and those in service around him. There had been rumors about Lafayette and his fidelity to his wife, but he had always behaved in the most discreet manner so as not to offend. Lee's actions were blatant, insulting, and, beyond that, had taken place in the room right next to where she entertained friends in private.

The bedtime discussion they shared that night was less than comfortable for General Washington. Martha demanded that the hussy be driven out of camp and that General Lee find separate quarters. She said that she would not sit next to him or across from him at any meal, and beyond that, she wondered why he was even being offered a return to second-in-command after not just this behavior but what she felt was nothing less than betrayal by his actions during the campaign in New York and New Jersey, where he had failed to follow orders.

"You can find a far better second," she had insisted, "a man you can trust, such as Nathanael Greene or Anthony Wayne. There is something about Lee that shows him to be a man of shallow and deceitful character."

She rarely ventured to offer advice about anything related to his position as commander of the armies, but her disdain of Lee was intense and had continued to trouble him.

He had, after that night, sent out more discreet inquiries as to Lee's behavior during his imprisonment. He finally had to admit that the answer was an uncertain one. There was a fair chance that in fact the intelligence could be false information, planted by the enemy to discredit a man he felt could still be a trusted soldier. He had finally decided in Lee's favor. What better way to take out a superior officer than to release him in exchange, then besmirch his name?

With prayers offered, the gathering sat down for dinner, Martha putting herself at the other end of the table next to von Steuben, who bore no love for Lee. The two men had nearly come to blows when Lee derisively dismissed the Russian soldiers with whom von Steuben had loyally served.

The thunderstorm from the west was fast approaching, the first cold gusts of wind a welcome relief, cooling after the long day of heat. All exclaimed over the fresh greens, the succulent lamb. Martha was beaming as some of those at the table immediately dug into the peach cobbler, saying it was delightful, even though the fruit was most definitely far from ripe.

The first heavy drops of rain rattled on the roof of the tent, several of the men getting up to lower the flaps on the side facing the storm. Washington motioned for the man lowering the flap near him to hold back. He loved watching an approaching storm. There was a wonderful majesty to it. As a boy he used to have fantasies that the peals of thunder were actually the roar of artillery, and he smiled at the memory of how he used to dash about leading imaginary charges until ordered into the house, the adults always so frightened and praying that a bolt from the divine power did not strike their house or barn as retribution for some sin.

He had never feared lightning, and was amused by the reports of Franklin's experiments, which some claimed were tempting the wrath of God Almighty. Always progressive in his thinking about the sciences, he was one of the first planters in Virginia to install the doctor's invention of lightning rods on his home and outbuildings.

The storm swept in, and finally he stood up himself to drop the awning and tie it in place, and returned to his meal.

"I will admit," Lee offered, as Washington returned to a conversation he had only been half listening to while watching the storm, "the men do look smart on parade. But to expect them to behave that well in battle?"

"I think we have a good start," Washington replied. "Lafayette's Guards in particular. They took to it with a passion, even offered to practice drill on the Sabbath, which I, of course, forbade."

"Yes, at this moment, the spirits of the men are indeed high. Of course, I could see that in those in the review. It is just that I know how morale of troops who think too highly of themselves can be shattered to the darkest depths by too hard a blow. You saw it after the defeat of Braddock. I saw it with the Forty-Fourth at Ticonderoga in the last war. After such defeats men jumped in fright at the sight of their own shadows. I just fear that this German, with his——how shall I say it without offense——his enthusiasm and high-sounding praise for our troops, is not tempering what he is teaching with an understanding of reality."

Washington said nothing.

"Our opponents can and will continue to deliver three volleys to our two, their Grenadier Guards and Hessians, four to our two." As he spoke, he waved his fork around and punched the air as if delivering the volleys. "And two ranks to their three? Sir, that is not orthodox at all. It lacks depth."

"Von Steuben explained, and I accepted, that training the men to volley fire three files deep to just two is cumbersome and would take too long. This new formation also makes it easier for the men to shift from column of fours to files of two for line of battle. I saw his point and agree. Besides, in a fight of even numbers we will always overlap their flanks if they should try for our center."

Their debate was interrupted by a yelp of pain and then angry growls and snarls. All looked over to where von Steuben's dog, Azor, was debating ownership of a bone, tossed from the table by the baron for his dog. Several of Lee's spaniels, which followed him everywhere, had attempted a quick snatch and run of the prize.

The huge mastiff easily won the debate. The gathering laughed and von Steuben, obviously cursing in German, shouted for his dog to come back. Lee gazed down the length of the table angrily at the baron.

"I pray, sir, can you keep your dog in check?" Lee cried.

"I shall, if you keep your pack in check," Lafayette translated, but Washington sensed, hiding his smile, that the retort had been a little more heated. The crowd clearly favored the big dog over the noisy spaniels. Azor had become something of a favorite around the camp, while Lee's dogs tended to be a yapping nuisance.

Lee, obviously made uncomfortable by the altercation and the tone of conversation with his superior, fell into a glum silence and this way finished his meal.

"Sir?"

Washington looked up. It was Hamilton by his side.

"Colonel Morgan has just ridden in."

The general stood up and went to the east side of the tent, which was still open, the rain from the storm coming down in sheets. Morgan seemed oblivious to the blow, taking his time tying off his mount to a tether line next to Washington's the other officers' horses. Only then did he come in under the tent, heading straight for Washington and saluting.

"Sir, we need to talk."

All were silent, watching the two men. For Dan Morgan to have ridden from his outpost on the lower Schuylkill meant something was definitely afoot.

Washington hesitated, about to tell the colonel to just report his news, but he looked around at the gathering. It was not his custom to receive dispatches, especially reports from his vast network of agents and spies, in front of others.

The storm was still at its height. Regardless, he motioned for Morgan to follow and walked the few dozen yards to a cabin that served as a dwelling for some of Greene's staff. A junior officer was inside, dozing, but as the general and Morgan stepped in, the young man, startled, jumped from his bunk.

"I'm sorry to disturb you," Washington offered, smiling at the confusion his entry had caused, "but may Colonel Morgan and I have a moment of privacy?"

The boy could only salute. Without bothering to put on his hat or boots, he hastily departed out into the rain, looked up at the sky, and then just darted off.

"It must be important if you feel you should deliver it yourself," Washington announced, looking back at Dan, whose features were aglow with delight.

He reached under his hunting frock and pulled out a leather dispatch pouch and handed it over.

"Half a dozen notes within, all from our reliable sources——our rope maker down at the docks, the servant in what is now Clinton's headquarters, the minister, and the girl keeping company with the Tory officer.

"All our sources say Clinton is leaving Philadelphia."

Washington tucked the dispatch pouch into the breast pocket of his jacket. He would examine the notes later.

"Attacking here?" he asked.

There was not as much anxiety as there would have been three months ago. If anything, he would welcome the fight now. His fortifications, thanks to sufficient tools at last, the digging of a thousand men, and the eye of von Steuben and the young French engineer L'Enfant, had given him a fortified line in depth, where only three months ago there was barely a ditch.

"No, he's evacuating!"

"What?" Washington exclaimed in genuine surprise.

Dan broke into a grin.

"It's in the dispatches. He's losing five thousand of his men. They are being sent all the way to Jamaica."

"We did have rumors of that. Hard to believe London is that foolish."

"Well, the rope maker confirmed it, and he has always been good with his information. Ship chandlers at times know even more than their captains, since they have to stock supplies and provisions for the voyage. The money we have spent making sure the man always had a good selection of rum and port on hand loosened more tongues yet again. The first of the ships might already be leaving port. That cuts Clinton's strength by a good third."

Washington nodded, taking it in and thinking hard about the implications and, just maybe, the opportunities inherent in this news.

"If anything," Washington whispered, "such news might lead me to venture an attack. By the end of the month five thousand more militia are coming in. That would give us nearly two to one odds in our favor."

"It's why Clinton is pulling out. Word is he has been ordered to do so from London."

Washington gave a dismissive sniff.

"Trying to run a war from four thousand miles away. They didn't under-stand that was impossible in the last war and they still don't understand it."

Morgan nodded.

"New York?" Washington asked.

"That's what the girl and the servant report. According to them, Clinton said that if he now stays in Philadelphia, under strength as he is, you might decamp, and strike across Jersey ahead of him. They fear that the French might land to the east or what is left of our northern army will come down."

He took out the notes Morgan had handed him.

"This girl and her servant——I don't want to know her name——are you certain she is reliable?"

Morgan grinned.

"Her paramour is a Loyalist, and close friends with a Captain André. André is close to Grey and was present at the staff meeting Clinton held with his commanders. I am certain she is reliable. She wanted to leave Philadelphia when we abandoned the city, even though her parents are for the Crown. Dr. Rush convinced her to stay and listen carefully. She has cultivated an excep-tional contact."

"Is there a chance she could be receiving false information——that they have figured her out? If so, the lass is running a grave risk. They will arrest her before they leave."

Morgan shook his head.

"Checks have been made on that as well. André is quartered in Dr. Franklin's house, as is the Loyalist, and the two are reported to be close friends."

He nodded and then scanned the other reports.

"So it is back to New York by land."

Washington looked at him and grinned, slapping an open palm with a balled-up fist.

"His supply train, too?"

Morgan nodded enthusiastically.

"Oh, how we harassed their supply trains last summer. Two or three rifle-men and a couple of men with axes to drop trees could tie them up for half a day. It will be grand, just grand!

"Along with Tory refugees, who will be allowed one wagon per family. They will be going so slow, and will be strung out in such a long column, that there may be many opportunities for us."

The storm outside was passing and Washington stepped out into it, enjoying the cooling brush of light rain drifting down. He looked back to the pavilion tent. All had stopped eating and were looking his way, sensing that something important was transpiring. All of them were eager to know what it was.

He calculated the moves, standing silent for several minutes, and then nodded, looking back at Morgan.

"You have a good line of couriers set up to bring news of any change."

"Made sure of it before I left. Anything happens in the city, we'll know within eight hours."

"It'll take them a day at least to ferry everything across the Delaware. If we cut straight overland, cross at Trenton and Bordentown the moment we get the word, we will be ahead of them."

He looked back at the gathering.

"Officers' meeting for a council of war?" Morgan asked.

He thought again for a long moment. Just as he had spies in Clinton's very headquarters and patriots within the city, he always assumed that at least to some degree the enemy had done the same. Several times watch posts had been discovered on the east bank of the Schuylkill just two miles away. Reports had come in after the agents were gone that at least one herder bringing in half a dozen starved cows for sale had in fact been with Grey's light infantry.

I must not let Clinton know that I suspect anything until he starts his move and is committed.

"Not a word to anyone," Washington finally said. "Go to my headquarters, there should be some food there, and then find a bunk and get some sleep."

"Looks and smells like good food up there, sir," Dan replied, nodding toward the party.

"And forty inquisitive souls who will pester you to death for news," he replied with a smile. "I promise Martha will set aside some roasted lamb and cobbler for you if there is no food down at headquarters."

He paused.

"And, yes, some of Lafayette's brandy."

"Thank you, sir."

"Good work, Colonel. Your country is in your debt."

Morgan went back to his horse, mounted, and trotted off for headquarters while Washington returned to his guests, smiling, saying nothing and settling back to what was left of his meal, attempting to eat calmly and, as always, show no rash emotions.

"It must be something important?" Lee finally asked, unable to contain himself.

"Later, sir," Washington whispered. "I'll tell you later."

Lee looked at him, trying to hide his disappointment, and returned to nursing his drink and his injured pride, and, while keeping a wary eye on Azor, he tossed a few bones to his spaniels.

CHAPTER SIXTEEN

✷ ✷ ✷

Philadelphia
June 23, 1778

"Did you really knock him cold?" Elizabeth asked.

He was still shaken by what had happened. Outside the window of their rendezvous hiding place, the city was in turmoil. It was still an hour before dawn but all were awake, for today the British army would evacuate Philadelphia.

He had not expected this last night with Elizabeth, but André had told him that without doubt his wisest course was to make himself scarce till dawn, when everyone would be on the move. Chances were the officer would not even remember, and if he did, in all the confusion of the day the issue would be sidetracked for awhile.

After packing up his own luggage and loading it onto one of the wagons for Grey's staff, he had posted himself in Ben Franklin's library, acting as sentry to protect what was within. Though strict orders had been given that there were to be no acts of retribution, looting, or vandalism as the army evacuated, more than a few on the staff muttered that this was, after all, the property of "a signer," and as such deserved special treatment.

In the middle of the night a major, drunk as usual, had staggered back from a final farewell night at his favorite stew house and brothel, and announced that he was going to borrow some of the books.

Allen felt that conceding a few books to the major might quell him and send him off, but the man had then proceeded to knock them off the shelves, an armload at a time. He intervened, using the strategy of offering the man a drink, which the major had taken, but then he had staggered over to the glass harmonica, holding the bottle, upended it, poured the brandy onto the instrument, then turned the bottle in his hand, holding it by the neck, preparing to smash it on the delicate crystal goblets within.

Allen had pulled him back and the struggle finally ended with a blow that knocked the major out cold. One of the sergeants of the guard was standing in the doorway, having come in to check on the commotion, and for a frozen moment Allen could see the very real prospect of a court-martial for striking a superior officer.

"Don't you worry about it none, Mr. Dorn," the sergeant whispered in a heavy Irish brogue. "I'll take the gentleman to his room, tell him later he must have fallen. If he even remembers enough to ask."

The burly sergeant hoisted the major on to his shoulder and carried him up the stairs, returning several minutes later.

"Asleep like a babe he is, though daresay he'll have a time of it chewing his breakfast," and the sergeant grinned conspiratorially. "I'll let the word slip that some barkeep at the knocking shop did it."

"Sergeant?"

"Yes, sir?"

"Why?"

The sergeant looked at him.

"That thing you play there," and he pointed to the harmonica, "it's the voice of an angel it is. Like to think that someday the good doctor will be back here and play it again."

"Thank you," and Allen extended his hand. The sergeant, surprised, took it firmly.

"Besides, word is that the doctor's son, our Loyalist governor of New Jersey, requested special protection for the house and General Grey did make them orders known. So we can say we was just following orders."

What the sergeant had said was true. Franklin's son was now the military governor of New Jersey for the Crown. Yet another family torn asunder by the war.

"I'd suggest you run along for a while, sir, perhaps see your fair lady one last time," O'Donald whispered, and then winked. "If the good Captain André comes in, I'll let him know. He's a good 'un and to be trusted."

The sergeant, standing watch, had enabled him to slip off, and with the strangely willing connivance of the family servant, he now rested by her side on a settee in the parlor, her parents asleep upstairs.

He had drifted off while holding her. They had said their farewell the night before, and he had not assumed he would have such a moment again, but when David answered his tapping on the back door and guided him in, and she had swept into his embrace moments later, all discretion and fear of her parents waking were cast aside.

They had drifted off for a brief moment, and now she chuckled at his account of the fight.

"Miss Elizabeth."

Allen looked up with a start.

It was David, standing discreetly in the hallway outside the parlor.

"Yes, David."

"Your parents, miss."

She sighed.

"Thank you, David."

She snuggled in closer to Allen.

"It is time, you have to leave."

"I know," and he felt his throat tighten.

"Will you write?" he asked.

"Of course. Though I daresay that Dr. Franklin's postal service might not run for a while between Philadelphia and New York."

She hesitated for a moment.

"Which way do you think the army is heading once across the river?"

"To New York."

"I know that; the entire city knows that."

"So why do you ask?"

"Just curious. The weather is hot. It will be a hard march."

Why was she asking? Her rebel sentiments were more than obvious to him, though she kept them in check. Officers for the last two weeks had been cautioned repeatedly to say nothing about the intended line of march. He knew as well that a careful game of false information had been laid out, as to the details of the march, so why was she asking?

"Call it feminine curiosity."

And now he knew without any doubt what she was about.

"That or you have been sending information all along to Washington." He paused. "You've been spying for Washington," he whispered.

She did not reply, simply feigning surprise and then anger.

"How dare you at this very moment of parting make such an accusation?"

He could tell that the anger was false, even though she pushed back from him, sat up, and pulled her hand away from him.

"Allen."

He was not sure what to say.

"I do love you. I really do."

"And I you," and he hesitated. Had she been playing him all along?

"Till now?"

He didn't reply.

"This damn war," she sighed.

"I know. This damn war! No matter which side wins, chances are I will never see you again, Elizabeth."

"What do you mean?" and he felt her hands tighten on his arms.

He shook his head ruefully.

"If we lose, do you think I can ever return to Trenton, or here?"

She looked at him and tears came to her eyes as she shook her head.

"And if we win, would you stay? Could you stay and marry me? Would you stay?"

Tears now rolled down her cheeks as she stifled back a sob.

"I would gladly marry you, Allen van Dorn. You are an honorable man and I love you. But could I stay here if we lose?" She lowered her head and shook it. "No," she whispered.

He gently kissed her on her brow.

"I'll always love you," he whispered. Standing up, he left her, following David to slip out by the servants' entrance and then out onto the street, heading down to the wharves. He had been ordered the night before to attend to the baggage wagons for General Grey and his staff as they were loaded aboard the ferry and crossed the river. He hoped he could remember where to find them.

The street was already lined with troops queuing up for the crossing.

The troops were hot with the damp morning heat, sweat pouring off of them as they stood in lines, waiting, burdened down in their heavy wool uniforms and full marching and battle gear, many carrying some extra loot in their packs and haversacks. Even without the booty they were taking, the average infantryman, between uniform, weapon, accoutrements, rations, and pack, carried upwards of eighty pounds, and after months of inactivity, except for the dragoons and light infantry skirmishing along the Schuylkill, the men were terribly out of shape. It was going to be a slow, exhausting, painful march across New Jersey back to New York City. This was a much less capable army than it had been when it marched proudly into Philadelphia half a year earlier.

Hundreds of boys and young men prowled around the edge of the crowd, grinning sardonically, offering taunts, a few of the more daring throwing horse droppings, egging on the "bloody lobsterbacks." Strict orders had been given that any man who leveled a weapon and fired this morning would be summarily executed. Light infantry had been deployed as a cordon, backed by officers and sergeants, repeatedly ordering the men to stand steady.

It took several long minutes to find General Grey; he, his staff, and their mounts were already aboard a ferry that was about to leave. The sight startled him; he had not realized just how late he had lingered with Elizabeth.

John André extended a helping hand as Allen leapt from the dock to the ferry, its crew preparing to shove off.

Grey looked at him, making a point of producing his watch, opening the lid, and gazing intently at Allen and back to the watch. He snapped it shut.

"A farewell with the young lady, lieutenant?" Grey snapped.

He struggled not to take offense and simply nodded. There was a flicker of a smile from Grey, and he wondered if the major had filed a complaint and the boom was about to fall, but Grey said not another word as he turned away.

He was obviously in a foul mood, and Allen felt it best not to offer any excuse. Grey stalked to the front of the ferry as the crew, having shoved off from the dock, went to their oars. The eight men, all of them slaves, bare backs glistening with sweat, dug into the dirty water of the Delaware with their sweeps, angling upstream against the current.

"Good-bye, Philadelphia," André sighed, making the gesture of blowing a kiss.

As they cleared the end of the wharf and the long row of oceangoing ships lining the docks, Allen saw that the broad river was alive with traffic, dozens of boats plying each way, back and forth across the river. Once clear of the closed-in heat of the dock and out on the river, now filled with whitecaps from a strong southwesterly breeze, the tension relaxed. Men began to talk, more than a few hurling insults back at the city, exclaiming their pleasure that soon they would be back in a proper loyal city.

Allen simply looked back wistfully.

"Did you see her again?" André asked.

"Yes."

"Ask her to marry you?"

Allen found he wasn't actually quite sure now.

He sighed and shook his head.

"I fear it is over. This war will drag on, she will eventually forget me."

André put a comforting hand on his shoulder.

"Not so glum, my friend. Adventure awaits. A new campaign. Chance for promotion and glory. For me to take the next jump, without proper backing at home, we need a bloody good campaign. And besides, regarding fair ladies, there will be others."

Allen forced a smile and said nothing.

"By the way, stay clear of Major Parsons," André whispered. "Claims he has some memory that you struck him."

Allen looked at André blank-faced.

"I'd have shot him myself if he had damaged our treasure," André whispered, patting Allen on the shoulder. "If he looks for a duel, my friend, I'll challenge him first."

"What?"

"You are fresh fish for him, my dear provincial friend. He'll think twice though before facing me. Have fought a couple already. No one killed, of course, but my honor was maintained, so don't worry. Besides, a gentleman needs to fight a duel now and again. Not quite your case, though, if you forgive me saying so. And I can't let it be said I didn't protect a friend when he needed it.

"Anyhow," he announced airily, "don't care much for the man. Got his commission because his father made his money in the slave trade. Not a gentleman at all."

Allen, flustered, did not know what to say. Could he ever fit into this world where even his friend called him a provincial?

He looked at the men around him and wondered what exactly it was they were fighting for. André spoke of adventure, a new campaign, and always the obsession all of them had for promotions, glory, and titles.

He thought of Jonathan and his comrades. Though he could not embrace their cause, given all the misery it had created in this world, nevertheless they did fight for something more. Even Elizabeth. In his heart he felt no real sense of betrayal or that she had, in some way, used him. She could have as easily gained her information from the flighty young Peggy Shippen, and most likely did. Yet she had just made it clear that if faced with choosing between him and what she believed in, she would chose that belief.

Could I do the same? he wondered. And in his heart he knew the dreadful answer. He could not. All his rationales for joining the Loyalist cause now seemed like so many empty words. Even his closest friend in this army would never quite see him as an equal, but would always view the world as an aristocrat, befriending and thus needing to protect a "provincial" friend from the son of a slave trader.

The nagging doubt that had been lingering all winter, festering within and, he realized now, fed by Elizabeth, came rushing in. *I cannot embrace the rebel side, but I no longer feel part of the side I am on.*

He lowered his head. André, thinking he was mourning the loss of Elizabeth, made a cheerful comment about the women who awaited their return to New York City and left him to his thoughts.

He thought again of Jonathan. Never had he felt so utterly alone.

Valley Forge
June 23, 1778

Peter Wellsley, no longer dressed in the castoffs given to him by the widow Hewes but in the proper uniform of blue and buff worn by the headquarters company of General Washington, stood at rigid attention at the approach of his commander.

Preparations for the march had been going on since the evening before. In the small stockyard nearly fifty head of cattle were being slaughtered, some of the meat passed out to the troops to roast on open fires. Meanwhile, with a fresh loaf of bread, a pound per man, coming out of the bakehouse, the poor souls laboring within for their General Baker were glad that this was the final night of such work for them. During the cold, dark days of January and February, the bakehouse job was one of the most sought-after in the entire army, for it was always warm, and at least there would be some fresh bread. But now, in late June, with temperatures soaring to ninety or more, and food again plentiful, it was hard for those men to stay at their tasks.

Yet still they labored, shifting from the baking of fresh bread to producing unleavened slabs of hard biscuits and hardtack for marching rations. The slaughtered beef not eaten in the feast of the night before would be salted down.

Extra cattle were already being driven ahead, preceded by foragers, armed with vouchers, who would sweep up additional supplies in advance of the army as it marched toward Trenton and from there into upper Jersey.

Haversacks were now stuffed with the freshly salted meat, a dozen palm-size slabs of hardtack, even a small ration of coffee beans, a luxury undreamed of throughout the long hard winter.

Ranks were dressed, marching columns formed, and a festive mood was in the air, for they were leaving this place at last. Few would look back nostalgically, except for those who had visited the cemetery yesterday and well into the evening, looking among the thousands of unmarked graves to where a brother, a comrade, a father might now lie. The hospital huts were still filled with nearly a thousand men too sick to march, men down with the ever-present flux and a myriad of other illnesses and injuries. When deemed fit, those still under enlistment would be sent up to join the ranks. If unfit or discharged, they would eventually be sent home when transport could be arranged.

There were more than a few tearful farewells, promises to write, or soldiers now healed going back to thank the women who had tended to them. He had sought out the old widow who today would move back into her house, and at the sight of him she burst into tears.

"Lad, I declare you've grown three inches and gained half a stone."

He offered to return her departed husband's overcoat and she had finally taken it, holding it between forefinger and thumb, declaring she would burn it, even though he had made certain to boil it the day before to insure that no lice lingered within its seams. As for the trousers, they were beyond hope, and he had thrown them aside when he had been issued his new uniform. He offered to pay her for the boots she had given him, and which he still wore, even though the soles were now paper-thin, but she would have none of it. Then, after saying a brief prayer over him asking for the Lord's protection, she had sent him on his way, wiping the tears from her eyes with her apron.

The general was now near him and he could see the look in the man's eyes. They were no longer careworn as he had remembered them across the dark months. His features were alive, eyes glinting as he gazed out upon the ranks drawn up on the parade ground, brigade after brigade drawn up in column of fours, the parade ground stamped smooth from their months of drill.

The general was not given to speeches. There had been plenty enough over the last hour, from Lafayette and Greene, even a halting one from Inspector General von Steuben, which had been met with cheers. The German drillmaster was now one of the most popular officers with the rank and file, noted for his growing command of Anglo-Saxon profanities, his giant dog who in reality had the heart of a lamb, and most of all for what he had taught them they could be.

Von Steuben rode behind the general and alongside Lafayette, whose Guards Brigade would lead the march.

The day was hot. Sweat coursed down Peter's face and the back of his neck. The uniform was heavy and far too warm, but he did not mind it, not with the memory of so many months of almost freezing to death, a fate that had literally taken several of his fellow guards while on sentry duty.

The general reined in and then gazed out silently at the columns drawn up. He was silent, saying nothing, all eyes upon him.

It looked as if he was about to say something, but Peter could sense there would be no words, for those closest to him could see the emotion that he was trying to mask as he gazed upon this new army, now approaching fifteen thousand strong. Phoenix-like, it had risen from the misery and ashes of this place ... Valley Forge would forever after conjure up anguish, cold, defeat ... but also endurance, dedication, and rebirth.

Washington drew his sword and, standing in his stirrups, saluted the color guard holding aloft his flag of command, beside it the new colors of the army and the nation, the thirteen red and white stripes and a circle of thirteen stars in a cantonment of blue. Next, gazing out at the troops, he offered a salute to them as well.

With that, wild cheers erupted. Again there were the strange variants, from the measured, disciplined huzzahs of the New Englanders to the wolflike cries of the men from the frontier. He stood tall in the saddle, acknowledging their cries, and then, sheathing his sword, the general turned and started off.

With a roll of drums, the lead unit, Lafayette's Guards, led by Washington's headquarters company, turned in a column of fours and filed off the parade ground, massed. Drummers and half a dozen fifers were to the front of them.

But Peter would no longer march with his comrades of the headquarters company, and there was some regret there, for they had been his faithful comrades for nearly a year and a half since Trenton. He along with a dozen other men of the company trained by von Steuben had been offered promotions as drill sergeants to six-month units coming in from their home states. Harris had urged him to take it, and even Lafayette had told him he could thus serve his country better, and so now he stood with old neighbors from Jersey, men of the Second New Jersey Infantry, who had arrived in camp four weeks ago. It was barely enough time to train them to the basics of marching and keeping line, many of the men chaffing at taking orders from a mere stripling half their age. It had even come to blows, a burly corporal from Amboy knocking him flat. He had not run off to report it. Instead he had stood up and glared at the man while wiping the blood from his mouth. He had told him he might damn well be able to lick him, but he would still take orders. And, no, he was not running off to the officers.

The men began to obey, the corporal from Amboy making sure they did so.

His regiment was ordered to step out and fall in behind Lafayette's Guards, and Peter stepped to one side, marching alongside the drummer. He called for him to keep the proper pace. Looking back, he grimaced as the line accordioned slightly, but the last files were now running to catch up.

They passed along the flank of the field fortifications. Knox's artillery had been stripped from the bastions, limbered up, and mixed into the line of march. They moved down the long slope back toward the headquarters. Several hundred spectators stood there: women of the camp, civilians, some invalid soldiers, more than a few on crutches and minus a foot or leg, lost to frostbite and not yet fully recovered to journey home. By the gate was the general's wife. As all shifted muskets to the salute, she waved her handkerchief and forced a smile despite the tears in her eyes. Behind her stood the old widow who had saved his life, crying as she caught a glimpse of him.

They passed the outer bastions, the road turning southeast, heading down to the ford over the Schuylkill. The route of the march by the end of the day would take them all the way to Trenton.

Home. Was it even home anymore? Perhaps he would be spared a few minutes to see his parents, and Jonathan's family, though he doubted they would greet him warmly. It was strange that, after this last year, after the last six months, this place they were leaving, with all its nightmares and tragedies, felt far more part of his soul than any place of childhood.

Clear of the outer line of fortifications, the ceremony of the march relaxed. Most of the drummers and fifers fell out of the lead and stepped to the side of road to fall back in with their individual units. Only a lone drummer and fifer at the front kept the beat, playing the ubiquitous "Yankee Doodle," "Chester," or "Old One Hundred" to keep up what was now to be the standard pace in fair weather of three miles to the hour. The order was passed to carry arms, some men slinging their muskets over their shoulders, others shifting them to more comfortable positions. Chatter broke out in the ranks; the men exclaimed about the building heat of the day, the lucky fact that they were at the very front of the column and thus would avoid the dust, and the ever-increasing carpeting of "road apples" left by the hundreds of horses and mules.

Peter looked back over his shoulder and thrilled at the sight as they rounded a bend in the road sloping down to the ford over the river. The column, already a mile long, stretched clear back to the parade ground. The ranks were tightly packed, the men eager to be off, to demonstrate their marching discipline. Some were singing and joking. Such a difference, he thought, a lump in his throat. He remembered how he had seen this place six months back, nearly to this day, when Sergeant Harris, now Lieutenant Harris, had all but carried him the last mile, through the snow and sleet. From the blessing of an old widow, he had been given a bath as if he was a child, and warm clothes and a bed.

They were leaving Valley Forge behind.

The road turned to the east and Valley Forge disappeared from view.

The road ahead, he sensed, was leading to a destiny that they must now fulfill, having been given, as a blessing, one more chance to prove themselves.

CHAPTER SEVENTEEN

✳ ✳ ✳

Near Allentown, New Jersey
June 25, 1778

Dawn was breaking as Inspector General von Steuben dismounted, handing the bridle of his mount off to Vogel. The first rays of the sun struck his face. It was more than warm, with clear promise of another scorching hot day to come. There had been little cooling during the night, and the Jersey air was heavy, humid. Most of those with him had shucked their heavy uniform jackets, tying them to their saddlebags. It was time to put them back on. Riding about in broad daylight without a proper uniform along the porous boundary of what was the British versus patriot line was a guaranteed way to be shot at by both sides.

He relieved himself inside the woodlot where they had stopped, came back out, and with a grin accepted Vogel's offer of a skin filled with claret.

Amazing, only three days before, he had been in Philadelphia! Riding with a detached guard that had swept into the town after the last of the British, he had entered a city in utter confusion. The Loyalists, some said up to two thousand, had fled. The patriots, not sure if this was some sort of ruse on the part of the British, greeted the advance guard with absolute joy. Once into the city he could see that vengeance was already being dealt out to some. Several women had had their hair brutally hacked off. A merchant, tarred and feathered——mercifully, he was told, the tar had not been boiling hot—— was being ridden around on a rail by some town toughs. He had disdainfully scattered those scum. Damn them, they could torment an old man easily enough, but when it came to real fighting, those types were never to be found.

The merchant, in gratitude for his rescue, had pressed upon von Steuben his last three bottles of claret, which had survived the British occupation. He left the city to ride back to Washington to report——and then had passed the orders to the detachments of militia that were wandering in to occupy the city——that any acts of reprisal were to be dealt with harshly.

The wine was tepid but refreshing, and he offered it to his traveling companions, Du Ponceau and Captain Ben Walker, a taciturn New Englander who recently had been assigned as an aide to his staff, with an escort of a dozen dragoons of Virginia cavalry to make sure he got back in one piece to report.

"I think that's Dan Morgan," Walker announced, pointing across a field of knee-high corn, lightly shrouded in morning mist.

"Let's go see," von Steuben replied, mounting and setting off at a fast canter, the cavalry struggling to keep up. Several of them cursed over this assignment of keeping the impetuous German out of enemy hands at all costs.

Von Steuben, with his growing understanding of crude Anglo-Saxonisms, grinned.

By God, it was good be in the field again. I feel twenty years younger, he thought joyfully, for it was like the old days: being sent out to gather intelligence, scout the enemy lines, probe, try and snatch a prisoner or two, bring in any deserters for questioning; playing the cat-and-mouse game of who is chasing whom as defensive pickets and offensive scouts probed and pushed back, probed and pushed back.

Morgan was mounted on a rather fine gelding, saddle and trappings indicating it was a recent capture from some either dead, or now dismounted, British dragoon. He smiled at von Steuben's approach, the two exchanging salutes. Walker, slipping alongside them, was a man who could translate directly from English to German, a surprisingly common skill in a country where Germans were the second most common group of immigrants.

"Bastards are strung out along that road for miles," Morgan announced with a cheery grin, leaning over slightly, spitting out a stream of tobacco juice. "I almost pity the sons of bitches," he continued. "They barely moved six miles yesterday; that thunderstorm in the afternoon turned the road into a swamp. They clearly have gotten out of condition during those months in Philadelphia. The city may have captured the British Army as much as they captured it.

"And you'll love this, sir. The Hessians are starting to break up under the strain of it all. Poor damned souls, they can't take the heat. We saw at least a couple of dozen dead by the side of the road. They just collapsed with all they're trying to carry. Picked up a couple of dozen deserters as well last night. Slipped out of their camp and ran smack into my men. Lucky sots, my boys didn't gun them down in the dark."

"Where are they?"

"Back over there," Morgan replied, nodding to the eastern end of the woodlot he had just come down through. "Heard you were scouting about, thought you might like to talk to them, so kept 'em here rather than send them back to the rear."

"Excellent."

Von Steuben paused for a moment to look south toward the village of Allentown. The air was obscured with the smoke from hundreds of smoldering fires. In the still morning air were the familiar sounds of an army encamped——the echo of wood being chopped, the neighing of horses, and a distant hum of voices. He could sense a lot from just the sounds; there were some things only a veteran of many campaigns could pick up on. There was no singing, no martial music, no laughter or shouting. Several drums rattled, the call for ranks to fall in.

"Ah, a little sport," Morgan announced, and he looked to where a man was pointing off to the southeast.

A light skirmish line was emerging out of the mist, several hundred yards off. The sharp crack of a rifle echoed, followed by three more shots. Von Steuben could not see where the shots came from, but they stopped the skirmish line cold. The men, crouching, retired back into the mists.

Morgan grinned.

"They're getting real cautious-like. I got six hundred of my best in an arc entirely around the front end of their army. Lot of Jersey militia under Dickinson are joining in. Bit of a fight two days back at Crosswicks, where we were getting set to burn a bridge. They pushed us back, but what a time it was. Those Jersey boys are like hornets, not at all like I heard they were a year ago.

"We've been burning bridges or knocking them down. The local farmers sure are furious with us, but every well is either knocked in, or we find a nice, dead varmint or two like a skunk or groundhog, put it in the bucket, and lower it down. First man that draws up the bucket for water gets an eyeful of a waterlogged rotting skunk in his drink . . ."

Morgan laughed and shook his head.

"Poor bastards in this heat. Only water from muddy creeks, it is a sight."

And then he sighed.

"Gotta pity the Tories, though, damn them. They should have left their little ones behind at least. No one would have harmed them, not like the massacres going on along the Mohawk right now. You see their little ones, trudging along, tongues hanging out, crying, you wanna at least show the white flag for a few minutes, ride up and give 'em a drink. When are we gonna keep children out of war?"

Von Steuben said nothing, remembering coming into a Russian village that had been overrun and looted by Turkish raiders. The children, the young girls . . . he blotted the memory out. At least this war had not yet degenerated to that level, though what he had heard about the fighting against the Indians out on the frontiers was almost as bad.

"Their disposition," he asked, forcefully changing the topic. As he asked the question, Walker drew out a notepad, ready to jot down the information.

"Looks like Clinton has split the army into two divisions. Cornwallis's division is right down there, not three hundred yards away, bulk of the men there, say six, maybe seven thousand.

"Head of the column is led by your German friend, von Knyphausen. Reckon he's about four miles or so to the east at a little crossroads, Imlaystown. Parked in between are most of their wagons. You might not believe this, but Dickinson claims he has some good men who just lie in a creek bed all day, watching a bridge they had captured and needed. They said they counted up to three thousand wagons crossing, said over a hundred wagons an hour were being pushed across."

"Three thousand?"

"Yup. Food, tentage, and loot. My God, Philadelphia must be stripped damn near bare, and the army wagons are mixed in with them Tories hauling everything they own."

Three thousand wagons. Absurd. Frederick with forty thousand to supply, perhaps, but for less than a third that number of men?

The night before, back in camp in Hopewell, near Princeton, where Washington had halted his army to await developments as to the British line of march, he had passed orders that the army was to strip down. Only essential supplies of additional rations and ammunition were to move forward with the army. Everything else, including tents, was to be left behind.

With the scorching heat, the men had been stripping down as well. Though it was against orders, more than a few had managed to somehow "lose" their new heavy wool uniform jackets, the usual excuse being they were stolen after the men had taken them off before jumping into a creek to cool off. Most of the men were carrying not more than twenty-five pounds total, and that

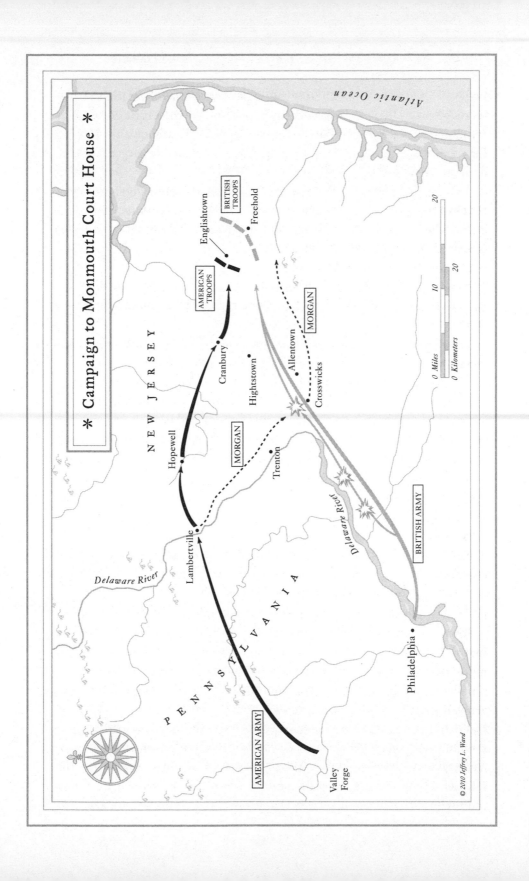

* Campaign to Monmouth Court House *

Atlantic Ocean

BRITISH TROOPS

Freehold

Englishtown

AMERICAN TROOPS

NEW JERSEY

MORGAN

Cranbury

Hopewell

Hightstown

Allentown

MORGAN

Crosswicks

Trenton

MORGAN

Lambertville

Delaware River

BRITISH ARMY

PENNSYLVANIA

Delaware River

AMERICAN ARMY

Philadelphia

Valley Forge

0 Miles   10   20

0 Kilometers   20

© 2010 Jeffrey L. Ward

included a musket and twenty-four rounds of ammunition. He knew that, by regulation, Hessian troops routinely carried eighty pounds or more . . . which might be fine for autumn campaigning in the Rhineland, but here? In this heat?

"The question His Excellency wants answered is, what is their line of march? Are they going to turn more northward, to Brunswick and Amboy, perhaps even turn up toward Newark, or will they hold to a more southerly course, perhaps to the Monmouth Highlands and Sandy Hook, and there wait for transport back into New York harbor?"

Morgan looked over at him and shrugged, the uniquely American, and at times French, gesture a bit insulting. But he had learned to not take offense.

"Got me, that's why I'm sitting here," Morgan offered, and he leaned over and spat again.

Von Steuben reached into his breast pocket, drew out a roughly sketched map of the region, and pointed out the possible lines of march.

"The general needs to know today."

He did not add that at a most frustrating council of war last night, the discussion had been exactly on this point, and opinion had been sharply divided. General Lee was calling for utmost caution, arguing that the army was still not yet ready for any kind of stand-up fight. He had suggested that, as of this morning, Washington break off shadowing the enemy, turn northward——using the Watchung hills as a defensive barrier to his right——and march up to lower New York, and, with the protection of the Hudson Highlands, await developments.

Wayne and Lafayette were on the other extreme, begging that it was time to go into the kind of all-out fight for which the army had, under von Steuben's tutelage, been training these last three months.

"Three months versus three years of training?" Lee sniffed. "Trust me, gentlemen, we are still babes compared to giants when it comes to training. Remember, I was a prisoner in their camp. I was on parole and allowed to walk about their camp and watch their daily drills. I know those same drills, for, remember, I served with them for more than a decade. Even chatted with some of my old comrades from my days with the Forty-fourth, and they are eager, more than eager for a chance to meet us on the open field. Believe me, gentlemen, we are no match. Not yet. Maybe three years more with your German and then I'd think about it. But, damn me, we can't do it this year or the next. This German's drill is far too informal for my blood."

Von Steuben had remained silent in spite of the direct insult, for Lee was, again, second-in-command by right of seniority, and his own position as inspector general and master of drill ranked far lower. But he could sense that Wayne and Lafayette were stunned by Lee's criticism.

Washington, much to von Steuben's chagrin, had after that advice from Lee shown hesitation and said he would wait another day to see developments. Lafayette whispered later to von Steuben that Lee was a strutting poltroon. He wished the man had stayed a prisoner. By the rules of war, Lee's commenting on anything he had seen while under the terms of parole was a violation of the ethics of a gentleman. It showed, yet again, the nature of his character.

"You say the Germans are in Imlaystown?"

"That they are."

Von Steuben, after handing over the map to Morgan, leaned over to study it yet again.

"That would indicate a move more to the eastward, to Freehold, and Monmouth beyond. Though there are roads here and here." As he spoke, he pointed toward the villages of Cranbury and Englishtown. "Clinton could turn northward, if Cornwallis should, this morning, come up the road I just traveled on."

He pointed to the map yet again.

"They can march to Hightstown and then to Kingston and the main postal road that leads straight as an arrow to Brunswick and from there to Amboy."

Morgan nodded.

"Or, if this morning he follows Knyphausen, it will definitely mean the more cautious and southerly route, as he tries to avoid contact and gain the Jersey shore for transport into New York Harbor."

Morgan leaned over and spat again.

"Exactly why I'm sitting here," he drawled, "and I reckon that's why you are, too."

Von Steuben felt a ripple of excitement. By God, he was smack in the middle of it. Across the mist-shrouded fields, but three hundred yards away, were his new enemies, Cornwallis and Clinton. At this very minute they were rousing their army to move. Would it be due north to Hightstown or east to Freehold?

He prayed it was north, though if so, he would have to race back to where Washington was camped, fifteen miles away. Lee would scream that they must retreat, but perhaps, just perhaps, the general he admired so much would listen to his own counsel, at last turn his army south, find some good ground.

There were several stretches of good open ground between Hightstown and Kingston where he could draw up and let the British come on.

If east, it would mean a hard march. Perhaps it was impossible now to get ahead, but they could most definitely fall on the flank and rear of the British if they should choose that more timid route.

"What do you think?" von Steuben asked, looking over at Morgan.

A couple more rifles cracked to their left. Both looked over. Several dragoons lingered in the mist near the town. There was a flash of a musket from them. A second or so later, the hum of a ball passing high overhead. Morgan laughed, shaking his head.

"Two hundred and fifty yards with a musketoon? They couldn't hit the broad side of a barn at that range."

He spat derisively in their direction. The dragoons fell back into the mists.

"I'd like to see the captured Hessians," von Steuben announced.

Morgan looked back over his shoulder.

"Gregory!"

A rifleman stood up from behind the split rail fence bordering the woodlot. All this time, von Steuben had not noticed that only a few dozen feet away, a score of Morgan's men were concealed.

"Take our inspector general here to meet his countrymen."

Von Steuben looked over at Morgan.

"I'm Prussian, not Hessian."

Morgan gave him a bit of a smile and shrugged.

Von Steuben rode up to the south side of the fence, saw no place to pass through, dismounted, and climbed over. Walker, Vogel, and Du Ponceau followed his lead. Azor took a look at the fence, tried to crawl under it, his bulk stopping him, drew back, whimpered a bit, and then finally sprang over it, a rifleman scrambling to get out of the way.

"Hey, von Steuben, you can ride that horse that's following you," the man cried, the others laughing.

He looked back with a good-natured grin, not sure what the man said, and called Azor to heel.

They made their way through the woodlot and picked up the scent of a cooking fire. He had not eaten since the night before, and there was the scent of bacon or ham on the wind.

He came to their encampment. A rifleman leaning against a tree simply nodded as they passed and pointed to a small clearing. Two riflemen were standing in the clearing, rifles tucked under their arms, one of them gingerly holding a slice of hot, greasy bacon and trying to eat it. Sitting and standing around the fire were nearly twenty Hessians, blue uniforms and yellow or red trim, most of them sporting the traditional drooping mustaches, all of them filthy and mud-caked. A corporal was squatting over a frying pan resting in a smoking fire, bacon sizzling, forking out slices and handing them out. Another man was peeling off slices of cold smoked ham and passing them out as well.

At the sight of von Steuben, in uniform, approaching them, a sergeant came stiffly to attention, shouting a command, the others standing. The man cutting up the ham dropped his treasure on the leaf-covered floor of the forest.

Von Steuben returned their salute.

"Stand at ease, men," he announced in German.

They did as ordered but looked at him warily.

"I am Baron von Steuben, inspector general of the Continental Army."

There were muttered gasps from several of the men, the sergeant snapping a command for the men to fall silent.

"I'd like to talk with you."

No one dared to reply.

"I assure you that you shall be treated according to the proper accords of war, so you have nothing to fear now or in the future."

He could see the uncertainty in their eyes. Some of them shifted fearful gazes toward the lanky, dirty, tough-looking riflemen guarding them.

"We came in and surrendered of our own accord, sir," the sergeant announced, still at attention because he was addressing a superior officer and was a fellow German.

"That is good," von Steuben replied. "I am serving on this side because it is the just side. The same as when I served with my king in the last war. But enlisted men such as yourselves must follow orders, of course."

The sergeant and the others seemed to relax slightly.

"Sir, I was with the Twenty-first at Minden," the sergeant announced. "Your regiment was on our right."

The baron smiled.

"The Twenty-first, stout lads. I remember you well."

It was a bit of a lie. The Twenty-first had come close to breaking under the hammer blows of that morning, and his own regiment was one of those that had come to their rescue.

"I was there, too," another man, a gray-mustached private, chimed in, and several others nodded. He could feel the tension easing.

"How did you get that food?" von Steuben asked, pointing to the frying pan. The bacon had been forgotten with his approach and was smoking and near to catching fire.

The corporal tending it squatted back down, pulling it off the fire, forked out a slab, hesitated, and then offered it to him.

He hesitated to take it; it was still sizzling. The corporal offered the fork as well, and von Steuben nodded his thanks, holding it up to take a bite.

"Found it in a barn," one of the men offered lamely. Von Steuben chuckled and they relaxed still more.

"And your captors allowed you to keep it?" He nodded toward the two riflemen.

"We fed them first," the sergeant offered.

"Wise move. These wild men of America can be fierce if not fed. And think of it. They're not such bad fellows. You think the Russians or French would have allowed you to keep that food if they had caught you?"

The men shook their heads.

"We weren't exactly caught, sir," the sergeant announced.

"You deserted, then?"

No one spoke for a moment.

"It is all right, men. Nothing to be ashamed of." Again that was something of a lie, at least according to his code of conduct. But he wanted information, and being friendly was always the quickest way to get it.

"I apologize for interrupting your meal. Most likely later today you will be escorted to the rear area and from there sent over to Pennsylvania. Let me give you some advice to make things easier. If you have indeed left your regiment, you know there is no going home for you, ever again."

The men now stood silent, some lowering their heads. To his surprise, one of them broke down and began to cry, muttering about the daughters he would never see again.

Von Steuben went up and patted the man on the shoulder.

"You will see them again. That I promise you, lad."

The man looked up at him, his sun-blistered face streaked with tears.

"When this war is won by the Americans there will be a new country here, open to all. Write to them and urge them to leave Hesse behind. Come here and start your lives over. This is a rich land, with room for all, for all who will join in the fight.

"That is my advice to you men. I know you are of stout heart——good, decent men. And yet your prince sells you to others to serve as nothing more than mercenaries. That is a violation of a code of honor, as I see it, and as you should see it. You were in the army to serve Hesse, not to be sent here to a war not of your own making. You have every right to do what you did.

"Offer to join the American cause. They need men of your training and discipline. You will win rank and advancement, I promise you that."

"And if we are ever recaptured we will be flogged to death as deserters," one of the men growled in reply.

"You have made a choice," von Steuben replied, sharply fixing the man with his gaze. "If you should wish, you can go back. Go ahead!"

He snapped out the last words sharply, friendly tone gone.

"Go back!" and he pointed to the south and the open field beyond. "I am a general with this army now. I will order your guards to let you go and they will obey me. You can still slip back. Say you were captured and escaped and wish to rejoin the ranks staggering along that damn road down there, with a hot day ahead, and no water. Any of you. Go now!"

No one moved. The complainer lowered his head, avoiding von Steuben's gaze.

"Then we understand each other," von Steuben replied, voice still a bit cold. "You have made your choice, and I now offer you a promise of hope. Offer to join the Americans' cause and they will welcome you. Serve with honor and courage. When victory is won, contact your families and bring them here. If need be, seek me out and I will help you, my fellow Germans, in any way possible. I swear that by God Almighty."

There were smiles, muttered offers of thanks. The two guards, not understanding a word, nevertheless sensed that something had transpired, and when he looked to them, there were nods as well.

"Sergeant!"

"Yes, General!" Again the man had snapped to attention.

"Take a walk with me."

The sergeant saluted, told his corporal to oversee the distribution of food, and fell in respectfully by von Steuben's side, walking half a pace behind him.

"When did you desert?"

"Last night, sir."

"How?"

"The men are nearly all of my company. Our captain, earlier in the day, died."

"How?"

"We think it was the heat, sir. That and too much rich food while we were in Philadelphia. He was not a bad man, but, forgive me, sir, not a very good soldier, and he was so fat he could barely walk. We were marching. There was no water, the rebels had destroyed every well along the way. The one stream we reached, they had slaughtered a cow, a couple of days before, and put it upstream from the ford. The smell of it was evil and no one dared to drink. There was offal all along the bank of the creek as well."

"Why didn't someone drag the cow out of the creek?"

The sergeant shook his head.

"Don't know, sir. So we had no water, and our captain, he started to drink. He had taken to drink when we took ship over here and never stopped. Even though he was riding, he just suddenly fell from his horse, holding his chest, and was dead. The company was given to Lieutenant Dietrich and, sir, forgive me, but he is the devil incarnate. With every order given, I was to flog the last man to obey."

"I know the type," von Steuben said with genuine sympathy.

"That was enough for me, sir. So once it was dark I passed the word to the lads that I trusted that I was finished with it. I made sure the sentry posts were men I trusted, and just before the middle of the night we slipped out of the camp. We'd only gone several hundred paces and were nearly shot by one of those woodsmen that had been trailing us. Corporal Robb knew enough English to keep us from getting shot. The woodsman brought us in and they sent us here."

"And the bacon and ham?" von Steuben asked.

"Well, sir, we found it along the way," the sergeant offered, and von Steuben sensed it was a lie. He let it pass, of course. All men forage on the march——it was how they stayed alive at times——and a good sergeant knew when to turn a blind eye.

"Tell me about the march."

"Hell, sir. Pure, bloody hell. This America——" He shook his head ruefully. "You either freeze your bottom off, or your brain is roasted. And the road! Most of the army has been moving along just one road, sandy or clay. The heat was killing us, and orders were any man who took off his jacket or, worse yet, claimed it was lost would, of course, be flogged. By yesterday, you would see a dead man by the side of the road every few hundred feet, some with faces black, tongues lolling out from the heat and no water."

"What were the men saying?"

Here was the key question. A good sergeant, more than any other man in any army, should know the tenor and tone of his men.

The sergeant laughed and shook his head again.

"Damn mad, sir."

"At whom?"

"Officers, and the damn British."

"Why so?"

"You should see the wagons that are slowing us down. Rumor is General Clinton has twenty wagons loaded with wine, brandy, rum, food, furniture taken from his headquarters, tents, even some women traveling in a carriage. Even the lieutenants have their own supply wagon, while the poor sots in the ranks stagger along, some carrying packs near as heavy as they are.

"I fought in the last war from '56 right to the bitter end. Wounded three times, I was. Would the king have allowed a march like this, sir?"

It was a slight breach of protocol for a sergeant to ask such a direct question, but it was also a compliment and von Steuben agreed, shaking his head.

"Do you think their army is going to turn north or hug the roads to the south and head for the Jersey coast?"

The sergeant looked at him with a bit of surprise.

"Sir, I'm only a sergeant. Officers don't speak of such things in front of me."

Von Steuben laughed softly. "Soldier's rumors, then."

The sergeant smiled. "Ten months ago, when they were all haughty and proud, and under Clinton rather than that scared rabbit Howe, we would be——" He hesitated. "Sir, I mean they would be marching straight north now, looking for a fight. The men all are saying that the last thing the damn British want at this moment is a fight."

Von Steuben had half assumed that, but this was important news. A good officer knew that, more often than not, the rank and file had things figured out before the generals had even thought of it. It was a superior officer indeed who could keep his cards so close that no one could second-guess him. Frederick could do that. Washington could do it. He doubted Clinton could.

A rattle of gunfire——from the sound of it, rifles and muskets—— thundered from the edge of the woodlot facing south. There was a pause, and then yet more firing. Things were beginning to kick up.

He turned and led the sergeant back to his men. The two guards, joined by half a dozen Jersey militiamen, were standing, looking expectantly to the south. It was obvious the riflemen wished to get into the fray. The appearance of the militiamen was different, though. They were gazing at the captured

Hessians with cold disdain. The Germans who had appeared somewhat relaxed after talking with him were now clustered together, obviously nervous.

Von Steuben came back into the group and looked at the militiamen, then turned to Walker.

"Tell them who I am. Find out what command they are with, and tell them that these men are honorable prisoners who must be escorted back to where the army is camped near Hopewell. Be certain to get their names and that of their commander, and tell them without any misunderstanding that after this campaign is over I will personally check to see that these men have been delivered safely. Tell them that General Washington himself wishes to see them. And, if I hear of any mistreatment, it will be they who will be shot."

He spoke loudly, in German, so that his fellow countrymen could hear.

"Thank you, sir," the sergeant whispered. "We've heard that militiamen don't take prisoners, or that if they catch us alone . . ."

He made a gesture indicating they would be gelded.

Walker spoke to the militia. There was some muttering, which Walker killed with a sharp command, pointing to von Steuben. At the mention of his name, the attitude seemed to change a bit.

"The best to you, men," von Steuben announced to the prisoners. "You have made the right choice. I pray someday we shall meet again under better circumstances."

As he turned to leave, all snapped to attention and saluted. He smiled, returned the salute, and set off back to the open field.

Reaching the edge of the woodlot, he saw that the riflemen, who had been concealed behind the fencerow, were up, moving into the fading mists, which, with the rising sun, were disappearing. At the northern edge of the village of Allentown, a line of light infantry skirmishers in red was deployed out, trading shots at long range. On the road itself inside the village, there was, as of yet, no movement. It was well after sunrise, the heat rising by the minute, but Cornwallis was standing in place.

What did it mean? Why weren't the British on the road to get most of the marching in before the heat of the day? Was discipline now so collapsed that they couldn't arouse their troops before dawn? Was Cornwallis waiting to clear back the annoying cloud of militia and riflemen before advancing north? Was the Hessian movement eastward just a feint?

Damn, he did not yet have an answer.

He rode over to where Morgan was standing in his stirrups, telescope raised, scanning the town, oblivious to the occasional shots zipping overhead and cutting into the ground at their feet.

"Could actually be their line of march, or a feint before they pivot to their real route!"

As he spoke, he lowered his glass and pointed to where, on the road that led toward Hightstown, a column of light infantry, flanked by a troop of dragoons, was drawn up with what looked to be a four-pounder, limbered and ready for the advance. The small column emerged from the town, infantrymen at the double, once clear of the last home, immediately swinging out into open-skirmish order, still charging at the double. British dragoons rode out to either flank, moving to envelope the skirmish line of Morgan's riflemen and the Jersey militia.

The militia, at the sight of the advancing cavalry, immediately broke and headed for the woodlot, rightly fearful of being caught out in the open by mounted troops who could ride them down and slash them to pieces.

The skirmishers pressed the advance, even though Morgan's riflemen dropped several before finally giving back.

The artillery piece advanced a hundred yards out into the open and within seconds its experienced crew had their piece unlimbered and pointed in their direction. The first shot was fired.

A second later, a four-pound ball shrieked between where Morgan and von Steuben sat astride their mounts, the round passing so close von Steuben could feel the flutter of it. There was a scream behind him. Turning, he saw that one of his cavalry escort was down, the horse having lost its right foreleg at the shoulder. The animal was in agony, kicking and thrashing as its rider was pulled clear by his comrades. One of them drew his pistol and shot the poor animal in the head, ending its suffering. The dismounted rider stood up in stunned disbelief and faced the artillery crew, shaking his fist and cursing them.

"I think we should show a bit of discretion," Morgan announced calmly. "That gun does seem to have us in its sights."

They turned and rode back across the field, von Steuben's staff and escorts behind, Morgan's riflemen and the Jersey militia following. The British advance had stalled out in the middle of the field and did not press forward, instead trading shots at long range. The British were at the disadvantage without any Hessian Jaeger riflemen, who could fire at nearly the same range as Morgan's men could with their Pennsylvania and Virginia long rifles.

But they did not press forward. The lone artillery piece stayed just barely out of rifle range, tossing either four-pound shot or grapeshot down the Hights-town road or into the adjoining woodlot. The cavalry finally did advance to either flank and at last forced Morgan and his riflemen and militia to fall back for half a mile until they gained a defendable stretch of a nearly dry streambed, where cavalry could not easily venture against determined infantry.

Allentown was now out of sight. Were these enemy skirmishers the advance guard for today's march, or a cover while the rest of the army continued to the east and the road toward Monmouth? This was a key bit of information that he must bring back to Washington today.

"I'm going to ride parallel to their line for a while," von Steuben announced. "See if they are really moving that way, if I can."

Morgan nodded.

"Can I find you here when I get back?"

Again that annoying shrug.

"Maybe. Depends."

"Send a report back to the general once you get a sense of their movement," von Steuben ordered, and Morgan shot him a bit of a cold look.

"Don't need to be told that. It's what I've been doing these last six months."

The baron offered a smile.

"I did not mean an insult, sir. Just that the general needs to know today, immediately, if they are heading east rather than north, so that he can move accordingly."

He turned and started off to the east, his staff and escort following at the gallop.

It was turning into a beautiful day and he felt a surge of joy. At that moment it almost didn't matter which direction they were turning. He had a job to do. It was a job he was suited to and there was that heady sensation that today, indeed, he could make a difference in this war that he now so passionately believed in.

On the Road to Hightstown
One Mile North of Allentown

"Damn, that was close!" Captain John André announced. Allen had instinctively ducked as a rifle ball cracked the air between them.

"Calm, sir," André chortled. "Always show calm in all things as a gentleman should. Look to our good general back there for inspiration."

Without lowering the field glass held in his right hand, André gestured back to the rear with his left hand.

Allen looked over his shoulder to where General Grey, mounted, remained a couple of hundred yards behind the light infantry skirmishers.

"Easy enough for him," Allen muttered. "We're in rifle range, he isn't."

"My fine young provincial friend. You put too much credence in these backwoods ragamuffins and their rifles."

"My fine English-born friend," Allen snapped back. "I know what they can do. Remember, I lived near here. Several of the men of my village had long rifles and could choose which eye they wanted to shoot at a hundred yards."

"And we are a good two hundred yards back," André replied casually.

Allen kept his eye on one rifleman in particular, who apparently had singled them out for attention. The man was casually leaning against the side railing of the bridge the light infantry were to take and secure, arm moving up and down as he loaded. Behind him, men with axes and crowbars were hacking at the decking of the small, twenty-foot-long bridge, tearing it up.

"Gun number one. Fire!"

The four-pounder a dozen feet to the left of where André and Allen stood kicked back with a roar. The rifleman on the bridge, and those working at destroying it, spotted the flash and dove for cover. Splinters kicked up near the rifleman from the impact of grapeshot. Allen watched the man with the rifle, who stood back up several seconds later as if nothing had happened and continued reloading.

The skirmish was picking up in intensity, but so far there had been only a few casualties on either side, the light infantry keeping their distance to well over a hundred yards. They were taking advantage of any cover, knowing they were facing riflemen. The cavalry was far out to either flank, having been flanked in turn by militia concealed in nearby fencerows and woodlots. The militiamen, though firing at extreme range with their muskets, had forced the attempt at flanking to turn back.

"Ah, John," Allen finally offered, seeing that their distant opponent had finished loading, and this time was sitting down, elbows on knees and drawing careful aim.

"I see him," André whispered, "and, my friend, General Grey sees us. It is our job to stand here and inspire the men."

There was a flash, and a second later André flinched. Startled, Allen looked over. The rifle ball had grazed André's epaulette and he was gazing down at it.

"Damn him, this uniform cost twenty guineas," he snapped.

Angry now, he stepped forward and drew his sword.

"Come on, men, enough of this playing about," he shouted, and he pointed the sword toward the bridge.

The rifleman was back up, reloading. The axmen worked furiously——planks were coming up, and, rather than toss them into the shallow stream, the party was hauling them away.

André trotted along the road, sword out.

"Come on now, men, to the bridge!"

Cursing under his breath, Allen followed.

It was already blazing hot. Sweat beaded his face. His shirt underneath the jacket and vest was soaked, as if he had been swimming. His mouth was dry, his tongue felt swollen.

He had to follow André, damn it, and he drew his own sword.

The cavalry from the flanks, having drawn back toward the center, wheeled. Their captain, seeing André going forward, shouted for the men to charge. The thunder of their hooves rumbled across the open field as they trampled down spring corn and knee-high hay that had been turning brown in the heat.

The light infantry, which had been hugging the ground and a low line of hedges that bisected the field, came to their feet. After several hours of skirmishing in the heat, they were tired. Many of them were panting. One had collapsed in a heap, though not from any wound; after lying an hour behind the hedge, without water since the night before, cooking in his heavy wool uniform, he simply gave out.

On the far side of the bridge Allen could see a few mounted men. Someone had identified one of them as Morgan. The man seemed unperturbed by the ragged charge, and, while still mounted, he raised his rifle and fired. Allen saw a man to his right go down, cursing, clutching his arm.

The scattering of riflemen and militia in the streambed got up on the far bank and ran. The axmen tearing the bridge apart gave way and ran as well. The rifleman who had nearly killed John, unable to finish loading, gave a wave, jumped the broken span of the bridge, and darted off.

André reached the south end of the bridge. Grabbing hold of a railing, he swayed, head lowered, panting. For a moment Allen feared he had been hit.

He came up to his side.

"Damn it, sir, why did you do that?"

André looked over at him and tried to grin, beads of sweat dripping from his face.

"Sorry, lost control of myself for a moment, I guess. Not looking for mention in dispatches, mind you, just that bloody man tore my good uniform."

Around them the cavalry were reining in. A ten-foot span of the bridge was gone in the middle and none dared to try and jump it. They turned their horses to either side, trying to force a way through the thick briars and saplings to get down to the stream.

The light infantry gained the bank. For them, getting through the tangle was easier, and most of them were down into the creek within seconds, discipline forgotten as men began to peel off cartridge boxes and set aside muskets so they could kneel in the stream.

Some of them began to curse.

"Damn bloody rebels!"

Allen saw where the calling cards had been left. Apparently during the night someone had thought to drop a cartload of offal——from the smell of it, pig manure——into the sluggish creek, and the decaying head of a butchered sheep was bobbing in the stream.

Most of the men didn't care, and scooped up handfuls of the water to drink, even as sergeants cursed at them to leave off.

"Rather impetuous of you, Captain André."

Allen, leaning over, still gasping for breath, and furious that he could not refill his canteen, looked up to see General Grey.

André smiled as he saluted, though it was obvious this effort had blown the last of his strength.

"Wanted to have a talk with that bloody rifleman who marred my uniform, sir," and he pointed at his shoulder.

Grey offered a smile and then gazed at the creek and shook his head.

"Order the men not to drink here," he announced. "Send a well-guarded watering party upstream a few hundred yards. Captain, picket the bridge, make it look like you are trying to repair it, but go no further."

"Sir?"

"This is only a diversion, young sir, remember that. Only a diversion. This army is moving east, not north."

"Yes, sir."

"André, I'm leaving you in charge. Mr. van Dorn, you stay with him."

He smiled.

"You can translate if we bring in any prisoners here."

Allen simply saluted but said nothing.

"The army is set to move within the hour, to follow Knyphausen's division. Once we begin the move I'll send word back for you to rejoin my ranks. Good day to you, gentlemen."

Grey turned and rode back toward the village.

Allen watched him go, and then winced as a rifle ball cracked the air.

He looked back to the north. The riflemen and militia had stopped their retreat at the next farm, the flash of smoke from the shot drifting up from the upper floor of the barn.

"So it's east, as you guessed," André said, looking over at Allen, his voice hoarse.

Allen simply nodded.

If the army had indeed turned north here, Grey would have been pushing the advance far more aggressively. He was most likely under orders to drive the rebel militia and their prying eyes just far enough back so that the line of march was no longer in view.

If Grey were to turn north, Washington would know in short order. He was without doubt somewhere just to the north of them——perhaps in Princeton, maybe even just up the road ahead in Hightstown. There and waiting, with good water all around them, while this army, burdened down, with every bridge a point of contention, with every well and creek polluted, staggered under the sun.

At least this way, Washington would have to march too, if he were looking for a fight. And there was something in his heart that told Allen that was exactly what Washington would do. Things had changed since last autumn, when, at the mere approach of light infantry and cavalry, the American militia would disappear, and even their riflemen keep their distance.

Another puff of smoke. The fence railing that André was bracing himself against splintered. Cursing, he stepped back.

There was a distant taunt, and André, eyes glazed from heat and exhaustion, looked northward and for once did not have the appropriate quip.

"Come, John, let's get you into the shade," Allen suggested. André did not resist as he led him away from the bridge and along the riverbank, above where the offal and sheep's head were stinking in the creek. He sat him down. A light infantry corporal approached, offering a canteen.

"Filled it far upstream, I did, sir," the corporal announced. "It should be fresh."

"Thank you. That's most thoughtful of you," Allen replied, glad to take the offering. The corporal looked at him with a bit of surprise, not having expected a courteous response.

André suddenly hunched over and vomited, then lay back, gasping, features pale.

Allen unbuttoned his uniform jacket. Underneath, his vest was buttoned and soaked with sweat, as was the finely made cotton shirt beneath.

He uncorked the canteen and sniffed the water. It was warm——not pleasant-smelling, but there was no rank odor.

"Come on, John, some of this now."

"Champagne, I hope," André tried to quip.

"Just drink."

He took several gulps and gasped.

"Damn, are you trying to poison me?"

"I'm trying to keep you alive."

Allen took the canteen and forced down several long gulps, then poured most of the rest of it onto André's face and chest. The water was green with algae, brackish. He forced him to drink the rest of it.

He seemed to revive slightly.

"Now just stay here in the shade, I'll see to things," Allen said, and motioned for one of the light infantrymen who was sitting in the shade nearby to come over. He gave him the canteen and asked him to refill it and see to the officer.

The man, obviously nearly in the same condition as André, did as ordered, while Allen stood up and went back to the bridge, keeping low.

A light scattering of shots had resumed, but not of the intensity of before. His side would advance no farther, and it was as if the other side, sensing that, was now indulging in just a little harassing fire for the sport of it.

He stood up.

The horseman on the far side, about two hundred yards off, seemed to be studying him with his field glass. After several minutes the man waved. Allen returned the gesture and then rode off.

They must know now, he realized. He gazed up the road, shimmering in the morning heat.

Hightstown, about five miles off. From there, Trenton was just ten miles to the south and west. Ten miles and an eternity away.

He could see their militia now out in the open. With the skirmishing dying down, some were sitting in the shade, under trees or on the west side of the barn.

He wondered if any of them were his old neighbors and friends.

Leaving the bridge, he went back to sit by André's side. His features were pale, waxy, eyes closed. For a fearful second, he thought he was dead.

"Passed out, he did," the light infantryman keeping watch said.

Allen lay down by his side, the world suddenly hazy, spinning.

He had no sense whatsoever of the passage of time when, two hours later, someone shook his shoulder.

"Orders, sir, we're pulling back, the army is moving out."

Eyes gummy, he opened them.

André was sitting up by his side, features still pale.

"Come along, Allen," André sighed, "another march awaits."

Leaving the bridge behind, Allen looked back over his shoulder.

The militia were still there, sitting in the shade . . . and watching.

As the British started retreating, the militia slowly got up and began following.

Hightstown, New Jersey
3:00 PM, June 25, 1778

Von Steuben was exhausted as he rode into the village. Until now the war had pretty well bypassed this place, other than for some few foraging parties passing through during the winter campaign of a year and a half ago.

It was a crossing place for roads that came up from Allentown and Trenton, branching from there to Freehold to the east, Cranbury to the northeast, and Princeton and Hopewell to the north.

Several dozen militia were gathered outside the tavern in the center of the village, which was bisected by a clear, fresh running stream, water trickling over the face of a mill dam just east of the main road. The sound of the tumbling water was refreshing, and as he wearily dismounted he asked Vogel to take his horse down to the stream to water him. Azor left his master's side and just plunged into the creek, splashing and rolling. Militiamen standing outside the tavern, laughing, offered the usual comments about the miniature horse.

Von Steuben walked stiffly up to the tavern. To his surprise, he didn't even need to ask for a drink. One of the militia came out from the darkened interior, bearing a pewter mug, foaming beer dripping over the side.

"You the German, ain't ya?" the host asked, and he nodded his thanks, taking the tankard and draining it in half a dozen gulps. He should have known better with this heat. The cool drink hit his stomach so that his head swam and he had to sit down on a bench, in the shade of the tavern's front porch, the men laughing at his distress.

The same offer of beer was made for his escort of cavalry and staff, Du Ponceau and Walker. Von Steuben fished in his jacket pocket, feeling the Continentals but at last finding a couple of Dutch coppers. He pulled them out and asked the innkeeper if they might have another round. Pleased with the offer of real money, the man scurried inside.

The militia stationed here were, typical of militia, boasting about how they were ready for a fight. If need be, they would drop the bridge in the center of town, and then knock out the mill dam, find a couple of old horses or dried-up cows, take them upstream, shoot them, and push them in. A barrier of up-ended carts and wagons blocked a low crest a hundred yards south of the stream. Another barrier was up on the north side of the bank.

Tactically, he could see it would be an excellent place for Washington's army to make a stand, if they could come down here in time, and if this should be the route of the enemy advance.

The militia actually seemed to be looking forward to their task of destruction. Obviously, they had never been in a fight before.

Von Steuben took the second tankard of beer, was about to drink it, and then saw Vogel slowly walking up from the streambed, leading their mounts. He stood up, went over, and gave the stein to his servant, who nodded, barely able to croak out a thank-you.

"Riders coming in!"

The cry echoed from the barrier at the south side of the village. Friedrich looked up and his heart quickened. It was Dan Morgan, trailed by several of his riflemen.

In the searing heat he was riding at a trot, and once clear of the barrier he tried to urge his mount to a gallop, but the beast was played out.

Seeing von Steuben in front of the tavern, Dan stood in his stirrups.

"It's east! They're going east!"

He reined in by von Steuben's side, his horse lathered, panting for breath, and dismounted.

"Someone give him a beer!" As if by magic the innkeeper was out, holding up a tankard. Morgan grasped it and tilted his head back, drinking deeply, half of the beer cascading down the front of his jacket.

"Would have sold my soul for that half an hour back," Morgan gasped, holding the tankard back out to the innkeeper.

"You sure they ain't comin' here?" the innkeeper asked nervously.

"No. They're running east."

"Thank you, God," the innkeeper cried. Some of the militiamen cursed, mostly the younger ones, but it was obvious that more than a few were without doubt relieved that the war was not coming to their town.

"How certain are you?" Walker asked, even as von Steuben pulled his map back out.

"Damn certain," Morgan replied angrily. "You think I'd come back if I wasn't certain?"

"Tell me," von Steuben asked, and he held the map before Dan.

"They skirmished us out to the bridge, about two miles north of Allentown. But came no farther," Dan announced, pointing out the position on the map. The innkeeper came out with a refilled tankard, and Dan took it, now using it to gesture at the map, spilling some of it on the paper.

"They sat there about two hours or so, didn't push farther. That had me pretty well decided then, but I wanted to be sure. They finally started to pull back. I rode about a mile east, crossed the creek through some woods, came out on the far side with my men, and we pushed back a dozen or so of their dragoons. Finally gained a good view of the road between Allentown and Imlaystown and it was packed. Not with wagons but their infantry. Moving slow but definitely moving."

"Could be a feint nevertheless," von Steuben ventured.

Dan shook his head as if insulted.

"Picked up a few more of their deserters, also dropped one of the dragoons, and captured him, and he talked before he died. They all said the same thing. What clinched it was a boy slipped out of the village. Brave lad, claimed he overheard a couple of officers saying they were glad to be getting the hell out without a fight. That it was full marching gear, fall in, and head east. I then circled back toward Allentown. Wagons are packing the road, but only a light guard of infantry and dragoons, no artillery, which was also on the road east. I tell you, von Steuben, it is east for certain."

He did not need any more convincing. Though Morgan might not think much of him, he knew the reputation of this man as a scout.

He grinned.

"I'll take it back to the general now."

Morgan looked at him, back at his horse, and then at von Steuben again.

"I need another beer. Another half a dozen beers. I'm as parched as the plains of hell."

Von Steuben folded the map back up, motioned for Vogel to mount up, and did likewise. He looked at his cavalry escorts. For every step he rode, they had ridden two, constantly circling back and forth, galloping ahead if they suspected an ambush. They were as played out as Morgan.

Du Ponceau, ever eager, was already on his mount. Walker set down his tankard and mounted as well.

He set off, and though he knew he might be pressing his mount beyond its limits on this hellish day, he forced it to a gallop.

Before dark, General Washington must have this news. He could picture it so clearly now; a classic maneuver was in the offing. An exhausted and increasingly demoralized enemy, strung out on a single road, and the coiled fist of an army, eager for a fight, smashing into its middle.

It just might be the victory that could win the war . . . and he would be right in the middle of it.

CHAPTER EIGHTEEN

* * *

The Road from Cranbury to Englishtown, New Jersey
3:00 PM, June 27, 1778

A thunderstorm was building with magnificent intensity to the west, the distant rumble almost like that of artillery. But if there was to be any artillery fire this day, it would be to the east, ahead of him . . . a sound he had hoped to hear by now.

George Washington, with a strong patrol of cavalry in escort, swept ahead, riding in silence, wrapped in thought. And now he was assailed with the first inkling of doubt since this campaign had begun barely a week ago.

The road was rough-worn, clay on the high ground giving way to sandy loam as it dropped down into broad ravines cut by meandering creeks. The signs of an army having marched on it earlier in the day were evident; deep ruts had been cut by heavy artillery. There was the churned-up dust from the passage of thousands of men. Here and there, men lay under the shade of a tree or had collapsed along the bank of a creek. Those who still cared struggled to their feet at the sight of his approach, holding up small pieces of paper, notes of permission to fall from the ranks. Others just lay gazing at him, comatose. More than a few had died from exhaustion, flies already swarming about them. Dozens of played-out horses stood alongside the road, lathered with sweat, trembling, some having found a creek to lie down and roll in . . . and more than a few of these were dead in those streams as well.

The heat was killing——as bad as, or worse than, the hottest days back in Virginia. At least at Mount Vernon there had always been the stirring of a breeze off of the broad Potomac to cool the afternoon air. On days of such heat in the afternoon he would call his laborers in from the fields, while he himself would retire to the front veranda of his home, to wait for the cool of evening to resume work.

War took no such pity on men or beast.

He worried for his own mount, could feel the way it trembled, its footing not sure. As the road dipped down into another ravine, a muddy ford ahead, he dismounted. Billy Lee and his staff did the same.

A young lieutenant was sitting on the ground under the shade of a willow, features ghostly pale, shaking as if taken with a chill. Beside him lay another soldier, the man older, and obviously dead.

The lieutenant looked up, saw his general, and tried to rise, but could not. Washington extended a hand to him, gesturing for him to remain where he was.

"Stay seated, lad."

"I'm sorry, sir, I'm so sorry," the lieutenant gasped, and began to cry. Washington handed the reins of his horse to Billy Lee. No need to tell him to make sure the horses drank slowly so they wouldn't get cramps.

He walked over to the lieutenant and knelt down by his side, motioning for one of his staff to come over and help the lad, who strangely had not stripped down but was still in his heavy uniform jacket. Hamilton helped the boy to peel the jacket off his sweat-soaked body, took the boy's hat, stepped into the stream, filled it with tepid, muddy water, and then poured it down the lad's back and chest. The boy continued to shiver, and Hamilton repeated the effort.

With that the boy turned to one side and vomited, and continued to cry.

"I'm so sorry, sir, I couldn't keep up. Captain Jacobs told me to fall out and to keep an eye on old man Parker," and he nodded to the corpse, flies already covering the dead man's face despite his best efforts to shoo them away. "But Parker died. I'm so sorry."

"Just lie back in the shade, Lieutenant," Washington replied soothingly, and stood back up, looking at Hamilton, who shook his head. He could see the boy was badly sunstruck and should be in a hospital, not alone out here.

It tore at his heart. If he detailed off a man to stay with every soldier who had collapsed along this road, he would be alone and then finally have to stop himself. He had to push on, no matter what the human cost.

Billy Lee had finished watering the horses. Pulling up some weeds and rushes from the streambed, he wiped the lathered sweat off of them, talking softly to the animals. It was ironic that they were, of course, receiving more attention than this stricken lad.

Major Laurens came over and knelt by the boy's side.

"You see this a lot where I come from in South Carolina, sir," Laurens drawled. "Let's get his body into the stream, but keep his head on the bank. The water should cool him a bit, and with luck he'll pull through."

Laurens lifted the boy up, waded into the stream, and laid him down. He did not hesitate to raise the body of the dead man, peel off his blanket roll and canteen, and use the blanket roll as a pillow to prop the boy's head up. Then he sloshed upstream a few dozen feet, filled the canteen, came back, and set it into the hands of the lieutenant.

"Lieutenant, keep drinking that water. You'll puke it up but it will pull the heat out of your body when you do. Just keep drinking and you should feel better in an hour or two."

The boy had nearly passed out from the shock of the water and was shaking uncontrollably.

Washington stepped back, touched by the gentle compassion Laurens showed. The major lowered his head, held the boy's hand, which was grasping the canteen, whispered a prayer with him, then stood back up.

Washington looked back at his mount, Billy Lee nodding that they were ready to move on.

"My prayers are with you, Lieutenant," he said, his words sounding hollow even to him. He turned, went back to his horse, and mounted. Billy Lee, ever prepared, handed over a canteen to the general.

"Sir, a long drink here in the shade before we set off will be good for you."

He nodded his thanks, taking the proffered canteen, and began to drain it down.

"Slowly, sir," Billy Lee whispered, "else you'll get sick from it."

He did as suggested and handed the canteen back.

Without another word he urged his mount across the ford, sparing a quick glance back at the lieutenant.

"Rather far gone, sir," Laurens sighed, "but he might pull through. I've seen worse."

"I pray we will see him back in the ranks again," was all he could say in reply.

Six months ago that same boy had been most likely freezing to death, praying for just a bit of warmth. And now what he would have given for just a flurry of snow or a piece of ice. How strange war is at times. The general sighed as he pressed on down the road.

Turning a bend in the road, they saw the small village of Englishtown directly ahead, and he felt a surge of frustration. Men by the hundreds were out in the fields and orchards, nearly every last one on the ground, huddled under any shade they could find. Along the bank of a narrow creek, little more than a ditch, men by the score were in the water, just sitting. Muskets, cartridge boxes, packs, and jackets were piled up on shore. It was not what he had expected at all.

He urged his horse up to a trot and came into the center of town. Half a dozen artillery pieces were parked to the side, horses not in their traces. Several company-size units were slowly marching along, heads lowered, men panting, not even noticing or responding as their general rode by. On the shaded front deck of a tavern he saw the man he was searching for and rode toward him. General Charles Lee was sitting in a straight-back chair, surrounded by staff, all of them holding tankards. At the sight of Washington's approach they stood up, Lee coming down the few steps, snapping to attention, and offering a salute.

"A pleasure to see you, sir," Lee announced. Those around him hurriedly buttoned up their uniform jackets, put on their hats, and then just as quickly removed them with a flourish of salute.

Washington returned the salute with a nod and a touch of the brim of his hat and dismounted.

"A drink, sir, to cool you?" Lee offered.

He shook his head.

"We need to talk," Washington announced coolly. Lee motioned for them to go into the tavern, but he refused, turning to walk instead around the side of the building, stopping at last beneath an apple tree out back.

"I thought this army was moving to attack now, today," Washington said.

Lee looked him straight in the eye and sighed.

"Sir, the situation does not yet present itself."

"How is that?"

The owner of the tavern had set a table and chairs under the tree. Those occupying the place gave way and retreated at the sight of the two generals.

Washington sat down in one of the chairs, and the innkeeper hurried out to serve him.

"Sir, an honor, sir," he gasped, sweat beading his face. "May I offer you some cooling refreshment?"

"Cool cider, please, if you have some?"

"Most certainly, sir. Straight from the springhouse." The man waddled off, returning a moment later with a wooden tray and half a dozen tankards.

Washington took one up, sipped it, and struggled not to sigh. It was indeed cool, almost cold. He removed his hat and took the liberty of unbuttoning his jacket, letting it open up to the still, humid air, which held more than a hint of the approaching storm from the west.

Laurens, Hamilton, and some of Lee's staff came to join them. Laurens, without being asked, produced a map of the area and spread it on the table, using a couple of the tankards to anchor the corners.

"Now, please explain why this army is not moving."

"Because the British have not moved."

"What?"

"Sir, their second division, under the direct command of Cornwallis, is but six miles from here." Lee pointed to the east.

"Why are you not pressing in as originally ordered?"

"Because I am following your orders, sir," Lee replied.

Washington looked closely at the man, and again he felt doubt. Lafayette would have pressed on, even if nine out of every ten men he commanded had collapsed from the heat.

Lafayette originally had been in command of this, his advance guard of five thousand infantry, nearly all his cavalry, and two batteries of artillery. He had decided to keep the army in two divisions just as the British were now do-ing.

Washington had sent Lafayette forward with his own advance guard of five thousand, while his own reduced supply train, and his remaining command of eight thousand, were, at this moment, resting at Cranbury, five miles east of Hightstown. There was still the chance that Clinton would push Cornwallis due north at the last minute and try to strike for Brunswick. The advance by Lafayette was to shadow that, and even to act as bait if the British should scout them out and decide to attack what they might think was an inferior force.

If so, he could be on their flank with his main force in less than three hours while Lafayette held them. If, on the other hand, the British continued to re-treat to the east, Knyphausen would have to move first, and like an accordion their line of march would stretch outward before Cornwallis, burdened with their supply train in front and around him, along with the Loyalist refugees. If that happened Lafayette was ordered to attack with everything he had, even though outnumbered. Then he would bring up the main bulk of the army to fall on the British flank.

Lafayette was not the most capable of his tactical commanders on the field, but he was, by far, the most eager and aggressive, and when Washington had given him the assignment, he knew that the young man would seek any opportunity to strike.

And then, last night, General Lee, to whom he had first offered the command of the advance guard, and who had refused it, saying that it was not befitting his rank and that he preferred to be with the main army, had suddenly reversed his decision, appealing for the opportunity to lead the advance. By so doing, he had hoped to lay to rest once and for all the rumors of his behavior when taken prisoner and held in captivity.

Lee had reinforced his argument, and the man could indeed be persuasive, by pointing out his superior rank. He said that his long years of experience in the British Army and even his personal acquaintance with Clinton and Cornwallis would give him an advantage.

Much to Lafayette's chagrin, Washington had to agree with Lee, and ordered him forward to take the command.

But now?

There were the seeds of doubt as to his decision. All appeared too relaxed, languid, torpid under this scorching heat. The marshes of the region were a breeding place for mosquitoes and annoying horse flies, which now swarmed around them. Lee swatted at them while with his other hand he pointed out the positions on the map.

"Clinton has gone to ground here, west of Monmouth, on good, high ground with clear fields of fire, as if awaiting us. It is very good ground, sir, for them——and I caution against an assault. They have not moved since this time yesterday."

"Have they constructed fortifications and abatis?"

Lee laughed and shook his head.

"In this heat? No, sir. I think they simply turned, hoping we'd rush into the attack, but also to rest out for this day."

"And Knyphausen?"

"He is four miles away on the far side of Monmouth."

"Has he moved at all?"

"The same, sir. No, though some of the wagons have been pushed forward under heavy cavalry guard, heading toward the Monmouth Heights and the harbor at Sandy Hook. It is definite that they are now heading toward the shore there for transport."

"So why are you not attacking now?"

"As I said, sir," and Lee's voice took on a slightly pedantic tone, "I know

Clinton, sir, and he is subtle. He has picked good ground on what he knows is a day of killing heat and told his men to find shade and rest. If I push these men forward now, sir, half of them will fall out and the rest will collapse if they try to fight a battle."

"The weather is the same for both sides, General Lee," Washington offered, "and they are far more burdened down than we are."

"Yes, sir, but we will have to march into battle with the temperature over one hundred degrees while they wait."

"Did you think of advancing in the morning instead?"

Lee nodded.

"But then the men still back at Cranbury would have had to march ten miles or more to come up and engage. May I suggest instead, sir, that we wait out this day? Besides, that storm will soon be upon us."

As he spoke, he gestured back to the west. The thunderstorm was indeed approaching, towering in its majesty and power.

Washington shifted his gaze from the map to Lee and then back to the map again.

Another peal of thunder slapped across the sky, the blazing afternoon sun at last darkening in the southwest as the forward edge of the storm advanced. The sun disappeared, and many men emerged from hedgerows and orchards, and from trees and the north side of the other buildings in the village. There was even a bit of a ragged cheer as the first cool gust of wind swept down from the heavens, flattening the spring hay.

"Sir, this storm promises to be a big one. To try and march now?" Lee offered. "The roads, especially at the bottoms of the ravines, will turn into quagmires an hour from now. I beg to suggest that your plan for movement is a most excellent one, but, please, I implore you not to be too hasty. There is wisdom in the adage 'haste makes waste.' In this case it will be a waste of thousands of good men."

Washington thought of the lieutenant he had left lying in the stream and, finally, reluctantly nodded. Lee smiled.

"I have a forward screen of scouts. This same storm will sweep on to Clinton and his army, too, forestalling all movement for the rest of the day for him as well. He may move, sir, but not much before midmorning tomorrow."

A heavy droplet of rain smacked the map, staining the ink. Laurens looked up at the darkening heavens, and with a nod from the general, he rolled the map up, putting it back in its leather case.

Lee sat back in his chair, his spaniels resting around him, panting and cowering with each peal of thunder.

"I assure you, tomorrow shall be a glorious day for our arms," Lee announced, raising his tankard of strong ale in salute.

Washington nodded thoughtfully. "Your orders are as follows." As he spoke he looked over at Hamilton, notebook out, his back turned to the increasing gusts of wind. "I expect your advance guard to have broken camp before dawn, be completely formed and on the road. You are to advance with all possible speed directly upon the British forces now encamped on the high ground west of Monmouth Court House. Whether they are preparing to move or not, you are to attack with alacrity and élan, your regiments properly deployed into battle order as they have been trained to do this past winter.

"You are to bring about a general engagement regardless of enemy disposition, be they preparing to retreat or hold the high ground, as you described. The main body of the army shall be on the road before dawn, coming forward with all possible speed. By your bringing about a general engagement, the enemy will be fixed in position and the forces with me shall fall upon their flank and rear."

He spoke with a steady voice, but his enthusiasm was obvious. Across nearly two years, if ever there was an opportunity to deliver a resounding defeat, perhaps even a war-winning defeat, it was now.

"You do realize, sir, that the combined forces of the enemy equal, and perhaps exceed, our own?" Lee offered cautiously.

"Our men are trained," Washington replied, slapping the table with his hand. He repeated emphatically, "Our men are trained. After so many months of suffering at Valley Forge, they are ready for a fight. General Lee, they are eager for a fight, to prove that they have endured a frozen hell, have been reforged, and will now stand and face the enemy. And you will have the honor to lead the way."

His last comment was an encouragement to Lee, and he looked into his eyes.

"Tomorrow, sir, you shall lead the way, and in holding the enemy in place and, I believe, knocking them off balance, you shall open the way to a victory that shall be spoken of in every court in Europe. The victory can be yours and I shall credit it to you if you do as I have ordered."

Lee gazed straight at Washington and simply nodded.

The rain was beginning to fall, heavy drops that smacked onto the table, kicking up tiny swirls of dust on the ground with their impact. A cold gust of wind swept across the fields and around the yard of the tavern. It was a blessed relief from the hellish heat of the day.

"Do we understand each other, sir?" Washington asked.

"Yes, sir, we do."

He nodded to Hamilton, who finished dictating the order and handed the note to Lee.

"I shall ride back now to Cranbury and prepare the army to move before dawn. Good day to you, sir."

Lee and those with him came to attention and saluted as Washington left them and returned to the front of the tavern, where Billy Lee stood patiently, brushing the sweat off of their horses while holding a bucket up for Hamilton's horse to drink. Out in the street of the village a crowd of men had gathered, in part to enjoy the cooling breeze and also out of curiosity as to what was transpiring. All came to attention as their general mounted.

He looked at the men and then rather uncharacteristically stood in his stirrups.

"Tomorrow will bring us victory, men," he shouted.

A ragged cheer went up, men taking their hats off and waving them in salute as he turned and urged his mount up nearly to a gallop.

He did not look back as he rode off, nor did he see Lee, standing by the side of the tavern, take his orders and, without looking at them, stuff them into his pocket. Lee then turned away and went back to the front porch of the tavern and called for another round of cool ale for himself and his staff.

Once out of the village of Englishtown, Washington settled his mount back to a slow trot. The storm was upon them with all its fury. Cold, delightfully cold blasts of wind raced down from the heavens, pressing the winter wheat flat and even bending the thick stalks of corn. A blinding sheet of rain raced toward him and he lowered his head, holding his hat brim, his mount shying for a second as a bolt of lightning slammed into a tree atop a low rise just a hundred yards ahead.

He knew the storm was making his staff and their cavalry escort, riding behind them, nervous. A man on a horse in open fields in such a storm could be struck down, but he had a sense that fate had decreed that such would not be his end. Dr. Franklin might debate the point with him, but on this day, death by lightning would not be his fate.

They crested the hill, those around him looking more than a bit nervously at the heavens as they rode on, the fury of the storm whipping about them. The rain was deliciously cooling and he could feel his horse being revived by it. The animal skittered with each crackling peal of lightning that struck the ground nearby or raced overhead. He urged him to a quick canter, eager to be back with the main body of his army and set the orders in place for their movement before dawn.

The cavalcade swept down into a sloping ravine, the clay road beneath them now slick and slippery from the pounding rain. As they forded the shallow stream, pockmarked with the driving rain, he looked to his right.

The lieutenant they had left there two hours ago was floating in the stream, facedown . . . dead.

He slowed, staring at him for a moment. Billy Lee turned his mount, splashing up the creek, dismounting to pull the body up onto the bank. Kneeling down, Billy folded the young man's hands on to his chest and then with two fingers closed his eyes, lowered his head to pray for a moment, and, remounting, came back to join the group.

"Too far gone," Laurens sighed. "Lad's brain was burned by the heat."

Washington said nothing.

The storm was sweeping past them, the rain abating. Steaming mist was already rising from the road ahead. He sighed. It was just a summer heat storm, not a line of storms promising cooling breezes once it had passed. In another hour it would be as hot again as it had been throughout the day.

He could already sense that tomorrow would be even hotter.

Near Monmouth Court House
3:00 AM, June 28, 1778

"John, come on, John, wake up."

Allen knelt in the mud by his friend's side, shaking him on the shoulder.

Ever since his bout with the heat two days ago, John André had not been his usual self. His demeanor was subdued, remote. Allen now saw that change along with more than a few of the men of their command. Men born and raised in England had never experienced such heat before. Last night at Grey's staff meeting it was said that at least a hundred or more had died during the march from Crosswicks to here, and much of the rest of the army was sick with exhaustion and heat, and from the unrelenting plague of stinging insects that hovered around them in clouds.

He had readily volunteered to take André's place on the midnight-to-three watch, and André had collapsed on the open ground, under the rude shelter of a wigwam made of nothing more than pine branches set up against the stout trunk of an old oak. The rude shelter had not, of course, kept out any of the rain, though in fact afterwards, when the heat came back, the mud was at least somewhat cooling, and André had dropped off into a deathlike slumber.

"Come on, John, up now."

His friend at last stirred and, groaning, sat up.

"Where in hell are we?" he whispered.

"Same place as we were yesterday."

"As I said, where in hell are we, or should I say are we in hell."

Allen managed to force a laugh at André's pale attempt at humor. He drew hope from it. Perhaps a bit of the old spirit was back.

"I think I'm going to be sick," André gasped. Staggering to his feet, he walked off a few dozen paces. It did not really matter where he went for privacy; they were surrounded in the woods by the men of Grey's command, along with the rest of the army. He heard André gagging and then relieving himself, someone nearby cursing him to go do his business somewhere else. André came back, and in the pale light of the setting moon Allen could see that his friend was indeed spent, white breeches and his "twenty-five guinea" uniform jacket caked in mud and filth.

André sat back down on the muddy ground with a weary sigh.

Allen offered him a plate upon which rested a biscuit and several slabs of cold bacon. André picked up one of the slices with his fingers, took a bite, suppressed a gag, and let it drop back on the plate.

"Next time, friend, I'd prefer a brisket of lamb, warm but not hot, or fresh-shot quail."

Allen chuckled.

"You are in the Americas, sir, and bacon cooked or uncooked is what we get here."

"Damn this place!"

Allen tried not to take offense and offered over a wooden canteen, uncorked.

André sniffed at it and sighed.

"That's better." He took a deep gulp of the watered rum and then another.

He coughed, suppressing another rebellion of his stomach, then took another long drink.

"Slightly better."

Allen offered the plate again and André shook his head.

"You eat it. That will last ten seconds in my stomach. If there for more than a minute I fear it will come out the other side. I fear I have the flux from the bad water and heat."

Allen nodded sympathetically but did not hesitate to wolf down the greasy bacon and polish it off with a gulp of the rum.

"Officers' meeting, sir," he announced, now taking on a more official tone. "General Grey expects you there."

"Lead on, then, my Virgil, lead on," André sighed, as Allen helped him to his feet.

Being a general, Grey had retained his tent, while the rest of the army was ordered to march without them and leave them in the wagons of the supply train. It was lit within by several lanterns. Before entering, André struggled to brush the mud off his breeches and smooth back his hair, Allen helping him.

Grey looked up as the two came in.

"You look like death, John," Grey offered.

"Why, thank-you, sir, and, bless me, you most certainly do not," André replied, and those gathered around the general laughed, though it was forced.

"As I was saying before you arrived," Grey continued. "The orders are straightforward. The men are to be roused now. Ranks to form at four and set off. The Germans ahead should already be up and moving, and with them the wagons, between our column and theirs. By nightfall we will have gained the Monmouth Highlands on the Jersey shore. Once there, we hold as the rearguard, while the rest of the army goes down to the beach to embark. A dozen ships are waiting to ferry us to New York City. Gentlemen, it shall be a hard day's march."

No one spoke.

"I expect the heat will be as bad as, perhaps worse than, yesterday. Keep an eye on the men. Let them know that any that fall out from exhaustion we will leave behind. As for the light infantry, do not skirmish them out unless absolutely pressed. We all know what fate will befall them if they wind up in the hands of the rebels, especially those led by that madman Anthony Wayne."

Again there was silence.

"And if the rebels do attack us?" one of the staff asked.

Grey snorted.

"In an open field?" He chortled. "Let them. In fact, I shall send them a personal invitation to do so. We will butcher the rabble. Now, that would be the right way to leave New Jersey. With a defeated army of dead rebels left behind."

Of course his words were greeted with a chorus of approval, but Allen remained silent. He suddenly realized that Grey was staring at him.

"A comment, perhaps, from our good Lieutenant van Dorn regarding his former countrymen here in his home colony."

Allen reddened as all turned to look at him.

"Go on, young sir, it is why I have you on my staff. Tell me what you think Washington and his horde will do."

"Attack," Allen said softly.

"Let them," came a reply from the major he had come close to fighting a duel with back in Philadelphia. "Let them and we will show them what for. Or are you afraid of them, Mr. Dort?"

The major deliberately mispronounced his name. Allen stared at him and did not reply, turning instead to his commander.

"Sir. I think they will attack with everything they have. We are a column strung out on a road for a dozen miles or more. Their forces are gathered."

"I will send them a personal invitation to attack," the major interjected. "A proper duel and we will send them packing. But then again they are merely provincials, have no sense of honor, and would run from a good and proper challenge from a gentleman."

No one spoke for a moment, for the implication was obvious.

Allen turned and faced him.

"Sir, if you seek satisfaction . . ." His voice trailed off as Grey barked a command for both of them to desist.

"Mr. van Dorn, you will direct your comments to me alone at this meeting, and the rest of you will be silent."

Allen stiffened, turned back to Grey, and nodded.

"Go on then. Your opinion."

"Sir. The rebels in last year's campaign were soundly defeated in every open-field engagement. But that was last year. We have heard the reports of their drilling since early spring. Sir, you asked me to join your staff to give my views on what can be called my former countrymen. I know their mettle. They are, without doubt, not drilled to the caliber of the men under your command, but they believe they are."

He paused.

"That, sir, is what I think shall be the issue this day. They believe, after so many defeats, that they are now our match. The march of this last week has done nothing to dissuade them of that belief. No one here can deny that we have left behind scores of dead, along with hundreds of exhausted, and, though we dare not admit it, most likely hundreds of deserters as well, especially from the Hessian ranks. That will embolden them. I think, therefore, that before this day is out they will swarm in to attack. We must be ready for that."

All were silent except for the major, who gave a sniff of disdain and deliberately turned away. Grey did not reproach the man, for back in England, the major's family line was far more intimate with the inner circle around the royals than his own, but all could see his frustration.

Grey nodded thoughtfully.

"I shall take your words into consideration, Mr. van Dorn."

That was all he said in reply, but Allen could see that Grey had taken his comment to heart.

"We march in an hour," Grey snapped. "Dismissed."

One Mile East of Englishtown
8:00 AM, June 28, 1778

Inspector General Friedrich von Steuben had been in the saddle for nearly two days without rest. After riding from Hightstown to report to Washington that Clinton was indeed turning east, he had indulged himself in a few hours' sleep. Without any specific orders, he had taken upon himself the role he felt best suited for at this moment. Gathering his exhausted staff, he had ridden off to yet again scout the enemy line of march.

He had ridden clear around the enemy column. The dragoons assigned to him had finally given up on their duty, begging that their mounts needed to be rested. He had simply ridden on. In the end it was down to the ever-faithful Vogel, Du Ponceau, and, of course, Azor.

Late in the afternoon yesterday, his decision to continue had nearly cost him his life. In the midst of the storm he had left his two companions and his dog to rest in a shallow creek bed as he rode forward for a closer look. He had nearly ridden straight into a vedette encampment of British dragoons, two of them mounted. They charged straight at him, one of them shouting, "That damn German!"

Drawing out his two heavy Russian-made horse pistols from their holsters mounted to either side of his saddle, he had leveled them, one in each hand. The lead dragoon shied off not a second too soon as his first pistol fired off with a roar. The second man reined back hard, the next shot striking his horse in the chest, sending it rearing back. He had turned and ridden off, and in the excitement had dropped one of the precious pistols.

The first dragoon, now joined by several comrades, had chased him across an open field, drawing closer. Only pistol shots from Vogel and Du Ponceau had caused them to rein in, suspecting a trap.

With a flourish he had jumped the narrow creek bed, looked back at his angry pursuers, one of them shouting for him to come back for a one-on-one duel, and waved his hat in salute.

He was forty-eight years old, and had not had so much fun in years.

For several anxious moments he could not find Azor, and feared he had run off. Finally his dog came out from the bushes, grinning in that funny way dogs do when their cowardice has been exposed. He returned to his master, sheepishly wagging his tail. Von Steuben had dismounted to rub the dog's head, even though he was soaking wet and stank. He rode on, he and his comrades laughing about the narrow escape, even though none would admit just how heart-stopping it had been.

Throughout the night he rounded in front of Knyphausen's column. Then, at three in the morning, that which he had been anticipating was now at last obvious. The enemy forces were beginning to shake out, preparing to march before dawn. Sweeping along the edge of the long column that stretched clear back beyond Monmouth, the evidence was clear. Teamsters were harnessing their mules and horses to wagons, by the light of smoldering campfires men were stirring, and, though the wind was still, the smoke in the air carried the scent of bacon, ham, and salt beef being cooked.

At times he ventured to within easy hailing distance for a closer look, Vogel and Du Ponceau repeatedly begging him to keep his distance. But he had to know for sure, and, other than bringing in some willing deserters, he had to see with his own eyes in order to make an accurate report. As the first glimmer of dawn showed on the eastern horizon, revealing a landscape cloaked in morning mist and smoke, he was at last convinced.

They were forming up to march.

And now, as he wearily rode into Englishtown, eager to report directly to Washington, to his dismay he saw that only now was the advance guard preparing to move out.

He had not been present when command of the advance guard was transferred from Lafayette to Charles Lee, and when he received news of that it had stunned him. Lafayette was still a very young man, but that was a virtue in an advance guard commander. It took the raw nerve and at times foolish valor that had yet been tempered by bitter experience to push an advance guard forward. Only now were the men under the command of Lee beginning to form up.

He spotted Dickinson, of the Jersey militia, and rode up to inquire as to their orders, only to be informed that there were no direct orders other than to probe forward cautiously, make contact with the enemy, and then await "developments."

Cursing loudly in German, he pressed back up the road, upon which, nearly four hours after first light, the first troops were finally beginning to move along.

Damn all! They should be on them even now. It was a moment all generals dreamed about. An enemy column, exhausted, demoralized, strung out on a road, with your own massed force ready to smash into them and roll them up, unit after unit. But he saw no such force now. Only men just recently roused, beginning to march forward, none of their regimental or brigade commanders with any sense of clear orders from their general other than "make contact, develop the situation, and then await further orders."

At last he rode into the village of Englishtown, the road clogged with disorganized men coming in from fields adjoining the town. Their spirits seemed high enough, but none clearly knew what they were doing other than marching east. And the heat. Already it was as hot at eight in the morning as it had been at noon yesterday. Hours that could have been used for marching before the boiling summer descended on them had been lost. In the Ukraine, both sides had known to take advantage of the cool of night and, when need be, sit out the midday heat. That advantage was being taken by the enemy, and squandered by General Lee.

He rode into Englishtown and asked repeatedly for General Washington, only to be told at last that the main van of the army was advancing from Cranbury but was still several hours away.

He had spent two days and nights without rest. It had been in fact a week solid of campaigning ever since riding into Philadelphia, and the push had at last caught up with him.

He needed Vogel's help to get out of the saddle. Du Ponceau went up to a house where a door was open. A woman was standing in the doorway, while out by the fence guarding the house, her children were lugging up buckets of well water and offering them to the troops slowly marching by. The men were grateful as they took out their tin cups and scooped up a cooling drink, shouting their thanks to the women and her children. Du Ponceau, without doubt displaying his usual French charm, chatted with her for a moment and returned.

"Madam Beaulieu graciously offers one of her beds for you to rest, sir," Du

Ponceau gasped. "She is a good patriot; her husband is French, no less, and a captain of militia. She will keep watch while we rest and inform us the moment the advance guard of General Washington and the rest of the army appears."

Friedrich needed to lean on Vogel's shoulder as he hobbled up to the house. Du Ponceau took their horses around to the barn to unsaddle and water them.

"Bonjour, monsieur," she offered as von Steuben gained the door. All he could do was smile, and doff his hat in reply, as she led the way into the house and to the rear and a small servant's room, bed freshly made.

She offered some breakfast but he refused, Vogel simply asking for some water. She returned a minute later with a pitcher, glistening with moisture, and two cups. He and Vogel drank eagerly and she withdrew, saying she would keep watch.

Von Steuben looked at the bed and then just collapsed, not even bothering to take off his boots and jacket. Vogel simply lay down on the floor. Azor looked at both of them, and then slowly walked outside to claim some more territory. The children laughed and offered him a bucket to drink from and then some scraps from their dinner of the night before. Du Ponceau, going into the room, found von Steuben on the bed, Vogel on the floor, both snoring loudly. Mustering what little energy he had left, he went back out to the front yard and simply lay down under the shade of a willow, requesting of Madam Beaulieu that she rouse him the moment she saw the approach of General Washington. Within minutes he was fast asleep as well.

As they slept, from far to the east came the distant echo of musketry.

CHAPTER NINETEEN

✳ ✳ ✳

Monmouth, New Jersey
June 20, 1778
10:00 AM

"Close it up boys, close it up." The chant was repeated over and over by the weary young captain, mounted on a swayback horse, riding along the line of march.

"Easy for him to say," Peter gasped. "Son of a bitch is going the other way."

The captain heard the comment, looked back at Peter, but said nothing and rode on, while those around Sergeant Wellsley chuckled.

Though he missed his old comrades from the headquarters company and especially his friend Sergeant Harris, men he had marched with and fought alongside for more than a year and whom he knew he could trust to stand by his side in battle, it was good to be back among those of his home state.

The day was already scorching hot, the temperature nearly equaling the worst of yesterday afternoon. As they marched, men were uncorking canteens and upending them. Sergeants were cursing them, telling them to save their water for when they'd really need it.

A low rise of ground was visible through the cloud of dust a quarter-mile ahead, beyond it coiling wisps of yellow-gray smoke. Distant shouts echoed, and the men around Peter talked excitedly. Another officer galloped by on the far side of the fencerow bordering the field.

"Come on, boys. Move it. Come on! We need you at the front."

Frustratingly, the column suddenly slowed to a stop, men bunching up, the regiment ahead coming to a halt. Confused cries ahead, curses, then the long roll of a drum. Another officer, mounted in the field to his left, waving a sword, pointing.

"Form line to the left!"

Peter, momentarily confused, looked around. The colonel of his regiment, who had been marching just in front of him, had momentarily disappeared from sight in the confusion. Then he saw him balanced precariously atop a split rail fence to his left.

"Over here, boys! Form up over here!"

The column Peter was in broke into a confused mass, swarming off the dust-cloaked road, pushing up over the split-rail fence, sections of it collapsing. Men spilled off, regained their footing, and rushed into a field of thigh-high hay, already toasted golden brown. Hundreds swarmed across the field in apparent confusion, men shouting excitedly, while on the far side of the low crest ahead, the rattle of musketry was turning into a continual roar, a cloud of smoke rising up. Along the crest men began to appear, running, staggering, looking back over their shoulders.

Peter found the colonel of his regiment.

"Line!" he shouted. "Get to the center with the flag, keep shouting the order to form line to the front!"

The gray-haired colonel, who had the look of a schoolmaster or preacher, his face red, florid, spectacles steamed, sweat streaming in rivulets down his face, nodded. Yet he remained atop the fencing, looking to the east.

"Christ in heaven, they're just on the other side of this ridge!" he cried.

"Form line!" Peter screamed, pulling the man down. The colonel looked at him in anger, and then realized what Peter wanted him to do. He nodded, shouting for the flag-bearer and drummer to follow him.

Together the four sprinted several dozen yards from the road, Peter looking about to see how the rest of the brigade was forming up. No commands from higher up had been given. He had caught a glimpse of Charles Lee an hour earlier, riding along the line of march, but nothing since.

He felt a knot in his stomach. Whatever was happening just beyond the low crest was coming closer.

"Here! Hold the flag up here!" Peter shouted. The colonel looked at him, nodded, grabbing hold of his regimental flag-bearer and fixing him in place.

"Form line!"

Frustrated, Peter stepped in front of the man.

"Second New Jersey Militia!" he cried, surprised by the power of his own voice, something else that von Steuben had taught them, calling it "command voice." "Regimental front, center on the flag!"

The swarm of men looked toward him.

"Come on, men! Remember the drill! Form line and get ready to give them hell!"

Some of the men recovered their wits and began to fall in, but the line was taking far too long to form. Peter stepped back half a dozen paces, saw where the First was attempting to form on the left, men still dashing in from the road. On the right, the other side of the road, the other two regiments of the brigade that had been leading the line of march were forming as well. However, some men had crested the low rise ahead and were pulling back, already rattled. Many of the men did not even bother to stop, but just kept on running to the rear.

The brigade commander, mounted, was in the middle of the lane, shouting curses at those fleeing.

Let them go, Peter swore inwardly. Focus on those still with you!

More men were now coming over the crest from ahead, no semblance of formation, some having already tossed muskets aside, running full-out. As they hit the battle line forming up, in places they started to trigger panic with cries that the British were charging.

Peter looked back at the men, standing before him wide-eyed, the colonel looking nervously toward the low crest.

"Prime and load your muskets!" Peter cried.

He was still shouldering his musket and he made a deliberate show of grounding his weapon, reaching into his cartridge box, pulling out a cartridge, tearing it open with his teeth, priming the pan, then ramming the rest of the cartridge down the barrel and reshouldering his musket.

His action triggered a response from the line. Men began to load, more than a few fumbling with their cartridges, a gap-toothed boy his own age looking straight at Peter, grinning nervously, forgetting to withdraw his ramrod as he reshouldered his musket. Peter trotted down the length of the line, musket at the shoulder. The colonel who was supposed to be in command just stood there, back to his men, looking toward the low crest as if mesmerized.

"Battalions!"

The cry was distant, barely heard. Peter tore his attention from the men he was responsible for, and saw the brigade commander now waving his sword and pointing toward the low crest. The regiments on the right, barely formed, surged forward, no real lines, just a surging tide.

Peter stopped by the side of the colonel.

"Sir, the brigade is advancing!"

The colonel nodded with the prompting, and held his sword high.

"Come on, lads!" he cried, pointing forward.

Peter sighed. A year ago he would not have even noticed, but now, after the months of drill, he knew that in the heat of battle, commands had to be precise, drilled over and over and over into the men so that they reacted without even really thinking. He dreaded what was undoubtedly ahead.

They surged up the slope, Peter turning, marching backwards, watching the line.

"Guide to the center! Guide to the flag!" he screamed over and over, and most of the men, hearing him, struggled to follow his orders. The drummer picked up the beat, almost to the tempo he had tried to train the boy to use.

A tree line on the next ridge was visible several hundred yards away, puffs of smoke hanging in the branches. Directly on the crest ahead a cannonball impacted, kicking up a spray of dirt, then bounding high overhead, clearly visible. Men ducked low. The crest was less than fifty yards off, then thirty, the broad, open valley ahead now visible. Smoke hung like a heavy curtain, motionless in the hot, humid stillness.

And then he saw them, a heavy skirmish line of British light infantrymen spaced three feet apart, each moving independently, firing, reloading, crouching down, firing again, then sprinting forward a dozen feet and repeating the action. As an elite unit they were used to triggering panic among their enemies even before the main attack line hit. They were supported, two hundred yards off, by several troops of dragoons who were trained to dash in with flashing sabers if and when their enemies were routed. On the opposite crest were at least eight to ten guns, barely visible in the smoke from their repeated discharges.

What was left of a ragged line of infantry——from their uniforms they looked to be New Englanders——was rapidly falling back, running, already coming up the slope. At the sight of them the men of his own unit slowed in shock.

It was going to be a very bad moment, Peter realized. Nothing was more demoralizing to green infantry than to have a defeated unit fleeing through their ranks.

He looked to the right of the line. The two regiments on the opposite side of the lane had gained the crest and stopped. Just as his own regiment reached the crest, the swarm of broken troops were upon them.

"We're ordered back! Fall back!"

Peter struggled to be heard above their cries.

"Hold, New Jersey. For Christ's sake, hold!"

Men began to peel away from his line, like leaves torn from a tree bowing over in a tempest.

"Hold, New Jersey! Hold!"

Within seconds he had lost a quarter of the men of the regiment. Others seemed ready to run, looking nervously at the advancing light infantry and, over their shoulders, to the safety of the rear.

The enemy skirmish line was a hundred yards off, advancing confidently. He could hear their shouted taunts as they slowed for a moment to reload at the sight of this new line awaiting them. Then they began to move forward.

Peter felt as if time was somehow distorting. A flood of thoughts washed through him in those few seconds. Surprisingly to him, he felt no fear. He felt nothing like the fear that had gripped him when for a few terrifying minutes at Brandywine it looked as if these same light infantry were about to overwhelm the headquarters guards and actually take Washington himself. But then, thank God, Lafayette and his men had swarmed in to the rescue.

He glanced back at the regiment of militia. They stood there, wide-eyed, most of them, about ready to break, but they maintained a semblance of the line he had tried to drill into them in a few short, precious weeks. The advancing enemy was only a heavy skirmish line, not solid regiments, though on the far ridge arrayed just behind the artillery he could see columns of those emerging from the woods and deploying.

The light infantry were too far ahead of the main line. And they were too few. We can smash them down, he thought to himself.

The range was down to seventy yards, extreme for a musket, but the time must be now! Some of the light infantry were kneeling down, taking aim, firing, one of the men in his ranks screaming, collapsing, tearing at his chest. In another few seconds they will panic, which was exactly what the superbly trained British light infantry was trying to trigger.

He looked to the colonel who just stood wooden, sword half-raised.

"First New Jersey Militia, poise your muskets!" Peter screamed.

As he did so he ran to the colonel's side, grabbed him by the shoulder, and shoved him toward the protection of the line. It was better than having him shredded by the fire of his own men.

"First New Jersey, take aim!"

Along with the flag-bearer and drummer, they now pushed into the middle of the line. He caught a glimpse of the light infantry before him. They had stopped their advance, some going down, hugging the ground.

"Fire!"

It was not really a volley, more a ragged burst, a rattle of musketry that swept the line. The smoke hung around them. Peter had not fired, intent on attempting to lead. He crouched low to judge the effect. It had caught the enemy light infantry off guard. Several of them were down, others were firing back, but they were not charging!

"First New Jersey, reload!"

A ragged cheer went up. The volley had had little real impact but the simple act of firing back had steadied the men. The smoke from their firing concealed them for a moment, and hid from them as well the terror of what they faced.

Peter stepped back in front of the line, running down its length, shouting encouragement.

Several of the men who had finished reloading shouldered their weapons and fired, the discharge of one peppering the side of Peter's face. If he had not seen the movement at the last second, he would have been directly in front of the man, his head blown off. Only turning and tucking his chin down low into his right shoulder at the last instant had saved his life.

"Hold your fire. Hold for volley fire!"

He spared a quick glance at the culprit, who was so intent on what he was doing he did not even realize how close he had come to killing a comrade.

Nevertheless, it made Peter realize that being in front now was far too dangerous. He shoved his way back through the line, making it a point to slap his musket hard into the side of the offender, who glared at him angrily.

"Watch where you shoot, you stupid bastard!" Peter snapped, and then he was behind the line.

"Second New Jersey! Fall back!"

The cry came from the road, the voice loud, clear. He looked toward the road, wondering who was giving such an insane order. They were on the crest; they had stalled the light infantry. The heavy infantry would have to advance across the open ground, and at least this militia could put half a dozen more volleys into them, while the broken ranks that had swarmed past them had a chance to reform.

"I am ordering you to fall back!"

The man shouting the command was standing in his stirrups, pointing his sword to the rear.

"It's a general!" someone cried.

Peter gazed at the man. It was indeed a general. It was Charles Lee.

The men around Peter hesitated, some beginning to pick up the cry. An officer beside Lee——it appeared to be the brigade commander——was arguing, pointing his sword forward. Lee cut him off with a violent sweep of his hand, almost as if he was prepared to strike the man down with his sword.

"I am General Lee! Fall back, men. Fall back! We're being flanked!"

And with that Lee set off at a gallop, heading to the rear.

At that instant the regiment around Peter broke, reminding him in a flash of memories of the panic he had witnessed far too many times.

"Hold!" he gasped, as if offering a protest, but no one heard him. He stood silent then, the entire regiment around him breaking and setting off at a run back to the west.

The enemy light infantry, which had hesitated, seeing the move, did not hesitate now and began to bound forward. From the far ridge the dragoon companies, seeing the retreat as well, began to surge forward, and yet again there was the distant bugle call, not the call for advance or charge, but the taunting call to a foxhunt.

Furious with rage, Peter shouldered his musket and for the briefest instant was tempted to turn about and see if he could drop Lee from the saddle.

He fixed his aim, though, on the advancing light infantry, took careful aim at a man aiming directly at him, and fired. A second later he felt a tug at his shoulder. He felt no pain at that instant but knew he had been clipped by a musket ball.

"Come on, boy! Run, damn it, run!"

It was the colonel of the regiment, grabbing him by his uninjured arm.

Instinct took the place of training. Peter turned and started the run. Behind him he could hear the growing thunder of hooves, the pounding kettle drumlike sound of cavalry coming in at a charge.

Form square. We're supposed to form square, he thought, but that thought was lost as he continued to run, gasping in the hot, humid, smoke-filled air.

The men with him plunged into a tree line bordering a meandering creek, jumping into the calf-deep flow, which was by now churned muddy. Men collapsed in the water, some just stopping there, unable to run farther under the blazing hot sun.

Around him hundreds of men seemed to be swarming to the rear, many casting aside muskets and peeling off uniform jackets so they could run faster. He caught another glimpse of Lee, now riding at a slow trot, shouting some undistinguishable orders.

"Damn you to hell!" Peter cried, tears of frustration clouding his eyes because his musket was soaked in the creek, barrel filled with water so that he could not even shoot at the man.

"Come on, lad." It was the colonel, still pulling him along. Looking back, he could see the line of dragoons, now spread out, driving their quarry before them.

"Told you it would never work," the colonel gasped as he pulled him along. "No sense in you getting killed for nothing."

The Road from Englishtown to Monmouth
11:30 AM

He had awakened with a start. The windowpane of his small, stiflingly hot room was rattling from the distant thump of artillery fire.

The fight was most definitely on!

He sat up, groaning. Though the past few days had filled his heart with an excitement and joy he had not known in years, von Steuben was again being reminded that he was most definitely a man well past middle age. The joy of being on the hunt a few days before was now replaced with infinite weariness. And yet, he could not shirk it now . . . today he sensed might very well be the most important day of his life . . . even if it was his last.

"Vogel," he croaked. The man was asleep on the floor, Azor curled up beside him. As he nudged Vogel with his foot, his servant opened his eyes.

Azor just gazed up at him and sighed.

"Come on, the battle has started," von Steuben said, barely able to speak because his throat was dry, almost constricted.

He went through the house and out onto the front porch. A column of troops was surging by. He caught a glimpse of a flag, men of Stirling's division, part of the main army. Most had their uniform jackets off, bundled up on their packs or simply cast aside in the boiling heat. The road was churned up into a cloud of dust, the men near ghostlike within it.

The woman of the house was nowhere to be seen. Under a willow he saw Du Ponceau fast asleep and went over, kicking him aggressively.

The man opened his eyes.

"Washington. Did he pass?"

Du Ponceau looked at him in confusion.

"Washington?"

"I asked the woman to tell me when she saw him," he offered. "Damn it, get the horses!"

He looked around and caught a glimpse of one of the children, coming from around the side of the house, lugging a pail of water.

"Boy," he cried. "Did you see General Washington?"

Frustrated, he realized he was speaking in German.

"General Washington?"

The boy started to talk, pointing east, toward the battle, but he couldn't understand a word. Vogel came out of the house, Azor following, stretching stiffly. Du Ponceau appeared, leading their horses. Von Steuben grabbed the bucket from the boy, offering it to his horse, which lapped up a few licks, and then in turn to Vogel's and Du Ponceau's horses, saving the last bit for Azor.

His two companions were mounted. He tossed the bucket to the boy and mounted. There was still no sight of the woman, and he wondered if, in all the confusion of the army passing, she had missed sight of Washington. Or might she have been a Tory at heart and just let him ride by? It didn't matter now.

He rode out the open gate as one regiment finished passing, another one just emerging out of the cloud of dust, their flag marking them as Pennsylvania. He waited for their approach.

"General Washington?" he shouted, and he pointed east.

"Think so, sir," a mounted colonel in the lead replied. "Ain't seen him but reckon he's ahead of us. Say, what the hell is going on up there?"

Von Steuben didn't give Du Ponceau time to reply as he turned and started east. His poor, overworked mount should have been rested for the day and not been driven back out like this in the heat, but there was nothing he could do about that now. He had to find Washington and report the enemy movements and his sense, as well, that Lee was not pushing ahead as ordered.

The street in the center of town was wide enough for him to trot alongside the column. Once out of the village, it narrowed. Now it was clogged with infantry, artillery, and wagons bringing up extra ammunition.

He forced his way off the road and into an adjoining field and set off as fast as his mount could carry him, barely above a canter.

The road to his right was packed solid with men, but they were moving forward in fits and starts, perhaps jogging for a hundred yards or so, men gasping in the heat, then coming to a stop, the way ahead jammed. March discipline, which he only wished he had had more time to instill in these men, was breaking down. A steady pace of three miles to the hour was far less exhausting than gaining a single mile in that same hour by running a few hundred yards, standing for minutes, creeping forward, stopping, then running again. Beyond that, this kind of marching demoralized the men, convincing them that their commanders were not in proper control.

The ground ahead was becoming difficult to traverse. There were sloping ravines covered with tangles of briars and overgrowth, and stretches of boggy ground out of which clouds of stinging insects swarmed, as if for them this battle was manna from heaven. He came up a long slope and ahead saw a church and then the sight he most feared, men falling back through the churchyard, some collapsing on the shady side or even crawling behind head-stones to seek the protection of even such a macabre shadow.

A regiment holding a fair semblance of order, actually marching back in column of fours, appeared. It was followed by another regiment, the second one dragging along several wounded lying in blankets, other men limping or cradling a wounded arm. Down off to his right several hundred yards away, he could see that the main column of Washington's advance was still tangled on the road.

Von Steuben forced a gallop toward the retreating men, Du Ponceau and Vogel by his side. Azor, unnerved by the rattle of musketry in the distance, reluctantly slunk along.

"What in hell is going on here?" von Steuben cried.

"We're flying from shadows." The reply came from a visibly distraught col-onel who was in tears and pointed back to the east.

"Lee is a poltroon, a damn fool, the son of a bitch," the man continued to cry. "There was no council of war last night, no orders given other than to march forward. We start to deploy, not sure of our position, and then he starts to cry for us to retreat. He's a poltroon, and, by Jehovah Himself, I will call that man out as a coward when I see him again."

Stopping in the shadow of the church to let his horse have a few moments in the shade, von Steuben half listened to the curses of the officers who began to gather round. The glare of the furnacelike sun was blinding as he tried to gaze across the field and marshy ground ahead. He could see a distant battle line of red, advancing into the marshy ground, moving toward their right, the American left. Down on the road, what sounded like a pitched battle had un-folded, the road and low ground obscured in smoke, shadowy lines moving out of the smoke. Men were pouring back to the west, some in panic, but many in fairly good order.

He looked again to the center and left.

"You will stop and rally here!" he shouted, looking back at the officers gathering around, some of them men he recognized from the long months at Valley Forge, others unknown, obviously commanders of militia.

"You know what to do, lads. You know how to fight those red-backed sons of bitches, don't you?"

He could tell that Du Ponceau was adding in a few more well-practiced strings of invective, and several of the men grinned, taking off their hats and offering a weak cheer.

"This is nothing. A mere skirmish, lads. Here is good ground. Now form your men into battle line like you've been taught, and be ready to move back forward to support the center or right!"

"Goddamn, at least someone knows what they're doing," came an enthusiastic reply.

He saluted, and rode out from the shadow of the church and past the hundreds of men who were slowing as they reached the low crest. He was not sure what to do next.

He stood in his stirrups, sword drawn. "Rally, you sons of bitches, you dogs," he cried out in German. Of those who knew him, or had heard of him, most did not understand a word, but they had heard stories that here was a man who could truly curse with the best of them, and they responded with a cheer, their officers racing about, shouting for them to fall back into line.

He raced across the flank of the slope, knots of men running past in the opposite direction. He really did not need directions now. The thick of the fight was on the main road ahead and he rode straight toward it, having to slow at times to push around men fleeing to the rear, or sometimes tangling up with other regiments from the main body of the army that were beginning to swing out into battle formation. And then he saw him, straight ahead, and indeed in the middle of the fight.

"Do not show your backs to them! Rally!"

Boiling with rage, General Washington rode back and forth across the area where he was trying to establish a new front to slow down the advancing enemy, who were less than three hundred yards off. Most of the panicked troops were now behind him, having far outrun their pursuers, who were keeping formation and advancing at a steady pace, believing they were driving a routed foe from the field.

He stood tall, gazing at the men who were reforming into ranks.

"You know me!" Washington cried. "And I know the mettle of what you are. And I now ask you . . . Can you fight?"

A ragged, halfhearted cheer greeted his words.

He looked to his right, where Anthony Wayne, explosive with rage over what had happened, was keeping two regiments of Pennsylvanians in line. Though the range was long, they delivered volley after volley.

He pointed toward Wayne's men.

"They have trained just as you have, my lads. Now will you let it be said that men of Pennsylvania can fight better than you?"

Even as he shouted encouragement, officers and sergeants were jostling men back into line.

"Now I ask you again. Will you fight?!"

This time his words were met by a cheer and then three huzzahs for the general.

"Get ready to give them everything you have. The rest of the army is form-ing up behind you in support!"

Wayne came galloping up to his side, swearing a blue streak.

"You must hold here, General Wayne," Washington announced, now lowering his voice. "The rest of the army is deploying out even now on the far side of that ravine." As he spoke he pointed back to the west, where, sev-eral hundred yards away, lines were beginning to shake out from column of march.

Wayne, face so soaked with sweat that it looked as if he had just emerged from swimming in a deep pool, nodded.

"Forgive me, sir, but God damn Lee! We had them by surprise and then he panicked, said our right was broken and we were outnumbered. I begged him, sir. I begged him in front of the men to hold, that you were coming up and would strike on the right in reply."

"I'm sorry, sir." His voice broke with rage and shame.

Washington extended a reassuring hand. He knew that for Wayne this fight was a personal test unlike any other. Though exonerated for what hap-pened at Paoli, Wayne had repeatedly sworn that in the next battle he would either have his revenge and regain his honor or die in the effort.

"Do not do anything foolish, General Wayne," Washington said sternly. "I need you today. Now, take command here."

"General Washington!" He turned to see another reassuring face. It was von Steuben, his staff trailing, the man's face a picture of fury.

"I am at your service, General," von Steuben cried, and he nodded.

"Move along the line, stiffen the men. This vanguard is to slow the enemy while our main body deploys."

"Sir, General Lee should be fighting this battle miles forward, overrunning the supply trains I saw last night."

Washington took it in.

"No time for that now. Go rally the men and then slowly pull back onto the main line, giving me time to get the rest of the army deployed. I thought I would find this battle three miles farther ahead and not here!"

Wayne and von Steuben saluted and rode back to the right . . . and then Washington saw him, crossing the field to the left, surrounded by staff, a knot of infantry falling back with him, his head lowered, his mount lathered with sweat.

At that instant, at the sight of Lee, the way he had led, the way he had fought battles, the lingering sense, across all the long years, that somehow, just somehow, the professionals who trained and fought in the armies of Europe were superior and perhaps even to be deferred to in some manner, forever vanished. Gone with it was any remaining core of self-doubt. While in the future he would seek counsel and advice, he would always do so with the knowledge that his instincts and his judgment would be the final arbiter of what needed to be done.

"General Lee!" he thundered, riding straight at the man. Lee looked up at him, eyes narrowing. Men who had been fleeing slowed to a stop, for, though in the middle of a battle being lost, they knew a new storm was about to explode.

"General Lee!"

Lee started to raise his hand to remove his hat in salute.

"In the name of God Almighty. What have you done here?"

"Sir. As ordered, I . . ."

"God's wounds, sir. I do not believe what I am seeing. What in hell are you doing?"

"Sir, the situation developed poorly . . ."

"Poorly? It is you, sir. Damn your soul, it is you, sir, who have behaved poorly."

Lee recoiled in shock.

"Sir, I object to that tone."

A pent-up rage, a fury that perhaps could be traced back across two years of frustration and defeat after defeat, at last exploded into the open.

Washington removed his hat, drew it back as if ready to strike Lee in a challenge, and then, thinking better of such behavior, hurled it to the ground.

"You are a strutting, arrogant, foul-mouthed poltroon. You came to this army boasting of all your skills and I was fool enough to believe in you."

"The men, sir, they began to break as I told you they would when facing the enemy in an open fight . . ."

"Damn your soul for your lying impudence. How dare you blame these good men for your failings?"

He looked at the enlisted men who now stood in a large knot around the two, silent, stunned that their General Washington, always so controlled in manner and voice, was speaking this way. The fact that his anger had finally taken such control over his emotions, that he was cursing at a fellow officer in front of enlisted men, if anything pushed him even further and made him even angrier.

"As Almighty God is my witness," he cried, looking up at the blazing hot heavens and then back at Lee, "this is the last time I shall ever listen to the likes of such arrogant strutting asses as you. I shall take my own counsel and I swear, by God, to listen to it. These men are soldiers and they will be led by proper soldiers and not by the likes of you, damn your soul."

He felt light-headed, fearing for a second that he would lose his grip on his saddle. The heat was nearly overwhelming his senses, that and a rage unlike any he had known or openly vented in years.

"Sir," Lee replied, his voice quavering but his eyes now filled with malice, "I am a gentleman and object to being spoken to in this way."

"Object? You dare to object. Well, sir, I object to your presence on this field."

"What?"

"General Lee, you are relieved of command."

"What?" Lee gazed at him, mouth open and closing like a fish out of water gasping for life.

"Mr. Lee, I relieve you from this battle, I relieve you from command. You are out of this army forever, as of this moment."

"I demand, sir, that you retract that. I shall seek a court of inquiry. I shall go to Congress itself for what you have said, for the insults you have leveled at me."

"Damn you to hell!" Washington roared, and he leaned forward menacingly, his massive frame towering over Lee. "Go to whomever you damn well please. Go to Congress, go to Gates, go to the damn king himself! Now get the hell out of my sight or I will personally whip you from this field!"

Lee shied back, one of his staff grabbing his reins, pulling him back farther.

Features paling in spite of the heat, Lee lowered his head and, with a raking of spurs so vicious that his horse whinnied from pain, rode off. Washington, still standing in his stirrups, glared at him as he left.

"By God," he heard one of the enlisted men gasp, "we got ourselves a fightin' general today."

He turned his gaze on the men, struggling to control his fury.

"Do you men still know how to fight?" he roared.

A primal cry erupted around him.

"Then fall in and show those redcoats over there"——he pointed back to the advancing British——"how Americans can stand and fight for their freedom!"

Breathing hard, face drenched with sweat, he turned back. His staff gazed at him awestruck.

He saw General Lafayette, silent, features immobile, and nodded to him.

"General Lafayette, you will assume command of Mr. Lee's men. General Wayne is holding the right. Those you can rally here are to hold, then only slowly give ground. The main body, even now, is preparing on the far side of the ravine. It is good ground and that is where we shall make our stand and then drive them from this field."

For once Lafayette did not offer his usual flourishes. He simply snapped off a salute and, turning, galloped off with a big grin on his boyish face. Lee was gone, and the army was going to fight like a real army . . . at last.

Billy Lee rode up and offered him a canteen, like Lafayette his features fixed, not daring to speak. He took a long drink, not objecting when Billy Lee poured some of the precious water out, soaking a large handkerchief and offering it so that he could wipe the sweat from his brow.

"Sir?"

It was one of the enlisted men. He vaguely remembered him, the boy who had been the guide at Trenton and then part of his guard. He was holding up his hat to return it.

"Thank you, son," and he took the hat back and put it on.

The boy was grinning at him.

"No, sir. It is I who thank you." Suddenly red-faced, the youth dashed off to fall in with the battle line.

"Give them hell, boys! Make it even hotter for them than this day already has," Washington cried. Turning, he galloped back up the long slope to the west to see to the deployment of his main line of battle.

Noon: In Front of the "West Ravine"

"Keep pushing them! Keep pushing them!"

Allen van Dorn stalked behind the skirmish line, Captain André at his side. The fight had been going on now for almost five hours. Most of it had been an open-field chase, typical of so many battles here in America. Within minutes of first contact with their advancing lines, two miles to the east, the enemy had wavered and then without warning had just simply broken.

It most likely would have been over by now except for the heat and the rough——and in many places marshy——ground that slowed their advance to a crawl. The light infantry was sloshing through sucking mud, at times sinking nearly to their knees. And all the time, plagues of biting mosquitoes and gnats covered them, getting into their eyes, ears, and nostrils. Their water was gone, some of the men in desperation scooping up muddy mouthfuls of slimy liquid out of their footprints in the marshes, and then taking the mud to cover their faces in an effort to keep the insects off. But within minutes the sweat pouring down their faces had washed the mud off.

And then, increasingly, men began to simply stop sweating. They would stagger along for a few more minutes and then just silently collapse, as dead as if they had been struck in the heart by a bullet.

He looked back anxiously at André, who seemed to have recovered somewhat from the heat of the previous day. But he knew the man was still weak from heat exhaustion . . . and he was feeling that same weakness. Allen longed to shuck off the heavy red wool jacket, but dared not. In the smoke and confusion, if he should be seen with just a white linen shirt, he might be taken for a rebel straggler, and with his local accent no appeal would spare him from being taken prisoner or, more likely, being shot or bayoneted on the spot.

For several minutes he had clearly seen General Washington in the fray, just north of the road, surrounded by a knot of officers. He had informed André, and the captain had tried to press the light infantry forward into range, but the men were exhausted. They were moving woodenly, slowing as they got barely into range and firing several ragged volleys, more than a few of them then crying that they were out of ammunition.

Their resupply wagon, which should have been following the main body of regiments advancing behind them, could not be found.

"Light infantry of Grey's command! Halt!"

The cry echoed up and down the line. And the hundreds of skirmishers and dragoons slowed to a stop, many of the men sitting down, some just collapsing. Those still capable tried finding shelter under the tangle of growth sprouting in the marshy ground.

General Grey was in the middle of the road, André heading over to him, Allen following.

"A good drive of the game," Grey announced, "but damn hot work it is. Damn rebels run too damn fast."

Fighting was still heavy down to the left, where a line of their own heavy infantry, coming into range, was now engaging. To the right flank, other units were closing in.

"Something is bracing them, though, sir," Allen offered, and Grey looked down at him.

"How's that?"

"They were running like sheep . . ."

"As they usually do," Grey interrupted.

"But they rallied just ahead."

"Yes, yes, saw that too. That damn Washington. Saw him. André, too bad our lads couldn't have gotten a bit closer, that would have really made hash of them this day. Shoot the lead dog and the rest of the pack will run."

Allen stiffened slightly at the way Grey had called Washington a dog. That was not the man he remembered seeing at Trenton, or the one who had showed pity to the brother of one of his fallen men, and offered him immediate parole and exchange.

"Yes, he was there, sir, and there is something different about them this day," Allen offered, ducking low as the enemy line, a hundred yards off, fired a volley, several balls humming by far too close.

Grey sniffed derisively.

There was a round of laughter from Grey's staff when not a single shot hit.

"Can we have a flag of truce for a moment," said the major that Allen detested, laughing. "You there, Allen, you're a provincial and understand their barbarous jargon. Go over there and tell him that 'Flintless Grey' and his light infantry are at their beck and call for a duel with bayonets, by God."

"You go tell him," Allen snapped, and then paused, "sir."

"You impudent pup. After this battle . . ."

"I am at your call, sir," Allen snarled back, "any time you wish."

"Both of you!" Grey cried. "I'll put both of you on report. And you, Mr. van Dorn, I'll put you up on charges if you dare to challenge a superior officer to a duel."

Allen glared at the major with contempt.

"Mr. Van Dorn!"

He turned back to Grey and saluted.

"My apologies, sir. Heat of battle."

"You say that you sense something. Well, by God, I have you on my staff to tell me about these rebel neighbors of yours, now tell me, damn it."

"Look at those lines forming, sir. They did not break and panic when we drove back their first attack. They are holding, and even some of those who broke before are standing now."

"And giving back in an orderly way, by God," the major interjected, and pointed forward.

He was right. The advance line of rallied troops was indeed now retiring, but doing so slowly, coming about every minute or so to fire another volley even though the range was far too long.

Directly ahead, what was left of the first wave of the American attack was falling back, not in confusion but rather moving to merge into the main line. From the other side of the field, British heavy infantry were struggling to advance through the marshy ground.

"Light infantry to rest. Get the men watered and resupplied with the ammunition, which should be coming forward," Grey announced.

He scanned the enemy position.

"We might have a half hour, an hour at most, and then the chase will be on again. Now move quickly, men!"

Allen looked back toward the retreating American line and wondered who was with them this day, and what now compelled them to fight in a manner he sensed was different from anything the British had ever faced from them before.

Englishtown
12:30 PM

His horse stumbled as he rounded the bend in the road, and then it started to collapse. Von Steuben did not even rein in. The poor beast simply stopped, head lowered, panting.

He dismounted and reached for the canteen he had picked up off the body of a dead man lying by the side of the road. Taking off his hat, he poured what little water there was left into it, and set his hat on the ground for the poor horse. He looked back over his shoulder. Du Ponceau was slowly trailing behind, joined by Vogel, who had been thoroughly shaken when a spent musket ball had struck him in the back, perhaps cracking one of his ribs. The poor man was petrified by the experience, and no matter how many times he and Du Ponceau had reassured him that the round had not penetrated and that there was no blood, Vogel kept reaching nervously back, expecting to find a hole.

There was a moment of fear as he watched the two approach. Poor Azor was nowhere to be found. Then at last he saw his beloved companion, who was engaged in his first battle and not doing all that well, slinking at times on his belly and yowling pitifully whenever a cannonball shrieked by . . . much to the amusement of the men that his owner had been rallying.

After helping Wayne with the right flank, von Steuben had ridden back to the center and again joined Washington, who was now with the main line along the top of the low ravine. The general had picked the ground well; it was an exceptionally good place to receive an attack. Washington had ordered him to ride back to Englishtown, there to rally the men of Lee's command who had completely broken and bring them back into the fight.

"And General Lee?" he had asked.

Washington glared at him coldly at the mere mention of the name.

"He is removed from command and from this army!"

"Yes, General!" von Steuben replied in English, and set off.

He waited another minute for Vogel to come up.

"Please find water for this poor beast"——he handed up the reins—— "and get him back to the house of that forgetful woman. Get his saddle off, rub him down well, and see if you can soak a blanket in water and put it over him."

He reached down and scratched Azor's ear, the poor animal trembling, tongue lolling out, dripping saliva.

"Water for Azor too and see if the woman will lock him inside until the battle is over. Tell her I will pay."

"Yes, sir," Vogel croaked. Von Steuben could see the man was played out, barely sweating, which was truly a bad sign.

"And into a springhouse there, if she has one, for you, my friend. Your day out here is finished."

"Sir, may I say you don't look too good yourself."

He forced a laugh. "I have not had this much excitement in years, that's all."

Du Ponceau came up, and von Steuben could see the man was plainly finished and indeed suffering from heatstroke, gasping for air, swaying in the saddle.

"You, too, my friend, both of you go rest."

"Sir?"

"Don't worry, I'll find you before I go back in."

It was a lie. He knew if he pushed them any further it might very well kill them.

As for himself, he wasn't sure either. He shrugged inwardly. If I die from this, he thought, it will be a good end, a soldier's end.

Besides, he still had orders to follow.

The street ahead was nearly empty, but to either side, under what little shade could be found, men by the hundreds had collapsed. From within several homes he could hear cries of anguish, and through an open door he saw a surgeon at work, taking off a man's arm, several men holding the victim down. By the side of the house were half a dozen severed limbs, those nearby watching wide-eyed.

Damn them. Soldiers, especially panicked men, should never be allowed to see what transpired in a hospital.

"Vogel?" he gasped. He looked around, ready to order his assistant to go over, close the door, and find someone to haul the limbs out behind the barn and start burying them. But Vogel was already out of earshot.

He did not have time for this, and staggered on up the main street, looking back and forth, the men lying to either side of the road watching him in turn. A few of them got up at the sight of him and began to slowly shuffle down the road, west, away from the battle. He ignored them.

He reached the tavern that he heard had been Lee's headquarters the day before. Under the shade of the front porch was a knot of men, in the middle of them Charles Lee. He was holding a tankard and leaning against a beam supporting the front awning of the inn.

Lee looked up at him as he approached. No one spoke, no one offered him a tankard, and he made it a point not to salute.

"Why are you here?" Lee asked warily.

"General Washington orders me to rally these men," he replied in broken English.

Lee shook his head ruefully.

"They are played out, sir. They've seen enough."

He was not sure what Lee said, but he sensed the tone of it.

"They are *Soldaten*," von Steuben snapped. "They will fight."

Lee gazed at him, and to von Steuben's dismay and shame, the man's eyes filled with tears and he began to ramble. He could barely follow what Lee was saying. He was obviously undone.

"I take command," von Steuben finally snapped, loud enough so that those watching even from the other side of the street could hear.

Without waiting for a reply, he turned his back on Lee and stepped into the middle of the street.

"Listen to me!" he shouted. "I am General von Steuben!"

His gaze swept those watching him.

"General Washington orders you to fight!"

A few responded, standing up.

He looked around yet again and then broke into a torrent of his finest curses, in German, an occasional few words in English coming through. Cursing the British, cursing the damn heat, cursing any man who was a coward who would not fight for his own home and liberty. A couple of men in the crowd actually started to laugh, a few of them who knew German translating for the others.

More and more came to their feet.

"You are dogs and I love you for it!" von Steuben cried in German. "Stinking, foul-mouthed Americans, but will you let it be said by those damn English that you are cowards?"

"The battle is this way and I will lead you to it and there give the lobsters a kick in the ass they will never forget!" He pointed back to the east.

More and more men came out from behind alleyways, from under trees and porches and from inside houses. Ever so slowly, they filled the street. Units were all mingled; it would take forever to have them form into their individual regiments and companies. He recognized several faces. They knew the drill. Once clear of the town he would simply swing them into a battle line and lead them forward.

If ever there was a moment to live for, he thought with a smile, it was this. By God, it was indeed better than Minden. If he had to choose between this moment and another chance to be decorated by the king himself, he knew which he would choose.

"Come, my children. Let us find a damn good fight!"

With sword raised high, he led them back into the fray.

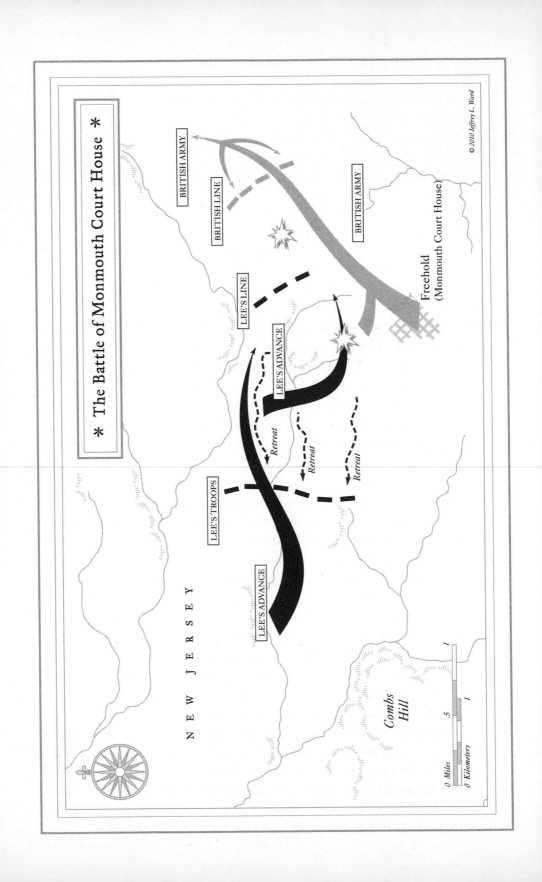

* The Battle of Monmouth Court House *

BRITISH ARMY

BRITISH LINE

BRITISH ARMY

Freehold
(Monmouth Court House)

LEE'S LINE

LEE'S ADVANCE

Retreat

Retreat

Retreat

LEE'S TROOPS

LEE'S ADVANCE

NEW JERSEY

Combs
Hill

0 Miles   .5   1

0 Kilometers   1

© 2010 Jeffrey L. Ward

CHAPTER TWENTY

* * *

"Here they come!"

General George Washington rode down the length of his battle line. The British had moved their artillery up to the opposite ridge on the far side of the ravine and the marshy ground beyond, and had been pounding his line for nearly an hour.

And the men had held.

Counter-battery fire from his own guns took out several of the British fieldpieces, each successful hit, visible to his ranks, triggering resounding cheers. Riding up to one battery to congratulate them on their successful shooting, he was stunned and impressed to see a woman manning the swabber for the barrel of the gun, exhorting the men around her to stand in the fight even though her husband had just been killed.

Throughout the barrage and counterbarrage the men had stood firm. Most of the regiments had been ordered to lie down, but there had been little comfort there, for they were out in broad, open fields, under the flaming heat of a noonday sun. Not one canteen in ten still had a drop of water in it. Drummer boys had been detailed off to take canteens and run back behind the lines to a distant creek, or seek out a nearby well or spring for refills.

Washington had established a command post under a grove of spreading elm trees, leaving most of his staff there to carry dispatches as they came in while he rode along the line to inspect. The British artillery had quickly spotted the position and turned an entire battery on it. Rather there than against his infantry, he thought, but still he was nervous for the men he had left behind until, riding close by, he saw, to his absolute delight, Billy Lee and several other servants wearing uniform jackets and hats, standing out in the open and posing as if they were the commanders, and thereby drawing the fire to themselves . . . and standing absolutely unflinching, to the cheers of the men watching as round shot bounded to either side of them and clipped through the trees overhead. Never once did the pseudo-officers duck.

And now the main attack was coming on hard and fast. Clinton and Cornwallis were pushing in every regiment they had. If Lee's attack had gone in as he had planned, they would have caught the British still in camp or strung out along the road for miles. With the time Lee's timidity or cowardice had bought them, the British professionals were now fully arrayed.

"As terrible as an army with banners," one of the men in the line in front of him gasped, as the smoke from the artillery fire lifted for a moment, revealing the advancing host.

A minister was out in front of the regiment——men of Stirling's command, a Massachusetts brigade——holding up a Bible. "Though a thousand fall at thy side, and ten thousand at thy right hand, it shall not come nigh unto thee," he intoned.

Washington removed his hat as he rode behind the line. Some of the men prayed on their knees.

Range was down to a hundred and fifty yards, and now out of the marshy ground the enemy came on, their drumbeat sounding the call, holding back, holding the pace of their advance back in the mind-numbing heat until they were within musket range.

"Up, men, up!" The cry echoed along the line. Men came to attention, muskets already loaded, the weapons at the shoulder. The sight sent a shiver down Washington's spine, a battle front a quarter-mile across, thousands of men. The moment of the supreme test was at hand.

Range a hundred yards, ninety, eighty. He could clearly see the British regimental banners, the flag-bearers waving their colors back and forth slowly to make them visible, since the hot, moisture-drenched air of early afternoon was absolutely still. Enemies he had faced before: men of the Grenadiers, their high, brass-capped hats glinting in the sunlight; men of the seasoned Forty-fourth; Twenty-third; the elite Coldstream Guards; Welsh Fusiliers; and, most feared of all, the Black Watch, in their dark tartans, pipers playing.

On so many a field, the mere sight of such an array advancing would cause men by the hundreds to melt out of the ranks and stream to the rear. Here and there a lone man did turn, throwing aside his musket, and start to run. But it was only a few, those in the ranks barely sparing them a backward glance. For the men running had always been the first to run. But today, on this day, no one else followed.

He could already sense it, a change, even an eagerness to be at it. The brunt of battle earlier in the day had been borne by the men of Lee's division, some of whom had been reformed by von Steuben and were now the reserve lines in the center. As for the rest, the men of Stirling, Greene, those of Wayne's regiments who had not been pressed forward earlier, this was now their moment. They had marched half a dozen miles in searing tropical heat. They had seen panic, panic that at Long Island had spread like a wildfire across a plain of dry summer wheat, but not now, not this time.

A cry started to echo up from the line, one man at first, then dozens, and then hundreds.

"Come on! Come on, you bastards! Come and try us! Come on!"

Officers shouted for the men to be silent, but their rage could no longer be contained. They had been driven, terrified, disdained, wounded, at times their friends murdered as they begged to surrender on a dozen fields. Only two hours ago some of them had run, but even they had not retreated of their own accord. Rather, they had been ordered back by the fear harbored by a man who would never be allowed to lead them again.

And now they were filled with rage . . . and with a bitter, angry pride. In the distance Washington could hear a booming voice, that of von Steuben, almost laughing, shouting something in German, the men cheering.

Eighty yards were down to seventy and still they were coming . . .

And still the Americans were standing.

"Battalion!" The cry raced along the line. To both right and left battle was already joined, volleys pealing, smoke obscuring all. In the center it was about to begin. Regimental names were being called out.

"Poise your muskets!"

The rattle of hundreds of weapons being raised up.

"Take aim!"

And now the thrilling sight of hundreds of muskets, as if guided by a single hand, being leveled, pointed downrange.

A last glimpse of the enemy. Some of the regiments stopped, others tried to press the advance to bluff their opponents into fear.

"Fire!"

An explosive tearing roar thundered along the line, regiment after regiment discharging their weapons as if a single finger pulled the trigger. Great gouts of yellow-gray smoke roiled out.

"Reload!"

The command raced along the line, officers stepping out of the ranks for a few seconds, crouching low, trying to see under the smoke. It was impossible to tell the impact. Ears still ringing from the massed volley, Washington could still hear the commands from the other side, nearly exactly the same, as their volley fire was returned by the British, flashes of their muskets, sheets of flame torching in front of him, the beelike hissing of the musket balls buzzing to either side of him. Along the line directly in front of him, half a dozen men dropped. A man staggered backwards, screaming, holding his hands to his face, blood gushing out between his fingers. He collapsed to his knees, continuing to scream. A few more men broke, turned, and ran, but the others continued to load.

"Faster boys, faster! Hold for the volley. Get ready!"

The enemy, faster at the reload, fired a second volley, and more men collapsed. But the line held and only seconds later the Massachusetts men leveled their muskets, aiming down into the cloud of smoke enveloping the field, and returned fire.

He pressed along the line. There was another volley from a British regiment, few shots hitting, for it was now impossible to aim due to all the smoke. One of his regiments went to the complex move of one line firing while the other reloaded, and the attempt paid off well when, out of the smoke, shadowy forms appeared, coming on at the double, holding perfect formation. The feared Black Watch! After the exchange of half a dozen volleys, they believed the time was right to come forward with the bayonet and rout a shaken and demoralized enemy.

The regiment facing them kept their nerve, and at a range of less than ten yards, the first rank leveled and fired a volley into the Scotsmen's faces. Dozens dropped in that second. The charge slowed. The men facing them screamed with rage now and, lowering bayonets as ordered, countercharged. And for the first time since the beginning of the war, one of the few times in their long and storied history of victory, the Black Watch gave back in confusion. Many of the Americans had inverted their muskets and were using them as clubs, and were now beginning to press down off the ridge.

"Not yet!" Washington cried, and started down the hill. A spontaneous charge, rather than a disciplined advance, could break the continuity of his own line and, in the confusion that followed, against an enemy he sensed was not yet broken, lead to a disastrous countercharge. He had witnessed it often enough on the frontier, the Indians masters at feigning a panicked retreat, only to lead their pursuers into a well-prepared trap and slaughter.

The men heard his cry and slowed.

"Gallant lads! Gallant. Hold the line. We charge when all are ready! Now we hold the line."

The men greeted his compliments with a cheer but only reluctantly retired the few dozen paces back up the slope, but in those few seconds all saw the wisdom, as enemy regiments to either side of the Black Watch turned their fire to oblique right and oblique left, crisscrossing with musket balls where proud regiments would have been advancing.

A few regiments broke into independent fire at will, but most held to von Steuben's training, seeing, on the field of battle, the wisdom of what he taught. The smashing hammerlike blows of a volley stunned like a well-delivered punch rather than mere slaps. When the enemy too began to surge forward, men from several regiments would be directed to fire at the oblique, doubling and tripling the blows on a particular unit, driving it back.

And, as each enemy surge was followed by their fire driving it back, the confidence of his men surged as it never had before.

Men became caught up in the hysteria of battle: shouting, cheering, some crying from a strange mixture of joy and anguish, for they were absorbing hammer blows as well. Men were dropping by the score. The wounded crawled or hobbled to the rear, but without help——the men were under strict orders that, unless in retreat, the wounded were to tend to themselves. Here and there he could see some of the women of the army, crouching low, moving up to help the injured. Yet more women were pacing behind the firing line, handing out canteens, grabbing canteens from men who were parched dry until, burdened down with two or three dozen, they ran off to the rear to refill them with muddy water and then lug them back up to the line. He saw more than one woman simply collapse, either from the heat or enemy fire.

Hundreds of men along the line were down. As he rode along the ranks he could see that it was not enemy fire felling them, it was the heat. In the thick, coiling smoke one could not see a dozen paces, and men felt as if they were choking in the smoke of a furnace.

It was nearly impossible to see anything clearly. The smoke seemed to trap the thunder of battle, pressing in on their ears so it felt as if they would burst.

Mingled in were the screams of the wounded and dying, the hissing buzz of bullets, the howl of round shot, and the dreadful thwacking sound of bullets hitting men, as if someone with an open hand was slapping another.

Some would feel a sharp tug on a sleeve or trouser leg, see blood, shake the limb, and then with a curse just resume loading and firing. More than a few of those, not realizing that the shot had severed an artery and that they were bleeding out, would continue fighting until the world grew dim and they fell.

Through it all Washington continued to ride back and forth behind the volley line, shouting encouragement or passing a quick order as couriers came up bearing news from the left and right flanks. On the right Wayne reported that he had started to turn their line and thought he saw a position for artillery. He requested permission to ask Knox to bring up the reserve batteries, and Washington readily agreed. In a momentary lull he could hear Knox's booming voice, urging his gunners forward.

He rode back up the line and caught a glimpse of the preacher, stretched out behind the line, hands folded over his Bible, a round bullet hole in his forehead out of which leaked brains and blood.

It had come "nigh on to thee," he thought sadly, as it had for many a man along the line, but, by God, they were holding and fighting in a manner he had never seen before.

His Americans were fighting like professionals.

As he rode along the line a cry started to go up: "Ammunition, we need ammunition!"

Each man had gone into the fight with twenty-four rounds in his cartridge box. Rarely had they held after firing but six to eight rounds. Now they had emptied their boxes and were screaming for more ammunition to be brought up.

Behind the line, men and women were lugging up boxes of cartridges, smashing the lids off with musket butts, scooping out hatfuls of rounds and going up to the volley line, stuffing cartridges into eager hands.

But after thirty or more rounds it was nearly impossible to continue to fire the muskets. In the heat the barrels were so hot that men suffered second-degree burns if they touched the metal, skin peeling off and cooking. The sharp edges of flints had been worn smooth and in some cases were cracking and shattering.

In the high humidity, after every shot the heat of the powder ignited in the pan by the touch hole, and then, cooling, triggered condensation so that the pan became filled with a thick black sludge that had to be wiped clean after every shot. Veterans knew to have a piece of rag tied around the strap of their cartridge box, using it to wipe the pan clean and clean the facing of the flint as well. In their excitement, though, more than one man would run his finger across the flint, pressing down too hard, and receive a painful cut that often sliced to the bone.

Musket balls, sized only three-hundredths of an inch smaller than the barrels, no longer could be dropped down smoothly. After ten to fifteen shots a man would have to lean into his steel ramrod to force the round down. Now, after twenty-five to thirty, the task was nearly impossible, the rounds having to be hammered down with repeated blows. With the extreme heat and sparks lingering in the barrels, more than one man lost fingers and even a hand when his musket fired prematurely. If he did not seat the bullet firmly but left it lodged in the middle of the barrel, at times the gun barrel would explode.

Men began to cast aside their own muskets, picking up those from men who had been wounded or killed early on, or men who had fainted or dropped their weapons and fled.

Sergeants began to pull men off the line, several at a time, and as women brought up fresh canteens of water, the precious fluid, rather than going down parched throats, was instead poured down barrels, the weapons so hot that water flashed to steam, gurgled and boiled as it trickled in a black sludge out of the touch hole by the pan. Some men tried to urinate down the barrels. But only a few could do so——the heat was so intense and they had sweated so profusely that they had nothing within them to give. A couple of men, attempting this delicate maneuver, simply burned themselves and hopped about in anguish, triggering gales of ribald laughter especially from the women staggering by, carrying the canteens and ammunition boxes and helping with the wounded. Bits of rag were wrapped around ramrods and forced down the barrels to try to clear them.

Within many of the regiments, less than half of the muskets——in some cases only a third——were still firing.

Washington could sense the fire slackening from the enemy side as well. Now was the most crucial of moments, something von Steuben had talked about in training exercises with him and officers of his staff and the various brigades, but which they never had time to drill for. Regiments were going to have to be pulled from the volley line and filed to the rear, where they could clean weapons and rest for a few minutes, have all canteens refilled, and be sent back in.

Wayne and others had questioned why they could not just "leap frog" the depleted regiments back, but von Steuben had been vehement in his reply.

"First, at such a moment, if men are told to retire, it might turn into a rout, and when they hit the reserve line, they might rout as well."

Wayne had sensed that the German was not telling the whole truth; that, at least in this army, until far better trained, if exhausted men were ordered to retire, they might very well bolt and run, taking the reserves with them.

"Second, under cover of intense musket fire and smoke, if one regiment is filed out and another placed into action with little or no interruption, it will shake the enemy's heart. For suddenly our fire will redouble while they are exhausted, and their morale will be shaken."

All had nodded in agreement with that point, having experienced it from the receiving end——when, out of the clouds of smoke, sharp fresh volleys ignited. If any of their own men were still hanging on, that was usually the moment they broke.

The British were already trading off regiments from their reserve, but at least from their vantage point farther up the slope, the Americans could glimpse what was being done, officers shouting reassurances to their own men to hold on and continue to pour it in.

Washington turned and rode back to where the reserve lines waited, concealed a hundred yards behind the slope. They were men formerly of Lee's command, now under Lafayette.

All they needed was his motion waving his sword and pointing forward. The young general did not need verbal orders. Men who had run earlier in the day stood up and began to advance, muskets shouldered high. At the sight of their general pointing the way they began to cheer.

Von Steuben, on foot, was out front as well, red-faced, gasping for air, but gamely leading the men forward, shouting at them in what they could only guess were the foulest of German oaths.

Washington rode up to von Steuben and leaned over and extended his hand, which von Steuben grasped.

"God bless you this day, sir!" Washington cried. "It is working. By God, it is working thanks to you!"

"*Jawohl, mein General!*"

And from the right there came a startling sound, which caused his heart to leap for a moment, but then he broke into the broadest of grins. Knox's artillery was opening up. A full battery of six-pounders positioned at a right angle to the enemy line was pouring down solid shot and grape from the crest of Combs Hill.

"Feed it to them, damn them!" he cried. "Feed it to them!"

. . .

"My God, what the hell is that?" Captain André cried, turning to his left. In the confusion and smoke of the battle directly to his front, neither Allen nor he had paid much attention to anything happening elsewhere.

Their men, hunkered down behind a hedgerow, were curled up into the narrow shade offered under the blazing early afternoon sun. They had found a brackish creek, dragging bleeding bodies and the half-drowned wounded of both sides out of it and, under John's strict orders, not harming the enemy wounded, before filling their canteens with the muddy water.

Ammunition had finally been brought up, corporals and sergeants smashing open the boxes and going down the line, passing out cartridges. Several of the light infantrymen died while in the shade, already too far gone from the heat. More than a few were in the throes of sunstroke, vomiting, shaking, their comrades stripping them down and forcing them into the muddy water to try to cool their bodies.

Allen, to the mocking disdain of more than a few of his British comrades while his back was turned, was taking canteens from the American wounded, going down to the filthy creek to refill them, and returning them, helping more than one man to sit up so he could drink.

"You one of them?" a man, shot in the stomach, gasped.

"Yes."

"You sound Jersey to me."

"I am. From Trenton. And you?'

"Springfield, damn your soul." The dying man pushed the canteen away from his lips. Allen lowered his head, put the canteen by the man's side, and went on to help the next man.

General Grey was nowhere to be seen or found, having gone forward with the Grenadier that had been assigned to his division, leaving the light infantry behind to recuperate from their morning exertions.

As the heavy lines of Grenadiers and Guards and the serried ranks of infantry had swept forward, Allen half expected that within minutes the battle would hit its climax and then sweep on. He dreaded the thought that he and the men he was with would be thrown back into the fight.

But the volley and countervolleys had thundered on for more than an hour. Men had cheered as the Forty-second, the legendary Black Watch, attempted a charge on the center, followed minutes later farther to the right by the Coldstream, supported en echelon by the Twenty-third. To the stunned disbelief of all watching, these troops had been repulsed from the low crest.

Men by the hundreds were now pouring back from the volley line. Dragoons had begun to ride back and forth behind the line, shouting at the men to "show blood to pass," and many were indeed wounded, reaching the creek bed where the light infantry rested and collapsing. Increasingly, though, they were men just simply exhausted and played out beyond caring. They could be flogged, beaten, threatened with the point of a sword or a cocked pistol and still they staggered on, or just simply collapsed. The reserve position was filling up with men dead or dying from the heat.

And now something was happening to the left.

Allen was helping an elderly man from, of all places, Bordentown, just down the road from where he lived. He was a distant kinsman of Elizabeth's. Using a discarded saber and blanket to fashion an awning to keep the sun off the man's face, Allen stood up to see what André was shouting about.

Through the clouds of smoke he could see brilliant flashes, followed a few seconds later by a howling clattering noise.

"Grapeshot into our flank!" André cried. "God damn them, how did they get those guns there?"

There was another volley from the battery and Allen could see shadows of movement in the ranks of heavy infantry.

They were beginning to fall back!

Those British light infantrymen still capable of action began to stand up. They were spectators witnessing a drama, but they knew they were about to be called back onto the stage.

Most of them had already cleaned their muskets, but many now resumed the task, dipping strips of rags into the muddy water, wrapping them tightly around their ramrods, and forcing them down the barrels to swab them clean. This was followed by a dry piece of rag to make sure the barrels were dry. Frizzens, pans, and flints were wiped clean. Though shaken, these men were far from ready to quit this fight, Allen realized.

Sergeants shouted orders for the light infantry to stand to at proper intervals and be ready, those too sick to fight and the wounded to make their own way to the rear. Wounded light infantry struggled to their feet, more than a few terrified of the fate that might befall them if taken prisoner, especially by Mad Anthony's men.

And now the flood hit them. By the hundreds, line regiments with glorious names were falling back, most moving in some semblance of order, stopping every fifty paces or so to deliver a ragged volley, regimental pride formed across generations preventing them from fully breaking even now, as artillery fire from the flank plowed into their ranks. A single shot could bowl over four, six, even eight to ten men into a bloodied, tangled mass.

"My light infantry!"

Allen looked up. It was Grey on the road, General Clinton by his side.

"Men. We will hold them here while the main body retires!"

Grey pushed his mount, barely able to walk, blood streaming from wounds to its right thigh and rear quarter, off the road and down into the narrow creek bed.

"We will hold them here as the main body retires!"

Never had he given such an order before! Always it had been for the light infantry to charge at the double-quick, "in and after them now, my lads, and show no mercy!"

But not now, not in this blinding heat and frightful cross fire pouring down from the hill to their right, and a resurging rattle of volley fire to their front.

"You said, earlier?"

Allen felt a hand on his shoulder. It was André.

Allen could not reply.

"Just remember, my friend. Never remind a general of a mistake you warned him about earlier. Bad form, you know, and not good for promotion."

André forced a smile and, with drawn sword, left him to go down the line.

"Now, men. Now!"

He was not sure who shouted the command, but it filled Peter's heart with a savage joy. He believed what was happening, for his own eyes told him so, and yet he found it nearly impossible to believe.

Four, maybe six hours ago he had seen his army, his comrades, behave as they had in half a dozen other stand-up fights. They had advanced with courage, but then within minutes were beaten down by the unrelenting volleys of the enemy, broken and demoralized. A cry would go up to retreat and it would turn to a rout. The victories at Trenton and Princeton had, in the first case, been won by total surprise and, in the second case as well, by a surprise and then a mad rush of desperate men closing with the enemy before the British musketry delivered in disciplined fire could tear them apart.

But now, this afternoon? It had been like witnessing a holy miracle. This time it was the disciplined, trained volley fire of his comrades, firing again and again and again, under a sun that was like the furnace of hell, that broke the enemy apart in an open-field fight . . . until, at last, their flank had been gained, just as von Steuben had promised it could be if they held the center. American artillery on that flank had done the rest.

The British were falling back and in places were actually trying to run, though run could hardly be the word for it. Both sides were exhausted, but the British far more so, burdened by their heavy uniforms, packs, and equipment. By the score they were throwing away their muskets, or just simply collapsing in the heat.

His men had filed in to replace the men of a Massachusetts brigade, their advance greeted with hoarse, croaking cheers. The tough men of the Bay Colony then stepped back, collapsing into the tamped-down hay, those still capable of any effort helping others to clean muskets, replace flints, taking canteens and passing them to the women with the regiment. In the case of a brother, son, or father, they were given permission to help carry their kin back to a safe place before returning.

Peter had not expected his men to fire in much of a disciplined manner, but they had made the best of it, able to deliver one good, scathing volley every minute or so. There had been a final, surging attempt by a British regiment to close and force them back, the ghostlike figures in the thick, cloying smoke, not more than a few dozen yards off, moving toward them. Their volley had hit his line hard, a couple of dozen men dropping, but the return volley, when the British had assumed the Americans would break, had shattered the British spirit, broken their morale, and sent them reeling.

The colonel of his regiment was played out from the heat, and from far too much fat on his body, and had already fainted away. To Peter's astonishment, the men of what he now called his regiment were actually responding directly to his commands. They had begun to surge forward and then he heard von Steuben shouting.

"Nein, nein! Volley *jaja!"*

Peter did as ordered and the wraithlike British line disappeared from view when his men fired. As the smoke ever so slowly lifted, they were gone.

They fired a half-dozen more times into the mist, and then there was a strange silence, except for the booming of the cannons to their right up on Combs Hill. There was no return fire.

No one spoke for a moment as his men loaded, Peter shouting a command for them to cease fire with their muskets poised.

There was no fire in response except for the occasional cannonball winging overhead or kicking up a cloud of dust and dirt in front of the line, the ball then bounding high overhead and far into the rear.

Still nothing. A hoarse cheer started to their right, from the artillery position, and it was picked up and choruses down the entire length of the line. Thousands of men cheered, at least those who still had the strength and voice to do so.

They had stood against the finest infantry in the world, fought them toe-to-toe in this furnace of hell, and now held the field, victorious.

Men began to slap each other on the back, some boasting already about how many of the lobsterbacks they had dropped. Others were lifting their eyes to heaven in prayers of thanks, some weeping. More than a few, the excitement and terror of the moment passing at last, slowly fell to their knees and lay down, pushed beyond all limits of their endurance.

"*Nein! Nein!* Not finished! Now, forward!"

Peter heard the command, caught a glimpse of von Steuben as the smoke was slowly lifting, and then saw Lafayette galloping down the length of the battle line, his horse lathered and near to collapse.

"Forward, brave men. Now drive them. Drive them!"

Some looked at him pass, incredulous, for had they not done all that was humanly possible this day?

Peter turned and faced the regiment.

"You heard him." His voice cracked.

"Charge bayonets!"

Men in the front ranks lowered their weapons, those in the back ranks held their muskets high.

Peter, armed with his musket, held it high like a sword and pointed it forward.

"At marching pace. Forward!"

There was no drummer boy; the lad had fainted away hours ago. He stepped off, counting out the cadence, looking back to see if any would follow, and his heart swelled. Nearly half did. The others were far too spent and simply collapsed, or remained where they were. Of two hundred with the regiment at dawn, fifty at most were still with him, stringing out into a single line and trying to keep formation as they swept down the hill. After fifty or so paces they crossed over the farthest advance of their foes. The ground was littered with bodies, some of them dead, most of them wounded or down with the heat. He saw a man raise his musket up, ready to club a fallen British soldier. Turning, he leveled his musket straight at the man.

"Damn your soul, I'll shoot you if you strike him!" Peter cried. "For God's sake, we're Americans, and we take prisoners!"

The man looked at him as if stricken, lowered his musket, and pressed on, Peter turning to lead the way, his heart struck by the cry of the wounded British soldier, speaking with a heavy Irish brogue, crying a blessing on him.

The smoke was beginning to lift, the air thick with humidity but almost breathable. He could sense that the air was slightly cooler here as they pushed to the edge of marshy ground, thickets ahead marking where a creek traversed the muddy ground.

And then a scattered volley swept out to them, several of his men collapsing, screaming.

Their damn light infantry!

"Volley fire on my command!" Peter cried as he backed up into the ranks of his men. Earlier in the day the surprise would have broken them, but not now.

"Take aim!"

Men brought their muskets down.

"Aim low, boys. Low straight into the thicket!"

"Fire!"

Their muskets rattled off. In the silence of the seconds afterward, he could hear screams from the other side. To either flank, though he couldn't see them, he heard more volleys.

"Reload!"

There was another scattering of fire, but not as intense as before. A man next to Peter silently dropping, head split wide-open by the impact of a .72 round ball fired at close range.

"Poise your muskets!"

Men raised their weapons up.

"When you fire, then charge bayonets!"

It wasn't a proper command, but, then again, these were not properly trained infantry of the line.

"Fire!"

Another volley rang out and then he leapt forward.

"Charge!"

Those around him, enraged by the surprise strike when they thought the battle over, broke into a run straight at the thicket. Several shots rang out and another man dropped, but this only served to further enrage them. In the shadows they could see men clambering up on the other side of the thicket and creek.

Light infantry!

"On them with the bayonet!" one of the sergeants near Peter cried. "On them!"

The charge surged forward into the thicket and a mad tangle ensued. Some of the British, pushed beyond exhaustion and unable to run, tried to hold their ground, men trading feeble blows with clubbed muskets and bayonets.

Peter, using the butt and muzzle of his musket, knocked brush aside and slid down, nearly falling into the creek, and then stood up.

He looked up straight into the gaping muzzle of a pistol, not a dozen feet away, aimed straight at him.

He flinched, braced himself for the killing blow, unable to raise his own musket in defense.

"Merciful God in heaven. Peter Wellsley!"

His gaze lifted from the muzzle to the man behind it. It was Allen van Dorn.

There was a slow, drawn-out frozen moment. Peter started to raise his own musket in defense, finger on trigger, but he felt wooden, slow, as if trapped in a nightmare sea of mud.

"Peter. My God."

He stood, unable to think. This was Allen. This was the older brother of his dearest comrade. This was his childhood friend and hero, dressed now in the uniform of the detested British light infantry, the muzzle of his pistol aimed straight at his eyes, trembling finger on trigger.

The moment stretched into eternity.

"Run, Allen, run," he gasped, "for Christ's sake, run!"

He could see Allen's eyes contract and he winced, as if Allen would indeed pull the trigger.

He raised the pistol up, fired it nearly straight up, and then turned and did as Peter begged. He ran.

A man slammed into Peter, knocking him to his knees. It was the soldier who had nearly clubbed the wounded man but a moment before.

"Down, sir!" the man cried, and even as he knocked Peter over he raised his musket, and drew careful aim on Allen's back.

Horrified, Peter saw the man's finger curl around the trigger.

"No!"

He swung his own musket up, striking the barrel, knocking the weapon high just as it discharged.

Terrified, Peter raised himself to look through the coiling smoke from the discharge.

The man had missed.

Peter looked up at his would-be protector, who gazed down at him angrily.

"Now just why in hell did you do that, damn it!" the man cried.

Peter could not speak, fearing his voice would break.

"Why?"

"He's my brother," Peter whispered in reply.

The man gazed down at him in surprise, and then turned and without comment knelt down in the muddy creek, splashing water on his face.

Peter looked to his left and right. The men were played out, the retreating enemy staggering through the marshy ground as they tried to run, here and there a man going down, collapsing, as those still with any fight in them continued to fire at their retreating foes.

He followed Allen with his gaze as he staggered off, until at last he disappeared into the smoke that blanketed the field.

The sound of gunfire drifted off. A command came from the right, from whom he did not know. For the line to hold, that Greene's men would now pursue.

The order was greeted with silence. No cheers now. Most of the men were sitting down in the mud, scooping up handfuls to plaster their faces to ward off the swarming insects, or swishing the sluggish stream with their canteens, trying to fill them.

"Sir?"

He looked up. It was the man who had tried to shoot Allen minutes before.

He was holding a canteen, offering it. The man gazed at him intently. He looked up. The man above him was no longer a soldier. He was simply a man old enough to be his father offering him a drink. He appeared to be nearly his father's age, unshaved for a week or more, beard gray, hairline receding, shirt and trousers plastered to him with sweat and mud.

Peter took the canteen and nodded his thanks, gulping down a long drink of the foul-tasting water, which at this moment tasted almost like nectar.

"Was he really your brother, sir?"

Peter thought of Jonathan and his frozen grave. And of——long before that, so many years before that——the lazy summers of a joyful youth . . . Allen acting the role of being annoyed when his young brother and friends pestered him and followed him, but then smiling, teaching them how to fish, to track game, shoot and clean it, to play like Indians in the woods. And when a lesson was too hard, Allen had always been ready to help them with their studies and readings.

"Yes," Peter sighed, and then lowered his head and broke into tears. "Yes, he was my brother."

He felt a hand on his shoulder.

"You're a damn good sergeant, sir, even if your brother is a bloody lobster-back. And I'd follow you to the gates of hell itself if you ordered us too. God bless you."

He paused.

"And God bless you for stopping me from the sin of murdering that wounded man. My blood was up."

Peter looked up at the man. He was perhaps nearly three times his age.

"My son died at Long Island," the old man whispered.

"I'm sorry."

"Damn this war," the old man sighed.

"Yes," Peter whispered. "Damn this war."

5:00 *PM*

"General von Steuben!"

Roused from his exhausted state, Friedrich von Steuben, sitting under the shade of a willow tree bordering the road from Monmouth, stirred. General Washington was approaching.

Von Steuben, every muscle, bone, and joint of his body protesting, slowly came to his feet.

"God bless you, sir, this day shall be remembered, and your name will be spoken of forever, if history does you justice," Washington smiled down on him.

Lafayette translated and von Steuben flushed with pride as he bowed, groaning inwardly from the effort.

"Do you think we can still drive them?" Washington asked, and then he paused.

"I mean, sir, I plan to still drive them."

The first was a question. The second, an order——and he offered from within a silent prayer of thanks, for Frederick himself would only have phrased it the second way,

"Your orders, sir," von Steuben replied, voice barely heard, his throat and lungs so parched and strained by the heat and action of this day.

"Rally what men you can. Push them forward. We have won a victory, yes. But not the victory I had prayed for. If we drive them we still might gain their supply train and thus finish them here and win this war."

"As you command, General," von Steuben replied.

Washington returned his salute and rode off, his own horse barely able to manage much beyond a walk.

Du Ponceau, Vogel, and Walker had somehow found him on this field. They wearily struggled to their feet. As ordered, poor old Azor had been left behind, locked up in the house where they had briefly quartered, and he could well imagine that his old friend would have no complaints about being left out of this final exhausting advance. Chances were he was happily chewing on a bone and enjoying the cool brick floor of the kitchen.

Once this last work was done, he would go back to fetch him, but not now, for his general had ordered him to press the attack.

"Come on, you stinking dogs," he announced, and then trailed off, nodding to Du Ponceau to continue to think up some appropriate words in proper American.

Not one man in five had the strength to regain their feet, but those who could did so, and pressed forward across the smoke-covered fields and marshy lowlands, most of those following sticking to the road rather than trying to struggle through the marsh.

They slowly advanced more than a mile, shadows lengthening, twilight beginning to descend. Well past Monmouth Court House, a mile beyond the ground where the battle had been triggered by Lee's less than halfhearted attack, a well-prepared fallback position presented itself: a rough barricade of logs, branches, and upended wagons.

Some of the men around him began to advance. Lafayette, the ever-exuberant Lafayette, rode up to join them, and though his horse could barely walk, with sword raised he pointed the way forward.

"*Mein General,*" von Steuben cried, voice cracking.

Lafayette turned and looked back to him.

Von Steuben pointed to the west and the lowering sun.

"The battle of this day is finished. They have had time to prepare a defense and our men are beyond anything mere mortals can do."

He sighed.

It could indeed have been a final victory, but God in His wisdom had seen it differently. But then again he was not a Calvinist who saw all things as truly preordained. A year ago this army would have broken under the hammer blows endured. He had seen men far better trained than these break. What they lacked in formal training, they more than made up for in will and courage, and their desire for freedom.

He could not help but feel a pride unlike anything he had ever known before.

They had fought the way he had trained them. They had faced some of the finest heavy infantry in the world and hammered them to a standstill, and then forced them to retreat, and this evening it was the Americans who held the field of battle.

They had won this battle. And from this battle they would win a war, of that he was certain.

"General Lafayette, please convey my respects to His Excellency General Washington. Please tell him that in my judgment our men this day have done all that is humanly possible to achieve.

"Tell General Washington he has won the battle. If the enemy should decide to try and stand again tomorrow, which I pray they will, please tell His Excellency he shall win again, and yet again."

Lafayette, who had seen so many defeats, could not reply. Eyes clouded with emotion, he could only nod in reply.

"Tell His Excellency the General that he has won a battle, and in so doing, he shall eventually win a war."

Three Miles East of Monmouth Court House
Midnight, June 28—29, 1778

All stood as General Grey came into the stiflingly hot parlor of the small, rough-hewn cottage that had been commandeered as his headquarters for the night.

"I have just come from a meeting with General Clinton," Grey announced.

No one spoke.

Allen had been sitting in the corner of the room, head bowed on his knees, nearly asleep. John André was by his side, again stricken by the heat, face pale. The poor man was deathly ill and several times Allen had helped him outside when he had to vomit. Whatever social class divided men, Allen thought, most certainly disappeared at such a moment, when a friend helped another, holding him up as he vomited convulsively.

André had not even stirred from his slumber by Allen's feet when Grey entered the room, and Allen did not disturb him.

"Orders, gentlemen."

No one spoke.

"This army is breaking camp even now and retiring to the east. By this time tomorrow night we should gain the safety of Monmouth Heights and that shall be an end of it.

"You mean, sir, we are not standing and taking back the ground ceded to-day?" a colonel of the Guards asked.

Grey fixed him with a cold gaze.

"No, sir, we are not."

"This is infamy and a stain on the honor of my regiment," the colonel gasped.

"To hell with the honor of your regiment," Grey cried. "Do you not understand, sir? We have been driven from the field. Driven! It is high time we fell back. Another day of this heat, and those damn rebels, devils all of them, attacking, and there will be no king's army left to speak of your honor."

The colonel did not reply.

"Do you understand me!" Grey shouted.

The colonel could only nod.

"We understand each other, then. The light infantry, as usual, will cover the rear of the column. The main van will march within the army, and this camp will be cleared long before dawn. All wounded and sick to be loaded aboard wagons, tentage and whatever else is needed to make room for them to be tossed aside."

"Burn them, sir?" the same colonel asked.

"No."

"But leave them to the damn rebels?"

"You damned fool! If we burn them, they will see it and attack. Think, man, think!"

The colonel, as if in a daze, simply nodded.

"Now hop to it."

Grey turned to leave the room and slowed at the sight of André on the floor. He looked at Allen.

"How sick is he?"

"The heat, sir. It truly did get to him these last two days. That and he has the flux now as well."

"Will he live?"

"If properly tended to, sir."

"I know you are friends," Grey said, his voice dropping. "Make sure he is on a wagon and you go with him."

"Sir? I can see him off and rejoin the troops."

"I heard you almost got yourself killed today," Grey said softly.

"Sir?"

"Oh, just a rumor of a rebel not ten feet away. You didn't shoot him and he stopped a man from shooting you."

Allen did not reply.

Grey offered a smile and patted Allen on the shoulder.

"You are out of this fight as well, Captain van Dorn. I still will need men such as you."

"Captain?"

Grey did not reply.

"See to your comrade. We'll talk once back in New York, but I want both of you out of this fight."

"Yes, sir," Allen whispered.

Grey took a few more steps and then turned to look back.

"By the way, your friend, the major you wanted to meet in a duel behind my back."

"Sir?" He stiffened.

"No need. He's dead."

"What?"

"The heat. Apoplexy. He was a useless sot anyhow."

Grey left the room.

He had barely thought of the noisome major. The man would surely have killed him in a duel.

He tried to think of Elizabeth, now far off in Philadelphia, but already she seemed like a hazy dream, perhaps lost forever.

But he could not escape the haunting look in Peter Wellsley's eyes. That look of confusion and contempt would live with him forever.

The others were leaving the room, once outside calling hoarsely for orderlies to bring up their mounts. Out on the road the army was already beginning to move, sergeants and corporals lining the road hissing and cursing for the men to be quiet as they broke camp and crawled away, to the Jersey coast, and the refuge of New York beyond.

The Battle of Monmouth was over, and Captain Allen van Dorn knew it would haunt him to his dying day. In his heart, he knew on this day that the side he had chosen to fight for was now losing the war. It might take months, it might be years, but something had changed forever. And in that changing, in his own life and world, he wondered if he could ever return home, if ever again he would see Elizabeth. His heart told him the answer.

He knelt down by André's side, shook him awake, and, half carrying his friend, staggered outside to find a wagon that would take them to safety, at least for today.

July 1, 1778
Philadelphia, Pennsylvania

The cavalcade had been crawling back into Philadelphia for several days now. Congress was returning from its exile in York.

There had been no cheering crowds to greet them. Nor was there any real disdain or anger . . . it was almost indifference. General Benedict Arnold, still not recovered from his wounds, had been sent into the city to reestablish order, with strict orders from Washington that there were to be no reprisals or arrests, other than of those agents known to still be active in service to the Crown and left behind to gather information or sow disorder.

Arnold might have been a little too aggressive in following that order——several hundred had been locked up——but even now lawyers were rushing to plead their cases, and a general amnesty had been declared for any who would affirm their oath of allegiance to the government of America. As for the Tory residents, nearly all had fled.

Dr. Benjamin Rush came in shortly after dawn. He noted with approval that his friend Benjamin Franklin's house had been spared. Hoping against hope, he turned the corner to his own residence, and there it stood. A few windowpanes broken, but otherwise intact.

Wearily he dismounted. No one inside was yet aware of his presence. Looking up and down the street, he saw many a house decorated with red, white, and blue bunting, and the new flag of thirteen stars and stripes. The town was in a festive mood even at this hour.

The food of midsummer was pouring into the city from the surrounding countryside and from across the Jersey shore. He could see that the supply of liquor was being replenished as well, with alehouses and taverns open and doing a flourishing business.

No one had recognized him, dirty, travel-stained, sweat-soaked as he slowly trotted to the rear of his home, into the small tack shop, and dismounted. Taking off the saddle and harness, he rubbed his horse down, filled a trough with water lugged from the well, and found enough fresh hay for his tired mount.

Picking up his medical bag, he walked back to the front of his house. He felt torn. Go down to the warehouses that were hospitals and tend to the sick left behind, or the wounded trickling in from the running battle fought across New Jersey? Go up to the meeting hall, where it seemed an eternity ago the Declaration had been signed? Or simply go inside and collapse into exhausted sleep.

As he stood debating with himself, a group of mounted troops turned the corner. To his astonishment it was led by Gates, who was followed by Conway.

They slowed at the sight of Dr. Rush.

"I did not know you had decided to venture back," Gates offered coolly.

"Duty is here now," was all Rush replied.

"Well, there is to be a meeting of Congress later today." He paused and nodded to Conway. "I have requested a hearing. General Washington made his rash move without proper consultation with Congress or the War Board. And most of the enemy escaped. Beyond that, he appointed his crony Arnold to command here. Conway would have been the more fitting choice."

Rush sighed and stepped closer to both of them.

"He won nevertheless," said Rush, and he felt a cold chill inside as he looked up at them. "And as for Arnold, you abused him after Saratoga and it was he who led the charge to victory, not you. So until he proves otherwise do not defame the man."

There was no denying he had cast his lot with these two men months ago, having lost faith in General Washington.

Gates sputtered, unable to reply.

Rush had made a mistake, a terrible mistake, and he had begun to frame what he would say before Congress. The sight of these two now . . . Rather than rejoicing in victory, in the freeing of Philadelphia and nearly all of Jersey, they were still ready to stab Washington in the back.

"I made a mistake," Rush finally replied.

"And that is?"

"I lost faith in Washington."

Gates looked stricken.

"And you, sir," he announced, fixing his gaze at Conway. "Find another job. I will vote to confirm this nation's gratitude to General von Steuben in the form of a permanent assignment as inspector general of the army."

"How dare you?" Conway snapped.

"I must dare," Rush retorted. "I must because I have been proven wrong and Washington right. Good day to you."

"We shall see about this!" Gates snapped.

"General Gates!"

He shouted out the name so that many up and down the street stopped and turned to watch.

"General Gates. This shall be a country ruled by government, not by generals. You may protest all you wish, but remember, sir, it is Congress that shall decide. God save us, we made mistakes; and I will admit before all that I made one of the worst of my life. But you, sir, you will submit to the will of Congress, and don't you dare to enter that hall today thinking even for a second that you can dictate otherwise. Your game and Conway's is over. Because, sir, regardless of our faults, General Washington never once faltered in his belief in what we must be.

"Now, good day to you, sir . . ."

Gates looked down at him as if physically struck. There was a frozen moment, and Rush half expected that this man or Conway would strike him. And then came a sound, a distant ripple that grew and spread. Those on the street broke into applause; some even cheered. There were no jeers or taunts, just the quiet reply of citizens who had endured defeat after defeat followed by ten months of occupation and now renewed freedom.

Gates and Conway rode on in silence, forcing their way through the crowd. Rush watched them leave. Gates would survive. He still had his followers, of course. But he had most definitely lost one these last few days.

He looked at the crowd. No one came forward to slap him on the back or shake his hand. They just stood there, applause dying away.

Humbled, he nodded his thanks and turned to go into his house.

An hour of sleep, perhaps, in my own bed, he thought. That would be good. And then . . . well, then to the hospitals first . . . and then to Congress for the work still yet to be done to win this war.

EPILOGUE

* * *

Monmouth Heights on the Jersey Shore
July 4, 1778

General George Washington collapsed the telescope he had used to study the distant shore of Sandy Hook and the British fleet anchored around it.

He handed the telescope back to Billy Lee, who slid it into its leather carrying case.

"They have slipped the noose," Washington sighed. "The last of them are away."

It was no surprise to him or to any of those around him. Once they had come within the protective range of the guns of the small British fleet left in New York Harbor to defend this redoubt, they had lost any hope of a final attack. The broadside of a single frigate, anchored off shore, might annihilate an entire regiment. Britannia still ruled the waves, and that included beaches near salt water.

Nevertheless, reports had at last arrived that French ships would force the approaches to Long Island Sound. Four thousand elite French infantry were expected in Rhode Island, the first of many who would soon, to the elation of Lafayette, be ready to march by their side.

Washington was elated as well, though he knew that for this Revolution to truly be a success, he must create victory with his own men and arms, if they were indeed to claim the victory as their own.

As word of the victory at Monmouth spread, fulsome praise poured in from Congress. Yet Washington would be forever frustrated that it was not the full victory, the war-ending victory beyond that of Saratoga that he had prayed for.

Whatever hopes that Gates and his cabal had carried were dashed forever. Washington's need to hold command of this army and thereby shape a Revolution that would truly unify these thirteen states into a free and independent Republic was insured. There would be, at least for now, no Caesar waiting in the wings to seize command and then seize power, as he suspected more than a few across the last winter had desired.

Addison's *Cato* was still right. It was a play that he hoped all would take to heart now and forever after. Freedom was worth dying for and tyranny was abhorrent to any free man.

"We will move north along the Jersey shore parallel to Staten Island and Manhattan, deploy out onto ground we have not seen in a year and a half," Washington announced. "Once secured, I'll ride back to Philadelphia. I think our trusted friend General Benedict Arnold, while he is still recovering from his wounds, is the appropriate military governor for that city."

He looked at his generals gathered around him.

"Unless one of you should wish to surrender your command in the field and indulge yourselves in the luxury of occupying a town, as our enemies who have run away back to New York have now done yet again."

A ripple of laughter ran through the group and he gazed at them, beaming with pride . . . Wayne, Greene, Stirling, Lafayette, and von Steuben.

"No volunteers?"

They laughed again and shook their heads.

"Gentlemen. May God bless you, and may your country never forget the service you have given to it across these last eight terrible months. Months of freezing cold, months of starvation, months of disease, but then months of building hope and pride, and then days of searing heat. You endured all. Victory shall be your reward."

And now his features were serious.

"But remember always the warning of Cato. And remember as well Cincinnatus. If someday a question shall ever arise as to what is our reward, it is this."

He gazed at them intently.

"It is this. That we are free. We are brothers in arms, who years hence shall remember the brotherhood we share this day, and that should be sufficient reward for any man. That alone is our reward. That alone is what we fight for."

He made a vague gesture back to the enemy fleet.

"Can they say the same?"

No one spoke, and more than a few lowered their heads. Lafayette struggled to hold back his tears.

He turned and, facing each in turn, first offered a salute and then extended his hand, clasping theirs warmly. There were chuckles when Lafayette, with unabashed emotion, offered the Gallic gesture of an embrace and then a kiss on both cheeks, which Washington accepted with embarrassment and a smile.

And last in line was von Steuben.

They saluted each other, von Steuben standing at stiff attention.

"Mein General," von Steuben gasped, voice thick with emotion. "History shall remember you forever."

His general smiled back.

"And, sir. I shall remember you forever, and thank you till my dying day . . ."

Voice thick with emotion, General George Washington lowered his head as he struggled to hide his tears of gratitude.

"America shall never forget you, sir. Never."

AUTHORS' NOTE

* * *

History defines the Battle of Monmouth as a strategic victory for the British Army: They were successful in disengaging from the American forces opposing them; but it was a tactical victory for the American cause because at the end of the day the British had been driven from the field.

That is far too simplistic an analysis.

For the first time since the start of the Revolution, thanks to the training of "Inspector General" Baron Friedrich von Steuben, American infantry stood in line of battle against the heavy infantry and elite troops of the British Empire and beat them at their own game.

Mythology of the Revolution created long after the guns had fallen silent has created a fantasy, passed down to this day in poorly written books and poorly taught and often boring history classes, that wily Americans were forever plinking away at foolish, indeed idiotic, British troops who insisted upon marching in columns. This myth is absurd.

The successful tactics of that era were predicated on the effective range of the muzzle-loading smoothbore musket, which was not much more than seventy yards. The gun was best employed by lines of disciplined troops, firing in volley. If indeed the American side was so brilliant and the British side so foolish, why, then, did it take eight years to achieve victory?

As to the tactics of nonlinear open warfare, the British light infantry, combined with Hessian riflemen known as Jaegers and mounted Hessian and British dragoons, were every bit the masters of such warfare, and in nearly all engagements would contemptuously drive the allegedly wily Americans from the field in panic.

It was Baron Friedrich von Steuben (and, yes, contrary to detractors, he was indeed a baron; reference the seminal work of Paul Lockhart, *The*

Drillmaster of Valley Forge, for details on that subject) who, during the winter of 1777—1778, in less than three months taught the American Army the rudiments of professional drill and the methods required to stand up to assaults from highly trained and disciplined elite British troops.

In the searing heat of the Battle of Monmouth that new method was tested for the first time. It worked. Volley fire, delivered at close range, did collapse the charge of the famed Black Watch (gallant allies in future wars who claim never to have backed off in a field of action, but if you should meet one of them, do not mention Monmouth!) and the Coldstream Guards.

The Battle of Monmouth was fought in heat nearly unimaginable—— except for our gallant forces facing action in the Middle East. It is estimated that the temperature reached 105 degrees Fahrenheit. This level of heat for armies wearing wool uniforms, the jackets alone for guard regiments of the British Army weighing nearly ten pounds. Water was nearly unobtainable except from filthy creeks and polluted wells.

The American side sustained approximately five hundred casualties, the British over a thousand. By the standards of later wars these numbers might seem small, but for the Revolution it stands as one of the bloodiest engagements across eight years of conflict. Not counted among the fallen, though, are men who were felled by the heat and its grim aftereffects, which usually hit within hours of drinking polluted water. Some estimates run as high as at least five hundred or more dead from heatstroke on each side, and upwards of half or more engaged in the battle collapsing while the battle raged, many of them taking weeks to recover.

As to the winter at Valley Forge: Figures are imprecise, but of the fourteen thousand men who marched into the completely unprepared encampment site on December 20, 1777, perhaps three thousand or more would die in the months to come from exposure, disease, and lack of even the most rudimentary shelter (the re-created cabins one sees there today were not completed for the majority of men until eight weeks or more after they arrived, since not even the most basic tools were available to them).

The role of women in the survival of our army is a subject only recently explored by scholars. For over two hundred years there has been a prejudice that "women of the army" were, as the euphemism of the times went, "of dubious virtue." Our army of the Revolution had a very strong religious streak to it. A common theme was that God would indeed only show His blessings upon an army and a nation that turned to Him for salvation. The women of Washington's army, perhaps upwards of a thousand of them at Valley Forge, were mostly wives, mothers, sisters, and daughters of men who were in the ranks. That is not to say that all were, as was said at that time, "angels of virtue," but regardless, their role was crucial, perhaps one of the most crucial of all in ensuring the survival of that army during its Calvary at Valley Forge. At Monmouth their role was crucial as well. Much has been made rightfully made of the legendary "Molly Pitcher," who was given the honorary rank of sergeant by General Washington after the battle. She was but one of hundreds of women who served that day, carrying water, bringing up ammunition, and tending to the wounded and sick. If not for them, without doubt, American deaths on that day would have been infinitely worse and the American Army might have been defeated once again.

As to Washington as commander throughout these most crucial months of the Revolution: He showed remarkable genius and a gambler's instinct, so crucial to victorious generals such as Patton, Jackson, and Robert E. Lee——no relation to Charles Lee, though descended from the famed "Light Horse Harry" Lee, who commanded Washington's cavalry forces when he led the attacks at Trenton and Princeton. But then at Brandywine and Germantown that instinct played false and he met with devastating defeats. It is easy today to assume that our heroic image and memory of General Washington stood as solid then as it does now.

That belief is to ignore the reality of history throughout the ages.

Oftentimes, men who are later judged to be icons cast in marble were mistrusted and indeed even hated by their contemporaries. Only victory at the end proved their wisdom and thus their place in history. This was true of Winston Churchill, who throughout the 1930s was detested by many of his countrymen for simply speaking of the dangers of Hitler, the response being that it was he who would create a war because of his Cassandra-like warnings. Abraham Lincoln was scorned by many as a butchering, bumbling fool until the final days of a war that had to be fought to preserve the Union and end slavery. Such has recently been realized as well of Ronald Reagan, who so prophetically declared, to the derision of nearly all alleged academic intellectuals of the 1980s, that Communism would and should be cast into the dustbin of history.

And so it was with George Washington. The conspiracy to destroy his reputation and have him removed from command was indeed real. Former friends——tragically, one of them Dr. Benjamin Rush, who would later mournfully recant his actions——did indeed move to have Washington cashiered from the army, to be replaced most likely by General Gates, perhaps indeed a Caesar waiting in the wings. If not him, most assuredly other Caesars did indeed wait.

Their efforts, thank God, failed.

The rest, as we know, is history. After looking at the reality of what did transpire during those crucial seven months of December 1777—June 1778, one can only conclude that it was nothing less than a miracle.

That it was indeed the Crucible of Victory.

Washington's Headquarters

Reenactors

Soldiers' Huts

Valley Forge National Historical Park is the site of one of the nation's most defining events, for it was here where the American Spirit was born. Today, visitors walk the same ground on which George Washington's tired and hungry Continental Army endured and overcame the winter of 1777–1778 and became the formidable fighting force that went on to win American independence.

For more information about things to see and do in Valley Forge, please visit www.nps.gov/vafo or valleyforge.org.

Valley Forge Convention and Visitors Bureau
ValleyForge.org • 800.441.3549